"There

I slid the chopper up next to the roof like I was docking a boat. I could see the two men clearly now. The older had a gun. The younger guy's hands appeared to be tied. I glanced over my shoulder briefly and saw Pardee reaching out to pull the prisoner aboard. I closed in and heard the *ping* of small arms hitting the skin of the bird.

A round came through the front glass to my right. I saw the shooter on the roof of the building directly in front of me.

"Okay!" Pardee shouted. "Let's get the hell out of here!"

I didn't wait to be asked twice. I took off at full speed directly toward the sniper. I saw the guy's eye go round as he threw down his weapon and flattened himself on the roof. We skimmed right over his head, probably missing him by no more than three feet. Once we cleared the compound I looked back and saw Pardee closing the door. We were sailing across the moonlit sky at full throttle and I realized right then I'd found myself a new life.

———

"A wild, romantic ride that will keep you guessing."
Lynda Curnyn, author of *Killer Summer*

LYNN MONTANA

RUNNING ON EMPTY

AVON BOOKS
An Imprint of HarperCollinsPublishers

This is a work of fiction. Names, characters, places, and incidents are products of the author's imagination or are used fictitiously and are not to be construed as real. Any resemblance to actual events, locales, organizations, or persons, living or dead, is entirely coincidental.

AVON BOOKS
An *Imprint of* HarperCollins*Publishers*
10 East 53rd Street
New York, New York 10022-5299

Copyright © 2005 by Lynn Montana
ISBN: 0-06-074255-0
www.avonromance.com

First Avon Books paperback printing: June 2005

Avon Trademark Reg. U.S. Pat. Off. and in Other Countries, Marca Registrada, Hecho en U.S.A.
HarperCollins® is a registered trademark of HarperCollins Publishers Inc.

Printed in the U.S.A.

10 9 8 7 6 5 4 3 2 1

Today

One

The temperature was a hundred degrees and I'd just climbed down from my plane, sweating like a pig, when Skylar Ambrose Tyler ambled toward me, a blissful smile on his face. Baron stood next to me, panting so hard he drooled like a leaky faucet on my left foot.

"Sky, what are you doing here?"

"I wanted to talk to you, Josie."

"About?"

"Us."

Uh-oh, I thought, *he's going to propose again.* Not that I was horrified. Just the opposite. It had been a couple of months since he'd last popped the question and I was beginning to wonder if he'd given up. Still, I found these occasions a bit nerve-racking. Sky's proposals were like chocolate—they gave me mixed feelings of guilt and desire.

"Josie," he said, taking my hands, "you are the most wonderful and the most beautiful woman I've ever known. You are fun in and out of bed. I trust you; I admire you. I have never, ever been bored by you. And if you'll be my wife, I promise I'll be true to you till the day I die. Please say you'll marry me."

This was the sixth time Sky had asked, and dammit, I smiled despite myself. I probably gave away my response, judging by the way his eyes brightened. The other five proposals had been equally flattering, though more long-winded, which, if nothing else, showed that practice does make perfect. Not that I was making a game of it. I just thought that before I said yes, it had to feel right and I had to be sure. It was a lesson I'd learned from painful experience.

My first husband, Pardee, had proposed only weeks after we'd met. It took a few more weeks for me to decide I loved him and, figuring that was all that mattered, I went ahead and accepted. Being hasty hadn't worked out well, so I was determined never to make that mistake again.

Maybe I overdid it a tad, putting Sky through six grueling proposals of marriage. But when you're snakebit, you're snakebit. Besides, I tend to be superstitious and six is my lucky number. I was born on the sixth day of the sixth month at six in the morning. So after Sky proposed for the third time, saying he was certain that three would be his lucky charm, I'd decided that if any man loved me enough to pop the question six times, then it would be a sign that he was the one for me.

And, not wanting to tempt fate by ignoring what I now considered to be a clear sign from God, I accepted.

"But I have some conditions," I warned, "so you might want to hear them before that grin on your face gets too big."

We were on the tarmac at Tyler Field, which was his family's private airstrip in the Salinas Valley, not far from

Monterey, where there was a Tyler family-owned bank, two office buildings, an industrial park and a neighborhood shopping mall. That was just for starters. Down in the Carmel Valley, there was a Tyler-owned golf course and country club.

I looked past Sky's shoulder over some of the richest and most productive farmland in America, knowing that spread out over a fifty-mile radius of the airfield there were maybe eight thousand acres that were Tyler-owned. None of this had anything to do with my decision to marry Sky, though it gave me the confidence of knowing I wouldn't have to support the guy. That was an important factor, given my marital history.

The airfield seemed like a funny place for Sky to pop the question. Again. But that's where he caught up with me, plus it was Monday. For some reason, Sky's proposals always came on a Monday, which sort of made me wonder if maybe he was superstitious, too.

The other factor could have been that I had on Daddy's leather flying helmet like I always did when I was flying. The cap—and a love for airplanes—had been in the Mayne family since my granddaddy's day back in the late 1920s in Kansas. Sky confessed that he fell in love with me the first time he saw me climb down out of my Grumman AgCat biplane, the flaps of my hat turned up over my red curls, looking, he said, "as saucy as a ripe tomato." My tight jeans had a little bit to do with it, too, I expect.

"Okay," Sky said, "what conditions?" He was a man used to closing deals.

"First," I said, "I'm not giving up my businesses. Either of them."

By that I meant Mayne Aviation, an aerial application (crop dusting) firm, which essentially consisted of my plane, me, a part-time tech, a desk, a file cabinet, a checkbook and receipts that exceeded expenses by about enough to pay the rent and buy groceries. The company had belonged to my daddy until his unexpected death during bypass surgery three years ago. I was now the Mayne in Mayne Aviation.

The other business was more a vocation. After I got out of the army I became a bounty hunter, a line of work that could only be described as, well, adventurous. My first husband, Pardee, and I basically chased down bail-jumpers and crooks who'd rather take their chances on the lam than face their future in court. The work took us all over the world and got me shot at ten times more than what I saw flying choppers in the Gulf War.

"I can see the crop dusting," Sky said, "that's in your blood. But why would you want to continue bounty hunting? I mean, it's dangerous and not exactly glamorous."

"It's not that I have a burning desire, Sky. I just want to feel free to do it if the mood strikes me."

I wasn't going to tell him that the thrill of the chase made me feel alive like no other thing in the world—not to mention that it was about the next best thing to sex I'd ever encountered. Now that I was in my mid-thirties, I didn't have the same bloodlust as when I was in my mid-twenties—due in part to maturity and in part to finally putting Pardee behind me. But every once in a while I'd get a call about a case and something would click in my head and I had no choice but to get out the Glock 19C, strap it to my hip and go nail a bogey.

There was something about the challenge of knowing it

was me against them, of tracking down some low sonovabitch and bringing him back in cuffs, that really did it for me. I was picky now, though. It had to be somebody I really wanted to see behind bars. And the reward had to be fat. Real fat. Skip-chasing paid for the extras, like nail polish, deodorant, a new rig every four or five years and, on one occasion, a new roof for my house. If I married Sky and his millions, the money wouldn't be justification enough. I had to fall back on loving it.

Sky gave me a look of consternation, which is pretty much what I expected.

"But I'm not through," I said.

"What else?"

"Baron comes with me, of course." The Red Baron was my copilot and companion.

"Josie, I love your dog. You know that."

"He sleeps on the bed, Sky. I couldn't break him of that."

"No problem."

At the mention of his name, Baron, the most gorgeous Irish setter you'd ever want to see, gave Sky a salutatory bark, which was about as friendly as he got with anyone other than me. Baron was as particular about my men as I was and, though he sort of liked Sky—if he hadn't I'd never have gone out with him to begin with—he was still jealous. Baron had made an exception for my ex, Pardee. He really loved the guy, which annoyed me to no end. I told Pardee it was because he was an animal himself. Of course, he took that as a compliment.

The Red Baron nuzzled my hip, making sure he got his due, and I scratched his ear. "I only cook if and when the mood strikes me, which isn't often," I said, continuing with my list of conditions. "Except breakfast. I don't mind cooking breakfast so much."

"Hey, Josie, do I look like I'm interested in a house-keeper? You'll have all the help you need and then some."

I wanted to keep my house, maybe sleep in it whenever I felt like it, too, but I figured that was beyond the pale. Sky might be willing to take an eccentric like me, but as he'd implied in his proposal, we got it on pretty good, and hell, it wasn't exactly unreasonable to expect that we'd be sharing the same bed every night.

The fact was, in lots of ways Sky was a darn good match for me—the main one being he was as easygoing as I wasn't. Still, he wasn't perfect. His lifestyle was lavish by most folks' standards and absolutely over the top by mine—which was another reason I'd turned him down the first five times he'd asked. Romantic as the notion seemed, I simply didn't know if I could handle a millionaire.

"That it?" Sky asked. "Or are there more conditions?"

The cell phone on my hip rang just then. "Excuse me," I said as I slipped the phone from the holder and gave the talk button a push. "Yo?"

I got a crackling sound, a faint male voice drowned in static.

"Hello? You're breaking up," I shouted. "I can't hear you." There was more garble, then the line went dead. I put it back in the holster. "That's the third time that's happened this afternoon." I looked at Sky. "Where were we?"

"We were discussing your conditions."

"Oh . . . right."

The plain fact was I hadn't given this a lot of thought, even knowing Sky'd probably be popping the question again. But this was my chance to set things up to suit me, because once a girl says "I do," a man's true intentions start popping up like weeds in a strawberry patch. I decided on a catchall condition.

"Just this, Sky. I don't have to tell you how I'm a little out of the ordinary as far as women go. I guess, to be honest, I'm downright funky."

"That's what I love about you, Josie."

"Some of it you may love, but I'm a package deal. I'm me, and what I want is to be accepted for who I am. What I'm saying is, don't plan on changing me. If you want a regular lady to share your life, you'd best look elsewhere, because I'll just end up being a pain in the ass."

Sky beamed. "You're adorable just the way you are."

"Same goes for you, by the way," I replied, testing whether I really meant it as I said the words.

The thing was, Skylar Ambrose Tyler really was a sweet guy. He was thirty-six, tall and lean and a touch on the pretty side of handsome. Like most fellas who'd been born into big money, he had an easy confidence that comes with knowing the world was his oyster. And he adored me.

Now, to most women that would be a dream come true—a nice, good-looking guy with a fat bank account and a worship-the-goddess attitude. Believe me, I liked it or I wouldn't have accepted his sixth proposal.

And what about love? you ask.

The way I figured it, I loved Sky about as much as I could love any man. Pardee had screwed me up in that regard. It's the plain fact. I had loved Pardee and it was hell. I don't know how a woman could be more miserable— discounting the sex, which was superb—than I was with Pardee. It took a while for me to figure it all out, of course, because love is mostly a self-imposed illusion. But the day finally dawned when I woke up, looked around, and said to myself, *What the hell am I doing? This is crazy.* And it was.

I had been through so much in my first marriage—the highs so high that there was no way that everyday life wouldn't seem like a low. But I couldn't live like that. Oh, I still wanted the excitement of my work, but I had come to realize that having a man I could count on was pretty much the whole ball of wax. How many truly good guys were roaming around unattached, anyway? The way I figured it, Sky came as close as I was likely to get.

"I consider this proposal preliminary," he said. "The official engagement will be tonight, if that's okay."

"Uh-oh," I said. "You aren't throwing a big party to make the announcement or anything like that."

Sky's smile was so wide and bright it made me want to give his dimpled cheek a pinch. "There'll be a party, all right, but it will be small and private. Just the two of us. I take it you're free?"

I chuckled. "Monday's one of my favorite TV nights, but there's nothing I can't record and see later."

Sky knew I was teasing. My sense of humor was another thing he appreciated. With Pardee it had been a little different. We'd make jokes at each other's expense, which I came to realize was just another form of hostility. The sex could be that way sometimes, too. It's incredible to think that I hung on for over six years, but there you have it—a great time in the sack can make a gal forgive a multitude of sins, for a while, at least.

There was a teeny little irony I didn't mention to Sky, though. Today happened to be the eleventh anniversary of my marriage to Pardee. Thinking about it, it was a small miracle that I'd lived this long, considering the life we'd led.

Pardee himself was still skip-chasing, according to accounts I'd heard. It had been five years since I'd last laid eyes on him—five blessed years—and here I was on the verge of changing the significance of this day for all time. I hoped it was a good omen.

"How about I send the car for you at seven?" Sky said.

I took a peek at my Seiko. "Lord, I better get a move on. I've still got one more run of pesticide and I need time to clean up." If I was going to get officially engaged, I had to do a little extra with my hair, shave my legs and come up with something special to wear.

"As far as I'm concerned," Sky said, "you could come just as you are."

"You are the sweetest man there ever was, Skylar. I hope you realize that." Taking him by the shoulders, I planted a wet one right on his lips and said, "Now if you'll excuse me, duty calls."

My new fiancé looked as happy as a bingo winner down at the trailer park, his grin almost reaching his ears. I skipped off, with Baron at my heels. When I got around to where my tech, Manuel, was topping off the tank with chemicals, I stuck my head back around the plane and called to Sky, who hadn't moved. "Considering it's a special occasion, you wouldn't mind if I bring Baron, would you?"

Sky Tyler just smiled and shook his head.

Two

The whole time I was doing my last application of the day, half my mind was on what I would wear that evening. It probably wasn't the smartest thing when racing along five feet above the ground at better than a hundred miles per hour, but what the hell, I'm a woman and women are multitaskers by nature. Fact was, I didn't have a single thing suitable to wear. Now, *that* was scary.

So I decided to drop by my friend Marta's place on the way home. She lived in Gonzales and was the only friend I had whose taste in clothes exceeded farm-wife chic. Marta and I were about the same size and, best of all, I knew she wouldn't mind loaning me something.

Marta, who I'd known since high school, rented a little bungalow on the edge of town, but she took care of it like it was a family heirloom. She'd really fixed the place up, painting the house a sunny yellow and the trim a bright white. There was a small lawn in front that always looked as if it had been just cut, and surrounding the grass were wide borders that were loaded with annuals of every color.

I admired Marta because she had pride, in both herself and her home. She never, ever took on a task unless she knew she could and would do it right.

By comparison I suppose a lot of folks would say that we were opposites, judging by the way I kept my own rather modest home and the haphazard way I dressed. But the truth was, when I cared about something, I was as picky as all get-out. Hell, I had to be. If the maintenance on my plane wasn't done just so, it could mean my life, or the life of some innocent person. Same was true of my bounty hunting.

But a shared desire to do things right wasn't the only trait that bonded us. Marta and I had something else in common, as well. She'd gotten addicted to a no-good man just as I had, only her Pardee was named Luis. He'd bought the farm in a knife fight at nearby Soledad State Penitentiary some time ago.

Marta had suffered the same way I had suffered. Only difference was I'd eventually met Sky and she'd taken to consoling herself with married men. Though not exactly the town slut, Marta was well traveled, which was why Sky didn't care for her. A part of me wished my friend had made other choices, but a bigger part of me understood she was living with her pain and getting through life the best she could.

Marta worked in a flower shop as a designer, and she had real good taste. She couldn't afford to buy expensive designer clothes new, so Marta haunted consignment shops and church bazaars like there was no tomorrow. Her wardrobe was fabulous.

I parked my four-year-old Jeep out front and told Baron to stay. With him standing guard over my two dozen Clint Black tapes, I knew my prize collection was safe. Baron barked, then stuck his head out the window, to get a better view of any potential threat, I suppose. I had gone through the little half gate in front of Marta's walkway when she spotted me through her kitchen window. She waved, then hurried to open the screen door for me.

"Josie, this is a nice surprise," she said, giving me a welcoming hug as I stepped inside. "I just got home from work. Want to join me for dinner? It's chicken burrito night."

Damn. No one in her right mind ever turned down Marta's cooking, except maybe to get engaged.

"Thanks for the offer, kiddo, but I'll have to pass. I'm going out tonight with Sky." I paused then, not quite sure how I should tell her my news. I decided to work up to it. "It's sort of a celebration, actually."

Marta knew how I loved her burritos, so I figured the funny look she gave me meant she was working on the problem. "Josie, don't tell me he proposed for the sixth time."

I nodded.

"And you said yes?" she asked, her brown eyes wide with excitement.

I nodded again.

"Oh, my gosh. I'm so happy for you!" She gave me another hug, but when she pulled back there was a tear in the corner of her eye. "Josie, I know you decided that six times would be a sign, but what about Pardee? When you talk about him I always hear something in your voice. Are you sure Sky is right for you?"

"I'm as sure as I can be," I said. "He is everything any woman in her right mind would want. He makes me laugh, he's good in bed, kind, and he seems to like me as I am. The fact that he's not Pardee, or even remotely similar to him, is a plus. If they were anything alike I wouldn't do it."

She gave me a sad smile of understanding, but didn't comment further on Pardee. She'd met him, gotten to know him, and liked him a lot—women do. He was just one of those kind of guys.

"Well, then let's find you a dress so you can celebrate in style," she said.

We went into Marta's small bedroom. It was neat as a pin, with the bed made and the cheap white chenille bedspread looking crisp against the sky-blue walls. On the night table next to her bed there was a huge photograph of Luis. I once asked her if she left it there when she had a gentleman over. She'd shrugged and said, "When they are married, how can they complain, no?"

She had a point. Marta started pulling out dresses. Most looked like they were suitable for a New Year's Eve party or a cruise, but there was a white dress that I really liked. It had a halter top, a low back and a short flouncy skirt. When I tried it on, Marta gave a nod of approval.

"Señorita, you look hot."

I checked myself in the mirror on the back of the closet door, turning this way and that. I did look good. Marta's bust was fuller than mine, but Pardee had said I had legs to die for, which was why he'd nicknamed me "Crazy Legs," because mine drove him crazy. Yep, this would do.

Marta had some white ankle-strap sandals with four-inch heels, but the shoes were a good size and a half too big for me.

"I'm afraid I'll have to make do with the medium heels I have at home," I told her. "But I sure appreciate the offer."

"It is just as well, Josie. If you wore the sandals, too, poor Sky might have a heart attack, and you wouldn't want that to happen before you got the ring on your finger." She giggled, pleased by the astuteness of her observation.

I hated to grab the dress and run, but time was short and I had to get cleaned up. Marta walked me to my car to say hello to Baron, and I promised to get together with her soon.

I rushed around like a chicken with my head cut off once I got to my house, which sat well off the highway in the middle of a field of brussels sprouts. My yard was lots bigger than Marta's, but instead of a flower border, I had only basic shrubs. The place was about the same size as hers—just one bedroom, a small bathroom, a tiny galley kitchen and the front room. But whereas she got most of her furniture at garage sales and then refinished it, I had some genuine antiques I'd inherited from my dad and grandmother.

Those few antiques were about all I had, other than my plane, that was worth anything. I had never been big on material things and happily made do with a cheap stereo, an eighteen-inch TV and satellite dish, a decent computer and my trusty Jeep. I had no jewelry to speak of except for my mother's tiny emerald engagement ring, which I kept in my safe-deposit box at the bank. My wardrobe was adequate for most occasions, save perhaps getting engaged.

After showering in a stall with a half-clogged drain, rusty water and a dozen cracked or broken tiles, I was beginning to appreciate the promise of the good life. Not that

I wasn't already aware of the things money could do. During the course of our relationship Sky had been generous, yet understated in a way that I admired.

The car and driver showed up right on the stroke of seven. I was still putting on my gold hoop earrings when the chauffeur knocked on the door. "I'll be right there!" I called. My house was small enough that a conversation with somebody outside was possible from any room, but I sent Baron to let the guy know I was on my way, just the same. He yapped plaintively at the door while I double-checked my lipstick.

Taking my great-grandmother's black and white silk shawl with ten-inch fringe—my father had told me she'd draped it over their piano in Kansas—I headed for the door. The chauffeur was waiting by the rear passenger door of the big Lincoln that the Tylers used to shepherd around visiting business associates and political dignitaries. They were a very political family, which was a problem for me, though Sky and I mostly avoided the subject, given my proletarian tendencies. Fortunately he didn't have his father's passion for the subject, so I didn't foresee screaming arguments during election year.

Baron bounded to the car as the Tylers' chauffeur, Marta's uncle by marriage, opened the door for me. Arturo smiled approvingly, but said nothing. When he got back in the car I asked where we were going.

"Can't tell you, Miss Mayne. Mr. Tyler said to keep it a secret."

My heart sort of bumped. I did like surprises. Sky was very creative that way. In January he took me to San Francisco for a sexy getaway weekend. Over dessert at Florio in Pacific Heights he suggested that we head right for the airport for a week in Tahiti. I was blown away, but as luck would have it that was the week I was getting a new six-hundred-horsepower Pratt-Whitney installed in the Grumman, which meant I couldn't go.

Off we went down my drive headed for the highway, two hundred yards from the house. The field of brussels sprouts belonged to Ned Plummer, one of Marta's beaus. Bisecting the field was the airstrip my dad had built. I no longer used it because it was so much easier to supply from Tyler Field. Baron and I did have a twenty-five-mile commute in the Jeep, however, whereas before the move we could almost roll out of bed and into the plane.

Arturo had put on a Clint Black CD, probably at Sky's request—he really was the most thoughtful man—so I listened to country music as we headed north on Highway 101, past vineyards and fields of broccoli, cauliflower and strawberries, many of which were among the accounts I serviced. When we reached Greenfield we turned west on Arroyo Seco Road, the back entrance to the Carmel Valley.

"We can't be going to the club," I said to Arturo. "It's closed Mondays."

"Can't say, Miss Mayne."

The only thing I could think of was someplace in Carmel itself. Baron sat next to me, looking out the window, as curious as I. "What's that man have in mind?" I asked my best bud.

Baron barked. He didn't know, either.

The distance traveled wasn't all that great, but it was slow going because the road was narrow and twisted along streambeds through a series of canyons and oak-studded valleys. Finally we reached the Carmel Valley itself.

The last of the May sunlight played on the hilltops,

whereas the valley floor was already bathed in shadow. To my surprise we turned in the entrance to the country club. I realized then the reason Sky had always proposed on a Monday was because he wanted to be able to celebrate at the club and that was the only day we could have it to ourselves.

I felt a bubble of emotion then that was so strong I had to take a deep breath to avoid shedding a tear. That was so like Sky—to plan something out down to the last detail. Of course, Pardee had been like that, too. Difference was Pardee's plans were always about some big adventure—never about romance. For him, romance with a capital *R* meant adventure with a capital *A*.

But Sky was into pleasing me. And as Arturo drove along the road with the long row of palm trees on either side of the roadway, I thanked my lucky stars that Sky was the man in my life.

I understood completely why he'd wanted to celebrate here. The property itself was magnificent, and far more than a golf course and clubhouse catering to the affluent set from the Bay Area. In the past couple of years Sky and his father had built a ritzy hotel and spa on an adjacent property. There were two major restaurants in addition to the snack shop for golfers, but I preferred the main dining room at the club because they had live music.

The building was all lit up, but the parking lot was completely empty. I was a bit relieved that Sky hadn't planned a big surprise party. I liked things kind of low-key. Arturo stopped at the entrance and Sky came out the door. He looked so suave and handsome in his white dinner jacket that I blinked, never having seen him in formal attire before. He had such a gallant air that I felt kind of inadequate in my slut dress.

Sky welcomed me with open arms, kissing me, then stepping back to admire what he saw. "Absolutely gorgeous, Josie!"

Holding my hand over my head, he twirled me around so that my skirt flared. Baron barked his approval. The three of us went to the door.

"You opened the club just for us? That's why you always proposed on a Monday, isn't it?" I said.

"The privilege of ownership," Sky replied.

There were more surprises waiting inside. The main dining room had been cleared except for a single table in the middle of the dance floor. On it was a white linen tablecloth, a single candle and a long-stemmed red rose. The lights had been dimmed, but there was a small orchestra of about ten musicians on the bandstand. They were all in tuxes and they were playing my favorite piece of music—Pachelbel's Canon. I'd discovered it ten years ago when it was used in a wine commercial, not realizing it was classical music until Sky had educated me.

I stood for a moment in awe. "Oh, this is incredible!"

"Nothing but the best for the most fabulous woman in the world."

I kissed him then, nearly crying. "How did you arrange all this on such short notice?" I asked as we walked over to the table.

"I've kept everybody on standby."

Sky helped me with my chair, the only man I'd ever known who'd done it consistently except my father, who'd been an old-fashioned gentleman, if something of a country boy. When Sky took his place across from me, his handsome face glowing in the candlelight, I found myself again on the verge of tears. He took my hand and kissed my fingers. I wondered if I might not have it in me to be a lady, after all.

Baron, meanwhile, had circled around, finally settling on the pad on the floor next to the table. Seeing it, I realized Sky had arranged it just for him. There was even a bowl of water. This *did* make me cry. "Skylar Ambrose Tyler, you are the most incredible man."

A waiter came with champagne and I decided I really had died and gone to heaven. Sky kept holding my hands and rubbing my fingers, all the while staring into my eyes like a man in love.

We took our champagne flutes and Sky toasted me and he toasted our love. I couldn't argue with that, I really couldn't.

It was so incredible to think this fairy tale was happening to me exactly ten years after I'd celebrated my first wedding anniversary wading through a croc-infested swamp in the Amazon. Pardee had promised we'd snag our prey and collect an easy hundred grand within two days of arriving in Caracas and be in Aruba in time to celebrate our anniversary on the beach.

A week later we'd chased the S.O.B. so deep into the jungle that our guide and tracker chickened out and headed back to civilization without us. I recall huddling under a makeshift shelter in the dark of night, the rain pelting down and soaking us to the bone, swarms of mosquitoes the size of hummingbirds bombarding us, snakes in the branches overhead and Pardee checking the luminous dial on his watch and saying, "We still got thirty minutes before our anniversary's over. Want to get it on?" That, in a nutshell, was my first husband.

Amazing what time could do for a woman willing to

learn from her mistakes. And yet, Sky Tyler still seemed too good to be true. I had to ask.

"This isn't a joke, right?"

"Josie, it's my dream. You're my dream."

He told me then that the chef had prepared a meal of all my favorites. After a big old shrimp cocktail we had the club's famous Caesar salad. Then, for the main course, Veal Oscar, which I'd tried for the first time when Sky had taken me to Florio. He'd remembered that I said it was the best-tasting thing—other than chocolate, of course—I'd ever put in my mouth.

Sky asked me to dance as we waited for dessert. He hadn't told me what it was, but I was betting on something rich and creamy and chocolate.

"Come on, give me a hint at least," I said as we swayed to the music. "Is it dark chocolate or light?"

He chuckled and drew me closer. "What makes you think it's chocolate? There are lots of other things for dessert," he said, giving me a wink.

I sighed but didn't answer. This was probably about as good as it could get in life. But then it occurred to me that Sky still hadn't said any more about our getting married. Earlier, he'd said the real proposal would be at dinner. Hmm. Was that what he meant when he said there were other good things for dessert?

"How long will the orchestra play for us?" I asked as the number ended. We headed for our table.

"As long as we want, darling."

Sky pulled out my chair for me and I took my seat again. "I guess I'm just not used to this high living, Sky. To me a classy party has always meant serving premium beer."

Sky laughed, as elated as a kid on his first bike ride without the training wheels. Then I noticed not one but two waiters approaching. Each was carrying a silver platter with a huge silver dome over it. They placed both platters on our table, topped off our champagne flutes and left.

"If that's dessert, I'll get so fat you won't want me anymore."

"No chance of that, Josie. I'll take you any way I can get you. But I thought it might be nice to give you a choice of treats."

He'd said "treat" not "dessert," and that made me wonder. Sky hesitated a long moment and then lifted the dome nearest me. Sitting on the silver platter was a huge slice of chocolate amaretto cheesecake from Lorenzo's, my favorite bakery in Carmel. For my last birthday Marta had given me a whole cheesecake from the place. I lived off the thing for a week, not eating anything else, which was a damn good thing, considering all the calories.

Next to the slice of cheesecake was a small white envelope with my name on it.

"Can I look in the envelope?" I asked.

"Sure, but I'll tell you right now it's a generous check for you to buy whatever you want as an engagement present."

That sounded promising. But my curiosity was getting to me. "And what's under the other silver dome?"

"A surprise. But if you take it, you can't have the cheesecake or the check. The choice is yours."

"If this is a test of my sense of adventure, Mr. Tyler, you should know which one I'll pick."

"Then have at it."

Right on cue the harpist began to play. I picked up the silver dome on the left and discovered a small peacock-blue velvet jewel box. The word "Tiffany" was imprinted on the top. My heart almost stopped.

"Care to look inside?" Sky said.

I opened the lid and found the biggest diamond I'd ever seen in my life. "Oh, my God," I said. "I can't believe this."

"May I?" Sky took the ring out of the box, moved around the table, and dropped to one knee as the harp continued to play. "By the way, you can have the cheesecake and the check, too. I was only kidding about you having to pick."

Sky cleared his throat and I muttered something, I don't remember what, probably, "Holy Shit." Whatever it was, Sky smiled and took my hand.

Baron, ever jealous, made a low growl and I shushed him.

Sky said, "Josie, I would be honored if you would—"

Baron was on his feet now, his growl becoming a bark.

"Baron, hush! Not *now*, for heaven's sake."

Sky tried again. "I would be honored if you would consent to—"

Baron began barking furiously, drowning out Sky, the harpist, even me. His fury wasn't directed at Sky, however. He was looking toward the dark periphery of the room. I looked to see what had upset him, spotting a shadowy figure just beyond the pool of light on the dance floor.

There was a low whistle, followed by a voice. "Hey, big fella, it's only me."

Baron went racing toward the figure. I knew the voice. It was the man I'd married eleven years ago that day. It only took three or four heartbeats for my outrage to come to a boil. I got to my feet as Pardee came out of the shadows. Baron was dancing around him.

Pardee would never be mistaken for a ghost, especially

not by me. He was as gritty and real and . . . well . . . out of the ordinary as the day I first met him. But he was here *now* of all times, as big and bad as life. To say I couldn't believe it was happening was an understatement.

I glanced down at Sky, who was still on his knee, his mouth hanging open, the huge diamond still in his fingers. I reached down, took the ring and slipped it on my finger just as Pardee arrived. Sky got to his feet.

"Pardon the interruption, folks," Pardee said. Then he looked me over. "Hey, lookin' pretty spiffy, Crazy Legs. Better than ever."

"What in God's name do you think you're doing?" I raged, incredulous.

Pardee's expression sobered. "I'm afraid we've got us a family emergency," he said with so much authority you'd have thought he was Dan Rather. "You and me gotta talk."

Yesterday

Three

I met Pardee going on twelve years ago. Sometimes I wish it was never. Other times, I know that but for Pardee I wouldn't be me, which is something to be grateful for, I suppose. Looking at it with hindsight, the negative side of the ledger seems a lot longer, but in fairness there were good times, too. I just don't remember them as well.

When I first laid eyes on the bastard—sorry, but he'd been one the day we met, straight through to the day we parted company—I'd been out of the army six months and was still trying to figure out what to do with my life. This was in Texas, where I'd been mustered out. Between flight pay, combat pay, and nothing to spend my money on for five years, I'd saved a tidy nest egg for a better tomorrow. But to keep from bleeding my bank account dry, I generated a little cash flow by hustling drinks three nights a week at Hoot and Holler, a country and western bar in San Antonio.

I hadn't wanted to go home to California because that's where I'd lost Todd, my high school sweetheart and love of my life, to the surf gods in a freak accident near Santa Cruz. I was there when it happened, leaning on the hood of Todd's VW Bug in my bikini and hooded sweatshirt, field glasses in hand, watching him and a couple of other guys racing a giant wave. I don't know whether Todd swerved to miss one of his buddies or if he just lost it, but he flipped out and disappeared under the surf. His board came up, but he didn't.

I grabbed a board and furiously paddled out to join the search. Twelve of us were at it for twenty minutes before we found his body. I held his hand, yelling at him not to give up as the paramedics tried to revive him, but there was no chance. I was devastated, convinced my life had ended that day.

The tragic loss was the original impetus for joining the army, seeing the world and escaping my sorrow. Since flying was in my blood, after my stint in the Gulf War I figured a job in aviation was the place to start. So I went to work on a dual civilian pilot's license for both chopper and fixed-wing aircraft.

As soon as I got my commercial rating I began answering ads for pilot jobs, but without success. Maybe that was because I was twenty-three, female and ignorant of just about everything but flying and soldiering. But I sure as hell wasn't going to be schlepping tequila and beer to drunk cowboys when I was fifty, so I was determined to find something.

A job counselor at the community college suggested I advertise in the paper, which I did, making myself sound like Tom Cruise in *Top Gun* but with an estrogen-enhanced sense of responsibility and judgment. I got one response. Pardee.

We met at a Mexican restaurant called Pollo Gordo, which was off the McAllister Freeway, not far from San Antonio International Airport. Pardee was already there when I arrived and halfway into a margarita. He did not get up when I approached the table but did offer his hand, nodding when I introduced myself, which seemed to be his way of handling social niceties.

It was immediately apparent that Pardee was not one for convention. He had a couple of days' growth of beard and shaggy blond hair that, though recently shampooed, was badly in need of styling. His shirt and pants were clean but wrinkled, looking as though they had been left in the dryer for a day or two before he put them on. Pardee seemed seasoned—"mature" wasn't a word I'd ever use to describe the man—and struck me as somebody who'd done his share of living.

He had a few days under ten years on me. We both had birthdays in June, mine falling on the Gemini side of the line, which now that I think about it probably explains why I have two sides to my personality—the one that craves adventure, fun, danger and spontaneity, and the sane one that wants unconditional love and a dash of what most people would call normalcy. Unfortunately, on the night I met Pardee, the saner side of me must have been on vacation.

"What do you want to drink?" he asked without ceremony.

Directness was another of his traits. Pardee did not have patience for anything but hunting. He could lie in wait for a kill long after a normal man would give up. And it didn't matter if his prey was animal or human. I sensed this in the first moments of our acquaintance.

"Iced tea," I replied.

Pardee did not smirk, but I could see a smirk go through his mind. He called over the waitress and told her to bring me a tea. Then he turned to me, smiling faintly as he pulled a folded piece of paper from his shirt pocket, opened it and flattened it on the table, running his coarse fingers over the coffee-stained spots on my résumé. "So, tell me, Josephine, did you really get shot down in the Gulf or is that bullshit you put in this to add flair?"

"Actually, it's 'Josie,' Mr. Pardee. I put 'Josephine' on my résumé since that's what's on my Social Security card, but I'm Josie."

"All right, fine, Josie. So, this story true?"

He did not offer his first name, which I did not discover until later was because he didn't have one . . . at least one that anybody could trust. I answered his question. "I got shot down, sir. Small-arms fire and RPGs."

"But you got rescued."

"We were under fire on the ground for about twenty minutes before they extracted us. Only thing that saved us was the gunship on the mission put down a suppression fire to hold the enemy at bay until Search and Rescue arrived. Everybody in my crew was wounded, with one KIA. I only had minor cuts from flying glass."

"What kind of ship?"

"Huey, sir. UH-1H."

Pardee gave me a lazy grin. "You can drop the 'sir,' Josie."

"Sorry, force of habit."

"You like the military?"

"Yes and no. I gained a lot. Learned a lot. The pay was regular."

"How'd you feel about being in combat?"

"Flying without getting shot at is less stressful."

"That why you got out of the service?"

"More the reverse, if you want to know the truth. I couldn't see going back to a regimen of training and marking time until there was a need to go into action again."

"You like war, then."

"I like excitement and doing something that counts. The army taught me to fly choppers and I'm damned good at it. I guess what I'm saying is I'm not into preparedness without a payoff. In the Gulf I got a payoff and it didn't seem likely that would happen again anytime soon."

"You're looking for more regular shots of adrenaline."

"Something like that."

The waitress brought my tea. Pardee scratched the back of his neck as he looked at my résumé some more. We ordered lunch. He picked up his glass, downed more of his drink, then leaned back in his chair, his arms crossed, and asked me what sort of work I expected to find.

To that point I'd regarded it as a job interview, taking Pardee pretty much at face value. He was unusual, which, of course, I noticed right away, but I was so focused on the process I didn't think a lot about him. This was the first serious job interview I'd ever had and I was pretty much flying in the dark, answering questions as directly and honestly as I could without really knowing what I was doing. But the way he looked at me then, the way his pale blue eyes settled on me, I knew something was going on in his head that had nothing to do with flying.

I couldn't say he leered, and nothing he did that day felt like ordinary flirting, but whatever was emanating from

him would be with us for as long as we were together.
Pardee later told me it wasn't my looks that got him so
much as discovering we both had the same yearning for
living on the edge. "Of course, it didn't hurt that you were
a fox," he'd said. When I'd relaxed enough to get in tune
with the vibrations, I, too, realized we were of a kind.

We continued with the game, Pardee going through the
motions of interviewing me in his folksy, eccentric fashion. "Think you can get the job satisfaction you need ferry-
ing oil executives between airports and drilling sites, or
delivering parts and supplies to rigs off in the boonies
somewhere?"

"That what this job is, Mr. Pardee?"

"Nope."

"Then what is it you're offering?"

Funny that the subject hadn't come up until then, but
when he'd called to set the appointment, I hadn't had the
presence of mind to ask about the position and he hadn't
volunteered a thing.

"The military equivalent of what I do is Special Opera-
tions," he replied. "I need to get access to places by extraordinary means, coming in by air being an example."

"To do what?"

He told me we could discuss the details later. I asked if
there were benefits.

"Nope."

"What's the pay?"

"It's by the job."

"In other words, no salary?"

"That's right. But you can make enough in a week or two
to go fishing the rest of the year."

That gave me pause. "It isn't illegal, is it?"

"Not really. Which is not to say it's like going to church, either."

I knew right then it'd be unorthodox, maybe shady, but instead of getting my butt out of there like a normal person would have done, I scooted to the edge of my seat, eager to hear more. My daddy had taught me right and wrong, but being a crop duster most of his life, he had a bit of dare in him—like teaching me to fly when I was ten and solo when I was fourteen. From the time I was a pup he'd say, "Don't hurt anybody if you can help it, Josie, but what you do with your own ass is your business."

Our lunches came and over burritos and enchiladas Pardee told me about the life of a bounty hunter. He made it sound adventurous and exciting, war without the killing. I was hooked on the mystique and feeling the thrill of the hunt. Maybe the best thing was the independence, the lack of regimentation and bureaucratic bullshit. That had been the downside of the military as far as I was concerned.

By the end of our meal I was ready to sign up. Maybe it was the uncertainty I'd been living with—the six months of eating burgers and pizza alone in my apartment, the tedium of the jerks at the bar, the persistent vacuum in my heart Todd had left when he disappeared under that monster wave. I can't say I felt an overwhelming attraction to Pardee, though I have to admit he *did* do it for me. It was more a gradual thing that kept sucking me in deeper and deeper as I found him harder and harder to resist.

Pardee and I were perverse soul mates, essentially, but we were also antagonists, rivals, enemies. The guy was a self-centered, sexist egomaniac with a corrupt, lying heart. We clashed and grated, fought and schemed, took our licks and our revenge on each other.

But not that first day. That first day the truth about us both mostly stayed hidden under a smokescreen of need—his need for a pilot with balls and a sense of adventure, and my need for a job that wouldn't bore me to death.

Pardee was distrusting enough that he took me to the airport after lunch and checked me out on a 205—the civilian version of the Huey I'd flown in the Gulf—that he'd rented for the afternoon. He directed me to fly to a ranch northwest of San Antonio near the town of Bandera, where he put me through my paces on an obstacle course of terrain features and abandoned buildings. At one point he had me chasing a Jeep up a draw, over a ridge and through a stand of piñon pine. It had all been prearranged. As he told me later, "A pretty face and a good story ain't enough. I gotta see you in action."

After we dropped the rented chopper off back at the airport, Pardee bought me a beer at a roadhouse and told me there was a guy holed up in Mexico who was wanted as a material witness in a homicide case in Zavala County. Pardee had a private contract to bring the guy back.

"It's only fair to tell you, Mexico's not the States and the liberties bounty hunters enjoy here don't apply there or in other foreign countries. So when you asked earlier if what I do is legal and I said that it was, more or less, I didn't mention there was a caveat."

When I didn't say anything for a moment, Pardee went on to explain further.

"What I'm telling you, Josie, is that I'm something of a maverick in the profession. Most skip-chasers won't work outside the States. Some even consider it bad form to accept a job that takes you abroad. No question it's risky, but the pay is better. Much better. Plus I sort of enjoy doing things that are out of the ordinary."

Pardee had probably never spoken truer words than those.

He hadn't scared me off, though. To the contrary, he'd struck the perfect note, appealing to my sense of adventure and my ongoing need to find something bigger than life, something to numb the pain of losing Todd. "Tell me more about the deal," I said.

Pardee told me he planned to go in by air and that he was prepared to give me fifty thousand dollars to do the flying. Two to three weeks of my time would be required for the preparation and execution of the mission. If all went well, there could be more jobs down the line.

I guess certain men have a peculiar effect on women, a power, an ability to take them out of their head to mental and emotional places they wouldn't normally go. That seemed to be the case with us. Even knowing it was a wild-assed thing to do, I said yes to Pardee's offer. The impulse wasn't exactly self-destructive, but it involved a surrender to a more dominant will. I was too young to understand it then, but in dealing with men, I've since learned, experience is everything.

From that point on, Pardee and I became inseparable. We were together 24/7 as we planned and prepared for the mission. It was more intense than any training I'd had in the military. Pardee was a natural leader who challenged me to be my best. We became close in the way teammates become close; we were bound by a common goal.

There were times when Pardee exuded sex appeal, turning me on without conscious intent. He never touched me, apart from a few playful pats on the butt, showing surprising ability to keep his eye on the ball. His single-mindedness intrigued me and had me yearning for more.

It wasn't until toward the end of our preparations that he became more specific about the mission. The subject, he told me, was on an isolated rancho and well guarded. A drug ring was involved; the local authorities would not be sympathetic to our endeavor. We were essentially mercenaries and privateers. I'd been sufficiently bitten that I probably would have gone along on the basis of that alone, but I asked for details on what the guy had done, preferring to think the cause was just. Pardee told me what I needed to hear, and it was a lie.

"Fernando Suarez is a drug trafficker who witnessed, and probably participated in, a brutal murder in Crystal City," he told me. "The Mexican government is dragging its feet, so you and I become the agents of justice."

I took what Pardee said at face value, I think because believing him was more important to me at that stage than the truth.

I'd had a couple of years of Spanish in high school, but Pardee, fortunately, was fluent, though his accent was atrocious, even to my ear. I asked him where he'd learned the language and he smiled and said, "No place I could tell a virtuous girl like you." I took that as a facetious reference to Mexican whorehouses, though I later concluded it may not have been as facetious as I thought.

On D-day we left San Antonio in a rented twin-engine Cessna 310, headed for Durango in central Mexico. Pardee's intelligence had Suarez holed up on a spread fifty miles southeast of town near the fork of the Mezquital River and the village of Nombre de Dios. Pardee had been to Durango two months earlier to gather intelligence and he had things pretty well scoped out. A leased Bell 205 had been brought up from Guadalajara and was waiting for us when we arrived.

We needed a cover, of course, and ours was shopping for ranch land. Pardee had arranged for a land broker to give us an aerial tour of the region, so we spent the afternoon of our arrival zigzagging over the countryside in the helicopter.

Pardee was no more a land baron than an astronaut, but after watching him play millionaire that day, I realized he was a con man at heart. Too bad I didn't make the connection between that insight and what was to follow.

We bunked at the Hotel Casa Sierra Madre, the swankiest place in town. Pardee had the best suite and I had a nice room down the hall. After the arduous day we'd had, he suggested that we dine in his suite rather than go down to the restaurant. Everything about Pardee had been so offhand and innocent that I hardly gave it two thoughts that he might have intentions. The first clue to what he had in mind was that he didn't lose the millionaire affectation, showing more class and sophistication than he had in the three weeks of our acquaintance.

The second clue was that he'd made an effort to look spiffy. He wore a neatly pressed khaki safari shirt and jeans. He'd shaved again and wore cologne.

Now, Pardee wasn't the best-looking man in the world, but he had presence and raw sex appeal. I think it was his don't-give-a-damn attitude that got me most. There was something about him that made him seem psychologically invincible—probably his self-assurance. And in the face of that swagger, I am sad to say that his many character flaws seemed to blur into inconsequence.

Icy margaritas were waiting when I arrived at the suite—the third clue. Pardee offered me one in an assumptive manner of a master indicating to a neophyte how it's done.

It's not like I was totally blindsided by this. I'd brought a pretty dress with me and I had it on. But it never occurred to me I should be concerned about getting involved with somebody I worked with because Pardee and I were in a union of spirit—psychological soul mates and comrades in arms.

Being a serious pilot, I never drank much. But on that night I wanted that margarita about as much as I wanted Pardee.

After two drinks and us sitting side by side on the little love seat, mariachi music coming in the open window, our knees touching and Pardee toying with my red curls, he said to me, "You want to bother with dinner, Josie, or do you just want to get it on?"

No, it wasn't the most romantic seduction line I'd ever heard, but then our relationship wasn't about romance. It was about necessity. I needed him and he needed me. It was the only explanation for all that energy crackling in the air. Even so, a certain amount of stroking was desirable, from my point of view.

"Did you bring me down here expecting it, like it was a given?" I asked. I wanted him to explain himself.

"I've found that expecting something is about the stupidest thing a person can do," he replied. "I tend to go where the wind takes me."

I put my hand on his thigh then, and, for the first time ever, he kissed me.

Four

The next morning Pardee was all business, the excellent thumping he'd given me seemingly forgotten. My feelings were hurt, but I didn't want to seem like a wimp, not on the eve of my maiden voyage as a bounty hunter. Also, I didn't want him to know he'd gotten to me. Emotionally, I mean.

That was the problem with being a woman. It was a lot harder to isolate sex from everything else and not connect the dots. Not that I was looking for major professions of love, mind you, but a token endearment or a few words of affection—"Hey, babe, last night was great"—would have done just fine. To ignore what happened hurt.

Pardee was in excellent spirits as he dressed for the day's performance as the gringo land baron. He reminded me of the Army Rangers I knew, professional soldiers who loved their jobs. Whistle while you work. I realized that what had happened last night was the equivalent of a gladiator getting a body massage before entering the ring. My job description had a wrinkle that had been omitted in the interview. Worse, I wasn't sure what to do about it.

The plan for the day was more phony ranch shopping. The snatch itself was scheduled for that night. Pardee and I would be together all day, knowing what had happened the night before, maybe thinking about it every time our eyes met. Did I ignore it, or did I try to clear the air?

Until I figured it out, I elected to pretend nothing had happened. After all, I was a gladiator, too. This was what it meant to be a soldier of fortune. I either played the game or I didn't. If I'd learned anything about men in the years since losing Todd, I'd learned that.

During my stint in the army there'd been three other guys, the relationships driven by the need for sexual outlet. The last fling had been in the Gulf, during the buildup; Ryan was a major in division staff. I was a warrant officer and, though I wasn't under his command, the relationship was inappropriate. We had to sneak. The desperation of it all was probably what fueled the passion. He was married, but he was also the first man I'd met who reminded me of Todd. Because of circumstances, it couldn't last long. We both went off to war. I never saw him again.

Maybe Pardee was a logical next step in my love life. My father used to say that things happen for a reason. I've always thought Pardee's role was to educate me. Well, I have to admit he certainly gave me an education.

The scouting for ranches that day kept my mind occupied. Flying was a good way to get away from yourself. Todd used to say the same thing about riding the waves. You had to think about what you were doing, but at the same time it was like being in a different world with different rules. Gravity wasn't even the same. Flying was like that, too.

The land broker, Señor Gonzales, a little guy with one of those pencil-thin mustaches and bad teeth, took us to lunch. Pardee flirted with the waitress, a busty girl in a peasant blouse that showed lots of cleavage. I took the flirtation more as a message to me than to her. I was beginning to understand.

After lunch we went back to the hotel to rest. I lay on the bed in my room thinking of Todd and Ryan and, especially, Pardee. I think what got to me was that the sex really struck a chord. There was a harmonic that went beyond the purely physical, the friction. It wasn't love. I knew love. It was more elemental than love. I think Pardee had scraped my soul.

Yet, the man remained an enigma, and that was problematic. He could burrow deep within me, but he couldn't open himself up. Or didn't want to.

But on that day after our first roll in the hay I was still trying to sort out the short-term implications and deal with my wounded pride. Though I'd initially resolved to ignore the incident, I began having second thoughts. Maybe I needed to clear the air.

I went down the hall and knocked on Pardee's door. When I heard the giggle of a woman, I turned beet red. Christ, he was getting it on with a whore. I turned on my heel and headed back to my room when a door opened behind me.

"Josie."

I turned. Pardee was leaning out the doorway, barechested. The man had a fabulous chest—broad, muscular, invitingly furry. It was probably his best feature. Snuggling against it was one of my favorite recollections. But not at that moment.

"Sorry to interrupt," I said. "I had a few questions, but never mind. We can talk later."

"Why not now?"

What was this guy? A pervert? "Aren't you busy?"

"Not really. Come on in," he said, beckoning me with a curl of his finger.

I went back down the hall, wary.

Inside I found a round-faced little maid cleaning up a mess on the floor next to the bed. Pardee, in his shorts, was back on the bed where he'd apparently been, propped up against a pile of pillows with topo maps scattered around him.

"Have a seat," he said, indicating the armchair next to the bed. "Maria's almost through. I had a little accident." He added something in Spanish to the maid, which prompted another gale of laughter.

I realized he must have knocked a tray with a pot of coffee off the bed and called housekeeping to clean up the mess. The maid, who'd pretty well finished, gathered the debris and cleaning basket, accepted a ten-dollar bill from Pardee and went on her way. He turned to me.

"What's up?"

I drew a momentary blank before managing to clear my mind and press ahead. "About last night," I said, hating the banality of the words.

"Yeah?"

There was no understanding on his face, no sympathy . . . or, for that matter, embarrassment. This, I could see, was a mistake. But I'd started and couldn't stop now, recalling the advice my dad had once given me—when in doubt, say what you think and say it plainly. "I hope there's no expectation for the future," I said. "I mean, when I signed on, that wasn't what I had in mind."

He looked at me with consternation. "What are you trying to say, Josie, that you have regrets?"

"I don't want it to have been a mistake, ruin things."

"Didn't ruin anything for me."

"I was thinking of myself, Pardee," I said with a glare. "I don't want sex to be part of the job."

"Oh, I see." He gave a shrug. "I respect the word no, Josie, if that's what you're worried about."

I could see he was putting it back on me. "Okay."

"Is there anything else?"

I felt like a kid who'd been kept after school. "No, that's it."

"Fine."

I got up and headed for the door, unable to get out of there fast enough. But he stopped me.

"Josie . . ."

I turned. "Yeah?"

"If I've seemed a bit cold and . . . well, brusque, it's because I'm trying to stay focused on tonight."

"I understand."

"I'm not sure you do. What I'm trying to say is that last night wasn't just another night. I considered it very special."

"Look, Pardee, you don't have to say that. It's not what I came for."

"Maybe not, but it's what I'm thinking. My intention was to get tonight behind us, then, once the pressure's off, turn to personal issues. As a matter of fact, I was thinking that as soon as we wrap up things here, maybe the two of us could spend a few days in Vegas. You know, unwind a little."

"I'm not so sure that would be a good idea," I said, my wounded pride now in full bloom.

"Why's that?"

"I'd rather that not be a part of our relationship."

"Funny, I'm thinking just the opposite."

"Is that your condition?" I asked.

Pardee shook his head and let a smile creep across his face. "Appears now it's just wishful thinking. Sorry about the misunderstanding. I'll see you at nineteen hundred hours."

That night was a lot like my first combat in the Gulf. Parts of it stand out in my mind crystal clear, others are just a blur. Pardee and I fell back into the role of comrades in arms with surprising ease. By the time we had our gear loaded into the bird and were airborne, the mood was as collegial as it had been the past couple of weeks. This was the part of a man's world I related to best; the one I'd come to know growing up.

Our plan—I should say Pardee's plan—relied on stealth and surprise, rather than an assault with overwhelming firepower. If it went according to plan, we wouldn't even have to leave the chopper. Pardee had a man inside who was going to take Suarez to the rooftop. On signal we would swoop in and pick them up before serious resistance could be organized.

Pardee told me that he'd considered an assault in force

with a myriad of gunmen, perhaps multiple choppers, but dismissed the notion as unrealistic, if only because it was unaffordable. This approach was costly enough. The ringer in the equation was the inside man, whose name Pardee had never disclosed. The danger, I realized, was that the guy wouldn't come through—or worse, that he would betray us. Pardee hadn't said so, but I knew there was a chance we could be flying into a trap.

It had been dark for an hour and we were maybe halfway to the objective when Pardee finally got the message on his walkie-talkie we were waiting for. But instead of the "go" we expected, our man gave us a caution light. He needed more time.

"I say we put down. No point in burning up fuel," I said.

"We might have a pretty narrow window of opportunity and have to move in fast."

"We could be heard or spotted circling around," I countered. "I can take us in close, then set her down, say three, four minutes from target."

We went with my suggestion. I brought us within about four miles of the ranch, then dropped into an open draw between some low, tree-studded hills. To avoid being seen, I waited until we were about fifty feet from the ground before turning on my landing lights to pick a safe spot. It turned out to be a corral, the steers scattering like cockroaches on a kitchen floor. Once the engine was off we could hear the cattle lowing all around us and smell the cow dung.

"Shit," I said.

"Literally."

For a while we just sat there, listening to the livestock in the pitch-dark.

"Reminds me of my childhood," Pardee muttered.

"You grow up on a ranch?" I'd figured him for a cowboy, and not just because his usual attire was boots and jeans and western shirts. He had the languor of a man who'd lived close to the earth.

"Sort of," Pardee replied. He hadn't talked about his past, avoiding the subject whenever it would have been natural to say something.

Seeing that he was sort of a captive audience, I took the opportunity to press him. "Where's home?"

"No place and every place, Josie."

"Where'd you grow up?"

"Nevada, mostly."

I didn't offer the same resistance when he asked about my family. I told him I'd been raised by my dad, my mom having died when a big rig plowed into her pickup on the highway. I was eight. Dad and I were both devastated. He couldn't get over the irony, the way my mother had always worried about his flying, crop dusting being among the most dangerous flying vocations known, worse than flying fighters in some wars.

Pardee asked if my dad and I were close.

"We once were. And we still are in spirit, I suppose. Dad was dead set against me going into the army."

"He want you to settle down, get married and have kids?"

"No, he wanted me to crop dust with him."

"Why didn't you?"

In answering Pardee's question, I said the truest thing I

probably ever said to him. "A girl has mixed feelings about a father," I said. "You love him, but you also know if you don't leave him, you'll suffocate." And this, I came to learn later, is pretty much true of all the men to follow in a girl's life. The tension always seemed to be between closeness and suffocation. "Maybe it's that way between a boy and his mother," I said.

Pardee's only response was, "I wouldn't know."

We heard a crackle come over Pardee's walkie-talkie. He exchanged a few words with his man on the inside and checked the luminous dial of his watch. Then he clasped his hand on my knee and said, "Five minutes to rendezvous."

I had the bird up and on the way in less than a minute. Pardee took his Mini Uzi 9mm submachine gun and moved back to the cargo door. I'd seen aerial photos of the ranch compound and had the complex memorized. We had night vision equipment just in case, but hoped we wouldn't have to use it. We'd be coming in dark, but expected the rancho to be well lit.

Flying southeast at low altitude, we came over a low ridgeline into a broad valley. The ranch house and auxiliary buildings were lying alongside a small creek that I could see snaking across the floor of the valley. As expected, there were plenty of lights in the compound. I glanced back at Pardee and gave him the thumbs-up. He nodded. I could barely make out his features in the obscurity, but there was something about his expression that reminded me of my dad. I quickly shook that off.

The terrain was mostly open, with only scattered trees, the majority situated along the creek. I happened to catch a glimpse of the moon coming up over the distant hills off to my left at about ten o'clock. The original timing for the snatch had been set prior to moonrise when the sky was darker, but the delay had nixed that. Couldn't worry about it now, though.

We were less than a mile from the objective. I pictured the folks at the rancho sitting up in their chairs as the *thomp-thomp-thomp* of our chopper grew louder and louder. It couldn't be a common sound in these parts, especially at night. I pictured them reaching for their weapons, me hoping they weren't too close at hand, hoping the element of surprise was working in our favor, that we'd be in and out before they could fully react.

Unless, of course, it was a trap.

We were close enough that I could see lights in the windows of the ranch house and the blush of moonlight on the rooftop. I searched for the figures that were supposed to be waiting on the tile roof, but saw nothing but a chimney. Less than quarter of a mile and no sign of our guys. I felt my gut go hard.

"I don't see them, Pardee!" I shouted.

I'd slowed considerably, dropping below fifty knots. Less than a hundred yards. I could see vehicles in the courtyard. Less than twenty knots. Movement on the ground. A big dog, it looked like.

Pardee slung open the door as we passed over the roofs of the outer buildings of the complex. Two figures suddenly rose from behind the top ridge of the roof.

"There they are!" I cried, unsure I could be heard over the roar. "I've got a visual."

We were hovering, inching toward the rooftop of the main structure where the men crouched. I looked for other personnel on the ground. The dog was bouncing around like drops of water on a skillet. Then a couple of men appeared, no weapons I could see. The men had to be shouting, the dog barking, yet I couldn't hear a thing but the roar of the aircraft's engine.

I slid the chopper up next to the roof like I was docking a boat. I could see the two men on the roof clearly now. The older one had a gun. The younger guy's hands appeared to be tied. Ten more feet. I glanced over my shoulder briefly and saw Pardee reaching out to pull the prisoner aboard. I closed in another three, four feet and heard the ping of small-arms rounds hitting the skin of the bird.

A round came through the front glass to my right. I saw the shooter on the roof of the building directly in front of me. Shit.

"Okay!" Pardee shouted. "Let's get the hell out of here!"

I didn't wait to be asked twice. I took off at full speed directly toward the sniper. It had to be like having a semi bearing down on you and I was glad not to be on the receiving end. I saw the guy's eyes go round as he threw down his weapon and flattened himself on the roof. We skimmed right over his head, probably missing him by no more than three feet. Once we cleared the compound, I looked back and saw Pardee closing the door. We were sailing across the moonlit sky at full throttle and I felt the same wonderful exhilaration as the first time I'd soloed in my dad's plane. I realized right then I'd found myself a new life.

Five

One thing a person who engages in dangerous pursuits learns early on is never to take anything for granted. The small army at the rancho had been taken by surprise, but not the constabulary back in Durango. That's where the ambush was waiting.

As we came into the little airport, there seemed to be a lot of activity considering the time of night. I saw vehicles and personnel moving around the buildings. The plan was to put down next to the Cessna, transfer crew and equipment and get airborne pronto. Pardee had moved up next to me and he saw the same thing I saw.

There were three police Jeeps arranged in a semicircle around the Cessna. There was no attempt to be subtle. I guess they figured us to come in and surrender.

"We got a backup plan?" I asked.

"Only to head for the hills."

"Then what?"

I was circling the field now. Ground control was shut down for the night. There was no traffic.

"Give me some options," Pardee said.

"We could fly this bird home, but we'll need to make a pit stop."

"Okay, head for the States."

I banked sharply off to the northeast and said a silent goodbye to my overnight bag and my favorite dress. If we made it home, I'd never see the stuff again. If we ended up in a Mexican jail, I'd never see the stuff again. Basically we were fleeing to save our ass.

I turned on the map light and pulled out a small-scale chart. After consulting my instruments, I told Pardee we had three hours of fuel and five hundred and fifty miles to base. "We should make it to Monterrey without any problem and can refuel there."

"Assuming the *federales* aren't waiting there for us."

"There aren't a lot of other choices," I said. "Monclova, maybe, but we can't be certain about the availability of fuel."

"Every airfield between here and the border will be alerted before we get there," Pardee said grimly.

"I don't understand. I know officialdom wasn't going to be helpful, but this strikes me as hostile. What gives?"

"You don't want to know."

That gave me a jolt. I knew instantly I'd been lied to because what Pardee meant was that he didn't want to tell me. "Yes, I *do* want to know," I shot back. "My butt is on the line right along with yours."

His expression was grim. He drew a slow breath. "The Mexican government refused to extradite Suarez back to the States, which meant resorting to extralegal means. That's why we've got the job, Josie. Basically, this is a kidnapping."

Yep, I'd been misled, all right. And I sensed it was much worse than Pardee was letting on. "Who is this guy, anyway?"

"The son of the minister of justice, Eduardo Suarez-Colombe."

"*What?* We kidnapped a politician's kid?"

"Yeah."

"Why?"

"The kid's a material witness."

"But not a drug dealer?"

"No. More like a student."

I turned so I could see the young man. He looked scared to death and as innocent as the stock benevolent-best-friend in a network sitcom. "Jesus Christ." I felt like a baby-snatcher and had a terrible mental image of myself rotting in a Mexican jail. "You lied to me, Pardee!"

"I exaggerated a little," he replied. "This guy has important testimony and his failure to cooperate is an obstruction of justice."

"You *lied*!"

"Whatever. Get us back to the States in one piece and I'll bump your cut twenty-five grand."

"Money isn't the issue!" I was livid, my eyes cutting through him like an armor-piercing round. "Listen, if I thought it would increase my chances of getting home, I'd put down right here in the desert and let you walk back. In case you haven't caught on yet, I'm pissed!"

I think Pardee smiled before he caught himself. "What's

the chance of us making it all the way to the Rio Grande without stopping?"

"Negligible."

"You sure?"

I took a look at the map. There was a point about halfway between Laredo and Brownsville where the river bent deeper into Mexico. The town of Roma was on the bulge on the American side.

"If we head for Roma, we could save fifteen or twenty air miles."

"Would that be enough?"

"Probably not."

"But maybe."

"Pilots don't like to think in terms of maybes."

"Try to think like a fleeing felon, Josie. It might increase your optimism."

That was a sample of Pardee's philosophy. The Dalai Lama he was not.

I adjusted the flight parameters to optimize fuel efficiency and range. Pardee tossed out all nonessential gear to reduce weight, then spent time in back with the boys. His man had a light flesh wound which Pardee dressed. Whenever the Suarez kid's eyes met mine, I felt like shit.

After a while Pardee came forward again, dropping into the seat beside me. We glanced at each other, it being clear there was nothing left to do but pray, not that I expected that particular skill to be in his repertoire.

"I've got to report in," he said.

He gave me the frequency and I set the radio and gave him my headphones. Moments later he'd made contact with our unnamed employer. I could only hear his side of the conversation, but it was enough to give me pause.

"We've had a change of plans, Jack," he said. "We're on our way with Suarez, but not in the Cessna and we won't be putting down in San Antonio. . . . Right now it looks like a place called Roma, which is ten, twelve miles west of Rio Grande City. . . . Yeah, that's right. We'll be lucky if we make it over the border because we're light on fuel. . . . It's a long story. Point is, the authorities here aren't too happy with us, and I expect they'll be mentioning that to the powers-that-be there. The immediate question is who do you know in the vicinity of Rio Grande City? . . . Okay. Any chance of organizing a friendly posse to greet us? . . . Right, but this wasn't anticipated. . . . It's our only shot, though. . . . Okay, fine. Much appreciated, Jack."

"So should I expect a visit from the Mexican Air Force?" I asked Pardee as he handed me back the headphones.

"Possibly."

"Does that concern you at all?"

"Well, they're not going to shoot us down because of Junior, so the most they can do is bluff."

"You had that figured out in advance, didn't you?"

"Yeah, only I expected us to be in the Cessna. I assumed the danger was if we'd failed to grab our man, but still had stirred up the hornet's nest."

"Well, we've got our man, but not enough fuel."

"I've got a good feeling, Josie. I think you and me are meant to pull this off."

"I hope you're right, but I'm not counting on it."

"Tell you what. We make it, and I'll treat you to Vegas."

"And if we don't, you won't?"

Pardee grinned. "Which side of the bet do you want, sweetheart?"

Our course took us fifteen miles north of Monterrey, which we reached at the two-and-a-half-hour mark. Within minutes two Mexican fighter jets intercepted and ordered us to land in Monterrey. I relayed the message to Pardee.

"Tell them to fuck themselves," he replied.

"I would comply," I told the flight commander over the radio, "but this bastard's got a gun to my head. I've been highjacked. They're forcing me to fly to the States." I ended the transmission.

"What's the purpose of that?" Pardee asked.

"I'm hoping to lay the groundwork for a lighter sentence."

"So you're a liar, too."

"Considering the company I'm keeping, God will forgive me. Let's hope the Mexican government is equally sympathetic."

Pardee laughed. "Honey, my money's on us making it. You're going to get your seventy-five thousand *and* your trip to Vegas. Trust me."

He was about the last man on earth I would have trusted on *anything* just then, but I hoped he was right. If we did make it to the Rio Grande, I was of half a mind to go to Las Vegas with the bastard for the sheer hell of it.

The fighters continued to shadow us, without further communication. I assumed they were consulting with command. People down in Mexico City were doubtless on the phone in their nightshirts, debating what to do. I hoped to hell Junior was a much-beloved son.

As we approached the town of Cerralvo, the fighters abruptly broke off contact, disappearing into the night. We were a little under thirty miles from the border at that point and, according to the instruments and my calculations, out of fuel.

"It's fumes from here on," I told Pardee.

"You've been throwing sevens, babe. We need one more."

I thought of the time in high school when Todd and I had driven to a secluded beach past Big Sur. After a wonderful day alone we'd headed back to Salinas, his old Beetle low on gas. The meter read empty and we were still a couple of miles from the nearest service station. "Don't worry, we'll make it," he'd said. I wasn't so sure. "We'll not only make it," he assured me, "but we're going to get married and live happily ever after." We ran out of gas a block from the station.

Pardee was consulting the chart. "Those lights on the horizon have to be Roma," he said.

"Or the towns on the Mexican side."

"You get close enough for us to swim and you've done your job."

I think I held my breath the next fifteen miles. As we approached the Mexican border town of Mier, the engine began to miss. We were still better than five miles from American soil. The missing got worse.

"These things glide?" Pardee asked.

"Not well and not far."

The engine coughed some more.

"If I put down here, we'll live," I told Pardee. "As it is, we're losing altitude rapidly."

"Since I'm the one who'll be getting the long sentence, I'm not very objective," he said calmly. "You decide."

The lights of Roma and the smaller American towns of Escobares, Garceno, Rosita and Las Barreras weren't that far, the north bank of the Rio Grande maybe a mile closer still, but from our present vantage point it seemed like half the distance to the moon. The engine was all but dead, firing just enough to keep the rotor turning. We passed over the southern edge of Mier at about five or six hundred feet. We could see the big bend in the river ahead, illuminated in the moonlight.

"Brace yourself!" I shouted as we reached the edge of the water.

We were at two hundred feet and dropping fast. The United States was still a Barry Bonds home run away.

"We're going to make it!" Pardee cried.

Yeah, but alive or dead?

I fought the controls, searching the dark shore for a spot, knowing I'd have little choice. The big chain-link fence on the American side was visible now. I had visions of crashing into it as we dropped toward it

"Brace for impact!" I shouted.

Two seconds later the front edge of the landing skid skimmed the top of the fence, pitching up the nose of the bird enough to keep us from tumbling. Instead we touched down and slid across the marshy ground, finally coming to rest against a bank.

For a few moments we sat in shock. Then Pardee whooped, took my face in his hands and planted a big one on my mouth.

"Look out, Vegas, here we come!"

Pardee got on the radio again and talked to his man in San Antonio. I gave him the location where I thought we were, at the tip of the peninsula due south of the village of Garceno. After he got off the radio, Pardee said, "Jack hopes to have somebody here in fifteen, twenty minutes."

"Jack must be the governor," I said.

"Better."

Without knowing them, I liked Pardee's friends. I was also feeling a little more charitable toward him. Surviving without ending up in jail could do wonders for the morale, I guess.

We decided to move up onto the top of the bank. Pardee and his inside man, whose name I then learned was Blanco, helped Suarez out the cargo door. It wasn't until I climbed out myself that he spoke for the first time. "Why have you done this to me?" he asked, bewildered.

"Because you wouldn't come back to testify voluntarily," Pardee answered.

"This is not right to kidnap me from my country this way," Suarez protested.

"Tell it to the judge, son."

I had no information on the background of the case, but I felt sick for the kid anyway. He couldn't have been more than nineteen. I'm sure I wouldn't have been very happy with the Mexicans if the situation were reversed.

Pardee and Blanco half carried Suarez up the bank. I followed.

It turned out there was a road less than a hundred feet away and scattered homes, though none close by. But we could see yard lights. While Blanco stayed with the kid, Pardee and I got what was left of the gear from the chopper, including a flashlight.

The bird had slipped around a bit as it had come to a rest against the bank. From the cargo bay you could look back across the river. I sat there for a second, staring at the moonlight on the water and the scattered lights in Mexico. Pardee sat down next to me, his leg right up against mine.

"Sorry your maiden voyage didn't go a little smoother," he said.

"You're saying this wasn't typical?"

"Naw. Sometimes these jobs are a piece of cake. Once I made ten thousand bringing in a bail jumper without leaving my house."

"How?"

"Tricked the bastards into walking into a trap with the law waiting."

I looked at his face in the moonlight. He seemed at peace, a man in his element. "How long you been doing this, Pardee?"

"I started as a kid. Been doing it on my own thirteen, fourteen years, I guess."

"And you love it."

"I can't begin to tell you, Josie," he said, sounding like a man in love.

We watched the water for a while.

"You were damned good out there, by the way," he said.

"I didn't do anything but fly until she ran out of gas."

"No, I mean overall, everything. I like your style."

I sensed it was a compliment genuinely felt. "Thanks."

"We make a hell of a team."

I didn't say anything.

"We going to work together again, or did I scare you off?"

"I didn't appreciate the duplicity."

"I wasn't sure how much I could trust you. As far as I'm concerned, you've earned your stripes. I'm willing to go in full partners with you, if you're willing."

I turned to him. "Just like that?"

"I told you, I was impressed."

"Thank you," I said.

We looked at Mexico some more and I felt a lot of energy radiating in my direction. I can't say it gave me an uncomfortable feeling, but I did feel uncertainty. Pardee toyed with my hair. The intimacy of the gesture gave me goose bumps.

"You ever been married?" he asked.

The question surprised me. "No."

"What would you think of marrying me?"

I gave him a double take. He wasn't smiling. I laughed. "You're kidding, right?"

"No, I'm dead serious."

Unable to help myself, I gave a hoot. "How can you even be thinking in those terms? Jesus, Pardee, I don't even know your first name."

He thought about that for a while, then said, "I don't use my first name and nobody knows it, but under the circumstances, I'll tell you." There was a good, long dramatic pause before he added, "It's Napoleon."

"*Napoleon?*"

"Yep."

"You're kidding."

"Nope."

I didn't believe him. And for good reason, because to this day I can't say what name the man was given at birth. On subsequent occasions when he was drunk he told me different stories, once saying his given name was Dwight and another time Charles. I'm not even sure the name Pardee is legitimate. But on that night he insisted it was Napoleon.

"When I saw your name on your résumé," he said, "I thought, Lord, can this be fate? I mean, how many Josephines and Napoleons end up together? Besides the originals, of course."

When we married, he produced a brand-new Nevada driver's license with the name "Napoleon Pardee" on it, but I think he had it made for my benefit. What I subsequently learned about the guy was that he didn't exist. Not in the eyes of the law. He didn't have a Social Security number. He'd never filed an income tax return, much less paid taxes.

Pardee had a company credit card for use when a card was absolutely essential, but mostly he paid cash for everything, from groceries to automobiles. I never saw him write a check, though he would buy a bank check or money order on occasion. For all I knew he was a criminal on the lam or he was in the federal Witness Protection Program. But on that moonlit night on the shores of the Rio Grande, he was Napoleon Pardee and he couldn't understand my skepticism about marrying him.

We didn't discuss it anymore that evening, but Pardee accomplished what he'd set out to do, and that was to plant the seeds. The son of a gun understood human psychology better than any man I'd ever known. It was amazing some of the things he could get people to do. Me in particular.

Our ride showed up about five minutes later, and we got on with the business of getting home to San Antonio. Just before dawn the four of us were in a Beachcraft Baron headed for hearth and home. A couple of law enforcement types were waiting for us at San Antonio International when touched down. They took Fernando Suarez off our hands. Pardee and I dropped Blanco off at a motel, then he drove me to my apartment.

I was bushed and relieved when he didn't ask to come in. Instead, he kissed me on the cheek—an odd end to a day that included a gun battle and a proposal of marriage—and said he'd be by later. It was ten in the morning when I finally climbed in bed, confused, but for the first time in years strangely happy.

For a while I lay there, asking myself if there was any way in the world I could marry this man. I knew the notion was insane. I didn't know Pardee. I wasn't even sure I liked him, but here I was, actually giving a proposal of marriage serious consideration.

In retrospect I think it was because he made me feel different—not loved, exactly, but different. When I was with Pardee, I lived outside my skin, in a world that was somehow bigger, brighter, more exciting. The man was wildness and craziness personified. Life didn't scare him, and I liked that.

Pardee was at my door at six that evening with seventy-five thousand in cash. He made me count it out on my kitchen table. I'd never seen that much money in my life.

"How about I take you to dinner before we head for the airport?" he said. "Our flight's not until ten."

"Flight to where?"

"Vegas."

"I thought that was still under discussion."

"You know that you're going, sweetheart, so don't fight it. Yesterday was just the beginning. We're in this for the long haul. I can feel it, and I've never felt this way about another woman before."

I later discovered, to my detriment, that that, too, was a lie. It didn't matter, though. The bastard had me and he knew it.

It was only a matter of time.

Six

When I was seventeen, Todd and I sneaked off to Santa Cruz to have sex for the first time at his aunt's house while she was on vacation in Hawaii. It was illicit and I felt guilty for having lied to my father about where I was going and what I was doing, but it was still a fairy tale because I was in love.

Seven years later I found myself in Las Vegas with a man who was best described as half crime fighter, half criminal, and half entrepreneur—that's right, with Pardee, the fractions never added up to an even whole. This time the fairy tale was the adult version. What the two situations had in common was that in both instances I felt I was in the grasp of something bigger than myself. Not that I was putty in Pardee's hands, but I wasn't able to walk away, either. The man was like flypaper.

Even before we settled into our fancy suite at Caesars Palace, the Mexican government had raised a big stink in

Washington, demanding the return of Fernando Suarez, plus our heads on a platter. Pardee's employer took the heat, warning us that we should be on the alert for retaliation. We'd stirred up a hornet's nest and it was doubtful we'd be able to return to Mexico in this lifetime. But I had no one to blame but myself. I'd known Pardee was a smooth operator and I hadn't asked the right questions.

Even so, being hunted was a new experience for me. I can't say it had me wringing my hands, and it was certainly different from the Gulf War, where I had the rest of the U.S. Army with me. But knowing I was being targeted was unsettling.

Pardee didn't seem particularly concerned, however. He was focused on having a good time and, being green, I tried to take my cue from him.

Las Vegas proved to be the ideal place to forget my troubles. It was the ultimate escape, a spring break for adults. The first thing Pardee did was order a magnum of champagne from room service. We got drunk and proceeded to fuck our brains out. I guess it was my attempt to purge myself, put my idyllic lost love for Todd behind me, and at the same time belie the falsity of what I'd had with Ryan and all the other men I'd slept with who weren't named Todd.

Pardee connected with my baser, more elemental nature. That was his great strength—and the source of his power over me. The notion of love never really figured into my thinking. I'd known love with Todd and that wasn't what this thing between Pardee and me was about. This had more to do with inevitability and ineluctability. Pardee was a goddamn magnet and I was a paper clip.

As you might imagine, the relationship had a built-in

deficiency—though it was years before I fully understood why that was so. Basically it was unequal. I surrendered my soul to Pardee, but he surrendered little in return, making damned sure I never fully understood him. That, of course, was by design.

After sex that first night in Vegas, I lay in a daze for half an hour on the sweat-soaked sheets before going in to run myself a bath. As I lolled in the huge Roman tub, Pardee came in to talk to me, sitting on the white marble floor, leaning against the door, seeming concern on his face.

"So, you okay, Josie?"

"If there were any vestiges of virginity left, they're gone now," I told him, fanning myself with a handful of bubbles. "That was the most thoroughly I've ever been screwed. *You* okay?"

"You were fabulous."

I didn't disbelieve him, but I'd have bet my pilot's license that I wasn't the only woman he'd ever said that to. I think with Pardee, the best a woman could hope for was to measure up.

Given our chemistry in the sack, I wouldn't have been surprised if Pardee had wanted me as a regular sex partner. But neither would I have been surprised if he'd thanked me for the good time and suggested that any sort of a relationship was too great a burden and that what we really needed was to say goodbye. Instead, he confounded me by going back to the theme of marriage.

"I've been thinking about it," he said, "and I'm convinced we've got real possibilities."

"Jesus, Pardee," I said, "good sex, even great sex, is no reason to get married."

"It's not the sex," he said. "Hell, you can get that anywhere. I'm talking about the way it feels when we're together, when we're focused on a job. I knew you were special after seeing you under fire. We'd make a great team, Josie."

"Hold on. Did I mishear you? You meant to ask me to be your business partner, not marry you."

"I've always worked alone," he told me, "bringing in outside help as required. I never teamed up with anybody, and never considered having a permanent relationship . . . until I met you."

"Work and marriage aren't the same thing."

"Before this job, I'd have agreed with you. Mind you, I'm not saying this is something we need do tomorrow. My point is, I have special feelings for you, and I want you to know that."

I think Pardee was giving me the sincerest compliment of which he was capable. At least, I took it that way. But I was still light-years—or a couple of months, as it turned out—from marrying the guy. First, I wanted to find out who the hell he was. That particular task turned out to be a work in progress that persisted until the day we called it quits. Nevertheless, I made a valiant effort to unearth all the facts I could when he took me to dinner that evening. We ate at Neros, the fanciest restaurant I'd ever eaten in at that point. I'd never been served by a guy in a tuxedo before and I have to admit I was a little intimidated. But there was a proposal of marriage on the table and I had to deal with it.

"Tell me about yourself, Pardee," I said. "And no copping out. I want to know everything about you, the good, the bad and the ugly."

He did give me an account of his life, in a manner of speaking. And there was probably some truth to it, but, based on what I later learned, not a lot. With Pardee you never knew.

Over the years I heard various versions of his life story. There was never a mention of his father in any of them, and I doubt Pardee even knew him. Sometimes he claimed to be a foundling, other times he made references to his mother, though she was always a mystery to me, and perhaps to Pardee, as well. Depending on his state of intoxication and his mood, I was told that she was a hooker, an alcoholic and a murder victim. For all I knew, she was all those things.

He made passing references to grandparents, but my impression was their role in his life was brief. What happened during his formative years was the deepest mystery of all and, if I had to guess, it held the key to who Pardee was and what made him tick. As with most things, the problem was more in what the guy *didn't* tell you than what he did.

After Las Vegas we returned to Texas, only to discover the Mexicans were even more pissed than we thought. For a week I had a creepy feeling that I was being watched. Pardee didn't have to tell me to be careful. I kept up my guard, not liking it one little bit.

One night, when he came by my apartment with a pizza and a six-pack, I asked straight out if he was feeling funny. "Yeah," he said, "something's going on. We're being watched. There's two or three of them as best I can tell."

"What do you think they're intending to do?"

"I don't think it's to tell war stories over a couple of bottles of Patrón. Josie, I've been thinking maybe you should get out of town for a while, at least until things cool down."

"What about you?"

"Somebody's got to keep 'em occupied."

Sure, there was an element of paternalism in that, and more than a little machismo, but the man didn't shrink from putting his butt on the line. You had to give him that.

Turned out he didn't have a chance to play hero, though. It was my night to shine. Having a third beer—instead of my usual two—turned out to be a lucky thing for both of us. I was in the bathroom when the boys from south of the border broke down the front door of my apartment. I heard the scuffle in the front room and I could tell Pardee was getting the worst of it.

Naturally my gun was in the bedroom, leaving me without a weapon at hand except for cuticle scissors and a nail file. I was torn between joining the fray and lying low, fear not being the issue so much as strategy. If they left without coming for me, I could make a dash for the bedroom and the Glock. On the other hand, now might be the time, while Pardee had them occupied.

I decided to go for the gun. When I burst out of the can, they pretty much had Pardee subdued. There were three of them and, seeing me, one of the guys chased me into the bedroom, scrambling over the bed after me.

By the time I got the drawer to the bedstand open, he was on top of me. Taking a handful of hair, he jerked my head back, trying to pull me away. I still managed to get the gun. As I spun, he grabbed both my wrists and pinned me to the bed.

I remember looking up at him in the semidarkness of the room. He was not terribly large, but he had a neatly trimmed mustache and was meticulously groomed. That stuck out because it seemed so incongruous. Having the advantage, he grinned, exposing a wide gap between his two front teeth. I think the awareness went through his mind that I was a woman and he had me in a compromising position. The hesitation was all I needed to bring my knee up and smash him in the balls.

He collapsed on me and I struggled to get him off. I did get my wrist free of his grasp as he tried to fight back through his pain, but the advantage was now mine. I clobbered him with the gun, knocking him to the floor.

Rushing to the front room, I discovered the other two had already dragged Pardee out the door and were headed across the parking lot. I could see they had him cuffed and each had him by an arm.

"Freeze right there," I shouted.

They glanced back and one fired a shot that whizzed over my head. I ducked behind a nearby car but couldn't return fire for fear of hitting Pardee.

By now they'd reached their vehicle, a big American sedan, and shoved Pardee in the backseat. I advanced as they jumped in themselves. Aiming at the tires, I squeezed off three or four rounds, flattening the front tire on the driver's side. They took off anyway and I ran after them, reaching the edge of the parking lot in time to see the sedan collide with a pickup.

It wasn't a horrendous crash, but it was clear the sedan wasn't going anywhere. Pardee's assailants jumped out and ran up the street. By the time I got there, Pardee had managed to open the door.

"You okay?" I asked, pulling him out and helping him to his feet.

Pardee looked a little dazed. He had taken a couple of hard blows, his right cheek was puffed up and bleeding. Somehow, he managed to grin. "Christ, Josie, you're even more useful than I thought. You wouldn't have a bolt cutter on you, by any chance?" he asked, indicating his wrists cuffed behind him.

"No, but I guess I'd better start carrying one."

The dazed driver of the pickup, a big hefty guy in his sixties with a belt buckle almost as big as his Stetson, staggered toward us. "What the hell . . ."

Pardee and I looked at one another. He grinned again and said, "You want to explain, or should I?"

Seven

The police showed up, but it took a while before they were able to cut the cuffs off Pardee. Until he was free, he was gentle as a lamb and more than a tad embarrassed. I often teased him about the way he looked—a lot more like the bail jumpers we brought in than the big-time bounty hunter he was known to be.

It turned out all three of our assailants escaped, though the police arrested one of them down in Laredo. The boys were Nicaraguan mercenaries, hired to deliver us to the Mexican authorities. It was never formally established who was behind it, but there was little doubt the responsible party was not too far removed from the family of Fernando Suarez, who himself remained a guest of the state of Texas.

It was doubtful the intent was to do a nice clean prisoner exchange because the government wouldn't have given a damn about us. No, the guys were after our skins, pure and simple. "The mystique of bounty hunters has its limits," was the way Pardee put it. Point was, Texas had gotten too hot for us. The next day Pardee asked if I wanted to go to Nevada with him, at least until things cooled down.

He had a ranch near Hawthorne at the edge of the Wassuk Range, and said we could hold out there as long as we wanted. "One nice thing about the high desert, you can see the bastards coming for miles," he explained. "With a couple of high-powered rifles and plenty ammo we could probably hold off the entire Mexican army."

I never did figure out how concerned Pardee actually was about the Mexicans and how much of it was part of his plan to get me to the altar. "There are a few problems to overcome, however," he'd candidly admitted. "Facilities at the ranch leave something to be desired."

That turned out to be a colossal understatement. For starters there was no ranch house, just a rusted-out old trailer. There was no electricity and no running water, but there were plenty of prairie dogs and rattlesnakes. Pardee said he'd buy a mobile home, plus he'd haul in a generator and dig a well. I guess I was supposed to be impressed.

This conversation took place in the front room of my apartment in San Antonio with the air-conditioning blasting at full tilt, a TV that could connect me with anyplace in the known universe playing in the background, a decent enough grocery store a couple of blocks away and eight fast-food restaurants within half a mile—in other words, all the conveniences of modern living. In contrast, Pardee was offering me accommodations that ranked just below a Bedouin tent.

He knew he had a tough sale, so he sweetened his offer.

"If we can find a little Piper, Cessna or something at a decent price, I'll buy it for you and build an airstrip so you won't need a mule team to get to the supermarket and the department store." Every girl has her soft spot and Pardee had found mine. My own plane, you say? Done!

He looked at me then with a twinkle in his eye and said, "I guess the question is whether we consider the arrangement temporary, or if we make it permanent."

"You're talking about getting married."

"I am."

I did have enough class to make him wait awhile. I decided to visit my father in California for a few weeks and invited Pardee to join me later. The unspoken intent was that I'd make my decision and, if it was a go, we'd get my dad's blessing. I spent a week in Monterey roaming the old haunts I'd shared with Todd and visited his grave.

It was at that point when I realized, finally, that I was on my own in this life. There would be no true love waiting around the next corner—not like the kind of love I'd shared with Todd, at any rate—because the innocence of that time, and of that girl, were dead. But the woman I'd become was alive and well and kicking. She had physical needs and the desire to live on the edge, just like Pardee.

When the guy finally showed up at the family homestead, I was thrilled to see him. My father, man's man that he was, felt a natural kinship with Pardee, which is not to say that he didn't have his doubts. "You sure the man's not a little too rough around the edges for you, angel?" was the way he'd put it.

My father, in his wisdom, had the situation pegged perfectly. No question Pardee was too rough around the edges for the daddy's girl that he—and for that matter, the rest of the world—knew me to be. But I'm convinced every woman has her dark side—a daring, subliminal side that certain men are able to tap into and liberate, if that's the word.

Often a woman's afraid of her shadow self, but there are some among us who crave to be in touch with it, to feel the fullness of the latent power within. More often than not, a man is the instrument of liberation, Bonnie and Clyde being the classic example. I guess Dad knew I had my Bonnie side because he was partly responsible for its creation.

The thing is, once the tigress is out of her cage, it's hard to turn her back into a proper lady. My father tried to warn me that a man who produced boatloads of thrills couldn't necessarily provide the kind of deep happiness that comes from within.

Had I only listened to dear old dad.

Pardee played his trump card by asking if I wanted to hunt down a bail jumper with him while I considered my future. The tigress in me couldn't say no.

We flew to Idaho and, after a week of searching, found our man. I didn't have to do any flying to save the day, but I was the one who lured the guy out of the mountain cabin where he was holed up, pretending I had a letter from his wife. Pardee and I made a fast thirty grand.

On the way home we stopped by his ranch. A brand-spanking-new double-wide was parked there, along with the promised generator. A well was being dug. What it meant was I could live the exciting life Pardee offered without having to forgo the minimal comfort of a roof over my head and a daily shower and shampoo. All my objections were being eliminated one by one.

The sunset that evening was gorgeous. The next day we had an appointment in Reno to check out a thirty-year-old Piper Cub. Pardee bought it. I flew us to Salinas to tell my dad we were getting married. Two weeks later we tied the knot.

On the day of our wedding we stood together on a cliff above the Pacific down at Big Sur. It was the exact spot where Todd and I had planned to marry. I later regretted making that choice because people aren't interchangeable and neither are dreams. But on my wedding day I was full of hope and happiness. And there was one thing I knew for sure—I wasn't settling. Pardee was as far "out there" as a man could be.

Sure, I knew that I'd barely scratched the surface on knowing who the guy was and what made him tick. I'm not saying that in the excitement and romance of the moment those things didn't matter to me. But I had discovered a deep connection with Pardee that had something to do with the way we both took big bites out of life, grabbing danger and excitement with both hands. I knew I'd never shared that with Todd or any other man. Nor was it likely that I ever would.

To my way of thinking back then, that sort of made us soul mates, corny as that sounds. Now, of course, I realize I put too much emphasis on the fact that the man wasn't boring. When I was around Pardee I always felt alive, and that was rare for me. After Todd died, I felt empty inside. Real empty. It took the excitement of a war or the thrill of a chase to make me feel as if I were among the living. When all was said and done, that's really what Pardee had to offer.

Ultimately the marriage didn't work because it was

based on what we were both trying to avoid—pain, emptiness, loneliness. We should have been trying to find some kind of mutual fulfillment. Still, we worked well together, building the ranch and skip-chasing. Hunting down bad guys gave us the adrenaline rush we craved and made us feel close. That's when the relationship really seemed to click—when we were on the hunt.

I kept busy turning the ranch into a real home. Pardee got a few head of cattle and made plans to do some serious ranching. But whenever either of us needed a little space, we found our own way. I would jump in the plane, get up in those big fluffy clouds that came rolling over the Sierra, and soar like an eagle. Pardee liked to get on his horse and ride off into the desert. What kept us coming back home was the power we had over each other.

So that's the way things were in the middle of year two when the biggest turning point in our marriage came in the form of an unexpected visitor.

Pardee and I had been doing a job in the San Francisco Bay Area. It seemed like most of our work took us to the wide-open spaces, but in skip-chasing you follow a trail where it takes you and sometimes it's into an urban setting. Although I'd been a country girl most of my life, hidden under my denim was an appreciation for nice things. My life with Pardee being what it was, I didn't get to tap into that side of me much.

Anyway, while we were in the city I made Pardee take me to a couple of nice restaurants and a play. He'd indulged my desire for a little culture, but I knew his mind was on his cattle, not on sharing an experience with me. Before we'd left home, Pardee had taken his truck into Carson City to have some major work done and he needed to pick it up. So on our way back we flew into Carson and I dropped him off before continuing on home in the plane.

It was dusk as I landed on our strip and pretty much dark by the time I secured the plane and hiked up to the house, lugging my case. If I'd been alert I'd probably have noticed the battered old pickup with the Texas plates up by the barn. But I was hot and tired and sore from the scuffle we'd had at the climactic moment of the capture down in San Jose. Our man was a capo in a biker gang that specialized in the manufacture and distribution of meth. His woman was so fiercely loyal I had to subdue her. It cost me a broken nail and a couple of bruises. The point is I was eager for a good long soak in the tub.

I was no sooner in the front door than my clothes started coming off. Unlike Pardee, who had a similar inclination to run around the house naked, I tended to carry my things directly to the laundry room. With a load ready to go, I dumped my jeans and shirt in the machine, turned it on and returned to the kitchen for a beer. I stood naked at the open door of the refrigerator, silhouetted nicely from the light inside, when I heard someone behind me. I froze.

I knew it wasn't Pardee. We almost never had visitors, which meant the Mexicans had caught up with us or it was a garden-variety burglar. With my Glock on the table in the front room and me looking like a birthday cake to a bunch of hungry six-year-olds, I figured I had to act quick. Though the room was dark, I knew I could find the drawer where the knives were and get into an offensive posture in seconds.

An instant before I flew into action I heard him mutter, "Jesus." I think it was awe in his voice, but I didn't take the time for an evaluation. I rolled over the table, landed on my feet by the counter, had the drawer open and the butcher knife out before he moved.

"Get the fuck out of my house!" I screamed as fiercely as I could. "Now! Or I'll slit you open."

"Jesus," he said again, rooted to the spot where he stood, his body language saying he'd never seen a naked woman before.

In my haste I'd left the refrigerator door open and enough light was cast into the room that I could make out his general physique. He was pretty big, better than six feet, but awfully slender. On closer inspection, I realized he was just a kid.

"Sorry, ma'am," he said, half turning to avert his eyes, though not before raking them over me again. "Ain't this Mr. Pardee's place?"

His voice was unthreatening and innocent. It was also flavored liberally with a Texas accent.

"Who the hell are you?"

"Quinn, ma'am."

He looked off at a ninety-degree angle, though his eyes darted furtively to the side, toward me, but not at me. I was beginning to see this wasn't an aggressor. In fact, he was more like the victim of a terrible mistake still in the making.

For my part, I was as embarrassed by my show of hostility and my language as I was by my state of undress. But there was nothing to cover myself with except a tea towel and a sponge. The laundry room was only a few steps away. I could hear the washing machine going. I couldn't recall if other laundry had been lying around. With mortification rapidly overtaking fear, I knew I had to do something about my nakedness before I addressed the problem of the kid's presence.

"Turn and face the front room," I commanded.

The boy did as I told him. "I'm really sorry, ma'am, but I thought this was Mr. Pardee's place."

"It is," I said, moving toward the door to the laundry room.

"Well, I didn't expect nobody to be here but him."

"Don't turn around," I said, "I'm turning on a light."

With the light on, I got a better look at Quinn—the back of him, anyway. He was in jeans and a western shirt, his tawny hair shaggy, his shoulders broad and sloping over his narrow hips. His body reminded me a little of Pardee.

I took a quick look in the laundry room, where I spotted dirty sheets and a couple of bath towels. I snatched one of the towels, wrapped it around me, tucked it in to fasten it and then, knife in hand, returned to the kitchen. The young cowboy hadn't moved a muscle.

"Who'd you say you were?" I asked.

"Quinn, ma'am. Can I turn around now?"

"Yes, but don't make any sudden moves. I'm armed."

The boy turned slowly, engaged my eyes as well as some of the rest of me. He didn't smile, a courtesy for which I gave him points. I figured him for sixteen or seventeen. The eyes and mouth were hauntingly familiar. At an instinctive level I knew what was coming.

Quinn said, "You don't know who I am, do you?"

"If I had to guess, I'd say you were Pardee's son."

The boy smiled. "Then he *did* tell you."

"No, it was a guess."

Was I surprised? Yes and no. With Pardee I'd come to

expect the unexpected because that's the way the man was, the way he wanted it. Revealing himself was an anathema, I guess because he felt safer when he was a mystery.

"Who are *you*?" Quinn asked politely. "Girlfriend?"

"Wife."

"Oh," he said.

"He didn't tell you about me, either."

The kid shook his head.

"I guess that makes us about even," I said.

"I reckon it does."

The moment had a surreal quality. I felt pretty damned strange standing there virtually naked in the presence of a stepson I didn't even know I had.

"Mind if I ask what you're doing here?" I asked.

"Basically, my ma kicked me out, said it's time I live with my old man for a while."

"Did your father know you were having problems at home?"

"Ma said she wrote to him."

I rolled my eyes. This was vintage Pardee. I was already looking forward to his attempt to explain.

I'd hear him out, of course. Then I'd count to ten and kill him in cold blood.

Today

Eight

Family emergency?" I said, seething. "Pardee, are you drunk?"

He gave me one of his mischievous grins. "Haven't had a drink all day."

"Then what in the hell are you talking about?"

Baron was yapping and carrying on, nuzzling Pardee's leg.

"Well, I'm damned happy to see you, too, big fella," he said, scratching my dog's ears.

Baron barked enthusiastically. I shushed him and told him to sit. Pardee had turned his attention to Sky, who was as flummoxed as I was pissed.

"Name's Pardee," he said, extending his hand. "I'm the husband, Josephine's Napoleon. And you're . . ."

"Sky Tyler." Bewildered, Sky took Pardee's hand.

"You're the new boyfriend, then," Pardee said, pumping Sky's hand. "I have trouble keeping up with this gal." He shook his head, bemused.

"Skylar happens to be my *fiancé*," I said, glaring at him as I pulled their hands apart. I held the diamond that had only been on my finger for seconds up in Pardee's face. "We're *engaged*."

"Oh, so *that's* why you were down on your knee, Mr. Tyler. We're talkin' *brand-new* fiancé. Well, damnation. Let me be the first to congratulate you." Pardee extended his hand again, but I stepped between them.

"What do you want?" I said, looking into his eyes with all the hostility I could muster.

Baron barked and I told him to be quiet. Pardee's expression turned cold sober.

"It's Quinn, sweetheart. They got him."

The blood came to a stop in my veins. I could tell by the look in his eyes that Pardee was dead serious. "*Who* has him?"

"The Mexicans."

His eyes glistened and I knew he wasn't bullshitting me. Pardee wouldn't joke about something like this.

"Shit," I said, unconsciously turning my diamond on my finger.

"Yeah, shit is right."

Baron whined and Sky stood silently by.

"Quinn is my stepson," I explained to Sky, the words out of my mouth before I realized that wasn't the way to put it. "I mean, *former* stepson. Pardee's boy."

"Josie and my kid are really tight," Pardee added. "I knew she'd want to know."

Pardee was right about that. But what a time for this to happen. On the one hand, I wanted to hear everything— every scrap of news that Pardee had about Quinn, how it had happened, what he wanted to do about it. On the other hand, this was my special night with Sky. My beautiful ring was barely on my finger, and here I was, immersed in a family discussion with my ex-husband.

I didn't have any secrets from Sky, but it would be a hell of a lot easier to deal with Pardee if I was free to speak my mind. Taking Sky's hand, I said, "Honey, will you excuse me for a few minutes?" I gave him a peck on the cheek before nodding to Pardee. "Come on," I said, heading for the door. "Let's go out on the patio and talk."

Baron barked.

"Okay. You, too."

My dog and my former husband followed me. "I'll be right back, Sky," I called over my shoulder. I took a quick peek at my new ring, hating it that I hadn't been able to appreciate it properly and savor the moment. "This better be legitimate," I muttered to myself, even knowing I'd rather it be a hoax.

I went out the patio doors. It was dark outside, though the moon had come up from behind the hills at the end of the valley, the silvery light angling through the trees. I was flushed from the champagne and the excitement, worried and angry all at the same time. I spun around as Pardee ambled toward me.

He looked me over, a faint smile appearing under his furrowed brow. "You look fabulous, sweetheart."

"Never mind that," I snapped. "For starters, I want to know how the hell you found me. Have you been following me?"

He stared heavenward, trying hard not to crack a smile. I could see it on his face and it made me want to belt him.

"I went to your place and, when you weren't there, I called Marta. She was shocked to hear my voice. It sort of came out in the course of the conversation that you were out with your beau and that it was a big night."

It didn't surprise me that Marta might have spilled the beans, given the way she felt about Pardee, but that still didn't explain how he'd tracked me down at the club. "Marta didn't know we'd be here," I said, suspicious.

"I know. When I told her about Quinn and that I had to speak with you tonight, she called her uncle. I believe he's your fiancé's chauffeur? Anyway, she found out where you were."

"And knowing you, you talked her into driving you over here."

"I had to twist her arm pretty hard, Josie."

I knew he was lying to spare Marta grief, but that was the least of my problems. "All right. Let's hear the story. What's with Quinn and the Mexicans?"

"Quinn was on his way from the Yucatán to Mexico City when he was kidnapped. There's a ransom demand, but my cynical side says this isn't about money because they want more than I could raise robbing banks for a month, and they must know that. The intent has to be to lure me down there."

"You're saying it's Suarez."

"Makes sense he or his family are somehow involved."

I studied Pardee, suspicion beginning to seep into my heart. The man was an inveterate con, but even though he wouldn't lie about Quinn being kidnapped, neither could I trust his motives.

Pardee probably sensed this because he said, "I couldn't keep it from you, Josie. Quinn's our son."

Technically it wasn't true, of course, but it might as well have been. Though I'd only had him a couple of years, Quinn was like my kid.

I suppose at some level I must have been hardwired to nurture, in spite of my taste for danger and excitement, because when Quinn came into my life I went into full mothering mode. The kid was impossible to resist—a big, lumbering, awkward version of Pardee but with a kind of innocence I doubt Pardee ever had. We'd grown very close during his time with us, and I'd tried hard to make a difference in his life.

The funny thing was, Pardee had been jealous in a way. Though he loved Quinn, he was selfish enough that he didn't want to have to share me with the boy, though I doubt he was consciously aware of it. And like many fathers and sons, there'd been a natural tension between them—an old bull, young bull thing.

Reaching into his shirt pocket, Pardee pulled out a folded piece of paper and a Polaroid photo. The paper was a ransom demand addressed to Ellie, Quinn's mother. The kidnappers wanted two million dollars. The picture was of Quinn, holding a recent copy of the *New York Times*. A gun was being held to his head. The sight of it made me sick.

"There's more to you coming here than letting me know what happened," I said. "You want my help, right?"

"I've got to go down there and get him, Josie. There's no other way I can see to do it. I figured you might have some ideas."

That was bullshit. He wasn't here for a consultation. During our years of skip-chasing Pardee did bounce ideas off me, true, but that wasn't my chief role. Basically we were a team, doing jobs together, top to bottom. And we were damned good. Now that he was facing the most important and challenging snatch of his career, it was only natural he'd want to maximize his chances. He wanted me in the saddle beside him.

"Dammit," I said, looking up at the moon and thinking of Sky. "This couldn't be coming at a worse time."

"It wasn't a time of my choosing, Josie."

I knew that was true. But I was upset and disappointed and couldn't help wanting to take it out on someone. "Why didn't you just call me?" I said. "This happens to be one of the most important days in my life and you've totally ruined it."

"That wasn't my intention. And anyway, I did try calling you from the bus, but I couldn't get through."

"The *bus*?"

"I would have flown, but to be honest, Josie, this is coming at a real bad time for me, too. I'm trying to save every penny I can for the operation." He actually looked embarrassed. "Fact of the matter is, I had to borrow three grand from Ellie for seed money. But a thousand's nothing. So I stopped in Vegas on my way here to pump up my working capital a bit."

"And you lost it?"

"You know it's rare for me to lose at poker, Josie. Had the damnedest run of bad luck. It was incredible."

"Jesus, your son's been kidnapped and you're gambling in Vegas?" I knew he was desperate because Pardee was not a frivolous person. "You're broke, aren't you?"

"Like I say, this came at a very bad time."

"Oil leases again?"

Oil leases had always been my former husband's weakness. It was what had lured him to Texas in the first place and it had been his undoing. During our marriage he'd lost half a million dollars before I finally put my foot down.

Still, I had never, ever known him to ask anyone—least of all a woman—for money.

He stared at his boots.

"How bad is it?" I asked quietly.

"Three years ago I had a good run," he replied. "On paper I was worth damned near two million. Then the tides of fortune turned. Three months ago, I pretty much bottomed out."

"The ranch?"

"Mortgaged to the hilt. Bank's threatening to foreclose."

"Jesus, Pardee."

"I'll do a few big jobs and get back on my feet," he said. "Year or two from now I'll be in high cotton again. But Quinn's kidnappers are not likely to wait for me to get solvent."

"I take it you wouldn't be averse to borrowing some money, then."

"If you could spare a few bucks, I'd be much obliged," he replied. "Not for my sake. For Quinn. And, of course, I'll pay you back every penny."

I knew this couldn't be easy for him. Pardee was a proud man and he would have to be truly desperate before he would take money from me. Sure, in the years I'd known him, he'd manipulated me like crazy, but he never stole from me, never out-and-out cheated me. And he'd never once asked for a loan.

"How much do you need?"

"Anything you can spare. I'm trying to sell off the last of my herd before the bank gets wind of it. I think I can get another five grand out of Ellie. You know what it costs to mount an operation."

"I can cash in some CDs and probably come up with fifteen or twenty, but after that it would mean dipping into my IRAs."

"Hell, don't do that, Josie."

"I'll need a day to get the CDs in my checking account, but I'll give you the check now. Let me get my checkbook. It's in my purse."

I started to turn away, but Pardee grabbed my arm, stopping me.

"Listen, sweetheart, I appreciate your generosity. There aren't many women who'd help out a former husband this way."

"You know how I feel about Quinn."

Pardee continued to hold my arm. "To be honest, though, the money's secondary," he said. "I was good before I met you, Josie, but when we were a team, I was twice as good."

I was flattered, which was Pardee's intent, of course. But I also knew what he'd said was true. At least he was man enough to admit it. I had to give him that. "I appreciate the compliment."

There was a little extra emotion in Pardee's eyes and I wondered if it was because of Quinn or me. Given all that had happened in the last ten minutes, I had to struggle to hold things together. And naturally, I felt pulled in two different directions. Because of Sky I resisted the urge to saddle up and ride off with Pardee, even though I cared so much about Quinn. Once I was alone, the excitement behind me, I'd worry about him like hell. But this wasn't the time for emotion. I had to get to the bottom line.

"You want me to go to Mexico with you, don't you?" I said. "Is that what you're really saying?"

"I couldn't ask that of you. Not Mexico."

"You have somebody else lined up?"

He chuckled. "Anybody who'd work for what I can afford to pay, I wouldn't want. Besides, nobody in his right mind would do anything with me in Mexico. You know that."

Pardee had a point. He needed me more badly than he'd suggested.

"Tell you what," I said, "I'll give you the money, but as for the rest, I need to give it some thought. Why don't you come by the house tomorrow and we can discuss it? If it's all right, I'll give you the check then."

"That'd be fine."

"Okay, see you tomorrow."

The bastard didn't have the grace to leave it at that. Reaching out, he brushed my cheek with his fingers. "It's true," he said, "I never have seen you looking so beautiful as you do right now. Not even on our wedding day."

I couldn't respond to that. I turned and went back into the club to be with the man I intended to marry.

Sky sat alone at the table, staring vacantly at his champagne flute as he tapped it lightly with a spoon. He looked sad. And why shouldn't he? This was his big night, too. Poor Skylar. He had no idea what he was getting into when he picked me to be his bride.

Seeing me coming, he got to his feet. He smiled. It was a bit tentative.

"Honey, I'm so sorry," I said, taking his face in my hands and kissing him.

Sky wrapped his arms around me. It felt so good. My fiancé was not the quintessential protective type, but he did make me feel safe and loved—I suppose because he was so committed.

"Everything all right, Josie?"

"No, everything's a mess. A genuine crisis. But I'll worry about it tomorrow. This is our night. I want to salvage it, Sky. Can we go back to where we were before Pardee barged in?"

"Seriously?"

"Yes, I want to hear you say the words."

Sky, looking so handsome in his dinner jacket, smiled his million-dollar smile and gave me the sweetest kiss. I hugged him ferociously in return.

"Hey, maybe we should invite your ex to the wedding," he said.

"Why?"

"I don't think I've seen you quite this enthusiastic before."

"Seeing Pardee made me realize just how special you are, Sky."

"Is that true?"

"Can't you tell?"

He took my hand and slipped the diamond off my finger. "As I recall, you were seated there," he said, indicating my chair, "and I was here." He dropped down on his knee and took my hand.

I beamed, shivers going up and down my spine. It was very quiet. Only then did I realize that the orchestra was gone. Sky had apparently sent them home. But that wasn't all that was missing.

Sky cleared his throat. "Josie, darling," he began.

"Honey, excuse me," I said, looking around. "Where's Baron?"

"I believe he went outside with you."

"That's right, but he didn't come in." I'd been so

wrought up that I hadn't noticed. "Hold that thought," I said, tapping Sky on the lower lip with my fingertip.

Slipping from my chair, I hurried over to the patio door. Opening it, I expected Baron to rush in. But he wasn't there. "Baron!" I called. "Here, boy!"

Usually one call was all that was needed before he came running to me, but there was no sign of him. I called a second and third time and went over to the low wall that ringed the patio. I peered out across the lawn, now brightly illuminated by the moonlight. There was no Baron.

About then Sky came out. He joined me in the soft, cool air, putting his arm around my shoulder. I called my dog again. "Baron! Where are you?" I glanced at Sky. "This isn't like him at all."

"Could he have gone with your ex?"

It had already occurred to me that's what had happened. Baron loved the guy. In fact, Pardee had given him to me as an "empty-nester" present when Quinn had gone off to college. Baron had always been my dog, but he had a special fondness for Pardee, sort of the mirror image of my relationship with Quinn, who'd been his father's son, but loved me best. That part of Baron's history I hadn't recounted to Sky. In fact, I'd told him as little about my marriage as I safely could without actually lying.

"If so, Pardee'll bring him to the house tomorrow."

"What's tomorrow?"

"We're going to discuss what to do about Quinn." I saw something pass over Sky's face, a thought he didn't express. I knew he didn't like Pardee's unexpected reappearance in my life any more than I did. The poor man, how could he? "I really hate having to deal with him," I said. "If it was anything or anyone but Quinn . . ."

"What happened, exactly? Was he kidnapped?"

Sky's question sent a shiver through me.

"Yes."

"And the problem's raising the ransom?"

"It's more complicated than that. But I don't want to talk about that now," I said, tears filling my eyes. "I want to get *engaged*!"

Sky chuckled and pinched my nose. "Josie Mayne, you're adorable."

"Well, I do, dammit."

"Okay, then. Josie, I love you more than you can possibly know," he said, speaking quickly, "and more than anything, I want you to be my wife. Will you marry me?" He held my diamond up for me to see. "What do you say?"

"Sky Tyler, I love you, and I would be honored to be your wife."

With that, he slipped the ring onto my finger and we kissed. Afterward he noticed the tear running down my cheek. "What's this? Tears of joy?"

"No, I really wanted you to do it on your knee like you tried to do before Pardee interrupted."

"That struck me as a failed strategy," he replied, "and I thought I'd better do it quick and dirty before a meteor hit the roof or something."

I laughed. "I can hardly blame you for that."

"Now that we're officially engaged and nobody can stop us, we can go inside and do the ceremonial thing, if you like."

"No, I've got you and my ring. That's all that matters. Anyway, it was my fault everything got messed up."

"It wasn't your fault, Josie."

"Yes, it was. I never should have married the guy."

Sky held me, which I was very grateful for, and said, "Now your life is tied to mine. It'll be a different story from here on out. How about if we go to my place and consummate this engagement?"

I glanced at my sparkler, shining in the moonlight. "I can't think of anything I'd rather do."

My fiancé and I went off, hand in hand. I was happy, but I knew the seeds of trouble had been planted. I refused to let that spoil the rest of our evening, though. I'd deal with my family crisis in the morning. Tonight belonged to me and Sky.

Nine

The unexpected appearance of one's former husband was not the ideal extra touch to an engagement party—in fact, it was the pits. But seeing Pardee did not bother me nearly so much as the shocking news about Quinn.

I really did love the kid, though of course he was hardly a kid anymore. Quinn was twenty-seven now and in graduate school. There was no way on earth I could be old enough to be his mother, of course, but I'd been his parent—albeit a stepparent—and I had given him my heart. The mere thought that the young kid I'd spent hours with over math problems or working on an essay for his history or English class was now being held for ransom with a gun to his head made me sick to my stomach.

But for Sky's sake, if not my own, I was determined not to dwell on Quinn, or Pardee, either. Tomorrow would be soon enough to face my problems. Instead, I admired my ring in the dim light of the car and I glanced over at Sky, who'd been super about the debacle Pardee's arrival had caused. My fiancé was emotionally mature and I respected him for that.

Putting some slack in my seat belt, I leaned over and gave him a kiss on the cheek. "Thanks for being so understanding, honey," I said. "Not many men would have handled an ex-husband showing up in the middle of a marriage proposal as well as you did."

"I accept the fact that it's all part of being with you, darling. You warned me you weren't very conventional. Unconventional people tend to lead unconventional lives."

I wanted to ask what he thought of Pardee, to get his take on the man, because I had no objectivity whatsoever. Most people considered Pardee an eccentric, which he was, or a flake, which is partially true, and most definitely an enigma—something he remained in my mind right up until the day I left him. But then a part of me always wondered if that wasn't because of the effect he had on me. Maybe others, who were more detached, could see right through the guy.

"So, how was it seeing him after all this time?" Sky asked, our minds obviously on parallel courses.

We were passing the Rancho Canada Golf Course at the west end of the valley, nearing the light at the Cabrillo Highway. In a few minutes we'd be at Sky's place. I wanted any conversation about Pardee to be over by the time we got there, so I addressed his question head-on.

"Annoying," I replied. "In one way or another Pardee almost always annoyed me. What was your impression of him?"

"Seemed like a very unusual person."

"You're being charitable," I said.

"I can see how you might have married him."

"Really?" I was genuinely surprised. "Why's that?"

"He's macho and independent. Good-looking in a rugged, earthy way. That sort of thing appeals to young women, I think."

I considered that. "You could be right. Pardee was my youthful folly and I outgrew him."

We'd turned south on the Cabrillo Highway, then right on Rio Road, which took us to Santa Lucia and the point overlooking Carmel Bay. Sky's place occupied the most spectacular setting of the many luxurious homes in the neighborhood. It was a modern glass marvel, surrounded on three sides by water, with a huge deck that wrapped nearly all the way around it.

I visited often enough that I kept some things there, but not to the point where anyone could say I was a live-in girlfriend. I'd kept Sky at a bit of a distance, not so much as a stratagem, but rather as a reflection of my true sense of propriety. I hadn't been desperate to snag him. When we first met, I was still too wounded because of Pardee to chase after any man. Sky was the one who had pursued me.

Our relationship developed gradually over time. Marta said it was because I would only let myself take baby steps, which, I think, is probably true—nothing bold, nothing rash, certainly nothing like the way I'd so easily succumbed to Pardee. When Sky met me and asked me out to dinner the first time, I'd suggested lunch instead because it sounded less . . . romantic, I guess.

So Sky had taken me to lunch. And the following week, he'd taken me to lunch and a movie. We fell into the habit of doing that every weekend until one Saturday when he showed up on my doorstep with a fancy picnic basket full of goodies he'd had a deli put together. He had a blanket with him, and we'd had lunch on my front lawn, looking at the field of brussels sprouts and talking about our lives.

We started going out to dinner, having more romantic dates after that, and the sexual relationship evolved naturally—out of our friendship and mutual respect. That might sound kind of boring to some women, but after being swept off my feet by Pardee and into a new life almost before I knew what had happened to me, I was grateful for a little sanity and decorum.

The bottom line was, I trusted Sky. We were always one hundred percent honest with each other. With Pardee I had wanted to be myself, but that always seemed to cause more problems than it solved.

Sky pulled into the garage and we went in the house.

"Care for something to drink?" he asked as I stood under the bright lights of the kitchen, admiring my ring again. I couldn't get enough of it, never having expected to own anything so beautiful.

"No, thanks, honey. I'm still feeling the champagne."

He came over and took me in his arms. "You know what I love about you?"

"What?"

"You'd feel the same about me if all I'd been able to afford was a two-hundred-dollar diamond chip."

I blew on my ring, then polished it on the edge of my skirt. "What makes you so sure? I'm already pretty attached to this thing."

"I know you, Josie."

He was right, of course. "Well, you know what I love about *you*?" I replied.

"What?"

"That you know the real me. That makes it more fun to be myself. I'd hate it if I had to pretend to be somebody other than who I am."

Sky opened his mouth to say something, but I put my finger to his lips, stopping him, because I was afraid he was going to make a comment about Pardee. I suppose it's hard not to think about people from your loved one's past. There were women in Sky's past, of course, a few of them local, but I didn't want to know about them, despite my natural curiosity. In my thirty-four years I'd learned that coping with today was tough enough without having to re-live yesterday, too.

"Take me to the bedroom and make passionate love to me," I told him. "Without further delay."

"How could any man turn down an offer like that?"

Our lovemaking was more spirited than usual. I'd had no reservations about that side of our relationship.

Did I think of Pardee while in the throes of passion? I can honestly say I didn't. He might have been lurking in a dark corner somewhere, just beyond awareness, but my at-tention, as well as my heart, was with Sky. I happily went to sleep in his arms.

At about two in the morning I awoke, feeling anxious. I'd been trying not to think of Baron, but I was aware of his absence from the bed and hoped to hell Pardee was look-ing after him. I could think of no reason why he wouldn't, but niggling doubt and Pardee went together like wine and cheese.

But even Baron got crowded out of my thoughts by Quinn. If Pardee was right about Suarez being behind this, we were talking about a lot more than ransom and a young man's future. We were most likely talking revenge, which meant that both Quinn's and Pardee's life were on the line.

I knew nothing about Fernando Suarez's present circumstances—hell, even some of the details of the original case were murky at this point. In fact, the last time I'd heard mention of him was a few months before Pardee and I split.

Suarez had ended up doing time on related charges when he refused to cooperate with the prosecution, and was released from prison after a couple of years. He returned to Mexico and, since the Mexicans had never made any further attempts on either Pardee or me after the incident with the Nicaraguans, we assumed the matter was pretty much closed.

It seemed we were wrong.

Unable to sleep, I went out onto the deck for some air and to watch the sea. I'd slipped on the nightgown I kept at Sky's place. It wasn't warm enough for the cool night air, but I decided to tough it out.

The house was situated on a rocky point overlooking the sea, the moon so bright I could make out the greenish hue of the water and the pale gold of the hills. Along the coast to the north I could see Pebble Beach, the dark foliage of the cypress, eucalyptus and oak standing out in contrast to the fairways and the pale sea cliffs below.

This was one of the most beautiful places on the planet. Soon I would be marrying a prominent citizen of this exclusive community and this would be my town. Despite myself, I couldn't quite believe it. Was this me? Did Sky really think I'd fit in?

He'd agreed I could still spend my days in my Grumman AgCat biplane dusting crops. I could still don Daddy's leather flying helmet and ply the skies with Baron in the backseat. I could keep my career, live my life as I chose, sharing it with Sky on mutually agreed-on terms. But I still worried that we were kidding ourselves.

Josie Mayne the pilot was one thing. Maybe we could get by that. But there was another Josie, too. There was the Josie who had gone to war, who got a rush chasing bad guys and, yes, the Josie who'd screwed Pardee at the Hotel Casa Sierra Madre in Durango, Mexico, at Caesars Palace in Vegas, under the stars on a godforsaken ranch in the high desert and a thousand other times in between. It wasn't so much Pardee that concerned me as the woman who'd first succumbed to him, then had trouble walking away.

The middle of the night, I could see, was a time of self-doubt. I held up my ring to the moonlight, wondering if Sky's fiancée wasn't as false as Pardee's wife.

"Couldn't sleep, I see."

Sky was at the door. He had on his bathrobe. "Yeah, thought I'd get some air."

He came over and leaned on the railing next to me and gazed out at the panoramic view. "Pretty at night, isn't it?"

"It's lovely. You're so fortunate."

"*We're* fortunate, Josie. *We.*"

I dared not share the doubt I'd been feeling. It wasn't the time. Not the first night of our engagement. "We," I said, acknowledging his point.

When I shivered, Sky put his arm around me. "Want a jacket or something?"

"No, you're keeping me warm."

He kissed my temple. "I love you," he said.

I looked up at him, brushing back the wisps of hair tossed by the breeze. "I love you, too, Sky."

He rubbed my arm vigorously to ward off the chill, and we looked out at a freighter moving north, four or five miles out to sea. I lay my head on his shoulder. I could feel his warm breath on my hair.

"You're upset, aren't you?" he said.

"Yeah, I guess."

"Because of your stepson?"

"Yes, I have a bad feeling."

"You must care for him a lot."

"I do, Sky. And it's mutual. Quinn was sixteen the first time I laid eyes on him. Pardee hadn't even told me he existed until the kid showed up at the ranch."

"What?"

"Yeah, I know, it's another pathetic example of how the man doesn't have even the slightest idea of what it means to have an honest relationship. But the point is Quinn was a good kid, decent and good-hearted. Basically, when I first met him, he was a redneck who'd dropped out of school and figured he'd make a life as a cowboy."

"But isn't he a college graduate?"

"Yes. In fact, he's in graduate school now, and mostly because of me, if I do say so. Like his daddy, Quinn is bright. But his mother hadn't exactly stressed the importance of education, and in any case we lived out in the middle of nowhere, with the nearest high school fifty miles away. Once Quinn decided to stay with us, I offered to home-school him.

"Honestly, it was a lot of work, but the rewards were great. The kid soaked up knowledge and I had to keep on my toes to stay ahead of him. I'd always been strong in math and science—my father had stressed both. Along the way I instilled a desire for learning, and polished up his grammar and his manners.

"With Pardee willing to pay, Quinn decided to go to college. Now he's getting his doctorate in anthropology. Even before I got my hands on him he had an interest in Native American culture, and I did everything I could to nurture that. Got him books on the subject, even took him to a couple of digs, though Pardee thought it was going too far when the object was a basic education.

"The past two years, Quinn's spent his summers working in the Yucatán. From the letters he sent me, he made it clear that his dad wasn't real comfortable with him in Mexico, but Quinn wanted to live his own life. I can't blame him for that, but it looks like the sins of the father may have caught up with him."

"Are you sure it's not just a ransom thing?"

"Pardee suspects it's really about him, and he's probably right."

I'd never told Sky the details of Pardee's and my brush with Mexican officialdom, but since I was being drawn back into things, I figured he was entitled to know what was going on. I gave him a brief summary of the Fernando Suarez affair.

"Ironically, it was the first job Pardee and I did together," I explained. "Wouldn't you know that of the dozens we've done since, that's the one that's coming back to bite us in the butt."

"Sounds like you consider it your fight, Josie."

I took a deep breath, wanting to find the words to help him understand how important this was to me. "I was as much a mother to Quinn as the woman who gave him birth. True, he was near grown before I entered his life, but if it wasn't for me, he'd probably be poking cattle."

"Did you stay in touch after he left home?"

"Sure. He was already in college when Pardee and I divorced, but we saw him holidays and he'd phone home regularly. After his father and I split, I'd make a point to talk to him once or twice a month. And he came to visit me a couple of times.

"I knew he was thinking about going to Mexico for the summer. The last time we spoke he told me how excited he was about it. I almost tried to dissuade him, but then I figured he was old enough to make his own decisions. But now, in retrospect, maybe I should have said something."

"It isn't your fault, Josie."

"Maybe not. I know you can't second-guess fate. But when I saw that picture of him with a gun to his head, I about died."

My voice cracked with emotion and Sky rubbed my arm again, kissing my hair. "His father'll figure something out, darling."

That, I knew, was true. But at the same time, it left me in a terrible position. I was caught between my love for Quinn and Pardee's need for help on the one hand, and my love for my fiancé and our new life together on the other.

Sky couldn't have known it, much less understood it, but the new Josie and the old Josie were at war.

Ten

By the time morning rolled around, I had built up a fairly significant obsession with Quinn's predicament. No matter how hard I tried, I couldn't stop the picture in my head of Quinn with a gun to his temple. The image was eating at me something terrible, and I knew it had to be eating at Pardee, too.

But I tried to be cheerful for Sky's sake. After all, it wasn't his problem. So I put a smile on my face and didn't complain when he told me that he had a business meeting in Monterey at nine, which meant I'd have to get a ride home with Arturo. I didn't have any aerial applications scheduled until the afternoon, so I wasn't in a hurry.

I was still in my nightgown, making breakfast, when Sky came into the kitchen, looking every bit the successful young businessman.

"You're pretty spiffy," I said, pushing my hair back off my face.

"And you're absolutely gorgeous," he replied, taking my

chin in his hand and looking deep into my eyes. "The most beautiful thing I've ever seen."

I had to laugh at that, knowing I'd only run my fingers through my thick curls to untangle them. But I held up my left hand. "Well, at least my ring finger is beautiful."

Sky beamed. My infatuation with the ring amused him. It truly was beautiful, of course, but it wasn't the size of the stone or the splendor of the setting that fired my enthusiasm. It was the symbolism, Sky's rather dramatic statement that he wanted the world to know I was committed to be his wife.

Pardee hadn't given me an engagement ring, just a thin gold band when we married. It wasn't that he was cheap. He'd asked once if I wanted a ring, and I'd declined. I'd never cared much about jewelry, so what was I going to do with big gaudy diamond? But that was the old Josie.

I poured us both some coffee and, while Sky drank his juice, I put the fixings for the omelette I had ready into the skillet. I looked over my shoulder to take in more of Skylar's smile.

"So, how you feeling this morning?" he asked. "I know you didn't sleep well."

"The morning sun always helps, but the problems remain."

Maybe Sky had sensed the resolve in my voice, because he went right to the pivotal issue. "What have you decided to do, Josie?"

I was glad my back was to him, but I straightened my shoulders anyway. "I'm giving Pardee some money to help with the expenses of the operation. Beyond that I'm not certain. But I won't turn my back on Quinn. What that means, exactly, will depend. First, I guess I have to discuss the situation with Pardee. But you need to know there's a chance I'll be taking some time off to devote to this, Sky."

I'd been working at the stove as I spoke and, when I didn't get a response, I glanced back at him. Sky's happy, upbeat expression had turned somber.

"Josie, you aren't going to Mexico, are you?"

His voice was so flat that my heart went out to him. Poor Sky. Engaged less than twenty-four hours and I was already talking about going off with my ex on an adventure that could end both Sky's and my dreams for a future together.

But what choice did I have? If I was the kind of woman who could turn her back on Quinn, would Sky have loved me?

"Honey, I can't answer that yet. I probably won't have to actually go to Mexico, but I have to wait and see how things develop. I suppose it's possible, though. I should tell you that."

"To the extent my views matter," he said, "I wish you wouldn't."

I could see he was upset. I folded the omelette over, lowered the flame, and went over to the table and stood next to him. "Sky," I said, unconsciously toying with his hair, "you're more important to me than anything, but it's also important to me that I be free to do what I have to do."

"Oh, you're free, Josie. That's not the issue. But it doesn't mean I don't have my preferences. Crop dusting is not without its dangers, but I accept that. The same with bounty hunting, though that one's a lot harder to swallow. But we're talking Mexico. It's not just another job."

"Yeah," I said with a sigh. "I know."

"Listen, darling, you're not superwoman and your life is not a James Bond movie."

"You aren't telling me anything I don't already know."

The skillet sizzled and I ran to the stove to take off the omelette. It wasn't exactly scorched, but it was a little better done than I intended. It would have to do, though, since there wasn't time to make another. I took it to Sky, putting it on his plate.

"Sorry," I said, "it's a bit overdone. I'm afraid I'm not much of a housewife. But you already knew that."

He put his arm around my waist and gave me a squeeze. "Josie, darling, it's taken me a lifetime to find you. I don't want to lose you. *That's* what's going through my mind."

It was around nine-thirty by the time Arturo turned into the long drive that led to my house. I was on the edge of the backseat in the big Lincoln, eager to see Baron. We neared the house, but I saw no ex-husband, and no dog frolicking on the lawn. I wasn't too worried, though, because Pardee would have to show up soon. He needed the money I'd promised him.

Then, just as I was beginning to wonder how long before I saw Baron again, he came bounding down the front steps. The car had no sooner stopped than I was out, on my knee and giving my puppy a big hug.

"So, feel guilty, do you?" I said as the limo turned around in the large gravel parking area and headed back toward the highway.

Baron yapped at me.

"Yeah, you ought to feel bad, you traitor."

I didn't see Pardee and wondered if he and Baron had somehow separated and Baron had made his way home on his own. I checked his paws to see if they were cut up, which they would have been if he'd run all night on the pavement, but they seemed fine. Standing, I headed for the house.

I was about halfway there when I saw something on the porch behind the hydrangeas. By the time I made it to the steps I could see that Pardee was stretched out on a lounge chair that he'd apparently brought around from out back. His Stetson was over his face and he appeared to be sound asleep.

I marched up the painted wooden steps to my porch but even the sound of my heels didn't awaken him. For some reason, that annoyed the hell out of me. So when I got to him, I gave the sole of his boot a gentle kick with my toe. Baron barked, adding his two cents.

That rousted Pardee from his slumber. Lifting his hat off his face, he squinted at me in the bright morning sun.

"Jesus," he said, "it's about time you come rolling in. Have you no shame, woman?"

"What's the idea of taking my dog without asking permission?" I had my hands on my hips and that unmistakable look of indignation on my face.

He lifted himself to his elbows and flexed his grizzled jaw, blinking the sleep from his eyes. "I did not take Baron. He followed me. I kept telling him to go back, but he stayed with me all the way to the highway."

"The highway?"

"Yeah, I hitchhiked. Took me damned near all night to get here. Not too many folks will give a ride to a man with a dog."

I smirked. "I thought Marta gave you a lift to the club."

"She did, but I couldn't ask her to stay. I guess I'd sort of expected to get a ride home with you. It was a bad assumption, I guess."

"That's putting it mildly." I crossed my arms over my chest as I regarded him. "So what happened, did you end up sleeping on the porch?"

"All night, sweetheart. Or what was left of it, anyway."

I shook my head. "That's pathetic."

"Yeah, I know. I probably should have rented a car, but I really expected a more friendly reception than what I got."

"Did you really? Even knowing I was with Sky?"

"I don't see how that figures into our problem."

My eyes narrowed. "*Your* problem. Or has it slipped your mind that we're no longer married?"

"Christ, Josie, give me a break. I wouldn't even be here if it wasn't for Quinn. Considering it's a business trip, I didn't see why personal issues had to be brought into it."

I shook my head again. "I'm amazed we lasted as long as we did."

"Don't get on your high horse, Josephine. You're the one showing up in the same dress you wore to a party the night before."

I felt my blood pressure soar. I shouldn't have let him get to me, but I did. "That wasn't just any party, that was my *engagement* party. And the man I was with was my fiancé . . . not that I owe you any explanation."

Pardee sat up, swinging his legs off the lounge chair and letting his boots clunk onto the porch. He yawned, running his fingers through his tawny hair. "That's right, the whole thing kind of slipped from my mind, what with standing out on the highway half the night and trying to get a little shut-eye on this thing the other half."

"It's your own damned fault. If you'd stayed away from the oil leases and the card rooms, we wouldn't be having this conversation."

He looked up at me, surprise on his face. "Jesus, Josie, you slipped back into the wife mode slick as an automatic going from third to fourth. Is it my smiling face or are you practicing up for . . . What was his name?"

"Sky," I said, glaring.

"Right." He grinned, friendly as could be. "Sweetheart, I don't want to impose any more than absolutely necessary, but I'd sure like to use your bathroom. And if you could spare a bite of breakfast that would be nice, too. Haven't had a bite to eat since lunch yesterday and I'm starved."

I gave him a long, hard look. "A friend of mine told me that former husbands will fade, but they rarely disappear for good. I now see what she meant."

"Hells bells, do I look like I want to be here?"

I dug my house key out of my purse. "You've got a point. And when you get a look at yourself in the mirror, you'll see what I mean."

I decided to suck it up. Reason told me that the best way to get through this was to avoid butting heads, which wasn't easy given that Pardee brought out the worst in me. But I resolved to bite my tongue. I had, after all, outgrown him. Besides, it was obvious that he wasn't enjoying it any more than me.

Since he'd been on the road for a couple of days and sleeping in his clothes, I told him to shave and get cleaned up while I fixed him some breakfast and got his check.

"Much obliged for the loan, Josie," he said. "It's damned decent of you."

"I'm doing it for Quinn."

That jab probably hadn't been necessary, but I was determined to be clear on the point . . . not that it didn't feel good to tweak him a little. That had been the essence of our relationship—taking potshots at each other until the tension rose to a breaking point and we had no choice but to burst into a full-fledged screaming fight—either that or screw one another into submission. Those days were long over, of course, but the impulses remained. Old habits die hard, I guess.

"I'm sure Quinn will be every bit as grateful as I am when he hears about it," Pardee said. Then he went off to the bathroom.

I sat down at the kitchen table to write a check, then realized I had to be sure of the amount. I called my bank to see what I could get for my CDs after penalties. It was less than I'd hoped. I decided to give Pardee fifteen thousand and asked the bank to do the necessary paperwork so I could come in, sign and get the money into my checking account that afternoon. I wrote out the check and left it on the table.

Then I decided it was time to change out of Marta's dress. Wearing it at ten in the morning did make me feel a little loose—and not only because of what Pardee had said. It just did.

On the way to the bedroom, I passed the bath. Pardee was in the shower, singing. The poor bastard had a terrible voice, but it had never stopped him from showcasing it in the shower. Thank God that was the only time he tried.

Baron sat just outside the bathroom door, half baying and half barking. It was hard to tell whether he was complaining or trying to harmonize.

"Jesus, Baron," I muttered as I passed, "you're overdoing it a little, aren't you?" I wondered if dogs needed an occasional testosterone fix, the same as women.

Feeling uncomfortable in the dress, I changed into my uniform—jeans and a work shirt—figuring I could shower later. My ring didn't look quite as natural with this outfit, but there was no way I was going to take it off. Not that Pardee would necessarily notice that I had it on—though Lord knows it was big enough that it could have blinded him. I didn't want any ambiguity regarding my situation.

After checking my hair, I headed to the kitchen to make Pardee breakfast. As I passed through the front room, I heard a cell phone ring. The sound was coming from Pardee's stuff, which he'd piled on the couch. I retreated to the bathroom door, where Baron continued his vigil, sycophant that he was.

The shower was no longer running, the serenade over. I rapped on the door. "Pardee, your cell phone is ringing," I announced.

"I'm buck-ass naked, sweetheart. Would you mind answering it for me?"

I rolled my eyes. God, men. "Where is it?"

"Should be in my jacket pocket."

I went back to the front room. Fortunately Pardee's denim jacket was lying on top of his things. The phone continued to ring as I dug it out of the breast pocket. I pushed the call button.

"Hello?"

"Yes," the caller, a man, replied, "I'm trying to reach Mr. Pardee. Do I have the right number?"

"This is his phone, but he's unavailable. Can I take a message?"

"This wouldn't be Mrs. Pardee, by any chance?"

"No, Josie Mayne. Who's calling?"

"Oh, Ms. Mayne, what luck. I was hoping to reach you,

as well. This is Andrew Waith, I'm an attorney in Austin. I represented Jack Hardy for many years before he passed away last November."

I had no idea what he was talking about. "So?"

"I'm afraid I have bad news. Jack's longtime employee, Ernesto Blanco, was shot dead two nights ago outside his home. The police think it was a professional hit. I thought it prudent to notify you and Mr. Pardee immediately."

I was about to say I had no idea who Jack Hardy and Ernesto Blanco were, and that if this had something to do with Pardee's oil leases it was no concern of mine. But then it hit me. The inside man in the Suarez case had been named Blanco and a man named Jack had hired us.

"Mr. Waith, do you have any reason to believe this could be connected to Fernando Suarez?"

"That's the concern, yes. I know Jack had felt an obligation to you and Mr. Pardee and didn't want anything happening to you. If you would pass this information on to Mr. Pardee, I'd be obliged."

"Sure," I mumbled, though my mind had already moved on to the implications of what I'd heard. "I'll tell him."

Waith gave me his number in case Pardee had any questions. I jotted it down on the pad by my house phone, and we ended the call. I didn't know Jack Hardy from the man in the moon, and I'd never seen Blanco after we'd dropped him off at the motel in San Antonio the morning after our return from Mexico, but this was striking a lot closer to home than I would have liked. I numbly stuck Pardee's phone back into his jacket pocket when the bathroom door opened.

Pardee was in his jeans, his feet and chest bare. It had been a while since I'd seen that magnificent, broad, furry chest, but it was shockingly familiar. The image, after all, had been etched in my brain over the course of two thousand days of togetherness. That was hardly a point worthy of concern at the moment, however.

"Who called?" he asked.

"A lawyer in Austin who used to represent Jack Hardy."

"And?"

"Ernesto Blanco was murdered a couple of nights ago. They think by a professional assassin."

Pardee looked as shocked as I felt. For a long moment he stood motionless, then he said, "Shit."

Eleven

I'd made my second omelette of the morning—wouldn't you know Pardee would ask for the same thing—and to add insult to injury, this one turned out perfect.

"You never were much of a cook, Crazy Legs," Pardee said, pushing the plate away, "but you could damned well make an omelette. I enjoyed that."

"Well, I'm glad you did. But would you mind dispensing with the Crazy Legs business? It's no longer appropriate."

"Why's that?" he asked innocently. "I checked them out last night and they look as good as they ever did."

Pardee gave me his usual smug grin then, one you couldn't exactly call flirtatious, but suggested he thought he was cute and implied you should feel the same. I chose not to argue the point, knowing it would only encourage him. I did give him a look of disapproval, though. I felt an obligation.

Naturally, he hadn't put on a shirt. He knew his chest was to die for. The object probably wasn't to be seductive, just to rub it in. I, after all, had left him, which in his book meant that I was the one who should be feeling guilty. (I didn't.) I wasn't about to give him the satisfaction of any kind of reaction, though—especially when there were other things on my mind. I sat down across from him.

"What do you make of Blanco being murdered?"

"He was a traitor to the Suarez family, so there was no love lost there. What surprises me is that it's been ten years."

"Almost twelve, Pardee."

"That long? God, how time flies. Seems like only yesterday I was breaking you in."

"Could we refrain from salacious comments and stick to business, please?"

"Josie, I meant break you in professionally, not sexually."

I flushed, realizing *I* was the one whose mind was in the gutter. "Whatever," I said, struggling to hide my embarrassment. "But getting back to Suarez, you think twelve years is too long to hold a grudge? They just now kidnapped Quinn."

"Yeah, but that's because he was a soft target and he was in Mexico. If they wanted Blanco this bad, you'd think they'd have found an opportunity before now."

"Maybe we should consider the possibility that what happened to Blanco might not have anything to do with Suarez."

"Yeah, that's possible. It could be about something else. He's done other dirty jobs for Jack over the years, I'm sure."

"You never told me anything about Jack Hardy. Who was he anyway?"

"One of those low-profile movers and shakers who exerts tremendous power behind the scenes. He knew politicians on a first-name basis, could even whisper in a president's or congressional committee chairman's ear and the next thing you knew, some tax break for the rich that especially benefited him was written into law, all in the name of lowering taxes to fight the tax-and-spend Democrats," Pardee said with a derisive laugh. "Why people can't see through that bullshit, I'll never know."

"Why do you care, Pardee? You never paid a tax in your life."

"Never took a thing from the government, either."

I had a rejoinder, but thought better of it and let it go.

But Pardee was on a roll. "Not that I blamed Jack for grabbing what he could. Hell, if people are so stupid as to elect politicians who'll give their money to guys like Jack, they deserve what they get. And the man did make deals happen; he had that kind of juice. You never saw his name in the paper, but everybody who was anybody in Texas knew Jack Hardy and what he could do for them."

"How was he involved in the Suarez deal?"

"He wasn't, Josie. Not directly, anyway. Fernando Suarez's testimony would have saved his son's butt, had he testified, and that's why Jack paid us. To save Junior. But Suarez chose to spend time in the slammer rather than cooperate. So in the end, all that came of our handiwork was a lot of bad blood."

"With Blanco and us in the middle of it."

"The murder and Quinn's kidnapping being ample testimony to that."

"So, I guess I need to start locking my doors at night," I said.

Pardee put his hands behind his head and leaned back in his chair, flexing his muscles. I did not look at his body. I didn't even want to look at his face. He was all too familiar.

"It wouldn't be a bad idea to stay on your toes," he said.

The phone call and our conversation had gotten my juices flowing. The urgency of Quinn's situation seemed to be growing exponentially. Last night I'd been worried. Now I was feeling antsy, ready to strap on my Glock and kick some ass. But first there was need for studied reflection.

"Tell me more about Quinn's situation," I said. "Have the kidnappers identified themselves?"

"They claim to be leftist rebels from the State of Oaxaca in southern Mexico, but who knows?"

"What about Fernando Suarez? What's he doing these days?"

"That's the interesting thing. I've done some checking and it seems the young man has risen nicely from the ashes. Matter of fact, he's the present governor of the state of Oaxaca."

"You're shitting me."

"Nope."

"An interesting coincidence."

"That's why I say this is probably about me, Josie."

"Us," I corrected. "I divorced *you*, Pardee. Not our enemies."

He chuckled. "Funny the way that works, isn't it? You can get rid of the baby, but not the bathwater."

I didn't want to get into the issue of our marriage. "So, are you going to strap on your six-guns and go down there?" I asked.

"I haven't figured out what to do yet. I got the names of the people to contact to discuss ransom arrangements. They've given us a month to come up with the dough. I hope we can find a more cost-effective solution."

It was obvious to me that Pardee was hoping that I'd go to Mexico with him, but that his pride wouldn't let him ask me outright. Normally I'd have enjoyed watching the guy squirm, but I knew he was suffering about Quinn as I was. Hell, just recalling that photo of Quinn with a gun to his head made me want to say, *To hell with it, let's saddle up.*

Yet the sparkler on my finger reminded me of my new life, with all its promise.

"You've got my check," I said, avoiding the bottom line. "What's next?"

"I've been working on this for several days, poring over maps, gathering intelligence. I gave a guy three thousand of Ellie's money to go down to Oaxaca and photograph a number of sites I identified. I've also talked to a friend of mine down there about aircraft."

"You learned to fly since we split, Pardee?"

For a second he didn't understand the question, then realized in mentioning aircraft he'd inadvertently tipped his hand. "No, that's just in case."

"In case what?"

The devil in me wanted to make him ask me to go with him. I was ashamed of myself, but not too much.

About then Baron, who'd been shamefully resting his chin on Pardee's bare foot, jumped to his feet and began barking like crazy as he headed for the front door. I looked out the window in time to see Sky's Mercedes come to a stop out front, the cloud of dust that had been following it drifting off to the east. If past and present weren't conflicted enough, I could see things were about to get worse. Turning my ring on my finger, I went to the front door.

Sky walked briskly across the lawn. My fiancé was pretty even-tempered and low key—the only passion I'd ever seen him show had been toward me. But there was so much determination in his stride that I couldn't help wondering if he was angry. Or perhaps it was something else. I'd find out soon enough

Baron slipped out the door and went to greet Sky, who acknowledged him with a nod and a word. They arrived at the foot of the steps and stopped there. "Is Pardee here?" he asked. There was something ominous in his tone.

"Yes, he is. In fact, we were just discussing what to do about Quinn. Come on in and have a cup of coffee with us."

"I don't mean to intrude, Josie, but I'd like a word with him, if that's all right."

Sky was being direct, but I didn't sense anger. He had a no-nonsense side to him and this was it. I couldn't imagine, though, what he wanted with Pardee.

Sky and Baron came up the steps. Sky smiled faintly as he went past me, but he didn't kiss me. He was in a business frame of mind. I closed the door. Pardee had come out of the kitchen and was leaning casually against the doorframe. Considering he was wearing jeans and nothing else, I could imagine what Sky was thinking. I didn't like it, but there wasn't a damned thing I could do about it now. My innocence would have to do.

"Morning, Mr. Tyler," Pardee said with a lord-of-the-manor-type self-assurance.

"Hello, Mr. Pardee."

"Just Pardee. Everybody calls me that." He grinned.

Sky shifted uncomfortably. It was an awkward situation. More so, even, than last night. I couldn't see things turning nasty, because Sky just wasn't that kind of guy. And even though Pardee wasn't above needling and being provocative, he didn't out-and-out pick fights.

"Who wants coffee?" I asked, jumping right in.

"I don't mean to intrude," Sky said. "I know you two

have important things to discuss, but I've been thinking about your son, Pardee. I share Josie's concern and I'd like to contribute to the effort to repatriate him."

Both Pardee's and my brows went up. But I was relieved Sky's intent was constructive.

"I'm sure money is critical," Sky continued. "So I'd like to pay Josie's share plus kick in some extra."

Pardee scratched his head, looking as perplexed as he was pleased. "That's mighty generous of you," he said.

"Forgive my ignorance, but I have no idea what it costs to mount a rescue operation. What kind of figure are we looking at?"

"A lot," Pardee replied.

"Twenty-five, thirty thousand?"

"For a minimal operation, yeah."

"How about if I give you a check for fifty, then? No point in cutting corners. And if more is needed down the line, let me know."

"Sky," I said, taking his arm, "that's so sweet of you, but this isn't your fight."

"If it's your fight, Josie, it's my fight, too. Now, don't get me wrong, I won't interfere. But if your life is at stake, we don't want anybody using secondhand guns and bullets and grenades that are past their expiration date, do we?"

"I appreciate your generosity," Pardee said, chuckling as he ambled over, "I truly do. But I can only accept your very kind offer under one condition."

"What's that?"

"That I be allowed to pay you back."

"Don't worry about it," Sky said. "I'm not without resources and there is always money available for a worthy cause. What could be more worthy than something Josie feels as passionate about as your son?" He took his check-book out of his inside coat pocket. "Who do I make the check out to?"

To his credit, Pardee looked at me as if to say, *Is this okay?* I nodded.

"N. Pardee would be fine, Mr. Tyler."

"Sky."

"Right."

Sky went to the sofa so he could write on the coffee table. I watched him, feeling a little funny—sort of like he was my patron, covering the expenses of my crusade. Having finished, he returned to where Pardee, Baron and I waited. He handed Pardee the check.

"I hope this helps."

"Much obliged, Sky. Remember, though, I'm paying back every penny."

"Don't worry about it."

I could see that Pardee was touched and grateful, despite his pride. Reaching into his pocket, he took out my check and handed it back to me. "I'd rather take charity than risk your life savings, sweetheart. Thanks to Sky, I won't need this."

I looked back and forth between the two of them, feeling like a girl who'd been asked to the dance by two different guys. "The important thing is that we get Quinn home in one piece," I said.

"I know it's none of my business," Sky said, "but as a silent partner of sorts, I'm curious about your plans."

"They're in the early stages," Pardee said.

"This probably sounds stupid, but is it unreasonable to think the kidnapper might release your son in exchange for the ransom money, even if you're the real target?"

"Who knows? But it hardly matters, given that they're asking for a million bucks. I'm sure that can be negotiated down, but wherever we end up, it'll still be a sizable chunk of change."

"Well, finance happens to be one of my areas of expertise, so if I can be of help, please feel free to consult me."

"Thanks."

Sky turned to me. I knew he wanted to know whether I'd decided to go to Mexico. I owed him an answer. Trouble was, I didn't have one.

"We won't know what's going to happen until Pardee and I develop a plan," I told him. "What I end up doing—whether I have to go to Mexico or not—will depend entirely on what we come up with."

"Will you have to leave here in the interim?"

We all had avoided meeting the issue head-on, and the time had come to discuss it. I figured it was just as well we do it in front of Sky. "Where's headquarters?" I asked my former husband.

"I guess the ranch. It's relatively safe there. And after that call, safety's a consideration."

Sky looked at me questioningly.

"We got a phone call a few minutes ago. A man who helped us with Suarez was murdered," I explained. "There's a possibility . . . a strong possibility . . . it could be connected with the case."

I saw the color go right out of Sky's face. I began spinning my ring, not liking the fact that Sky was upset or that we all had to make choices that were uncomfortable. But it was not a time for me to be faint of heart. Sky already knew that our engagement was not going to change my commitment to my career. This was about Quinn, true, but it was also about what I did for a living, who I was, the way I wanted to live my life. And though his generosity was admirable, I wasn't going to let that change who I was.

"Since the initial work will be done at operation headquarters, that's where I'll be," I said.

"How long will you be gone?"

"Several days, I imagine."

"I see. When will you be leaving?"

I glanced at Pardee.

"Yesterday wouldn't be too soon," he said.

"Today sometime," I said to Sky. "I've got an application this afternoon that can't be rescheduled, which means a couple of hours in the air. And I need to go by the bank and take care of some business. Then I guess we'll be heading out."

"Okay." He glanced alternately at Pardee, then at me. "Well, I know you have lots to do, so I'll be getting out of your way. Good luck," he said, offering Pardee his hand.

"Thanks," Pardee said. "And once again, I'm much obliged."

"Happy to help."

"Let me assure you that Josie's going to be fine," Pardee said. "We're both professionals and that's the way we're approaching this."

I was grateful for the comment. He didn't have to say that, but he knew what Sky had to be thinking—his new fiancée going off with her former husband. But Pardee was right, there was nothing to be concerned about, and it was good for Sky to hear it from him.

I took Sky's hand. "Come on, honey, I'll walk you to the car."

Sky and Pardee said a final goodbye and we went outside. Baron tagged along, loping beside me.

"I can't tell you how much I appreciate what you've done," I said as we walked toward the Mercedes.

"Considering my feelings for you, I had to do it. I love you, Josie."

I gave his waist a squeeze and leaned my head on his shoulder. "It's situations like this that show a person's heart, Sky. I love you even more than before . . . if that's possible."

"All I want is your promise that you'll take good care of yourself. I can't afford to lose you."

We'd reached his car. I took his hands. "I promise."

He smiled sadly and gave a little nod.

"I want to say something, Skylar. I know what you must be thinking, and I appreciate the fact you haven't complained. If we're going to be husband and wife, trust is essential. You have no reason to worry about me being with Pardee because it's you I love.

"Point I'm trying to make is that maybe this crisis coming along when it has is a good thing, because if our love can't survive me doing a job with Pardee again, then we're in trouble. I want you to know this is about rescuing Quinn. There is no other agenda."

"I understand that."

"Do you?"

"Josie, I know you're doing what you think you have to do for your stepson. I didn't expect our relationship to be tested quite this early, either, but as you say, better sooner than later."

He was so good it brought tears to my eyes. "Can I ask a big favor of you, Sky?"

"Sure. Anything."

"With the exception of you, nobody in the world means as much to me as Baron. Would you take care of him for me while I'm gone?"

"Of course. Do you want me to take him with me now?"

"If you wouldn't mind."

I got down on my knee and gave Baron a hug. Some people might have thought it silly, but I actually cried. "Listen to me, you two-faced bastard," I whispered in his ear. "I want you to be good while you're at Sky's. Behave yourself and try to do whatever he says. And it would be nice if you made an effort to get to know him a little better, too."

Baron barked.

"Will you make an effort? Please."

Another bark.

"Thank you. And remember. A man doesn't have to be an animal to be lovable."

Baron gave a low growl and a sideward look.

"Trust me," I told him. "I know." After kissing the top of his head, I stood.

Sky opened the rear door and I told Baron to get in. He tilted his head, looking uncertain, and I pointed to the backseat. He hopped in. Sky closed the door. I put my arms around Sky's neck and gave him a big juicy kiss.

"I love you, Sky," I said.

He managed a smile and got in his car, started the engine and drove away. I watched until they reached the highway. When they were out of sight, I turned toward the house. I could see Pardee in the window, watching me. But that was okay because I didn't expect him to give me any trouble.

Not big trouble, anyway.

Twelve

I walked back to the house, feeling sad and alone, but also relieved that Sky had accepted my decision with such grace. Even so, I felt the low-level anxiety that comes with gearing up for a mission. Of course, that was probably increased by the fact that I would be partnering with Pardee again.

Though I knew he was a professional down to his toenails, I also knew it wouldn't be easy working side by side with my ex-husband. Add to that the fact that we were rescuing a family member, and the situation became very complicated. The unanswered question was how it would play out.

Pardee had stepped out onto the porch, his face about as blank as he could make it. He'd lived with me enough years to know my feelings would be all over the board on this one, and I think he was smart enough not to risk upsetting me any more than he already had. It was a good call.

"I'm going to grab a quick shower and pack," I told him.

"Okay, I'll sit out here and enjoy the air."

I suppose the polite thing to do was to tell him to make himself at home while I was indisposed, but I wasn't in the mood to send out friendly signals. Being matter-of-fact was the way to go.

Back in my bedroom, as I picked up Marta's dress, which I'd tossed on the bed, I couldn't help but marvel at all the things that had happened in the few hours since I'd borrowed it. Had the dress been lucky for me, or unlucky? One thing was certain—I sure hadn't expected to see Pardee while I was wearing it.

I'd drop the dress off at the cleaner's on the way to the bank, and then leave the claim check with Marta. That meant going by the florist shop where she worked after I concluded my business at the bank, but I knew she wouldn't mind being interrupted because she'd be dying to hear about last night. Besides, if I was going to be out of town for a while, I wanted to tell her goodbye.

I didn't exactly get a respite from Pardee when I was in the shower. He'd used the lavender soap Sky had given me for Valentine's Day and he'd left the cap off of my new bottle of herbal shampoo. I put him from my mind, though, and thought about Marta. I suppose some people might feel betrayed by what she'd done, both in helping Pardee to find me and then driving him to the club. But I didn't have it in me to be angry with her.

Marta was such a romantic that she probably wanted to give Pardee a last shot at sweeping me into his arms and carrying me off to his castle to live happily ever after. If Luis were still alive, I have no doubt that's what she'd have wanted for herself. Poor Marta just wasn't realistic when it came to men.

But I'd lived too long, and knew Pardee too well, to indulge in fairy tales. In spite of Marta's fervent belief that romance and true love could triumph over anything short of death, I knew my ex-husband was no Prince Charming. Besides, I wasn't the one who needed rescuing, Quinn was.

So I wouldn't hold Marta's actions of the night before against her. But I still wanted to tell her that, just in case she was concerned that I was upset or angry or planning never to speak to her again.

I towel-dried my hair, letting my curls go every which way naturally, and put on a pair of clean jeans and a white cotton shirt with long sleeves. The question was whether Pardee would go with me to take care of my business in town and then to the airport for my final aerial application, or whether he'd rather stay here until I was finished. I went to ask him what he preferred.

I found him lounging on my sofa, reading the morning paper, and asked whether he wanted to come with me or stay at the house. He was eager to get started for the ranch and said he'd come with me if I didn't mind, so we could leave for Nevada directly from the airport. The decision made, I packed enough clothes to last me for a while, grabbed a few toiletries, then let Pardee take my case to the car while I closed up the house. I planned to leave a key with Marta so she could check my mail and water my houseplants. With Baron safely in Sky's hands, I was free to leave.

The ride into Gonzales didn't take long. Pardee seemed to be preoccupied with his thoughts as I drove, though he might have been listening to the Trisha Yearwood tape I had on. It was a song about a man with a cheating heart. I saw no harm in dropping little reminders of who he was in my eyes.

Pardee came into the bank with me, but stayed in the lobby, helping himself to a cup of coffee while I transacted my business. The assistant manager, Erika Williams, was her usual efficient self, having all the necessary documents ready for me. She noticed my ring and she noticed Pardee. God only knows what was going through her mind, but I didn't have the time or energy to worry about it.

Next, we drove up the street parking near, but not right in front of, the florist shop where Marta worked. "If you don't mind, I'll go in alone," I said.

"Suit yourself."

"Want the music on?" I asked.

"Okay if I pick out another tape?"

I smiled and went inside to see my friend.

Marta was just finishing with a customer when I came in the door. As soon as the woman left, Marta rushed around the counter and hugged me.

"Oh, Josie, I hope you aren't mad I took Pardee to the club, but when he told me about his son, I was sure you'd want to know immediately."

"I'm not angry with you," I said. "The timing was unfortunate, that's all."

I held up my left hand for her to see the ring. Her eyes got so round I thought they were going to pop.

"Oh, my God! Even Mrs. Crocker's diamond isn't that big." Mrs. Crocker was the richest old dowager in town and a regular customer. Marta did the flower arrangements for all her dinner parties.

Knowing that Marta would eat up the drama of the situation, I told her how Pardee had shown up at the magic moment, just as Sky was proposing.

"How romantic." She paused then, giving me an inquiring look. "Or were you pissed?"

"It practically ruined the evening for me, but at least he had a fairly decent excuse."

"You know what it reminds me of?" Marta said with a sigh.

I was afraid to ask.

"That Errol Flynn movie when Robin Hood rescues Maid Marian from the sheriff of Nottingham."

I knew she loved the movie—I think because Robin Hood worked somewhat outside the law and so had Luis. "Pardee is obviously the good guy, in your mind," I said. "Unfortunately, I'm the Maid Marian, Marta, not you. My ex-husband is definitely not the good guy in *my* movie."

"I still think it's romantic, even if it's the sheriff who gave you the ring."

I laughed. "Believe me, if you knew Pardee like I do, you'd understand why I'm marrying Sky."

"It's your life, but I still think your ex is cool. How did he like the fact that you're getting married?"

"He didn't like it, but so what?"

Marta gave a little smile and shrugged.

Well, she could romanticize it until the cows came home, but that didn't change the fact that I was the one stuck with the problem and I knew what I wanted. It was sort of ironic, though, that Marta had thought Sky was every girl's dream . . . until Pardee showed up on the scene. It went to show how silly women could be about a man—me included, I suppose, considering I'd made the mistake of marrying him in the first place.

Now, though, I had just one thing in mind. I wanted for us to rescue Quinn and then get back to our own lives—

him with his loose women and his flaky oil leases and me to Sky Tyler.

I gave Marta the receipt from the cleaner's and asked her to take in my mail and water my plants. She already had my house key, so we hugged a final time.

"Don't do anything I wouldn't do," she said. Then she added, "which leaves you lots of free rein."

I laughed, shook my head and returned to the Jeep and Pardee.

The drive to Nevada with my ex-husband was not your usual everyday kind of experience. They say that traveling with somebody brings you closer, even if the person is a stranger. That certainly isn't the case with former spouses. I found myself resisting the temptation to fall into old habits and patterns, and it wasn't easy. It took discipline to ignore the fact I'd once shared my life with the guy and to keep things businesslike.

Unfortunately, Pardee didn't feel the same need to resist his natural inclinations. From his point of view, calling me "sweetheart" or "Crazy Legs" wasn't being disloyal to anyone, and he didn't care that I considered it improper. Controversy was no big deal to Pardee. If he felt okay about something, that was all that mattered.

After giving it some thought, I decided to broach the subject of proper conduct between us, if only to get things out in the open. I gave him my speech about it being a new day in the most polite and diplomatic manner possible, then concluded with, "It's not about feelings, Pardee, it's about creating an effective working relationship so we can get Quinn home."

I was driving and it was dark, so I couldn't get a visual

reading on his reaction. For several moments he didn't say anything, then in typical Pardee fashion he said what he was thinking, and he said it without mincing words. "Who are you afraid of, Josie, me or yourself?"

"I'm not afraid of either," I snapped, angry that he was putting me on the defensive when he was the one crossing lines.

"Then why the bullshit? You already divorced me. I don't expect this to change things. And if I say something that seems overfamiliar, it's not because there's intent behind it. Just force of habit."

"Okay, fine," I said, seeing no point in turning the conversation into a full-blown argument. I was on the record as to how I felt, and that was enough.

Neither of us said anything for half an hour and the next thing I knew Pardee had fallen asleep. I was relieved in a way, not fully appreciating until then how tense I was in his company. But I was also annoyed that Pardee had chosen to ignore my discomfort and let the chips fall where they may. I knew with certainty that it was the one thing *I* couldn't afford to do.

It was after midnight by the time we reached Carson City. I had driven the whole way up to that point and was getting tired. I could have awakened Pardee and asked him to drive the remaining fifty or so miles out to his ranch, but I decided to stop for coffee and stretch my legs instead. While he continued to snooze, I ambled back and forth in a McDonald's parking lot, thinking of Sky and Baron and looking at my ring. Quinn, I decided, certainly chose a damned inconvenient time to get kidnapped.

Pardee didn't awaken until I turned off the highway and

headed up the long gravel road that led to the ranch house. He rubbed his face and muttered something like, "We here already?" but I didn't pay much attention. I was trying to deal with my return to the home where we'd spent most of our married life.

Were it not for the bright moon, I wouldn't have been able to see the hauntingly familiar landscape. Being here again gave me the willies, especially when I realized it felt a whole lot more natural being on Pardee's ranchland than at Sky's fancy house by the ocean. The realization scared me. There was nothing about Pardee that should compare favorably to Sky. Nothing.

I pulled up in front of the double-wide and we got out. The place was dark, the air cool. A light breeze redolent with the scent of the desert washed over me. Memories flooded my mind. I thought about the jillions of times we'd returned home after having gone out on some thrilling mission to snag a bad guy and collect the bounty. I recalled how we had often raced back home after having gone to the city for dinner because we were so anxious to tear each other's clothes off that we could hardly wait to get in the door. I knew it was not the sort of thing I should be pondering, even if my feelings were now in a totally different place. This flood of memories showed just how tenacious the past could be.

Perhaps it had been naive of me to imagine that it might be otherwise. The past might be inescapable, but that didn't mean I had to be a prisoner to it. Remembering wasn't the issue, I realized. How it affected me was.

Thinking back on my marriage, it was easy to dwell on the negatives—there'd been so many of them. And of course, the man and his furry chest weren't around to remind me how exciting our life had been at times, or the way we trusted each other so completely when we were on a mission. Nor had there been any immediate reminders of Pardee himself—the way he gazed right into my eyes, watching my face, when he made love to me. Or the way he so easily reduced me to a throbbing mass. Time had turned Pardee into an abstraction, but the past two days had changed all that.

My feelings having come into sharper focus, I now regretted having come to the ranch. Dealing with Pardee back at my place had been challenging enough. Dealing with him here, where we had made our home together, would be nigh on impossible. I knew right then I was in for a rough time.

But apparently I was the only one in the grip of the past. While I was thinking about all the things I shouldn't be thinking about, Pardee had grabbed his duffel and stumbled up to the door, still half asleep. He left my things for me to carry in. Which was fine. I didn't expect any special treatment. Wouldn't have wanted it.

As I gathered my stuff, I realized we hadn't discussed sleeping arrangements. Quinn's room had been the guest room before his arrival at the ranch and after he'd gone away to college. I assumed I'd sleep there.

On more than one occasion Pardee had slept in the "spare room," as he called it, usually when we'd had a fight. His periods of exile would end when he'd concluded that my pique had run its course. He was damned good at judging when it was the right time, though I suppose it was in part because I sent out a number of unconscious signals. I think that half the time the drama was a deliberate attempt on both our parts to spice things up. But that was then, I hastily reminded myself.

Pardee never did have much in the way of housekeeping skills, and as soon as I stepped inside I realized he hadn't improved one iota. The house was dirty and smelled bad. I could see the first order of business would be to make it livable.

He came out of the kitchen with a beer in his hand. "If you want a cool one, help yourself," he said. He leaned against the doorframe, one booted foot crossing the other.

I glanced around at the mess. The remnants of two or three meals were on the coffee table. Old newspapers, mail and both dirty and clean clothing were scattered all about. "Jesus, Pardee, you could have made an effort."

"I didn't know you'd be coming back with me," he replied. "And I knew that even if you did . . . well, you'd already be here and it wouldn't matter."

The logic was typical. Vintage Pardee. "You may be right, but I'd think your pride would kick in at some point."

"Are you suggesting your opinion of me could get any lower than it was when you walked out on me?"

The man was both infuriating and incorrigible. On the other hand, comments like that were the dose of reality I needed. I wouldn't have to worry long about memories of the good old times coming back to haunt me. "Well, you can just clean the place up in the morning," I said. "I'll help, but I'm not going to do it for you."

Pardee smiled. "Okay, fine."

I was pleasantly surprised by his quick capitulation, though I tried not to show it. He took a long draw on his beer.

"So, what's stronger, the positive or negative memories?" he asked, as though he'd been in my head the past fifteen minutes.

"The negative." I spoke quickly.

"I should have figured." He headed for the master bedroom. "I'll clear out my stuff so you can move in."

"I'd rather stay in the guest room," I said.

Pardee stopped. "Why? The master bedroom's more comfortable."

"I'd prefer it, that's all," I said.

He shrugged. "Suit yourself."

"Are there clean sheets on the bed?"

He stroked his chin. "I can't rightly say. Haven't been in there for months. Can't remember the last person who slept in the bed, if you want to know the truth."

I believed him, though I suspect he could have named everybody who'd been sleeping in his bed—I should say all the women. There doubtless had been several. "I'll check," I said.

The guest room was dusty, but the bed was made, after a fashion. I pulled back the spread and checked the sheets. They appeared clean. If it wasn't so late, and if I wasn't so damned tired, I'd have washed them anyway. But I was pooped.

Pardee had followed me, coming as far as the door. "This'll be fine," I told him.

"You sure?"

"Yeah. Good night," I said.

He nodded. "Make yourself at home, Josephine." Then he ambled off.

I plopped down on the bed, taking solace in the fact that sleeping here I would feel closer to Quinn, who was the justification for this, after all.

I went to the bathroom and washed my face. A shower would have to wait until morning. I returned, closed the

bedroom door, got undressed, climbed in bed and told myself to relax. For the next several days, the creature com-
forts were out the window. For all intents and purposes, I
was going to war. The trick would be keeping the casual-
ties from friendly fire to a minimum.

Thirteen

I awoke the next morning to the smell of coffee, flap-jacks and bacon. Except for his chili and grilled steaks, Pardee's cooking repertoire was restricted pretty much to breakfast. After a quick shower, I dressed and went to the kitchen, where I found my former husband scrubbing the sink, the sleeves of his work shirt rolled above his elbows, the front of him spattered with soap and water. I'd noticed the front room had been straightened some. He was making an effort.

"Mornin'," he said. "Sleep well?"

"Yeah, I was exhausted."

"Me, too, but I slept quite a bit in the car on the drive up."

"I noticed."

"Sorry if I was a little testy yesterday. I'm afraid I'm not the best of company these days," he said.

I knew Pardee was worried sick about Quinn, but he hadn't talked much about his feelings. He rarely did.

"This can't be easy for you," I said.

"I was thinking about it last night in bed. I don't know if I adequately thanked you for pitching in, but I want you to know I'm truly grateful, Josie."

"I know you are."

He nodded somberly. "How about some breakfast?"

"Sounds wonderful."

"Coffee?"

"Please."

"I'm up to my elbows in soap and grease," he said. "Would you mind pouring yourself a cup? Everything's more or less where you left it."

"Sure."

"Soon as I'm finished here, I'll make you some flap-jacks," he said. "Griddle's hot. Everything's ready."

I opened the cupboard where we'd kept the mugs. The one I'd always used—a pink one that Pardee had gotten for me at the state fair with "Crazy Legs" written on it—sat right in front. I reached behind it and got a plain white mug.

"Can I fill your cup?"

"No, thank you, sweetheart. Had my quota for the day."

I sat at the table with my coffee and watched Pardee cleaning the sink. Every once in a while he'd glance over at me and smile.

"If it's okay, I may wash the sheets on my bed," I told him.

"Sure. Did it turn out they were dirty?"

"Not as fresh as they might be." In point of fact I thought I could pick up the faint smell of perfume on them, though it might have been my imagination. I wasn't going to mention that to Pardee.

"You haven't said anything about your personal life," I said. "Is there anybody special at the moment?" I tried to sound upbeat and sisterly.

"Naw, not really. Things have been pretty much like they were before you and I hooked up," he said. What he meant to say was he'd knock off a piece when the mood struck him, but he kept his distance from emotional involvement.

There was neither sadness nor rancor in his voice, and I figured he'd adjusted to the single life. He was reasonably happy, or at least content. If there'd been periods of sadness and loneliness since we'd split, it didn't show, but it was a safe bet he hadn't gone without the pleasure of a woman long. The funny thing was, Pardee wasn't what you'd call a womanizer. His success wasn't so much a matter of *needing* to seduce somebody as the fact that he *could,* often without a whole lot of effort.

True, a woman did figure into the demise of our marriage, but she wasn't the actual cause of our breakup. I'm not sure I completely realized that at the time, though. I was probably too hurt and too angry to look at the situation dispassionately, but over time I came to realize that our differences ran deeper than a single dalliance.

Until we had to face the empty-nest problem, we'd been too busy to face up to that fact because Quinn's presence had masked the deficiencies in our marriage in one sense, and exacerbated them in another. I suppose it is like that in a lot of marriages.

"I don't understand what's wrong, Josie," Pardee said after one of our early post-Quinn fights. "You should feel relief now that the burdens of having a kid around are behind us."

"Don't you see?" I said. "I've been a mother for a couple of years and now that it's over, I don't know who the hell I am or what I want."

"You're my wife," he replied, as if that was supposed to enlighten me.

"Yeah, Pardee, that's who I am to you. But who am I to me?"

He never could have understood the difference in a million years, because our marriage had always been about him and his needs. We made a damned good team when we were chasing down a scofflaw. We had a great sex life, too, even when we were barely speaking to each other. But I finally came to realize that I wasn't fulfilled as a person because in so many ways I was alone. Try as I might, I couldn't make him understand the importance of sharing one's heart.

And then Pardee gave me the excuse I needed to leave. He started spending time in Reno, supposedly visiting Quinn. When I found out a showgirl was occupying his time instead, I packed my bags and left, filing for divorce immediately. We saw each other for the first time in months at a court appearance. Pardee apologized for hurting me, but made no attempt to dissuade me from going through with it. "I'm sorry I never figured out how to make you happy," he said outside the courtroom.

"I think it's pretty clear what happened. I didn't mean enough to you," I told him.

Looking sadder than I'd ever seen him look in our life together, Pardee had offered me his hand, then kissed me on the cheek and walked away. I stood there with tears running down my face, feeling as sorry for him as I did for myself. The greatest tragedy in the whole sad affair was the loss of what might have been.

While I did the breakfast dishes, Pardee worked at straightening the rest of the house. We agreed to put an hour into it, then break to go over the intelligence he'd gathered. That might sound strange, given how anxious we both were to rescue Quinn, but years of working together had taught us to intersperse our planning with physical activity, so as to give our unconscious mind a chance to mull over possible plans.

Pardee gathered his files and we went out on the front porch to study his maps and photographs. Mornings it was pleasant out there before it got hot, and it had always been a favorite spot of ours to strategize. As Pardee liked to say, "More than one bail jumper's fate has been sealed on our front porch."

He showed me the materials. It felt so familiar interacting with him that way, so natural, that it bothered me a little. I don't even think it was so much Pardee as what we were doing. Bounty hunting was in my blood.

I loved to fly and I got a certain amount of satisfaction crop dusting, carrying on the tradition begun by my father. The life I'd been leading was not without interest and excitement over and above the occasional skip-chase assignment I'd undertake. With Sky I'd had some interesting experiences, learning and seeing things I'd never been exposed to before. But preparing for battle with a guy like Pardee was utterly unique. There was nothing like poring over a map or studying a schematic of a facility in preparation for the biggest hit of all—the actual operation.

The funny thing was the buzz, the hit, wasn't about Pardee the man. It was about the thrill of the hunt, pure and simple. Pardee just happened to be a person I shared it with, my partner in the enterprise.

But there was danger in that. Work often involved a form of intimacy that came with the closeness of comrades in arms. I had to be careful that my enthusiasm didn't spill over into areas where I didn't want it to go.

We'd been working for maybe an hour when we exchanged quips and laughed at a shared recollection, all but giving each other a high five. The warmth in his smile reminded me of our better days together. And when our eyes met I felt a little jolt. It alarmed me.

I decided on a hasty retreat. Getting to my feet, I yawned and stretched, then said, "How about we take five?" I checked my watch. "I want to give Sky a call."

I went inside and got my cell phone. Pardee had gone to the john, so I went back outside and down the steps, deciding to take a stroll while I tried to reach Sky. Ambling in the general direction of the barn, I dialed Sky's office number in Monterey. His assistant answered.

"Hi, Katie," I said, "it's me, Josie. Is Skylar in?"

"He's on the other line," she said. "Do you want to hold or should I have him call you back?"

"Do you think he'll be long?"

"It could be a while. He's going over bids with a project manager."

"Okay, have him call me when he's free, would you, please?"

"Sure."

I hung up, disappointed. I really wanted to hear Sky's voice. Not that I was in danger of succumbing to Pardee. I just didn't want to feel too comfortable around him. And I didn't want my old life upstaging my new life, even though I was absolutely certain Pardee no longer meant anything to me.

I half kicked the dirt in frustration, aware again how bizarre it was to be back here, when a flicker of motion caught my eye in the sagebrush behind the barn. It was the wrong time of year for deer and the darting movement I'd seen was too quick for it to have been a steer. Plus, whatever it was had disappeared.

Then I saw it again. This time I got a glimpse of a hat and something shiny, like metal—maybe the barrel of a gun. My first thought was of Ernesto Blanco and what had happened to him. Turning on my heel, I headed back to the house.

Just as I reached the porch, Pardee came out. He saw the expression on my face.

"What's wrong?"

"I just saw a guy up behind the barn," I said, mounting the steps. "He was definitely in the sneaking mode."

Pardee opened the door again. "Let's get inside."

Once in the front room, Pardee went right to his gun case. As he unlocked it, I went to my room and got my gun, which I'd left on the nightstand. When I returned to the front room, I saw Pardee had a rifle in his hand. He tossed it to me, then took another rifle out of the case.

"Here's some shells," he said, handing me a box.

While I loaded, Pardee went to the window. There was a pair of binoculars on the table under the window. He picked them up and scanned the terrain out front.

"Just one guy?"

"Yeah, and I think he had a rifle. Only got a glimpse."

"Keep an eye out the front," he said. "I'll have a look in back."

Pardee was gone a couple of minutes. I was looking through the binoculars when he returned.

"There're a couple of vehicles coming up the drive," I said. "Four-wheelers. Just turned off the highway."

"Well, there are at least two guys in the brush up behind the house. Both armed. I think we're surrounded, Josie."

"Any point in calling the sheriff?"

"Nobody could get here in time to make a difference unless it turns into a siege. I'm going to keep an eye on the boys in back, to make sure they don't sneak up to the house. I might fire a warning shot to keep them at bay. If they return fire, then we call the sheriff."

"Why not call now?"

"The sheriff and I aren't on the best of terms." Pardee headed for the back without further comment.

"Care to explain that last remark?" I called to him as I continued to monitor the progress of the vehicles coming up the long drive leading to the house. They were still better than a mile away.

"A deputy came to the house to serve me papers early last week," Pardee replied. "I ran him off at gunpoint."

"That was smart."

"What can I say? I was pissed."

"What was it about?"

"I imagine the bank. They aren't too happy with me."

"Christ, Pardee, you're a magnet for trouble."

"Tell me about it." After a pause, he said, "I'm opening the window to take a shot. One of these bastards is moving in."

I heard the crack of a rifle echoing through the house. Pardee gave a hoot.

"That slowed the bastard up. If they come in now, it's going to have to be on their bellies. I wonder why in the hell they're doing this in broad daylight."

"I'm wondering the same thing."

No shots had been fired back. I assumed that was a good sign.

The vehicles on the drive were getting closer. The second one was obscured in the dust trail, but I could see the first one. There was a light bar on the roof and it looked like an insignia on the door.

"Pardee—"

The crack of another rifle shot echoed through the house.

"There's three of them, Josie. Just spotted one coming up the slope from the north."

"I'm not sure, but I think the cavalry's coming to our rescue," I called back. "The vehicles are law enforcement."

"Really? Well, I guess that saves us calling them."

The drive went into a little draw a hundred yards from the house and the two vehicles entered it, disappearing from sight. When they didn't come over the ridge, I started to get a funny feeling.

"Pardee, did you get a good look at the guys back there?"

"Why?"

"They weren't in uniform by any chance, were they?"

"What are you talking about?" Pardee came back into the front room.

About half a dozen figures appeared in the scrub trees on either side of the drive at the edge of the draw. Next thing, we heard the sound of a bullhorn coming from that direction.

"Pardee!" came a gravelly voice over the bullhorn. "This is Sheriff Watkins. We've got you surrounded. Leave your weapon in the house and come out with your hands up."

"Oh, shit," Pardee said.

"Apparently they *are* pissed," I said. "How far behind are you on the mortgage payments?"

"Maybe five, six months."

I rolled my eyes. "You realize this is going to mess everything up. They might even haul you off to jail. And I have no desire to bust you out so that we can go down to Mexico, only to get thrown in jail there."

"I didn't expect this."

"Considering you're such a brilliant planner, I trust you have a contingency plan."

"Now that I've got some bread, I'll catch up with the bank. That should take the heat off. This is all about money, you know. If I make the banker happy, the sheriff'll be happy."

"I'm not sure this is what Sky had in mind when he gave you the fifty thousand."

"It's not what I had in mind, either. But I can't very well go after Quinn if I'm cooling my heels in the can here, right?"

"Pardee," came Sheriff Watkins's voice over the bullhorn again, "come out with your hands up, or we'll come in and get you. This is your last chance."

"Shit," Pardee said, "I suppose I'd better go out and talk to them."

"I've got a better idea. We'll both go out, only *I'll* do the talking."

"Josie, it's me they want."

"Trust me, honey, they'd much rather talk to me."

"You might have a point."

Fourteen

Dan Watkins was a burly guy of maybe sixty with a head of coarse gray hair and a thick gray mustache. He did not look pleased as we headed down the drive to where he and his posse of deputies waited for us. The three men who'd circled behind the house followed us at a distance, their guns at the ready.

"What's the problem, Sheriff?" I said.

"And who might you be, young lady?"

"Josie Mayne. I'm Pardee's ex-wife."

Watkins's brows went up. "He wasn't holding you hostage, was he?"

"No, Pardee and I are both bounty hunters. We've teamed up to rescue Pardee's son, Quinn, my stepson, who has been kidnapped and is being held for ransom down in Mexico."

Watkins grinned. "Is that a fact?"

Being a planner myself, I'd brought the copy of the ransom note and the photo of Quinn with us from the house. I handed them to Watkins.

"You see, Sheriff, Pardee's been under a lot of stress lately, trying to gather the money to finance the rescue operation. And naturally, we're both worried about our son. If things have been a bit strange around here recently, that's why."

After studying the note and photo for a full minute, he handed them back. "Is running off one of my deputies at gunpoint what you mean by 'a bit strange,' Ms. Mayne?"

"I'm sure I don't need to tell you that dealing with bankers can be a pain in the ass, Sheriff. As you can imagine, though, it's especially tough when you're in the middle of a family crisis."

"This isn't just about the bank. My men reported being fired on from the house." He called to the deputies behind us. "How many shots, fellas?"

"Two."

"That's an assault on a peace officer," Watkins said. "A criminal offense."

I knew Pardee wouldn't be able to hold his tongue after that and he didn't. "No," he said, "it was a man protecting his wife and home against some guys sneaking around in the brush without identifying themselves as law enforcement."

"You seem willing to stick a gun in the face of a uniformed officer trying to serve court papers, Mr. Pardee. I'm not about to get my people shot up for lack of precautions. This time we came prepared. And I'm taking you in."

"Sheriff," I said, "I understand why you're upset, but hopefully you can see how difficult this is for us."

"I've got a job to do, miss."

"But isn't your primary obligation to the bank? I mean, you're just trying to enforce their rights, aren't you?"

"That's what this was about at first, yes."

"Then isn't the important thing to please the good, tax-paying voters at the bank? Arresting Pardee isn't going to bring them much satisfaction, but a check covering what's owed them would make you a hero, wouldn't it, Sheriff?"

Watkins eyed me, stroking his chin. "You prepared to give me a check to take to the bank?"

"That's exactly what I intend to do."

The sheriff was considering that when my cell phone rang. "Excuse me," I said, digging it out of my pocket. "Hello?"

"Darling, it's me."

"Sky, honey, how are you?"

"The more important question is, how are you? Is every-thing all right?"

"Yes, I just wanted you to know we made it here safely. Pardee and I have been working hard on our plan and even Sheriff Watkins, one of Nevada's most prominent law en-forcement figures, has come by to see us. In fact, he's here now. We're confabulating, so I can't talk long."

"Katie said you'd called, so I just wanted to make sure you're okay."

"Everything's fine, Sky. I called to tell you that. And also to say that I miss you."

"I miss you, too, darling," he said. "And I love you."

I turned away from the men. "I love you, too, Sky. But now I've gotta run. Talk to you later." I hung up and faced the sheriff. "Sorry, that was my fiancé. He's financing our operation."

Sheriff Watkins and his deputies exchanged looks. They all had grins on their faces. Watkins lifted his hat and scratched his head. "If you'd like to get me that check for the bank, Ms. Mayne, we'll get out of your hair."

"Certainly, Sheriff. I'll just run up to the house and get my checkbook. I won't be but a minute."

"Go ahead."

As I walked away, I heard Watkins say to Pardee, "You made a mistake when you allowed that young lady to get away, partner."

"True," Pardee replied. "But I've got her help now, when I need it most."

I took satisfaction in both comments. What woman wouldn't?

I was only gone a couple of minutes. I found that Pardee and the cops had loosened up enough that they were exchanging war stories by the time I returned.

After the sheriff and his deputies mounted up and took off, Pardee and I walked up to the house. "I have to admit you handled that pretty damned well," he said.

"Thank you."

"Just goes to show how well we work together."

"No, it shows how you need to get a handle on your finances and improve your public relations skills, especially when you're dealing with the cops."

"We were getting along just fine."

"I'm talking about first impressions."

"Josie, I like to do things my own way. Always have and reckon I always will. I think you know that." Grinning, Pardee put his arm around my shoulders and gave them a squeeze.

I removed his hand. "I saved your butt for Quinn's sake, Pardee. Don't get any ideas."

"I'm just working on my public relations skills, sweetheart."

"Well, save it for the people who don't know you."

* * *

Before lunch, we studied the topo maps Pardee had gathered. After we ate, I suggested we do some more housecleaning. "Cleanliness is next to godliness," I said. "Plus, it's good for morale."

"I remember when we had lots more palatable ways of lifting our morale than scrubbing toilets," Pardee quipped.

"Yeah, well, those days are over."

Pardee said he had ranch work to do, so when he grabbed his hat and went out the door, I retreated to my room and called Sky again. We chatted for quite a while. I didn't tell him about Pardee's troubles with the bank or the sheriff's real reason for coming by. Sky already knew Pardee was a flake.

After our conversation I lay back and closed my eyes, thinking I'd grab a catnap, but I didn't awaken until dark. Leaving my room, I expected to find Pardee in the kitchen, cleaning his guns while he listened to the radio, but he was nowhere to be seen. Concerned, I got my gun and strolled up to the barn. No sign of him there, but I noticed his old pickup was gone.

Maybe he'd decided to drive into Hawthorne for a night on the town. I was annoyed until I realized there was no reason I should care. Anything to distract him from me was a plus.

When Pardee hadn't showed up by ten, I ended up fixing myself a light supper and ate it in the kitchen, listening to country and western music and recalling the final months of our marriage when Pardee spent his time in Reno screwing the showgirl while I sat at home alone.

Quinn, like most kids who go away to college, left us

pretty much in the dark about what was going on in his life. I'd talk to him on the phone from time to time, but he was usually too busy for a meaningful conversation. Pardee's solution was to drive up for a visit, take in a basketball game with him—a sport I didn't much care for and therefore had no interest in—or take him out for a steak dinner. In the process, he'd garner enough intelligence on Quinn to satisfy me, yet mask what he'd been doing on the side.

I suppose I'd known at some level what was going on, but I simply didn't want to believe it. Maybe it was denial. Or maybe I needed to be ready to pull the trigger on the inevitable. Funny how people find a way to make happen what they know must be done, but can't consciously do without manufacturing the needed excuse.

As I was getting into bed, Sky called and we talked for an hour like a couple of smitten teenagers. It was after eleven-thirty by the time we ended the conversation with mutual professions of love.

For a while after that I lay in the dark, listening to the wind whistling in the eves. Occasionally I heard the neigh of a horse up in the corral or a coyote howling at the moon. Eventually I fell asleep. I slept soundly until sometime in the small hours of the morning when I heard Pardee come in the front door, bumping into the furniture in the dark, cussing under his breath.

I didn't wake up enough to check the time. I didn't want to know.

Not surprisingly, Pardee was the one who slept in the next morning. In fact, it was after ten before he finally dragged himself into the kitchen. I'd just finished cleaning out the refrigerator, having thrown away some stuff that looked like it dated back to my era, when I turned to look at him. He wasn't a pretty sight. One cheek was bruised and swollen and he had a cut on his chin. His left hand was puffed up like a mitten.

"Aren't you a little old for bar brawls?"

"It wasn't my fault."

"Yeah, just sitting there minding your own business, right?" I couldn't resist the sarcasm.

"Josie," he said, easing himself painfully into a chair, "I don't mean to embarrass you, but you're sounding an awful lot like a wife."

I gulped and turned three shades of red, realizing he was right. "Sorry, Pardee. I guess it's because you're such an inviting target."

"Yeah, well, last night really wasn't my fault. The gal wasn't wearing a ring. How was I supposed to know she was married?"

I chuckled.

"Wasn't funny. The bastard loosened a tooth," he said, reaching back into his mouth with his thumb.

I wasn't going to tell him that that was what came from choosing the wrong company. "You're lucky he only beat you up."

"Him and two friends."

"My."

"Plus, I had fifteen years on them."

"I'm surprised you didn't end up in the hospital."

"One of them did, and the other two limped home. You're lookin' at the winner, sweetheart, not the loser."

"In a manner of speaking, Pardee."

"Here," he said, pulling a check out of his shirt pocket and extending it toward me.

"What's this?" I looked at the check. It was the one I'd given the sheriff yesterday.

"I went by the bank and settled up with them. Don't think it's a good idea for us to intermingle our finances."

"You used Sky's money."

"What happens between him and me is business. And I will pay him back. I gave him my word. With you and me it's different. You may have divorce papers, but as far as I'm concerned it's nothing but government paperwork."

I think I actually took a step back.

"Don't get your shorts in a knot," he said, dismissing the horror on my face. "I respect the fact you've chosen somebody else. And I can't help it if I still love you. I accept your feelings as part of the way things are and move on. So you can relax."

"Then why did you tell me that?"

"Because it's true." He rubbed his grizzled jaw. "By the way, what's for breakfast?"

I poured Pardee some coffee, made him toast and scrambled a couple of eggs, all the while trying to decide whether to tell him that the truth regarding a person's feelings wasn't the only thing that mattered. Any love he felt for me didn't count for much at this point and there was no good reason to open his mouth in the first place except to be a shit disturber—which I already knew him to be.

In the end I elected not to say anything. That was the kindest course, and I knew in my heart it was better to feel sorry for him than try to educate him. Besides, if he really did love me and suffered because of it, that was sad.

The irony was that had he been able to share his feelings like this when we were married—had he let me inside a little, instead of always playing games, skirting the truth—

we might still be married. But then, I wouldn't have Sky and a brand-new life to look forward to, a life that was built on trust and honesty. Besides, I knew Pardee well enough to know that he was capable of using the truth to manipulate me just as easily as a lie, if it suited his purpose.

Still, assuming it was true, I felt a begrudging respect for him being able to profess his love. Pardee could be squirrelly, but he had both a moral and physical courage, which I respected. As they say, after he was made, they threw away the mold.

I had another cup of coffee while he ate. Pardee did not give me sappy looks. He seemed neither sad nor happy. If anything, his mind seemed to be elsewhere. Maybe on Quinn and the operation, maybe on the girl last night.

"Was she pretty?"

"Huh?"

"The woman you took a beating for."

"She had big tits."

"That's important."

"It is."

There was a bit of history behind that exchange. I'm fairly average in the bust department and Pardee proclaimed himself a boob man early on. He'd told me that my legs and my butt were my salvation. More than once Pardee had insisted he married me because of my crazy legs. I half believe that, though I think he was also addicted to the sparks that flew between us. Of course, at one time I had been, too. At one time.

"I think I've figured out how we get Quinn," he said, licking the jam off his finger.

"Oh? How?"

"We agree to pay the ransom, but insist on swapping the

money for Quinn straight up, like a prisoner exchange. We pick a remote location and, to make sure we don't get trapped, we do an extraction by air after having walked or driven in. Nothing fancy, real straightforward."

"Then you figure on me going to Mexico with you."

"That's why I'm laying out the plan. I could find another pilot, but . . . well, I don't have to tell you, Josie, a lot more is involved than flying skills. We're talking familiarity, trust, an instinctive understanding of how the other person thinks. I'll be frank. I want to maximize my chances."

"At my expense."

He shrugged. "I won't deny it."

I'd known from the start it would come to this. And how I'd respond had been a foregone conclusion as far as I was concerned, and probably in Pardee's mind as well. But we'd had to go through the process. Now we'd done that—Pardee told me he still loved me only moments before and now he wanted me to risk my butt and my future with Sky to go with him to Mexico. I had every reason in the world to say no, except for one. I had to do it for Quinn's sake. I knew that. Pardee did, too.

"Okay," I said, "I'm in, but I want to clarify something."

"What?"

"Your decision to include me in the operation is strictly tactical, right?"

"What do you mean?"

"It doesn't have anything to do with what you said before . . . your feelings for me."

"Hell, no," he said, dismissing the notion emphatically. "You think I'd take undue risk and put my butt on the line for the sake of sentiment? You know me better than that, sweetheart. Give me credit."

Naturally, he chose to turn the question and embarrass me. "I just want to be really clear on where we both stand and why," I said, salvaging what dignity I could.

"I haven't forgotten how to separate business and pleasure," he assured me with a grin.

"Fine."

"So, everything copacetic? We on the same page?" he asked.

"Yes, but if I'm going to Mexico, I want to tell Sky, first thing."

"I understand."

"There is something about your plan I don't follow, though. Where are you going to get the ransom money? You won't be able to walk into some mud hut with a suitcase full of telephone books."

"I've been working on that. While you were napping yesterday afternoon, I put in another call to the kidnappers. I got the ransom reduced to half a mil, under the condition there's no more delay. I figure we leave tomorrow, day after at the latest."

"Forgive my skepticism, Pardee, but half a million dollars is still a lot of money. How do you propose to come up with that much?"

"I have a plan."

"Care to share?"

"Not yet."

"Why?"

"Let's just say for your own good, Josie."

That was code for, *You don't want to know.* Pardee had said the same thing on our first job together. In the end that had turned out okay, but at the time I'd been mad as a wet hen that he'd been less than forthcoming. In the years since then, I'd learned the value of taking him at his word. There were in fact times—and this was undoubtedly one of them—when blissful ignorance was the best alternative.

At least, that's what I told myself.

Fifteen

I told Pardee it was his turn to do the dishes and clean up, regardless of how shitty he felt. So while he was working, I took my cell phone for a walk and called the man of my dreams with word of my decision to go to Mexico.

Sky was not pleased, but neither was he surprised. "I know about your love of flying and bounty hunting," he said, "but promise me that this will be your last trip to Mexico."

"Okay, it's a deal."

What was unsaid, of course, was whether I would survive *this* trip. But there were some things that people in love simply didn't discuss, and the prospect of never coming back was one.

"When do you leave?"

"Possibly as early as tomorrow. But I'll phone you again and let you know."

"Call as often as you like."

I could tell Sky was upset and I felt badly. "So, how's it going with Baron? Are you two bonding?"

"I'm doing my best to spoil him, but I'm not sure it's working. I think he likes my steaks better than he likes me."

"Poor Sky, abandoned by your fiancée and abused by her dog. Hang in there, honey. I promise I'll make it up to you."

"Yeah, I've already discovered that the secret to dealing with you, Josie, is patience. Lots of patience."

"You are regretting you asked me to marry you, are you?"

"Absolutely not. But I am regretting I let you leave."

"I have to do this, Sky."

"I know. I'm just venting my frustration."

"I love you, Skylar."

"And I love you, darling."

When I got back in the house, Pardee was sitting at the kitchen table, soaking his hand in ice water. What a contrast he was to the man to whom I'd just professed my love.

"Will you live?" I asked.

"Quinn had better hope so."

I sat down across from him. He gave me a thoughtful look. I wasn't sure what he was thinking. It could have been about me, or it could have been about the operation. At times Pardee was very difficult to read.

"I've been thinking maybe we do the swap on an oil platform."

So, he was thinking about the operation. "Why an oil platform?"

"First, there are a number of them strung along the Gulf Coast. Second, they'd be readily accessible. And third, control. I could take a boat to the rendezvous place with the ransom money. You could swoop in and touch down on the platform to get us when it's time to go. What do you think?"

I considered his suggestion. "Well, the deck of the platform would be open, which would make my job easier, but how would a bunch of leftist guerrillas get access to an oil platform? Unless you managed to find an abandoned platform, getting in and out would be tricky for both them and you."

Pardee pulled his hand out of the water, nodding as he flexed his fingers. "All good points."

"How about an island?" I said.

"You'd still have the problem of ingress and egress," he said.

"I wasn't thinking of an island in the Gulf. More like a small one in a lake. When I was studying the topo maps I noticed there were a number of good-sized lakes up in the mountains where both you and the kidnappers could gain access with greater security than in the open sea. And after the exchange, they could melt back into the jungle with the loot and you'd have a better shot of escape if it was a trap set by the authorities."

"I like that," Pardee said. "Unfortunately, there's not time to send my man on a scouting trip to get photographs."

"Pardee, it's time you enter the electronic age."

"What do you mean?"

"The Internet. If you had a goddamn computer we could research from right here."

"You know how I feel about computers, Josie."

"Well, maybe you need to shake your phobia. Ever since I've been skip-chasing on my own, I've been using the Internet for research."

"So, I was replaced by a machine, eh?"

"Only for some purposes. I do have Sky."

He gave me a wan smile. "Yeah, I've been replaced by a machine and a bank account."

My eyes flashed. "That bank account is financing your son's rescue, Pardee. You should be thankful."

"You're right. I didn't mean to sound ungrateful. It was more a comment on you than him."

"On *me*? What are you saying, that I'm marrying Sky for his money?"

"What else?"

I abruptly got to my feet and I was fuming. "What gall!"

"Calm down, Josie, I'm not knocking the guy. I'm sure he's got qualities besides generosity and a rich daddy."

"For your information, Sky is the sweetest, most considerate, caring, loving man I've ever known."

"And the richest."

"Yes, the richest, but that isn't even a factor. If anything, his money is a problem for me. Or, it could be a problem if Sky wasn't so understanding. The point is I love him."

"You loved me once, too."

"Past tense."

Pardee took his hand out of the ice water and flexed his fingers again. "Well, things have a way of changing, don't they?"

"They certainly do!" I took a turn around the kitchen, glaring at him.

"Come on, Josie, for crissakes. No need to make a federal case out of this. I was just making conversation."

"Well, I don't like the topic you chose. My relationship with Sky is none of your goddamn business and I have no desire to discuss it with you. I would appreciate it if you'd keep in mind that I'm here for one purpose and one purpose only. Quinn."

"Okay, fine."

"And I'd like to stick to business."

"I said okay and I mean it. Business it is. I believe we were discussing ways to research possible rendezvous points."

I drew a deep breath, trying to calm myself. A couple of days together and already we were at each other's throats as though we were still married. It went to show how right I'd been to leave the bastard in the first place. Not that I'd ever had any doubts about that.

I returned to the table. "Let's go to the library," I said. "If you're going to escape the Stone Age, that's the place to begin."

"Can't think of a soul I'd rather have show me the way." Naturally he smiled as he said it.

The bastard.

We were able to get lots of useful information using the Internet hookup at the county library over in Carson City. Pardee was so impressed with my newfound research abilities that he bought me a late lunch at Donnie's Grill in Hawthorne. The waitress seemed to know him. I dared not ask how well.

The high point of the meal came before the first course when a busty blonde who'd been eyeing us from a corner booth came walking by the counter where we sat. She was in a skimpy tank top and short little skirt. "So, Pardee," she said, "I see you haven't wasted any time replacing me."

"Cammy, you don't deserve the time of day from me, never mind an explanation," he replied without looking at her.

The blonde, who was more blatant than pretty, threw

back her shoulders, giving me a hard appraisal. "Haven't seen you around here before," she said.

"Josie's from California and she's my wife," Pardee said, still staring straight ahead.

"Ex-wife," I intoned.

"Right," Pardee said, glancing at the woman for the first time. "Now you've heard what you wanted to know, Cammy, so why don't you run on home to your husband?"

"I swear, I didn't know Rick would get pissed off like that. Usually he doesn't care if I go out dancing and have a little fun."

"I don't think the dancing was the problem. It was what we were doing in the back of my truck."

He'd said it loud enough for half the people in the place to hear. Cammy looked around, embarrassed, though I doubt there wasn't a soul in the town who didn't already know the story.

"I had a little too much to drink, that's all," she said.

"Yeah, right. Goodbye, Cammy."

The blonde tossed her hair and stomped off. Pardee and I sat there for a while, not speaking.

"You're right," I said finally, "she does have big tits."

Pardee did not smile, but I knew deep down he was reveling in his glory. He'd always loved it when women flirted with him in front of me. It didn't affect me the same way now as it had when we were still together, of course. In fact, I hoped for his sake he'd managed to get his rocks off before Cammy's husband showed up.

Watching him eat his steak and home fries, I thought of my dining experiences with Sky. My palate was not only more sophisticated now, but I ate healthier than I used to.

In fact, I'd changed in many ways. Much as I appreciated the fact I'd grown—took pride in it, even—I had to admit there was something comforting about the down-home life. This was the way I'd grown up, after all.

Pardee was rougher around the edges than I'd ever been. But deep down, in my heart of hearts, I had to admit that his way of living didn't scare me the way Sky's sometimes did. Not that I would have traded the new life I'd built for myself for the old one I'd shared with Pardee.

Still, I couldn't deny that Sky's millionaire lifestyle did have its drawbacks—I'd lived long enough to learn that nothing was perfect—but I liked it that being with him meant growing as a person, being introduced to new experiences. That was something Pardee wouldn't understand in a thousand years. If I didn't believe that, I'd be wrong to wear Sky Tyler's ring.

On the way home Pardee and I stopped to do a little last-minute shopping for our trip. We picked up some packets of camping food, batteries and film for his camera.

"If you had a digital camera, you wouldn't need to be buying so much film," I told him.

"You already have me thinking about a computer. That's enough progress for one day."

"Yeah, your entry into the modern world is happening at light speed. What's it been, five, six years since you heard they'd come out with color TV?"

We were in the Jeep outside the hardware store and Pardee playfully grabbed my neck, acting like he was going to give me a real shaking. I gave him a whack, the way I would whenever we engaged in playful fisticuffs back

when we were a couple. There'd always been a lot of phys-
icality in our relationship, I suppose in part because the
sexual dimension had been so intense.

But there hadn't been a lot of touching since his unexpected appearance a few days ago, so this little wrestling
match was as unexpected as it was natural. I was giggling
the way I always did, trying to punch him in the stomach
while he grabbed my arms, stopping me. Our faces ended
up inches apart and Pardee looked into my eyes like he was
about to kiss me.

I felt it coming and turned my head away. "Don't,
Pardee," I said.

He let go of me, settling back in his seat. I started the engine as I did a slow burn. I was pissed at myself, not him.

"Sorry," he said as I pulled into the street, burning a little rubber in the process.

"It was nothing," I said, "just a little slip."

I didn't specify on whose part the slip had occurred, but
I suspect Pardee knew as well as I that the one who'd made
the mistake was me. Neither of us said much during the
drive back to the ranch, but the underlying tension was the
strongest it had been since Monday night when Pardee
came walking out of the shadows and right into the middle
of my engagement party. This time the problem wasn't
what he'd done. It was how I'd reacted.

And more especially what I'd felt.

But how had I let this happen? That was the real question. Was it a case of slipping into the familiar, such as or-
dering a down-home-cooked meal like the ones I'd eaten
on a regular basis back in my years living with Pardee? I'd
enjoyed the steak and fries, all the while knowing that kind
of cooking was no longer a part of my healthier diet.

But indulging in fattening food and indulging in sex play were two entirely different things. I could afford to fall off the wagon and eat unwisely every once in a while. I could not afford to let down my guard with Pardee—even once.

Sixteen

As we drove back to the ranch, the hot desert air blowing my hair, all I could think of was how uncomfortable I was about the way things were going. It sure didn't seem to bother Pardee, though. He was sprawled out in the passenger seat, his hand on my headrest, his forearm lightly brushing my shoulder. I didn't bother to object since he made it seem incidental, but I was aware of his proximity.

Too damn aware.

It seemed like every time I took a step forward, I'd immediately take one back. Earlier I'd made clear my feelings about Sky, which was good. But then I'd allowed myself to get into that little wrestling match with him. That was bad. Or worse, stupid.

The solution was to give Pardee absolutely no cause to question my true feelings. The one thing I could count on was that he wouldn't give me the benefit of the doubt.

We came to the entrance to the ranch and I turned off the highway onto the gravel drive. We'd only gone a couple hundred yards before Pardee sat up and pointed off to the north.

"Looks like we have company."

I glanced over toward the airstrip. Sure enough, there was a twin-engine Cessna sitting there, gleaming in the late afternoon sun. "Who do you suppose that is?"

"Haven't a clue," Pardee said. "But I'm a little surprised he got down in one piece. The runway's not in the best of shape."

Pardee had sold my plane when we divorced and the landing strip hadn't been used since. I would have bought the plane from him, but I had my dad's Grumman, which wasn't good for much of anything but crop dusting. But it was a plane, and a girl could spend only so many hours flying. A second plane would have been much too frivolous, not to mention expensive.

I hadn't brought along my Glock, but Pardee did have his sidearm, which he took out of the glove box. "Not that I expect any bad guys would come flying into our airstrip," he said.

"Not all bad guys are necessarily smart," I said.

"Exactly what I was thinking."

We approached the house with caution. Pardee suggested I stop in the draw where the sheriff and his people had halted their advance earlier, so we could scout out the situation on foot. We moved up through the scrub brush and trees, the way the cops had, until we reached the rim of the draw. From there we had a clear view up the slope all the way to the house.

There were two men on the porch, one taller and more slender. And also a dog, a big red dog. I recognized Baron instantly. Then I realized who the taller man was.

"It's Sky!" I cried, as thrilled as I was surprised.

I charged out of the brush. Baron saw me first and, after a bark or two, he bounded down the hill toward me at full speed.

We met and he leaped up, practically knocking me down. I hugged him and he lapped my face. There's no joy like that of a devoted dog seeing his master after a separation, unless maybe it was the master's joy.

"What are you doing here?" I asked, intending to address the same question to Sky.

Glancing up toward the house, I saw that he was already halfway to us. I ran to greet him, with Baron loping at my side. We embraced, spinning around. Baron yapped, circling us.

"I already asked Baron what you two are doing here," I said between kisses, "and he wouldn't tell me."

"That's because he doesn't know."

"What *are* you doing here?" I asked more seriously. "Not that I'm not thrilled to see you."

"It's real simple, Josie. I couldn't let you go off to Mexico without seeing you one last time."

"I plan on coming back, you know."

"Yes, but . . . well, how could I pass up the opportunity? Anyway, I discussed it with Baron and he agreed wholeheartedly that we should come."

"*I* can get away with that one, Sky, but you can't."

"How's that?"

"I know Baron-speak and you don't."

He grinned, taking my face in his hands and kissing me again. Sky smelled good. He always did. After the long hot drive into town and back, I was wilted, but I hugged him enthusiastically anyway.

"Where's Pardee?"

I looked back down the slope. "He must have gone back to get the Jeep."

"We saw you coming," Sky said. "Where have you been?"

"Went into town for supplies and to do some research at the library."

"I was afraid we might have missed you."

"Is that your pilot?"

"Yeah. Dad was using our plane, so I chartered this one and a pilot who is damned good, fortunately. The landing was a little tricky."

"Sky, why didn't you call to say you were coming?"

"I wanted to surprise you, darling," he said, beaming.

I figured that was true enough, but with my surprise and excitement abating, I found myself slightly annoyed. There were hints of suspicion in Sky's questions, which led me to believe that he'd come to check up on me as much as for the pleasure of seeing me one more time before I left for Mexico. As I debated with myself as to how I felt about that, Pardee drove up in the Jeep.

He clambered down and strode over to us. Baron went into a frenzy and Pardee bent down to thump his flanks affectionately. "Long time no see, partner." He stood upright and grinned at Sky. "Well, this is a surprise," he said, offering his hand.

"Yeah," Sky said, shaking it, "Baron and I felt rude and decided to be uninvited guests. But don't worry, we won't stay long. I have to be back in Monterey tonight so I can make an early appointment tomorrow morning."

"You can stay on for dinner, can't you?" Pardee asked.

"I don't know about that," Sky replied.

"Josie's a fabulous cook. You can't miss one of her meals."

"You obviously didn't get that black eye complaining about the food, then," Sky said lightly.

Pardee chuckled. "No. Ran into a door, as a matter of fact." He gave me a wink. "I do confess to being a little drunk at the time, though."

He laughed. Sky and I didn't.

"Frankly," Sky said, "I've got a business proposition for you, Pardee."

"A business proposition?"

Sky glanced at me and, seeing my surprise, said, "Well, of sorts."

"In that case, come on and hop in the Jeep, then," Pardee said. "We should go up to the house and have us a cold one. A fella can't talk business if he's parched."

Feeling I needed to take charge, I got in the driver's seat. Pardee got in back with Baron, who lapped his face as enthusiastically as he'd lapped mine. Sky climbed in next to me. We exchanged smiles, but I had a wary feeling.

Once we reached the house, Sky introduced his pilot, a man named Talbot. We all went inside and Pardee promptly went to the kitchen for the beers. Talbot had asked for a soft drink, since he'd be flying. I asked how he'd located us, as our field wasn't on any charts.

"Radioed the sheriff's office," Talbot said. "They were quite familiar with Mr. Pardee and described the location with precision."

"I'm not surprised."

"I would like to walk the strip before we take off," the pilot said. "Could I borrow your vehicle to run down there?"

"Certainly." I gave him my keys. He took the soft drink Pardee brought for him and left.

Sky and I sat on the sofa and Pardee dropped into his easy chair. Baron immediately went over and rested his chin on Pardee's knee. Pardee stroked his silky mane.

I saw Sky's expression as he watched the two of them. I rarely noticed anything that suggested feelings of inadequacy in Sky, but I saw something now. He must have been thinking about all the steaks and time he'd invested in Baron, only to see him eating out of the hand of a seedy cowboy in dusty boots. Poor Sky.

"So, what's your proposition?" Pardee said. He was always one for getting right to the point. Actually, in that regard the two men were very much alike. I don't believe I had realized that before now. Maybe that should have bothered me, but I realized it was only natural they'd share some qualities—in particular Pardee's good qualities—and that shouldn't be something to avoid in a new relationship. I didn't want to throw out the baby with the bathwater.

Sky took my hand. "I've been agonizing over Josie being involved in such a dangerous operation," he said. "She's probably the most competent woman alive in this line of work, but nobody's infallible and anybody can have a run of bad luck. So, to spare both of you the risk and hardship of a dangerous rescue mission, I'd like to pay your son's ransom.

"No conditions, no obligation," he continued. "The money would be an out-and-out gift. You can tell the kidnappers I'll wire a million dollars to any bank account they specify, anyplace in the world. All I ask in exchange is that Josie come home with me and Baron tonight."

I about dropped my teeth. I looked at Pardee, then at Sky. "Honey, you aren't serious, are you?"

"I'm dead serious, darling. I'd gladly give Pardee a million bucks to release you from your commitment."

"Sky, I'm not under contract. I'm doing this for Quinn."

"I know, sweetie. Maybe I didn't phrase it quite right. I understand that you're doing this to secure your stepson's freedom and I'm all for it. I respect the fact that both of you are trying to do everything possible to get Quinn back home. But what I'm saying is if we can do it with cash instead of bullets, why not?"

I could see Pardee struggling to keep a straight face. My ex knew me well enough to recognize that poor Sky had stepped in it big time, as far as I was concerned. If I'd been close enough, I'd have kicked Pardee in the shins. He was enjoying this way too much.

"Sky," I said, "I think you and I need to go for a walk."

My fiancé was perplexed. "Have I said or done something wrong? I'm only trying to help. Sure, I've got a selfish motive in wanting to keep you safe, but Pardee will be spared too. And maybe his son, as well. I mean, won't he be in greater danger if you have to use force to free him?"

"Skylar, that isn't the point."

"Then I don't understand."

"Come on," I said, rising, "let's go outside."

Sky got up, looking a little bewildered. Pardee was frowning as hard as he could, just to keep from laughing, I was sure. Sky's offer was as endearing as it was naive, but it was something else, too, and that's what I needed to talk to him about.

We went outside and I made Baron stay in the house with Pardee. Sky and I strolled as I gathered my thoughts.

"You're angry with me, aren't you?" he said.

"I can't say I'm angry, Sky. But I am a little annoyed. It feels to me like you're trying to buy my freedom."

"Well, no, I tried to make it clear that I—"

"Yes, I know what you said. But why did you make your offer to Pardee? He doesn't own me and this isn't a competition for my allegiance. I'm not a prize racehorse."

"Of course you're not. And that's not what I intended. I guess my mistake was not talking to you first. But to be honest, I was afraid you'd turn me down for pride's sake. I figured Pardee would be able to look at it more dispassionately, like a simple business deal."

"You're making it worse, Skylar. It sounds like you're saying that because he's a man, he—"

"No, Josie, that's not it. I addressed my offer to him rather than you because I don't have feelings for him. But I *love* you. And I know this sounds weak, but the truth is I don't want to lose you, Josie."

I could see we were talking past each other. His intentions were good, but he just didn't get it. My pride wasn't the issue.

The hell of it was I wouldn't have an easy time of it explaining that the kidnapping probably wasn't about ransom. Pardee and I both figured it was far more likely that the object was to lure us to Mexico. In short, it was about revenge. But if I told Sky that, it'd send him off the deep end. So instead I did what I'd resolved never to do with Sky—I lied.

"Pardee has already explored the possibility of transferring funds. The trouble is these people aren't sophisticated and they're very distrusting of anything we suggest. They want cash, put directly in their hands, and they won't consider doing it any other way."

"Surely there's a way to explain to them how—"

"Trust me, Sky, there isn't."

"Then why not send somebody else to deliver the ransom?"

"They specified Pardee bring the money personally."

"Why would they care?"

I was getting deeper and deeper, which always seemed to happen when you strayed from the truth. "Because the way they figure it, the boy's father would be a lot more interested in his release than in setting a trap. For all they know, an outsider could easily be a cop."

He pondered that for a while, then said, "Is there any reason why you can't at least try it my way?"

"Pardee's already talked to them, Sky."

"Are you sure . . . I mean . . . could it be that Pardee . . ."

"That Pardee what?" I said.

"Are you sure he's telling you the truth? I mean, maybe his primary objective is to get you to go to Mexico with him."

I stopped in my tracks. "Skylar, you're jealous. That's what this is really about, isn't it? You're testing me."

"No, darling. This isn't about us. It's about the danger. I'm afraid of the Mexicans. No question about that. And you have to admit I've got good reason to fear. And yes, I admit it, I'd rather you not go down there with Pardee. I hate the thought of you being with him, to be honest."

I was so disappointed that my eyes filled with tears. Sure, Sky cared so much that he was willing to give away a million dollars for me, but what I wanted was his respect and his trust. Money had never been what our relationship was about.

"I've been faithful to you," I told him. "Absolutely nothing has happened between me and Pardee, and absolutely nothing will."

"Josie, that's not it."

"Yes, it is. You might not want to admit it to yourself. You want to know the best way to show your love? Trust me, Sky. It's natural to worry and be concerned, but given the fact that I'm going to do this, that I *have* to do it, the best thing you can do is to give me your blessing and wish me well."

He looked at me long and hard. Finally he said, "You're asking a lot, you know that."

"Maybe this is an important test for us both."

"Okay," he said, "if this is the way you want it, this is the way it's going to be. I wish you Godspeed, Josie. I'll be thinking of you and eagerly awaiting your safe return."

I beamed and my tears overflowed my lids. "Thank you, honey."

"And you know what? I'm going to pass on Pardee's invitation to dinner. Talbot is eager to get in the air before dark. So I'm going to get Baron and the two of us will walk down to the strip."

I wiped my eyes and nodded my approval.

"Unless I've ruined things for us, I'll just have to content myself with the expectation of your return home," he added.

"You haven't ruined anything," I said, feeling much better.

"Good."

"But I do want to ask a favor of you." I slipped my engagement ring off my finger. "I'm afraid to take this to Mexico with me and I don't want to leave it here. I'd feel better knowing it was safe with you, just like Baron."

I put the ring in his hand and he looked down at it for a moment.

"It's just for safekeeping," I assured him. "When you give it back to me, I'll probably make you get down on your knee again so I can relive the full experience."

That seemed to please him. "It's a deal." I gave him a big hug. "On that note," he said, "I'll go fetch my stepdog and be on my way."

I couldn't let Sky go without another kiss. And I didn't.

Seventeen

After the ups and downs of the day before, morning, as far as I was concerned, couldn't come soon enough. I wanted to get to Mexico, do the job, and put this behind me. Unfortunately, Pardee had more in the way of surprises in store.

The thing I'd learned about reprobates was that there comes a point in time when they invariably expose themselves for what they are—the bad news is that it's usually after they've bamboozled you. It was no different with Pardee.

Waiting for me at the breakfast table was a passport with my picture in it under the name Denise Raymond, and a ticket to Veracruz, Mexico. Pardee also had a fake passport for Quinn, likewise under a phony name. He confessed that he'd had them made over two weeks earlier.

"You were pretty damned sure of yourself having a phony passport made up for me, weren't you?" I said sarcastically.

"I wasn't a Boy Scout, but I do believe in being prepared." He gave me a self-satisfied grin. The bastard.

My eyes narrowed. "What would you have done if I'd refused to join your expedition?"

"I'd have gone on to Plan B."

"Which was?"

"Going down there alone."

On the one hand, I was flattered that he wanted me along so badly that he'd laid out big bucks he couldn't really afford for a passport that might not even be needed. But I was also embarrassed at being so predictable. I don't know if that said more about me or Pardee. "Who's Denise Raymond, if I might ask?"

"Nobody."

"You just got the name out of the phone book?"

"Actually it was my girlfriend in the second grade. The first girl I ever kissed."

"No obvious symbolism there."

Pardee shrugged.

"Is there?"

"Firsts," he replied.

"I wasn't your first anything, Pardee."

"You were my first true love."

I smirked. He got my point.

"So, what else have you prepared that I should know about? Might as well lay it all on me."

Pardee spelled out his plan and I discovered he was very well prepared indeed. Not only had travel arrangements already been set—we were flying as far as Dallas together, then on separate commercial flights to Veracruz—but accommodations had been prearranged, as well.

"I figure the authorities will be expecting us to arrive with our gear in a private aircraft," he explained. "So, while they're checking out the private aircraft arriving at every airfield in southern Mexico, we'll throw them a curve and walk right in the front door."

"What about weapons and equipment?"

"Stockpiled and waiting with friends."

"Why Veracruz?"

"Two reasons—first, it's not Oaxaca, but it's close, and second, I have reliable contacts there. That was partly my rationale for the oil platform. But your arguments for an inland lake were convincing, Josie. The one you recommended after our trip to the library, Presa Migel Alemán, is in the state of Oaxaca, but it's actually closer to Veracruz than it is to the city of Oaxaca."

"Why separate flights? To be less conspicuous?"

"That's partly it. I'll be going in first, so if they happen to grab me it's unlikely they'll look for you later."

"Where are we staying?"

"At a small *pensión* operated by an old friend of mine. She mainly caters to long-term guests during the high season. This time of the year the place is practically dead, so we should have it pretty much to ourselves. It's not fancy, but it's comfortable enough."

I didn't ask any questions about his woman friend—or the nature of his prior experiences in Veracruz—though I was sure it would be a colorful story. Pardee's almost always were.

After a light breakfast, we loaded the Jeep and headed for Reno. He had a kind of calm intensity that I'd often seen on the eve of a hunt. Back when we were a team, I'd get high on the anticipation, and I was feeling it now. With the green flag about to fall, my warrior instincts kicked in, same as Pardee's.

In a way—a big way, to be honest—that reassured me,

because our lives would depend on how well we worked together. Yet in another way it bothered me. What of my new life with Sky? What of our future?

I hadn't called him again, though I'd lain awake in the middle of the night for a couple of hours, thinking about him. I'd only had my engagement ring for a few days, but now that it was gone my finger felt bare.

The longer I'd lain there awake, the more I hoped I was right when I'd told Sky that this experience would be good for our relationship. Like I'd told him, if our love couldn't survive this test, we probably didn't belong together. But I'd said that feeling the confidence of a woman in love, a woman who'd given careful thought before she'd accepted Sky's proposal of marriage.

Now I wondered if I might have been naive. All the careful planning and thinking and weighing of pros and cons in the world wouldn't matter one iota if, at a deep, fundamental level, we weren't right for each other. Sure, most normal couples wouldn't have their love and trust tested like this. But I wasn't exactly what you'd call normal. I didn't lead a normal life—didn't want to. Sky would have to trust me as I was, take me as I was, or it wouldn't work in the end.

I knew I couldn't dwell on that now, though. No matter how things turned out with Sky, right now I had to get my mind on the task at hand. Focus. That was the way to get through this and back home to the life I'd made for myself.

We boarded our flight to Dallas and Pardee promptly fell asleep, which was what he always did on commercial flights. It didn't matter if he'd just gotten out of bed after a solid eight hours of shut-eye, as soon as he cinched up the seat belt, he'd close his eyes and start snoozing away. He woke up when the plane landed in Phoenix. He went to the bathroom, then talked the flight attendant into giving him a soft drink, even though drink service was long over.

"It's my dimples," he said, grinning, as he dropped into his seat. "Gets 'em every time."

"What dimples? You don't have any."

"No? Well, it must be something else, then."

I could tell Pardee was as stoked as I was. Part of it had to be the relief of finally being under way. And, too, maybe he was enjoying working with me again after such a long hiatus. I suppose I felt that way about it, too. Pardee was a good partner. At work and at play.

There was no denying that something about the hunt—the adrenaline, the guns and the sex—went well together. Of course, I wasn't thinking about the more intimate part of it now, even though I did worry about the way our professional and sexual lives had tended to flow together in the past. I simply told myself that would have to change.

After a very brief layover, our flight continued on to Dallas. Pardee woke up shortly before our approach into DFW. He yawned and checked his watch. "We aren't going to have a lot of time before my flight to Veracruz, so let me brief you on what to expect when you get there. Your flight will be met by a woman named Vera. She'll be holding a sign reading 'Raymond.'"

"Vera from Veracruz, huh?"

"Right. She'll bring you to the *pensión*. If all goes well, I'll be waiting for you there myself."

"And if it doesn't?"

"Unless Vera has other instructions for you, get on the next plane back to the States and remember me in your prayers."

"Is that all you're going to tell me?"

"The less you know, the better off you'll be, sweetheart."

"Seems to me you said the very same thing on our first job."

"That's because I cared about your well-being then, and I care about it now."

This was feeling a little bit too much like déjà vu for comfort, but I withheld comment.

We landed at DFW and I went with Pardee to the international terminal. I had an hour and a half to kill before my flight, so I walked him to his gate. They'd already called his flight.

"I'll see you in four or five hours, sweetheart," he said. "With luck I'll have a pitcher of margaritas waiting."

He had such a happy-sappy grin on his face that I didn't even bother to object to the suggestion. "Seeing as you're point man and the first to encounter enemy fire, take care of yourself," I said.

His smile turned vaguely sad. "You, too, Crazy Legs." He leaned over and kissed my cheek. "See you in Mexico, huh?" Giving me a wink, he turned and headed for the jetway.

I watched until he was out of sight. Then I walked along the concourse toward my gate, taking stock of my feelings. I could still feel Pardee's lips on my cheek. And damn, if I didn't like what I felt. I knew it was mostly the circumstances—the melancholy of past associations, the unifying influence of a common cause, the exhilaration of proximate danger. But if I were a hundred percent honest, I'd have to admit there was more. At a visceral level, Pardee still did it for me. He could still push my buttons, still get a reaction just because of who he was.

It didn't mean anything cataclysmic because it changed nothing. His deficiencies remained. If his reappearance in my life taught me anything about love, it's that love for one person did not necessarily negate love for another. I loved Sky Tyler and I intended to marry him, but I'd be a liar to deny Pardee still intrigued me. I was as attracted to him as I'd ever been, but time had changed one very important thing—I was wiser now.

And I knew with absolute certainty that I'd made the right decision when I left Pardee. He might have my number, but he didn't have my heart.

I stopped at a shop and bought a magazine and a candy bar. It was one of those chocolate-needy moments. Marta always said those tended to come when a woman realized she might be at a disadvantage, usually due to some man. And Marta, as usual, was right.

When I arrived at the waiting area I got my cell phone out of my purse. I polished off the last of my candy bar and was about to call Sky one final time, but something stopped me. I'm not sure what. I guess it was my mood.

I'd felt like this before, just before heading overseas for the Gulf War, or when going on a combat mission. In effect I was in the staging area and I had my game face on. I didn't want to lose my edge. Besides, Sky knew how I felt about him. I'd let that last profession of love at the ranch be my final word on the subject.

It was time to go to war.

Eighteen

In one sense my flight to Mexico seemed to drag on forever, but in another the landing seemed to come before I was ready. I admit to being nervous. Hell, if they arrested me, I could spend several years in a south-of-the-border prison. Not a pretty thought.

I fought my nerves by thinking of Quinn. He was the innocent victim in all this. And if Fernando Suarez was behind this, like Pardee suspected, he certainly knew how to carry a grudge.

Our landing in Veracruz was bumpy. I hoped it wasn't an omen. I was in the middle of the stream of passengers entering the terminal building. There were two cops in khaki uniforms at the gate. I held my breath as I approached them, not making eye contact.

I'd gone maybe ten or fifteen yards past them when I heard one of them shout.

"*¡Señora! ¡Espere!*"

I continued walking.

"*¡Señora!*"

I knew this was it. I quickened my pace. There was a whistle, then running behind me. Someone screamed. In the corridor ahead two more cops appeared with guns drawn. People all around me were ducking, shoving and diving out of the way. I got knocked to the side as the cops behind me came thundering down the hall. But instead of pouncing on me, as I expected, they ran toward a young woman in jeans and carrying a backpack, who was frantically, but unsuccessfully, trying to open a side door. The four cops converged on her, grabbed her and dragged her away.

I stood there for a few seconds, my heart pounding to beat the band. Along with the passengers around me I gathered myself, shocked that I was still in one piece. It was like being narrowly missed by a speeding truck. People around me muttered in English and Spanish, some angry for having gotten a start, others excited that something out of the ordinary had happened. I was just grateful it wasn't me.

A bit calmer, but perspiring, I continued on through passport control, then got my suitcase, which nobody searched—not that it would have mattered, since I didn't have anything with me that would have given away our mission. But the customs guys didn't even ask if I had anything to declare, waving me on through.

After warily walking past another cop at the exit, I turned my attention to the waiting throng outside customs. I saw a couple of signs but none said "Raymond," or "Mayne," or "Josephine," or, for that matter, "Pardee's pilot."

I stood there, looking around, until I started feeling conspicuous. The incident inside the terminal building had proven to me that there were cops aplenty around and they seemed to be alert enough. That didn't auger well, as it meant they might also be on the lookout for me.

Then it occurred to me that Vera might be waiting outside the terminal building, so I headed for the main entrance, hoping I'd be even less conspicuous out there. It was dark now. A bunch of vendors hawked their wares and taxi drivers were trying to hustle a fare, but there was no one with a sign that said "Raymond."

I waited in the sultry, tropical air, ignoring the looks from the men, hoping against hope this didn't mean Pardee had been caught and the mission aborted. I was about to give up and go back inside the building to inquire about flights back to the States when I saw a plump, middle-aged woman in a bright red caftan come running along the sidewalk. What caught my eye, apart from the fact she was hurrying, was that she was carrying a sign. I couldn't see what was written on the cardboard, but I decided to take a chance.

"Vera?" I said as she passed me on her way to the entrance.

She stopped, gave me a quizzical look, then in a clipped British accent said, between breaths, "Oh, of course . . . you must be Miss Raymond." She held up the sign reading "Raymond" and beamed. She was in her late fifties with a doll face and rosy cheeks.

"Yes."

She dabbed her brow with the handkerchief in her hand. "I'm terribly sorry to be late, love," she said, taking my arm. "It's my car. Ran out of petrol, of all things. Gauge isn't working properly. Bloody nuisance, that. Have you been waiting long?" she asked, as we made our way to the head of the taxi stand.

"No, not really," I said, not wanting her to feel guilty.

"Splendid. We shan't be inconvenienced greatly on the way back if all goes well," Vera said. "I rang up road assistance, but didn't think I should wait for them. Sometimes it's five minutes and sometimes it's two hours. Couldn't miss you, now, could I? With any luck at all, they'll be waiting at the car with some petrol. Left them a note."

The driver of the first taxi held the passenger door to his vehicle open for us. Vera spoke to him in perfect, rapid-fire Spanish. The man was not pleased with what she had to say. From what I could gather, he didn't want a short fare after such a long wait in line.

"These chaps can be bloody maddening at times. But then, I suppose they must earn the best living they can. Still, we can't be bothered walking, now, can we?" Vera said, taking my arm again. "Come along." She led me across the street to where a Gypsy cab, actually an old, beat-up VW van, sat waiting, the sleepy-looking driver leaning against it. A fare was quickly negotiated. The driver took my bag, we climbed into the grimy torn seats and we were off.

"My automobile is just a short distance up the road and this gentleman has agreed to sell me some petrol if the road assistance lorry hasn't arrived," Vera explained, mopping her face again. "So how was your flight, love?"

"Fine. Uneventful."

"That's lovely. Uneventful flights are the best, especially these days. Did they feed you?"

"Yes, I had dinner on the plane."

"My condolences."

"At least I'm not hungry."

She gave my hand a pat, then, lowering her voice, said,

"It's so good to meet Pardee's wife at long last. You're every bit as lovely as I expected."

I wasn't sure whether I should correct her "wife" comment or assume it was part of our cover, so I let it pass. Pardee still had the unfortunate habit of referring to me as his wife. I decided it didn't matter what Vera thought, though.

In half a mile we came to an old two-toned coral-and-white Chevrolet with fins that sat by the side of the road. The car dated back to the fifties at least. "It was my late husband Raoul's car," Vera explained as we got out, "and I can't bring myself to part with it. Marilyn—that's what he named her, after Marilyn Monroe—has almost a million miles on her and is practically the same age as me, and still runs like a top. Parts are a problem, however." She gave a cheery laugh. "Same as me."

Vera oversaw the transfer of my case to the Chevy, plus the addition of a few liters of fuel to the gas tank from a storage can. She paid the driver, giving him a good tip, judging by the huge smile on his face, and we climbed into the car, which was pristinely clean and in surprisingly good shape. We were soon on our way.

"I gather Pardee arrived without a problem."

"None whatsoever," she replied.

I wasn't sure how much Vera knew about what we were doing, so I avoided discussion about the job. I figured Pardee was a safe enough topic. "How do you know him?" I asked.

"That's quite a story indeed. I'm surprised he hasn't told you. Then again, perhaps I'm not. Most chaps are reticent about past loves, I suppose. It was my daughter. Irene. This was nearly fifteen years ago.

"I'm convinced Pardee saved her life," Vera went on, as she craned her neck to see over the steering wheel. "That's what it amounted to. Irene had been working as a travel consultant here in Veracruz when she first met Pardee. They had a fling, but they were young and it didn't last long. After he returned to the States, Irene took up with a wealthy Panamanian on the rebound.

"I told her she was daft, but she ended up going with him to Panama. As it turns out he kept her there against her will. Irene managed to get word to us of her plight and my husband Raoul engaged Pardee to go down there and bring her back. It was all delightfully romantic. I had hopes for a while that they might marry, though I suppose it was wishful thinking on my part."

This sounded like the Pardee I knew, though I wasn't surprised he'd never told me the story. "What happened to Irene after that?"

"She eventually married a lawyer here in Veracruz. They had a child, Anna, and were very happy until Ramon was killed in a freak boating accident out in the Gulf. This was a few years ago."

"I'm sorry."

"As you can see, though, we're all very much indebted to Pardee. I love him like a son and, truth be known, I don't think Irene's ever stopped loving him. But don't repeat that last bit, okay?"

I didn't know who I'd repeat it to, but that was fine. "Sure," I said.

"Not that it's any of my affair, mind you, but reading between the lines, I judge that you and Pardee are going through a rough patch."

"You could say that, yes."

"I do hope it works out, love. Pardee is so frightfully admiring of you and couldn't speak highly enough of your skills as a mercenary, not to mention your kindness toward his son."

It sounded to me like Pardee had given her his usual cocktail of half truth and half lies. I saw no point in making an issue of it, though. Lord knew, the man wasn't likely to change at this point. Besides, he evidently had his reasons.

We'd entered the city and Vera pointed out some of the sights. The part of Mexico I was familiar with was the northernmost desert and mountainous region, having become acquainted with it on that fateful first mission with Pardee. Tropical Mexico was a totally new experience.

I'd heard that Veracruz had a vibrance and a rhythm all its own. From what I could see it was more authentic than the newer resort areas like Cancún and Cozumel. There were numerous old buildings from the colonial era, and it was apparent the city had a rich history. According to Vera, it went back to Cortéz. "This was the first European colony in the new world, you know." I hadn't.

Marilyn Monroe, having no air-conditioning, was most comfortable with her windows down. It made for a breezy ride, but we were rewarded with the rich sounds of the streets. Salsa music seemed to be everywhere and as we rode I could hear the cry of street vendors, the clang of a trolley bell and even the bellow of a ship's horn in the harbor.

Veracruz did not seem like a dangerous place. To the contrary, it seemed friendly and welcoming. And I suppose it was—to Denise Raymond. Josie Mayne, though, was another story entirely.

Vera's *pensión* was located in the old quarter. The structure must have at one time been the grand old colonial-style home of a wealthy merchant—probably dating from the middle of the nineteenth century. Now it was a somewhat careworn boardinghouse. The building was surrounded by a wrought-iron fence which enclosed a small garden in front. Like the house, the garden was a bit neglected, but had color and a certain charm.

Vera drove the Chevy through the gate located on one side of the house and stopped in the gravel drive under a big mango tree. We got out. I retrieved my suitcase from the backseat and we headed for the front door.

Even before we reached it, the door swung open and we were greeted by an Indian woman with bronzed, deeply wrinkled skin. Vera rattled off instructions in Spanish and the woman took my case, heading immediately for the staircase.

"Come along, dear," Vera said to me. "Let's find that husband of yours and I'll see about a cool drink."

Not being used to the humidity, I was feeling hot and sticky, but rather than going upstairs first to freshen up, I decided to check in with Pardee. I had an urgent, albeit morbid, desire to hear the rest of the story he'd concocted about us.

After making our way through the lavishly furnished though slightly worn sitting room, we came out on to the veranda, which overlooked a tropical garden. Pardee sat at a game table with a girl of about ten, both of them hunched over a chessboard.

"Here we are, then!" Vera announced cheerily.

"Ah, you made it safely, sweetheart!" Pardee said, rising. He came over and gave me a spousal hug and a kiss on the cheek.

"I don't recall annulling our divorce," I said under my breath.

"We'll discuss it later," he whispered. Then, aloud, "So, have a good flight?"

"Yeah, it was fine."

Vera introduced me to her granddaughter, Anna, a pretty little girl with dark brown hair and a twinkle of Northern European stock in her gray eyes and lighter complection. I took a look at their game in progress.

"Looks like you've run into a prodigy," I told Pardee. I'd learned chess in the army and Pardee and I would play occasionally, though we'd given up when he got frustrated because he could never win. He was a whiz at Chinese checkers, so naturally that's what we tended to play.

"I didn't want to embarrass the kid," he said.

"Get used to it, Anna," I said to the girl. "All men have adequacy issues."

She gave me a quizzical look.

"Stick to chess, but don't play poker with him," I said. "You'll be much better off."

"Oh, but we already played poker, señora. I won twenty pesos."

I glanced at Pardee.

"She insisted on draw poker," he said with a shrug. "And as you well know, Josie, Texas Hold'em is my game."

"Good for you, Anna," I said.

I was fairly certain Pardee had taken a dive. That was part of his game, when dealing with women. As he'd once said to me in an unguarded moment, "When it comes to the fairer sex, the object isn't so much winning as getting them to play." Our relationship was testimony to that.

"Are you ready for your margarita, Pardee?"

The voice came from the doorway. It was an attractive woman of about my age, holding a tray containing a pitcher and glasses. Her light brown hair was pulled up on top her head, her eyes were pale blue. She was in a low-cut cotton dress with spaghetti straps. She was quite shapely.

"Irene," Vera said, "come meet Pardee's wife."

I'd met his old girlfriends and lovers before, so it wasn't exactly a new experience for me, though this was the first time it had happened since our divorce—not counting the woman in the restaurant back in Hawthorne, of course. She didn't really count, since there was some doubt whether the relationship had ever been officially consummated.

But seeing one of Pardee's old loves now, I have to admit, it didn't feel a lot different to me than it had in the past. I eyed Irene and she eyed me. We both smiled tightly.

I had long since divorced the guy, which should have meant that I had no cause for feeling any hostility toward Irene—though she couldn't have known that. And in spite of the fact that she'd had a husband and a child, jealousy was in the air, crackling between us like a downed power line in a rainstorm.

Irene put down the tray and shook my hand. "Welcome to Veracruz, Mrs. Pardee," she said. "Is this your first time here?" Her accent was light and musical to the ear.

"Yes, it is."

"As your husband can tell you, we have a wonderful city."

"Yes, what I've seen of it has been lovely."

"We are in the old quarter here, but the tradition is rich. Veracruz is a place with a lot of history, as I'm sure my mother has told you."

The comment could have been taken two ways, which, I

now assumed, was what she intended. Funny how defensive I felt, even though I'd gladly have given her Pardee with my blessing. Naturally, he was beaming through it all.

I considered declining the margarita, grabbing a quick shower and calling it a night instead. But an ornery streak in me—directed at just who, I couldn't say—kept me there. Vera, Irene and I ended up at the far end of the veranda in wicker chairs while, at her insistence, Anna and Pardee finished their game. It didn't take long for the girl to finish him off.

I'd spent several minutes answering questions about our life on the ranch—a feat of mind requiring only a change of tense—when Pardee finally joined us. We watched as Anna headed upstairs to bask in the glow of victory.

"She's damned good for being so young," Pardee said, as Irene refilled his glass for the third time.

"Ramon believed she is a prodigy and wanted badly to send her to a school for the gifted, but I was against it." Irene spoke in a light tone, but her expression was sultry as she eyed my former husband.

"I'm thrilled that I have both my young ladies here with me," Vera said. "It's not easy for two widows."

The conversation shifted to the operation. I quickly discovered that our two hosts knew almost as much about his plans as I.

"Irene's already located a chopper. It belongs to a geological firm she's done work for here in Veracruz," Pardee explained.

"That is a good break," I agreed. We both knew that the authorities would be on the alert for aircraft rentals. This would be a less risky way to go.

"How will we get control of the bird? I assume they aren't going to just hand it over to us."

"You'll either have to take it by force or guile, sweetheart. It'll be your pick."

The "sweetheart" sort of stuck in my throat. "As you know, *dear*, I don't like bashing heads unless it's necessary."

"Irene has an angle that should make it relatively easy for you."

"It turns out they're selling the aircraft," Irene explained. "I only found out a few days ago. Perhaps you can pose as the pilot for a buyer, take it for a test flight and neglect to bring it back."

"It will mean coming up with a plausible story," Pardee added. "How you want to handle it is up to you. Irene will tell you all she can about the company and show you where the chopper is. That should keep the two of you pretty busy tomorrow."

"What will you be doing?" I asked Pardee.

"Contacting the kidnappers and making final arrangements for the ransom."

Not being sure just how free I was to talk openly in front of our hosts, I didn't question Pardee further about the money, though we both knew there was no way on earth he could come up with half a million in cash. "When do we go into action?"

"If things fall into place, I'm hoping for day after tomorrow," Pardee said.

"It's unfortunate your trip will be so brief," Irene said. "But we are grateful we were able to see you again."

I didn't have to know the woman to see that her feelings for Pardee were much stronger than she was letting on. She was one of those people whose passion simmers under the surface like a volcano ready to explode. I could also see that Pardee was sensing it, too. And enjoying it.

His ability to turn women on just by being himself was his greatest joy. And it worked like an aphrodisiac. I'd seen it countless times and was often the beneficiary. Some of our most spirited lovemaking came after some woman, whether a stranger or acquaintance, threw herself at him.

My feelings about it now were different, of course. I reminded myself that the more attention he paid to other women, and the less he paid to me, the better off I was. I sincerely wished Irene well.

I made polite conversation awhile longer, but once I'd finished my margarita, I professed to be tired and in need of a bath. Vera had the maid show me upstairs to her "best room." Much to my consternation, I found Pardee's things already there. Worse, there was only one bed in the room. It was a king. I was willing to sacrifice for the team and I'd even lie for Pardee, if necessary, but I had my limits and sleeping with the bastard was definitely one.

Nineteen

I showered and was ready for bed, but I didn't want to go to sleep until I'd made it clear to Pardee we wouldn't be sharing the same bed. The last thing I wanted was him climbing in with me as though the last five years had never happened.

I considered my options. The easiest solution would be for him to ask for another room for himself. But he might not want to have to explain to Vera and Irene. If that was the case, he could either sleep on the floor or on the lounge chair out on the balcony. I wasn't hard-hearted. He could choose. But he had to come upstairs so we could discuss it, and God only knew when that would be.

Not having had the foresight to bring something to read, and there being no television in the room, I decided to go out onto the balcony for a breath of fresh air. The *pensión* was north of the harbor and not far from the water. From the balcony I could see snatches of dark sea through the trees and surrounding rooftops. The neighborhood had obviously degraded over the years. A few large old houses remained, but most of the buildings in the area were small apartment houses.

Salsa music drifted over from the nearest boulevard, but it was nearly drowned out by the cacophony of the tree frogs in the garden. As I stood at the railing in my nightgown, I could hear voices drifting up from below. I heard Vera say good night and I heard Irene and Pardee's reply.

There was a minute of silence, then I heard Irene say, "Your wife is quite lovely."

"She's a very special lady."

"You're happy together, then?"

"Josie and I have had our problems like most couples, but we also have a lot in common. On balance we get along okay."

I flushed at this, wanting to lean over the balcony and shout, *Pardee, you lying sonovabitch!*

"Then it wasn't she who gave you that black eye?"

"No, my horse knocked me into a post in the barn while I was cleaning his shoes."

Hearing that, I smirked. The truth and Pardee were never comfortable together.

"She is very nice, but she seems a bit formal with you," Irene noted.

"That's just Josie's style, sweetheart. When we're on a job, she's all business."

At least he got that right.

"Well, I'm happy for you," she said. "To be honest, I never thought you would marry."

"Why's that?"

"I thought you'd never give your heart to one woman.

You're a very independent man, like Clint Eastwood in his movies. And though it was a long time ago, I have not forgotten a moment of our time together. You broke my heart, Pardee. But you must already know this."

"I certainly didn't mean to hurt you," he said. "And I'm sorry if I did."

This I believed. Pardee never intended to hurt anyone. Not that it stopped him from doing what suited him. And, if somebody got screwed inadvertently . . . well, shit happens.

"But you also saved my life," Irene said. "So I guess we are even."

"I was very sorry to hear about your husband dying. It must have been very difficult, especially considering your daughter."

"It was a great tragedy, of course. I loved Ramon, but he wasn't the love of my life."

From my eavesdropping vantage point I could read Irene perfectly and I suspected Pardee was reading her, too. I wondered whether he'd hone in on her remark or let it pass.

After a hesitation, he said, "Fate plays terrible tricks sometimes."

There was a long silence below, making me wonder what they were doing. Then Irene said, "Is Josie the love of your life?"

This I had to hear. I leaned forward in anticipation of his response.

"I would have to say so, yes. Sometimes it takes a while to realize it, but it's true."

A bubble of emotion welled up from nowhere. I'm not sure why. Pardee was capable of saying anything at any time and there was no way to know if it could be trusted.

Yet, here he was telling another woman that I was the love of his life. It moved me. And it was weird that it did.

"Are you the love of *her* life, Pardee?"

My ears perked up at that, as well.

"I wish I could say I was, but I'm not."

What? Compulsive honesty? From Pardee?

"That's very sad," Irene said. "You deserve her love. She may be beautiful, but she is also very foolish."

"Can't argue with that."

It took all my willpower to keep from hollering, *Well, I sure as hell can!*

"Is there any chance you and Josie will part?" Irene asked.

I waited for his response right along with her.

"You never know."

"I don't mean to cause trouble," she said, "but if that should ever happen, I hope you will remember me. Perhaps I could help you through your sadness. God willing it won't come to that, but I owe you so much that I hope always for your happiness. This is the kind of woman I am."

I flushed. How transparent was that? I mean, the woman was pouncing on him before my body was even cold! What did she think she was doing, moving in that way? Hypothetically speaking, of course. The reality was my body was so cold, I'd already moved on to my next life, but she didn't know that. Besides which, there was a principle involved. Had the woman no shame?

"I appreciate you saying that," Pardee replied. "I regard you as a very special person. You've always meant a lot to me."

I wanted to gag. What a goddamn hypocrite. I would have bet my house the sonovabitch would come upstairs and try to finagle his way into sleeping with me, his "wife" and the "love of his life." What a snake.

"Then you have fond memories of when we were together, as well?" she said.

Jesus, why didn't she just put her hand on his crotch? If Pardee loved me so much, why was he sitting there letting her verbally undress him? It just went to show that "love of my life" crap was crap. Maybe the whole thing was a setup. Maybe the scoundrel was using me to get his old girlfriend all hot and bothered. That would be like Pardee. Just like him.

"I have wonderful memories of our time together," he said.

I rolled my eyes.

"I confess I often thought of you," Irene said, "even when I was with my husband. Did the same ever happen to you?"

I was squeezing the railing so tight, my knuckles were turning white. I couldn't wait to hear his answer.

Pardee cleared his throat. "It would be a lie if I didn't say yes, Irene. Over the years, I've thought of you many times."

That was it! I not only wanted to scream at him, but I wanted to swing down off the balcony and throttle the S.O.B. Not that it mattered to me now, of course, but he was desecrating our marriage, belying every profession of love he'd uttered. Of course, as Sky's fiancée I didn't give a shit, but I was outraged on behalf of the old Josie, the wife I'd once been. What a scheming, two-faced liar!

And I bet what he was telling her was true. He might have made love to me, but who was he thinking about? Irene? Sure, Irene and probably two dozen other women

I'd never even known existed. How wise I'd been to divorce him, and how foolish to have stayed with him as long as I did. Love of his life, my ass.

"I must be honest with you," Irene said. "This conversation is difficult for me. I think I will go to my lonely bed now and dream of the past. Can I ask one small favor before I go? Can I have a little kiss, an innocent kiss of friendship, to send me happily to my dreams?"

"For you, of course, Irene."

My eyes went round and I leaned out over the balcony as far as I could, hoping I might get a glimpse of them. I wanted to see just how innocent this little "kiss of friendship" was going to be.

Stretching my neck as far as I could, I could see their feet on the veranda below me, but I couldn't see more—not without hanging from the railing by my knees. But then, just as I was about to give up and go back inside, there was a sudden crack and the railing gave way, shearing off the rusty bolts that fastened it to the wall. As the railing fell, I somehow managed to grab the remaining stanchion. It, too, began to give way, going over like a tree falling down in slow motion, creaking and groaning until it pointed down toward the abyss below, with me hanging on the end of it like a big fish on a small pole.

There were Pardee and Irene, seated on the wicker sofa. And there I was, dangling before them. Irene's eyes were open wide and her mouth was agape. Pardee's expression was classic.

For a second or two we were all frozen like that, me looking at them and they looking at me. This was embarrassing at so many levels, I had no idea where to begin. About the only sensation I felt, apart from the strain on my shoulders and arms, was the hush of balmy air on my bare legs, which swung freely under my billowing nightgown.

I don't know where it came from, but after a moment I had the aplomb to say, "Excuse me, but I could use a hand."

Pardee jumped to his feet and came to the edge of the veranda, where he leaned out and grabbed my thighs, pulling me in. I let go of the stanchion and slid down into his arms. He held me briefly, then had the audacity to smile.

"You give new meaning to the term 'eavesdropper,'" he said.

"More like the original meaning."

He continued to beam, pleased as punch at my unorthodox arrival.

"Would you mind putting me down?"

Pardee gently deposited me on the floor.

I stepped back and ran my fingers through my hair, realizing there was nothing I could do or say to improve matters. Having no other choice, I fell back on instinctive politeness. "Please forgive the interruption," I said to Irene. With that I walked back into the house, through the salon and up the stairs to my room. My cheeks burned as I sat on the bed and quietly cursed the day I was born.

It was fifteen minutes before Pardee showed up. I lay in the middle of the bed like a mummy in a tomb, staring at the ceiling. I expected a wisecrack from him, but he said nothing, going into the bath only to come out five minutes later in his shorts and carrying his clothing, which he hung over the back of a chair.

"Why are we staying in the same room?" I intoned. "And

why the bullshit about us still being married? Does lying to your friends give you some kind of perverse satisfaction?"

"No, it's an unfortunate necessity."

"How so?"

"I figured being here with my former wife would be awkward."

"Awkward for who, Pardee?"

"The plain fact is I didn't want to hurt Irene."

"*What?*" I scoffed. "You practically seduced her."

"That's ridiculous. I was trying to be considerate. Josie, that woman's had the hots for me for years. Us being married made it easier to ask for help. I didn't want to give her the wrong idea."

"So you brought your *wife* along, then proceeded to play footsie with her behind my back? If that's not giving her the wrong idea, I don't know what is."

"We were just being friendly."

"Oh, so that's what you call it. Tell me, how many women were you *friendly* with while you were married to me? Besides Miss Reno, of course."

"Does it matter?"

The question brought me up short. "Well, I suppose it doesn't really *matter,*" I sputtered, "but it's the principle of the thing."

"What principle?"

"Oh, for God's sake, you know what I mean."

"No, I don't."

I was really getting angry now. The man could be positively infuriating. What made him think everything had to be explained logically? Couldn't he see that feelings and logic had nothing to do with each other? "If I have to explain something that ought to be obvious to you, there's no point."

"Try me."

"Listen," I said, "if you want logic, Quinn is all that matters. That's who we should be focusing our attention on, rather than how noble you are for playing around behind your wife's back in the name of chivalry. The point is, I have to look at that woman at the breakfast table. It's not easy enduring the indignities of being your wife. And I say that from experience."

"Josie, you're making no sense whatsoever," he said, pulling back the covers to get in bed.

I yanked them from his hand. "What do you think you're doing?"

"Getting in bed."

"You're not sleeping with me, Sir Galahad. Either get your own room or sleep on the floor."

"It's a big bed, Josie. I won't touch you."

"How naive do you think I am?"

"How desperate do you think *I* am?"

My eyes rounded with indignation. "You asshole!"

"I didn't mean it that way," he said, dismissing my fury. "What I'm trying to say is I accept the fact that you're my ex-wife and that you're marrying Sky. Right now all I want is to get a good night's sleep and rescue my son. Maybe I shouldn't have set things up this way, but I needed Vera's and Irene's help, and I didn't want any misunderstandings or distractions. Us being married was easier and cleaner and it enabled me to avoid needless emotional complications."

"Like friendly kisses?" I huffed.

"Just answer me this," he said, "are you jealous or just glad for an excuse to take a shot at me?"

"Neither."

"Then what's your problem?"

"My problem is *you*, Pardee. Being around you is a problem. Why do you think I divorced you, dammit?"

He considered that. "Do you believe that my primary concern is Quinn?"

"I suppose so."

"Have I done one improper thing since we've teamed up on this operation?"

I had to think about that one for a moment or two. The pecks he'd given me, the incidental touching, the little wrestling match in the Jeep were fairly inconsequential compared to what might have happened. Plus, I knew the things that had happened thus far were at least partly my fault. "I guess not," I said reluctantly.

"Then what makes you think I'm trying to pull something now?"

This was vintage Pardee. How he managed to make the most ridiculous propositions seem perfectly reasonable, I'll never know. He was the last man on earth I should be allowing in my bed, yet here I was, about to capitulate. I was convinced Pardee knew how to play on a woman's weaknesses, especially her sense of compassion, better than any man alive.

I purposely did not look at his chest. "Are there any extra pillows?"

"You sleep with pillows now?"

I never had, and it annoyed me that he was so intimately aware of my foibles. I think this was why former spouses despise one another—they know too much. But there were far more embarrassing things on the list than my pillow preferences. "I intend to divide the bed in two," I replied.

Groaning, Pardee went to the big armoire on the opposite wall, where he found three extra pillows. He threw them to me and I built a wall down the middle of the bed that might have given the Germans more trouble than the Maginot Line. Once he was in bed we couldn't see each other, which was just the way I wanted it. I had one additional statement to make. I took my purse from the bedstand and got out my cell phone.

"I'm going to call Sky," I told Pardee, "so could you refrain from talking, please? He wouldn't appreciate our sleeping arrangements."

"How do you plan to call him?"

"On my cell phone."

"It won't work in Mexico, Josie. Different system."

"Crap."

"Don't despair," he said, getting out of bed. He went to the dresser and brought me a different phone. "Vera got two of these for us, so we can communicate."

I thanked him. Pardee got back in bed, disappearing behind my fortifications. I dialed Sky's home number.

"Hi, honey, it's me," I chirped when he answered. "We're here. Everything's going fine. I wanted you to know."

Sky was delighted I called. He updated me on Baron's latest adventures, even put my beloved copilot on so I could hear him sniff the phone and bark at my disembodied voice. As before, Sky and I cooed and exchanged professions of love.

Somewhere along the line Pardee fell asleep. I could hear snores emanating from the enemy side of the divide. My former husband had always been a snorer, so the chances were it was a legitimate reaction to my telephonic lovemaking, though with Pardee you never knew.

Sky and I ended our call after a while, wishing each other good night. I turned off the light, thinking of my fiancé, my ring, my dog and missing them all. But I also thought of Pardee sleeping just inches away and how uncomfortable that made me feel. I was annoyed, angry, embarrassed. I'd behaved stupidly, falling from the balcony, getting flustered, jealous, fighting and sniping with Pardee like I cared.

He'd been exactly right—I was behaving like a wife, a jealous wife. And he was eating it up, laughing up his sleeve. But there was a bigger danger. Pardee had a nose for weakness. Once he saw an opening, he'd move in for the kill. The hell of it was I knew this, and still I'd let it happen.

Twenty

I awoke the next morning to discover my defensive fortifications were still intact and Pardee already gone. I was happy about that on both scores. I still wasn't looking forward to seeing Irene again, though. On my way to the bath, I glanced out at the balcony and confirmed that the railing was no longer there. I cringed inwardly, my folly seeming even worse in the light of day.

The weathered little maid was making my bed when I came out of the bath. I couldn't imagine what she thought of the embattlement I'd built down the middle of the bed. People around the world found the independent attitudes of American women odd anyway, so she probably regarded this as just another indication of how bizarre we truly were.

Once she'd finished with the room, I dressed and went downstairs. I found Vera on the veranda having a cup of *lechero*, the Veracruz version of *café con leche*, or hot milk in a bit of extremely strong coffee. She sat serenely staring out at her garden. Hearing me, she turned.

"Ah, good morning, love," she said in that distinctive cheery manner of the English.

"I'm terribly sorry about the railing," I said. "I'll be glad to pay to have it repaired."

"Don't give it a second thought," she replied. "I was relieved to learn you weren't hurt. You are okay, aren't you?"

"The only real damage was to my pride. But I do insist on paying for repairs. It's the least I can do under the circumstances."

"Thank you, but Pardee has taken care of it and I've already engaged a repairman. Everything should be restored to good order by the time you get back here this evening. Would you like some of our delicious local coffee, dear? Or tea, perhaps?"

"Coffee would be nice."

The maid was given my request and I sat with Vera to enjoy the relative mildness of the morning air. By day the large garden looked less forbidding and Vera suggested I might wish to take a stroll in it sometime during our stay. She confirmed that Pardee had left early to tend to business, that even though Irene was taking the day off from work, she was now running some errands that couldn't be put off. Anna was at school, of course. "Irene told me to tell you she'd be back around eleven to take you to see the helicopter," Vera informed me.

I was glad. It would feel good to do something meaningful. To this point I'd come off as a ditz, and there was my pride to consider. It was time to get back to being me.

A few minutes after I got my coffee and a plate of heavenly-smelling cinnamon pastries, the workmen arrived to fix the balcony railing. While Vera was occupied with them, I ate, then took a walk in the tropical garden.

The overgrown foliage and the abundance of birds reminded me of that job Pardee and I had done in the jungles of South America a year into our marriage.

It had been one of the most physically grueling hunts I'd been on. Afterward, we'd gone to Aruba for a little R&R. I recalled lying on the beach with Pardee after a night and morning of vigorous lovemaking. He'd turned to me and said, "After this, Josie, you can handle anything. You've proven yourself."

I'd never been a hundred percent certain whether he'd meant I'd proven myself in the field, or in the sack, or both. For some reason the ambiguity had appealed to me, though, and I'd never asked exactly what he'd been referring to.

Irene arrived to take me to case the location of the aircraft. There was a palpable tension between us. Not that Irene was frosty or hostile, but underneath the businesslike facade I think she resented me. Though nothing was said about the eavesdropping incident of the night before, it was clear we were both embarrassed—me for trying to hear the conversation and Irene for so blatantly coming on to another woman's husband. (Or so she thought.)

I resented Pardee for putting all of us in this crazy situation. The truth had been turned on its head, which made things even tougher for Irene and me. The hell of it was, there wasn't a damned thing I could do about it.

What concerned me even more was that Pardee still had feelings for me. He'd told me he still loved me and I'd taken him at his word—not that his word was worth all that much, but the growing body of evidence seemed to reinforce my conclusion. I'd tried not to think about it, but I could now see that it was driving everything. Worse, I'd let the situation get to me. I'd gotten defensive because I knew how dangerous Pardee could be. He understood my vulnerabilities better than any man alive and that gave him leverage.

The solution was simple, if not easy to achieve. I had to convince him that I really had moved on.

With respect to Irene, the tragedy was I couldn't tell her what was going on. We weren't competing for Pardee's affections, yet we were trapped in his web of chivalric lies. That didn't mean we weren't still antagonists. We were, after all, women, and we both had our pride, even if our differences were an illusion.

Irene's car was in the shop being repaired, so we took Marilyn Monroe. The worst of the heat was yet to come, but it was sultry enough that the windows had to be down for comfort. We engaged in minimal small talk until I asked about the situation with the chopper.

"I'm a travel consultant for various companies. The one with the helicopter is the Mexican subsidiary of an American firm, Industrial Geology International, or IGI," she told me.

"And it's for sale."

"That's right. You'll have to deal with the director, a man named Marco Rigi. He's a typical Italian, obsessed with sex. He's under the illusion that every attractive woman alive exists for his pleasure. That's the bad news.

"The good news is he's about a hundred and sixty centimeters tall. Five feet three inches. Still, he is very tenacious. You will have to be on your guard if you don't want to find yourself in his arms."

"Sounds like you're speaking from experience, Irene."

"Yes. I must constantly charm him to keep the account.

It's not pleasant, as he can be quite determined, but I manage to keep him at a distance. I don't know what he would expect from you as a sort of customer."

"I hope only sweet talk."

"With Marco you never know."

I thought I detected a touch of cynical glee in Irene's tone. I suspected she wouldn't be particularly upset to see me harassed a little. If she had to suffer, why shouldn't I?

"Do you have any suggestions on the story I should use with Mr. Rigi?" I asked.

"You would know about helicopters and the companies that use them better than I."

"Where is IGI headquartered in the States?"

"Houston."

"Good, maybe I can talk to him about Texas. I assume he speaks English."

"Very well."

"Is the sale being handled from Texas or here in Mexico?"

"I think the decision is made in Houston but Marco coordinates things here. I could not ask too many questions without arousing suspicion."

IGI was located in an industrial park outside of the city. Irene stopped under a large shade tree across from the company compound. From where we sat, I could see the helicopter—a 200 series Bell with a metallic paint job and a big "IGI" painted on the side—sitting on a pad behind and to the side of the main building. The compound was surrounded by an eight-foot chain-link fence topped with razor wire. There was a fairly serious-looking guard at the vehicular gate. Irene was right in her assessment: Deceit was definitely the way to go.

She and I sat silently while I surveyed the scene.

"Out of curiosity, did you mention Mr. Rigi to Pardee?" I asked.

"No. He said you were the aircraft expert and I should discuss the details with you." She hesitated, looked down at her hands, then up at me. "Do you mind a professional question?"

"No."

"If it turned out the only way to get permission to use the helicopter was to sleep with Marco, would you do it for Pardee and his son?"

The audacity of the question surprised me, but I decided on an honest answer. "I'd find another way."

"But if there was no alternative."

"Would *you*, in my shoes, Irene?"

She gave an ironic smile. "In your shoes, Josie, I would probably do many things differently."

At that moment I could have wrung Pardee's neck. His tall tale had caused one problem after another, but Irene's latest comment was the living end. I had to fight myself to keep the truth from boiling out of me. And the worst part of all was that I was partially to blame for not having come to an understanding with Pardee in advance of our arrival. I should have insisted that we agree on our cover story. Now I was paying for my oversight by being made the fool, which was humiliating—especially in light of the sacrifices I'd made.

"Oh, look," Irene said, pointing to the entrance of the building, "there is Marco now."

A small but sturdy man in a dapper white suit and Panama hat had come out the door and was walking briskly past the flagpole flying the Mexican flag. He was headed toward the small parking lot containing half a dozen vehicles.

We were too far away for me to see him well, but I got a good enough look to know I wouldn't want to go to bed with him for the team or, for that matter, to save my soul. I realized Irene had taken cynical pleasure in the suggestion.

"We have no other pressing business," she said. "Do you wish to follow him? You might learn something valuable."

"Sure."

We followed Rigi for a few miles to a village on the coast.

"His favorite restaurant is here," Irene said. "I believe this is where he likes to meet women for lunch and, if he can convince them, for a brief stay at a nearby beach hotel after. I confess to having lunch with him here once when I was trying to get the account."

I did not ask if her lunch meeting involved postprandial festivities. I had no reason to embarrass Irene.

As she predicted, he pulled up to a beach-style restaurant, got out and hurried inside. We parked in a shady spot nearby.

"Do you wish to go inside for a closer look at your prey?" she asked, enjoying the situation a little too much.

"No, I think I'll pass, thanks. But I'm thinking it might not be a bad idea to phone him soon and make an appointment. I assume you can give me his number."

"Would you like to call him now? I have his cell number. Pardee gave you a phone, did he not?"

"Yes," I said, considering the suggestion as I reached for my purse. "You think this is a good time? He might not want to be disturbed."

"Trust me, Marco loves to talk on the phone and play big shot to impress women. His secretary jokes when I call that he can't talk to me because he's on the phone with the Pope. He will take your call."

I found the cell phone Pardee had gotten for me. Irene gave me the number.

Marco Rigi answered with, "*Pronto. ¿Sí?*"

"Mr. Rigi," I said, "my name is Denise Raymond. I'm in Mexico and I just got a call from a friend who is in the market for a helicopter. He heard you were selling your Bell and asked me to check it out for him. Is it still available?"

"Yes, Miss Raymond, it is. Are you a pilot?"

"Yes."

"And you are in-a Veracruz?"

"Yes, I am."

"When-a would you like-a to see my helicopter?"

His English was excellent, but he had a very strong accent. Like many Italians, he seemed unable to avoid adding an extra syllable to the end of half his words.

"I was hoping tomorrow morning."

"This-a can be arranged."

"Good. Would ten be a good time?"

"Permit-a me to look at my appointment calendar, if-a you please. One moment." He was only off for a short while. "Yes, ten would-a be excellent. May I ask-a please, who is your friend?"

"Ryan Lynch," I said, giving the name of the major I'd had the fling with in the Gulf.

"And-a the company name?"

"Lynch Exploration out of San Antonio."

"I do not know this-a name."

"It's a small company."

"Very well. I look forward to meeting you, Miss Raymond. I have not known-a many women who are-a pilots."

"Our numbers are growing, Mr. Rigi."

"Perhaps you-a can educate me, then, Miss Raymond. Until tomorrow."

I ended the call and looked at Irene.

"I can see why Pardee married you," she said. "You are more than just a pretty woman who can fly airplanes."

I assumed it was a compliment.

"Now I will take you back to the *pensión,*" Irene said. "I must go to my office for a while and you will need to discuss your work with your husband."

There was a distinctive note of bitterness in her last remark. I wanted to say to her, *Irene, you're better off without him, trust me.*

I couldn't say anything, of course. Besides, who the hell was I to talk? Look how long it had taken me to wake up to the reality behind the enigma that was Pardee. Lord, I'd spent six years with the man as his wife, working with him in close and often dangerous circumstances, and I still didn't know his given name.

Twenty-one

By the time I was back at the *pensión*, the workmen had replaced the balcony railing. I looked at it, recalling all too vividly my embarrassment of the night before, and decided not to test it for sturdiness. I'd done all the cliff-hanging I cared to attempt for this trip. Not that I would be able to forget about it. The incident would live on in memory, popping into my mind, turning my cheeks red, even when I was eighty.

With little to do, I strolled in the garden and chatted with Vera about our common interest in antiques until she, too, left on an errand. I felt anxious about the impending mission, and definitely anxious to get going. It was always hard for me to keep the edge I needed to do my job but still stay loose until it was time to saddle up.

I considered phoning Sky again, but I didn't want to trouble him out of boredom. Instead I thought about Quinn and worried about the myriad of things that could go wrong.

Tough as this crisis was on Pardee and me, our suffering

surely paled in comparison with what Quinn was going through. I hadn't wanted to think about the way his captors may have been treating—or mistreating—him. The poor kid was probably feeling guilty, knowing his father and I would risk our necks to free him. It was worth whatever we had to endure to get him home in one piece, though. There was absolutely no doubt about that.

If there was a positive to come from this incident, it was that I now understood what Suarez had gone through when Pardee and I had snatched him all those years ago. Sure, the situation wasn't the same, and the kid wasn't a complete innocent, like Quinn. But at a human level the emotions were undoubtedly the same. His mother surely suffered as I was now suffering. His father had obviously felt the same outrage that Pardee felt.

The irony of that was haunting. People often make fun of New Age Californians and their talk about karma, but this was enough to make a believer of me. Fugitives weren't choirboys or Girl Scouts, but they were people. I would never forget that again.

Anna came home, interrupting my reverie. She'd visited a friend after school and spoke with me for a few minutes out of politeness. I could tell, though, she was more eager to see Pardee than talk to me—more proof, I suppose, of the power of the man's charm. I wanted to see the guy, too, but not for a game of chess. I needed to find out what the hell was happening and where things stood. My ruminations about Quinn had ratcheted up my anxiety level a notch or two.

Vera returned, followed a short time later by Irene, but still no Pardee. Nobody had spoken with him since early morning and I was starting to get concerned. God only knew what he was up to and there was always the possibility something had gone wrong. I think my worry was beginning to spread around the household.

Vera and Irene opted for a cocktail and, though I was tempted, I had juice with Anna instead. Some prospective guests arrived to inquire about a room and Vera dealt with them, but they ended up not staying. "It's very slow this time of year and the competition stiff," she explained.

We decided not to wait dinner for Pardee and the four of us ate. I glanced around the table at my companions, realizing it felt like a bizarre, semi-Hispanic version of *Little Women*. After the meal we retired to the veranda. I stared out at the darkness, alternating between visions of myself hanging in midspace from the bent stanchion and Pardee being slapped around at an interrogation room at the jail— "Who are your accomplices, Señor Pardee? You would not attempt this alone."

Much to our relief, Pardee arrived a short time later, toting boxes and bundles and a large metal suitcase that appeared quite heavy. He carefully set it aside. I think we all wanted to hug him, but in the end only Anna took the plunge. "How about a game of chess?" she effused, looking up at him with childlike innocence. "Tonight you get the white pieces."

Irene told her that Pardee had to eat first and besides it was too late for a game. "Perhaps tomorrow," she said, even knowing that Pardee and I would be gone by then, and never likely to return. I was beginning to understand Irene's sadness and I felt sorry for her.

We were all gathered around the large dining table to watch Pardee eat. It felt like *Little House on the Prairie* now, with Pa home. My role in the imaginary vignette was unclear. "Pilot" was probably the most relevant description, but "wife" carried the most emotional weight for everybody there.

When he'd finished eating, Pardee, speaking for us both, asked that we be excused because we had work to do. The two of us lugged everything he'd brought with him up to our room. Once the door was closed, he took off his shirt. Back when we were still a couple and living at the ranch, he would have taken off his pants as well, but out of nominal respect he stopped at the bare-chested stage. It wasn't forbearance on his part because he knew the effect his chest had on me. But what he didn't know was that I was operating under a more cautious and self-aware set of rules now.

"So, how did it go today?" he asked. "You going to be able to get us a bird?"

I gave him a brief rundown on what had happened, embellishing Marco Rigi's negative attributes a bit for dramatic effect.

"Well, if the guy demands sexual favors, just pull out your gun and take the damned chopper at gunpoint."

"And have every cop in the country on the alert within minutes?"

"I'm sure you'll find a way to finesse it," he replied.

His total lack of concern amused me. But then, what could I expect? Men had no idea what it was like trying to do business with sexual predators.

It was time for Pardee to do *his* show-and-tell. "Talked to the kidnappers on the phone," he said. "At first they didn't like the idea of the lake. Told me they had to think about it. When I spoke to them again several hours later, they'd changed their minds and agreed to the proposal."

"That's odd."

"Not really, if you think about it. My guess is they needed to clear the plan with the authorities."

"Then you think it really is a trap. And Suarez is behind it."

"Most likely. But that's been the assumption all along."

"So nothing's changed. If it's a trap, it's a trap."

"They've still got Quinn."

I pondered our dilemma. "What if they don't bring Quinn to the site? I mean, if the cops are in on this, they might just lie in wait for us."

"That's possible, but the only sure way to lure us close is to let us see his face. The thing we have going for us is that even if we lose, we win."

"What do you mean?"

"If they capture us, they'll have no reason to keep Quinn."

I chuckled. "Yeah, I guess we can celebrate either way."

Pardee tweaked my nose. "I don't know if I'd go quite that far."

"So when's this going to happen?" I asked.

"We agreed that the exchange will take place at high noon. I turn over half a million cash and I get my boy."

"How you going to swing the half mil?"

Pardee lifted the heavy metal suitcase onto the bed and popped open the lid. Inside was more cash than I'd ever seen in my life.

"My God, where did you get this?"

"Quinn's old man has his resources."

"I thought you were dead broke."

"I am, sweetheart."

"How'd you get it, then?"

"First tell me, if *you* were the kidnapper, would you take

this in exchange for a struggling anthropology graduate student?"

I glanced down at the bundles of cash. "If it's half a million and that's what I wanted, I suppose I would."

"But you'd check it out pretty closely, wouldn't you?"

"I guess."

"Go ahead," he said.

I wasn't sure what he was getting at, but I picked up one of the bundles. The bills were hundreds. I rifled through them, thinking maybe it was a Murphy roll, but rather than blank paper there were bills all the way through. I dug down to a deeper bundle and checked it out, too. Same result.

"Satisfied?" Pardee asked.

"What are you telling me? That's it's counterfeit?"

"Pull out a bill from the middle of a bundle."

I did. Hardly being an expert in such matters, about all I could say with any confidence was that the bill was obviously fresh off the press. "I guess it looks a little suspicious, if only because it seems so new."

"They are new, Josie. Check the name under Franklin's picture."

I looked closely. Damn if it didn't say "Pardee."

"Jesus," I said with a laugh, "where'd you get this?"

"Had it specially made through a guy I know down here. And it wasn't cheap, though bills more closely resembling legal tender would have been much more expensive. There are a lot of anomalies on the back of the bills. Basically, it's funny money, but I'm hoping it'll be good enough to pass a quick examination by guys under pressure. The outer bills in each bundle are real. With luck, they'll just rifle through the way you did."

"Then they *are* Murphy rolls."

"You got it."

"You're a scoundrel, Pardee."

"You know that, but let's hope the kidnappers don't."

The rest of the stuff he brought home was weapons, ammunition, explosives, surveillance equipment and other supplies. Pardee said he couldn't find me a Glock, but he did get me the closest 9mm he could find. I checked it out, weighing it in my hand, and then put it on my bedstand.

Pardee put all the stuff away, then spread a small-scale map out on the bed. We sat cross-legged, facing each other, the map between us.

I have to admit his energy excited me—me the professional, that is. This was the Pardee I appreciated most. Going over the final details on the eve of an operation was a real adrenaline rush. If I could have this *and* Sky, life would be perfect. Even knowing that was the stuff of fantasy, I was on a high. There was nothing like the closeness that came with common purpose and a shared goal. The only other place I'd experienced anything close to this was in the Gulf War.

"I rented a Jeep," he said. "First thing in the morning, I leave Veracruz and head up this highway, turning here on Route 145 to this side road to Temascal," he said, tracing the route with his finger. "I checked today. I can rent a boat on the lake near the town, which I'll take to this island. It took a while, but I was able to get some aerial photos of the area. There's a point that's open on the southeastern tip of the island. I beach the boat there and that's where I'll meet the kidnappers and Quinn.

"You, meanwhile, will have secured the chopper and will be flying in a holding pattern. If all goes according to plan and I get Quinn, instead of returning to the marina and the Jeep, we'll go to this open area on the opposite shore of the lake, rendezvous with you there and the three of us will get out of Dodge.

"However, should something go wrong . . . say, it's an ambush on the island . . . you have the option of coming for me or, if that doesn't appear feasible, you abort and get the hell out as fast as you can. No point in coming in if it's hopeless." Pardee looked me hard in the eye. "What do you think?"

"I'd like it a lot better if I had a spotter. It won't be easy to fly and keep an eye on what's happening on the ground."

"Well, you'll just have to do the best you can."

"I'm not so sure, Pardee. Let me see those aerial photos. And dig out a large-scale topo of the lake area, would you?"

I studied the photos, checking the terrain on the periphery of the lake. Then I checked the topo map against the photos.

"What are you looking for?" Pardee asked after a minute.

"A place where I can put down and watch the action from the ground. I'd like a hilltop with a vantage point. But it needs to be bare enough to land and open enough for easy ingress and egress." I pointed to a spot on the map. "This hill looks like a possibility. I'd prefer something closer, though. I don't suppose you have a telescope in your bag of goodies."

"I do indeed. It's not large but better than the binoculars."

"How old are these photos?"

"A year or two."

"Long enough for this barren hilltop to get overgrown with scrubs, but not trees," I said. "I think I'd prefer to put down there than circle overhead, if you don't mind."

He reflected.

"And don't forget, if I'm airborne for any length of time, I could give our intentions away," I added.

"Good point," he said. "Well, if you're more comfortable with that scenario, then let's go with it."

"Fine. I'd like to study these a little more."

"While you do, I think I'll grab a shower."

Pardee was in the bath about fifteen minutes. When he came out, I was already in bed, my chastity fortifications in place.

"Still don't trust me, huh?" he asked, eyeing the pillows.

"Pardee, I'd trust you with my life, but not my virtue. No way."

His smile turned sad. "I made a terrible mistake letting you divorce me, Josie."

My stomach dropped. It was starting to feel like that moment back at my place when he told me he still loved me. I liked and hated the notion, equally. My best strategy, I decided, was to be firm. "You had no choice."

"Yes, I did."

"How so?"

"You may not have trusted me with your virtue, but I should have made damned sure you trusted me with your heart. It was the biggest mistake I've ever made in my life."

Oh, God, I thought as my resolve weakened, *I really don't need this.* "Let's stick to rescuing Quinn," I said as firmly as I could. "You promised you wouldn't do this and it's not fair to go back on your word. I know you couldn't care less whether people consider you a gentleman or not, but please, please do the honorable thing this once. If you really care about me, Pardee, you'll keep your promise."

"Yeah," he said with a sigh, "you're right. Forget I said it."

"Thank you."

"But can I say just one more thing?"

"What?"

"You always said one of the things about me that bothered you most was that I never revealed myself, that I kept too much inside, right?"

"I guess."

"Well, you aren't the only one who's changed, Josie. I thought you ought to know that."

Twenty-two

Of all the things Pardee had done since reentering my life, the remark about failing to make me trust him with my heart was the lowest blow of all. And yet, in a funny way, it was the most endearing. Though he'd apologized often enough over the years, he'd never before put his finger on the fundamental problem of our relationship with such insight and regret. I felt compassion for him, despite myself. He shouldn't have done that. He should have spared me but, in a fit of honesty, he hadn't.

I'd lain awake for a very long time that night. I knew Pardee wanted me back. He was feeling the same things I was feeling, plus more. The difference was that he was alone and I wasn't. Pardee could get all the women he desired, but what he really wanted was a woman who was also his buddy, his partner, his equal. The closest he'd ever come was me.

Sure, a side of me still responded to Pardee. But I also knew how he fit in with the person I was today. My real worry was Sky. He was the man in my life and I loved him. But was I being true to myself? *That* was what had been eating at me, even more than Pardee's games. Why I hadn't seen it before, I didn't know.

I was relieved when dawn came because it meant the battle was upon us, and I could concentrate on more pressing concerns. This operation wasn't about Pardee and me. We both had to remember that.

"You awake, Josie?" Pardee said softly from the other side of the barricade.

"Yeah."

"I've got to get going soon, but I want to say something before I shove off."

I hoped it wasn't going to be another expression of regret about lost love.

"What?"

"I signed some papers a couple of weeks ago, leaving the ranch to Quinn with you as backup. If he and I don't survive this, the place is yours."

"Pardee, don't talk that way."

"You have to be aware, just in case. And there's something else. The odds are I'll be walking into a trap. If that's the case, I want you to get in the bird and hightail it out of there. There's no point in us both going down. Just go and don't look back."

"Don't be ridiculous, Pardee. That's not the way we work. Never have."

"Well, we are now."

"Not if I don't agree."

"Quinn is my kid, Josie, and this is my show. If you want to know the truth, I've been regretting I got you involved. I was being selfish, glad for the excuse to be with you again.

Maybe you already figured that out, but I want to come clean. If I've hurt you by things I've said and done, I'm sorry."

"I've known you're a selfish bastard forever, but I still wish you wouldn't talk this way. Besides, Quinn's my kid, too."

"I know you care about him, but—"

"There's no but about it," I said. "End of discussion. Okay?"

"Just promise me you won't make any decisions based on emotion. That was one of the first things I told you when you were green, remember? Be smart, first, last and always. I want you to promise me you'll do that."

I was so choked up I could hardly speak. "Okay," I croaked, "I promise."

"Thanks, sweetheart. Thanks for everything. I'm going to get dressed now and go."

Pardee got up, half naked in the faint light of dawn. I lay there as still as death, my eyes glistening with tears, knowing I'd heard his last will and testament. I don't think he was playing with my emotions. Pardee was preparing me. For all his selfishness over the years, this was his greatest act of kindness. He wanted to go out with honor and in style. I had to admire that, much as I hated the message.

It didn't take him long to get ready. I had plenty of time, so I stayed in bed. He ran some of his gear down to the Jeep, then came back upstairs for the case with the phony money. Before he went, he came and sat on the bed next to me.

"I left you the scope and a duffel so you can bring a few necessities with you in the chopper. It's unlikely we'll be coming back here."

"Yeah, I know."

"You've got your gun." He reached in his shirt pocket and pulled out some bills. "Here's a thousand bucks in case you run into trouble getting home."

"I've got money with me."

"Some extra won't hurt. Take it."

There were some things you didn't argue about with Pardee.

"You're acting like you expect the mission to fail," I said. "You've never done that before and I wish you wouldn't now."

"This is different than other jobs, Josie. Because it's for Quinn, I'm doing it with my heart, not my head. I'm not used to this."

"Well, if you want to save Quinn's butt, you'd better start thinking like the old Pardee. And dammit, stop feeling sorry for yourself."

He grinned, which I was glad to see. "Yes, ma'am."

"I'm serious."

"Okay. No more melodrama."

I looked up at him as he leaned over me in the dim light. Pardee took my hand.

"I know you always hated it that I never gave you a straight story about my name," he said, "so, as a token of my respect for you, I'm going to tell you the handle that's on my birth certificate."

"I don't want to know your real name," I said.

"Huh?"

"I don't want to know it. 'Pardee' is how I've always known you, and I'd like it to stay that way."

He shook his head, bemused. "Josie, you're one of a kind," he said, caressing my cheek with the back of his fingers. Still smiling, he leaned down for a kiss goodbye.

I could tell he intended it to be a friendly kiss, but it didn't end that way. His mouth lingered. And, despite all my good intentions, I gave in to the emotion of the moment, reached up, put my arms around his neck and kissed him back.

I didn't know why I caved in so easily. Maybe it was nothing more complicated than a desire to be honest about what I was feeling. It didn't mean I wasn't in love with Sky. But I felt a kinship with Pardee, too. And of course there was also that unrelenting attraction that I'd stopped trying to deny. But mostly I was feeling the closeness of comrades in arms. We were in this together, putting our lives on the line once more—this time to save Quinn.

I guess kissing him goodbye was just something I needed to do.

Pardee touched my face, his eyes glistening the same as mine. Then he got up and went over to his case of counterfeit bills. "See you at the lake."

I lifted myself to my elbows. "Good luck, Pardee."

He gave me the thumbs-up and went out the door.

I wondered if I'd ever see him again. It mattered to me a whole lot more than I thought it would. Because like it or not, I realized that I didn't want this to be our final goodbye.

Irene and Anna were gone by the time I got downstairs with my duffel. I was in jeans, hiking boots and a short-sleeve cotton blouse. Vera greeted me with her customary cheerfulness. We had breakfast, the traditional English variety with eggs, fried tomatoes, sausage, toast, marmalade and tea. "You're in for a rigorous day, love, and should eat a proper breakfast. I've packed a box lunch for later, as well."

Vera called me a taxi. We said goodbye at the front door.

"It's unlikely you'll be back, isn't it?" she said sadly.

"If we survive, we'll doubtlessly be persona non grata down here for all time."

"What a pity. Well, it's been lovely getting to know you, dear. As I told Pardee, I wish the two of you the very best."

"Thank you, Vera. For everything."

We hugged and I went out to the waiting taxi. As we drove away, I looked up at the shabby house with its faded splendor. It was not a place Sky would have appreciated—not that he would have been snobby about it, because he wasn't unkind. He simply lived in a different world than most of the people on this planet, including me. Crossing the divide that separated us would be our biggest challenge as a couple. I saw that more clearly now than ever.

As the taxi made its way to the outskirts of the city, I refocused on the task at hand. The first hurdle I had to face was Marco Rigi. Never having been a coquette, I wasn't looking forward to pretending to be one, even if it was for the greater good.

When we pulled up in front of IGI—late because of an accident on the road out of town—I was horrified to see that the bird wasn't sitting on the pad where it had been the previous afternoon. I had visions of our entire plan collapsing. I considered calling Pardee to alert him, but decided to wait until I knew for sure what was going on.

I paid the driver and went in the entrance to the building. A pretty receptionist with big black eyes and fat black curls greeted me. I asked for Rigi and gave my name. She invited me to sit, but I started pacing instead, wondering why they would have taken the chopper away if they knew I was coming to see it. The extra margin of time I'd built in was already lost and the pressure was on.

It was twenty agonizing minutes before Rigi appeared. I'd never been to Italy, but of course I'd heard stories about Italian men. They were supposed to be attractive and fun-loving—some of them a little too fun-loving for a woman's own good—and Rigi turned out to be a specimen with all the worst traits and none of the good that I could discern.

The poor man was rather homely, with fat lips, puppy eyes and a half-bald dome. He wasn't all that old— probably early forties—but had the look and demeanor of an old lecher.

I already knew a lot about him thanks to Irene, but the picture she'd painted wasn't nearly as dismal as the reality. That sort of surprised me, as I'd thought at the time she was relishing making me miserable about the prospect of dealing with the guy. I realized now that she had soft-pedaled it. Rigi was over the top, to put it mildly.

"Ah, señorita!" he said, breezing into the reception area, pulling up short as he looked me up and down, the libidinous wheels in his dirty mind already spinning at top speed. "What-a delightful surprise-a."

"Hello, Mr. Rigi, I'm sorry to be late, but there was a bad accident on the highway."

"There is-a absolutely no *problema*," he said, using the Spanish word. He moved forward, still painting me head to toe with his eyes, his grin already satanic.

Taking my hand, Rigi pressed it to his lips. Being so short, he didn't have to lean over far. In fact, I was able to stare down on his shiny pate, which glistened with perspiration under the threadlike strands of black hair plastered to his scalp. The scent of a potent cologne radiated from his body. It wasn't exactly gagging, but it wasn't pleasant, either.

"I am-a so happy to make-a your acquaintance."

"Likewise, Mr. Rigi."

"Please, señorita, it's-a Marco, *por favor.* Marco, eh?"

I gave him a smile that I hope split the difference between come-hither and businesslike. "Yes. Thank you. Huh, Marco I don't mean to be pushy, but I will be able to see the helicopter, won't I?"

He was still holding my hand and seemed reluctant to give it up. "But of course-a, Denise. You don't-a mind if I-a call you Denise, do you?"

"No, of course not. Please do."

Quite happy with that, he kissed my hand again, after which I managed to extricate it from his grasp.

"So, where is the bird?" I asked.

"Not far," he said evasively.

I wondered if he'd somehow gotten wind of what I was up to. Knowing I didn't have time for a lot of subtlety, I decided to address the issue head-on. "I'll not only want to inspect it, I'll want to fly it as well." I very pointedly looked at my watch. "And unfortunately I don't have a lot of time."

Rigi stroked his chin. "I was-a hoping we could have-a lunch and get better acquainted, Denise."

"I would love to, but there's not much point if I don't like what I see when I check out the chopper. I'm sure you understand."

Rigi frowned. Then, taking me by the arm, he pulled me over to the sofa. We sat and he leaned close, speaking in a confidential tone. "I must-a confess, there is-a a little problem. You see, I spoke-a to my people in Houston about this-a Lynch Exploration. They checked in San Antonio and find-a no record of it."

I'd outsmarted myself. Rigi might be a reprobate, but he was no fool.

"That's probably because it's so new," I told him, lying without blinking an eye. "I don't even know if Ryan has registered it yet. For the first several months he operated under his personal name, but things were going so well, he incorporated and is expanding rapidly. This is all very recent."

"I see."

Rigi was clearly suspicious. Given the time pressure I was under, extraordinary measures were called for. It was time to pull out all the stops. "But if you'd rather me not trouble you, Marco, that's fine. I'm only doing this as a favor to Ryan. And the reason I'm in a hurry is because he's leaving shortly for California to look at another helicopter. He said I should call him before he goes." I again checked my watch. "But I can always tell him you were too busy."

I planted what I hoped was a wistful expression on my face. "What a shame, though. I was hoping to stick around for a while, enjoy Veracruz. I love to dance. There must be wonderful nightclubs here for dancing."

Rigi's eyes got round. "You like-a to dance?"

"And eat. I was hoping to find a good seafood place on the beach."

"But Denise, I know-a the perfect one! You must allow me to take you."

"I wouldn't dream of it, Marco. Unless, of course, it is to

discuss the helicopter. Ryan paid for my trip, you see, and I couldn't possibly take any personal time unless I did my job and returned with a report."

"But how would he know? You could give a story, no?"

I blinked. "Do I look dishonest, Marco? Would you want me to deceive you?"

"Of course-a not."

"Well, then I have no choice but to go to the airport and head home."

"But I didn't say you couldn't see-a the helicopter. Houston said not to allow it to be flown until they check out the company. Come, you can see it. I will-a show you now."

"I'd have to fly it, Marco," I said, digging in my heels. At this point it was all or nothing.

He stroked his chin. "Perhaps we can-a find a way."

I picked up my duffel.

"You can-a leave this in my office."

"No, this goes with me everywhere."

"As-a you wish."

Rigi grabbed his Panama hat and led me through the building and out the back door to where the chopper had been moved. I walked around it, making a show of checking it out.

"Are the maintenance records available?"

"But of course."

"I'll need to check everything out. Ryan's a stickler for detail."

"I understand."

"Now, how about the test flight?"

He dug into his pocket and took out the door key, holding it up. I reached for it and he snatched it back. "Only if I go with-a you, Denise."

"You won't let me take it out alone?"

He had a pained expression. "If it was up-a to me, I would-a say yes, no-a question. But I have-a my instructions. Houston said not at all, no-a way. But I am thinking perhaps I can-a make a little exception if you agree to go with-a me to the beach-a restaurant. We can-a fly there, no?"

"I don't think that would be a good idea."

"Why-a not?"

I didn't have a good response to that. I could see Rigi was turning out to be more cagey than I expected. I'd reached the moment of truth. Did I reach into my duffel and pull out my gun, taking the bird at gunpoint as Pardee had suggested? The trouble was it created almost as many problems as it solved. The police would be alerted immediately. Maybe the thing to do was get in the air and worry about Rigi later.

"Well," I said, "if lunch is included, why not? I'd love your company, Marco."

He brightened at that. The fish was on the line again. Amazing how dumb men suddenly became when there was an immediate prospect of a little nooky.

"Please-a, Denise," he said. "Allow-a me to open the door."

We climbed into the bird and I took a few minutes to check out the instrumentation. The fuel situation was not bad, but neither had the tank been topped off. While the engine warmed I took a quick look at the logbook.

"Have-a you been flying for long?" he asked.

"Soloed when I was fourteen."

He laughed. I reached back and pulled out my map from the zippered pocket on the duffel. Rigi seemed perplexed as I consulted it.

"We won't be-a going far," he said.

"I always like to orient myself before taking off, regardless how far I fly," I explained.

"Obviously, you are a good pilot."

I smiled. "You ready?"

"Please."

We lifted off and I made a slow turn to the southeast in the direction of Presa Miguel Alemán, the huge reservoir located in the foothills about a hundred clicks, or sixty miles, to the southwest of Veracruz.

"What do you-a think?" Rigi asked after we were in the air a few minutes.

"Flies nice," I replied.

He leaned over to look down toward the ground. "The Gulf is-a behind us, you know. This is the wrong way for the beach-a restaurant. That's where we are-a going, no?"

"I wanted to go a little farther afield first, if you don't mind."

Shrugging, he relented, letting me have my head. I checked the time. I should already have been on that hilltop above the lake by now. I was about fifteen minutes behind schedule.

We were well clear of the outskirts of Veracruz, the populated area thinning out rapidly. I started looking for a place for the maneuver I'd planned. Another five minutes and I spotted a clearing in a heavily wooded area. It seemed like the ideal spot. I started taking the bird down.

When Rigi saw we were getting close to the ground, he said, "What are you-a doing?"

"Thought we could take a little break," I told him. "I've got a picnic lunch in my bag."

"No, I don't-a think this is-a a good idea, Denise."

"You'll love it, Marco. Nature makes me very passionate. And we would have more privacy here."

His brows went up. I set the chopper down in the middle of the clearing. There were no signs of civilization, which was perfect. Reaching back into my duffel, I got my gun. Rigi turned apoplectic when I pointed it at him.

"Sorry, Marco, but this is where you get off."

"This is a very bad-a joke," he said, more hopeful than certain.

"It's no joke, amigo. Now get out. I'm in a hurry."

"You are-a stealing my helicopter?"

"No, just borrowing it. Come on, move."

"I refuse," he said, folding his arms defiantly.

I pointed the semiautomatic at his head. "You think I won't blow you away?"

His eyes looked like they were about to pop out of his head, but he took a deep breath and refused to budge.

"Now, goddammit!" I screamed.

He finally seemed convinced I was serious. His hands shaking, he removed his seat belt and reached for the door beside him. Just as it opened he suddenly turned and tried to grab the gun. I could have shot him two or three times, but the last thing I wanted to do was hurt him. Things were already bad enough without adding homicide to my list of crimes.

"No woman will-a take my helicopter," he said through his teeth as we wrestled.

He was small, but stronger than me. Our faces were close and we were both straining to wrench the gun free. Remembering what Pardee had once said—"All's fair in love and war and bounty hunting"—I leaned over and took a big bite of his ear, drawing blood.

Rigi screamed in pain, his hat flying out the door. While he was distracted, I got my foot up and gave him a shove, pushing him out of the aircraft. Reaching over, I secured the door, then lifted the bird into the air. I had a final glimpse of Marco Rigi. He was sprawled in the grass and wailing. *Don't fuck with female pilots,* I thought. *It's bad for your health.*

As I sped toward the lake, I regretted having to bite him. On the other hand, Rigi was a predator. I rationalized that I'd given him his comeuppance for Irene and a hundred other women who'd endured his unwanted advances. The bastard would forever carry the mark of Josie. That was his penance.

Now I had to hope that the distraction hadn't been too costly to the operation. I took out the cell and called Pardee. The phone rang and rang and rang, but there was no answer. A sense of doom welled inside of me. I said aloud what I felt. "Shit."

Twenty-three

My hilltop turned out better for a landing than I could have hoped. There was some vegetation, but it wasn't bad. I had the bird on the ground and I was out, setting up the telescope on its tripod within minutes. I had the binoculars around my neck and the semiautomatic wedged under the waistband of my jeans.

From my vantage point, the island where the exchange was to take place was a good three miles away. It wasn't an ideal spot for observation, but it was sufficiently remote so as not to attract the attention of the kidnappers, or the authorities—assuming Pardee was right about it being a trap. The telescope was powerful enough that it was like watching a goal-line stand from the opposite end zone of a football stadium. I wouldn't be able to read the numbers on the players' jerseys, but I could make out what they were doing.

I immediately spotted the flat open beach we'd picked for the rendezvous site, but there wasn't a soul around. I searched the shoreline for a boat, but couldn't find one. Had the cops grabbed Pardee at the marina, or even on the road to the lake?

Shifting my attention away from the island, I started scanning the lake itself for clues. My hope was to spot kidnappers, Pardee—anyone who might give me a hint as to what was happening. The observation point was on the southern shore, the marina where Pardee planned to embark was on the northeast corner of the lake, so I began my search in the northeastern quadrant.

There were a few boats scattered across the lake, but most were stationary, probably fishermen. Then I picked up a motorboat, moving at fairly high speed, headed toward the island. As best I could tell it had a single occupant. It could be Pardee. God, how I hoped it was.

I'd been anticipating the worst, probably because of Pardee's gloom that morning, but this sighting gave me hope. It could be a false alarm, but I decided to try to contact him by phone again.

I got an answer on the third ring, but the connection was bad and the voice I heard kept breaking up. Between the lapses, I thought I heard a "Josie . . . you here?"

"I'm in place," I shouted. "Is that you in the blue and white motorboat?"

More static, then, "Roger that."

"Your guardian angel's watching," I told him.

I thought I heard a laugh. Over the crackling I could make out a couple of words, one of them was "love." I wasn't sure I wanted to know more.

I had the telescope focused on the blue and white speedboat and followed its progress westward across the huge lake. It was getting a bit closer to my position, which may have explained why the man on board started looking like Pardee. Either that or the power of suggestion had kicked in. I was thrilled.

After several minutes the boat neared the southeastern tip of the island, the place Pardee had designated for the exchange. I prayed that the kidnappers would show up and that Quinn would be with them.

Pardee reached the tip of the island. Slowing, he beached his boat, climbed over the side and waded to shore with a line, which he tethered to a log. Then he reached over the side of the boat and lifted out the metallic case with the funny money, returning to the beach, where he stood waiting.

I scanned the broad expanse of sand to the tree line, but saw nothing. The kidnappers could have gotten cold feet, which was certainly possible if they weren't in cahoots with the authorities. That would be a real pisser. Sure, it would be better than a trap, but it still wouldn't get us Quinn. As the various scenarios rolled through my mind, I knew Pardee had to be pondering the same thing.

A few minutes passed before I saw movement in the trees thirty or forty yards from where Pardee waited. Three men emerged from the undergrowth. One had a rifle, a second a handgun, which was pointed at the third man, who was taller than the other two. It had to be Quinn.

The three moved across the open area toward Pardee. Quinn was walking in front of the other two men and his hands appeared to be either tied or handcuffed behind him.

Pardee had picked up the case and moved toward the three, stopping about ten yards from the boat. I could see a shimmer of light at the small of his back. He'd stuck his gun in the waistband of his pants, the same as me, only his was in back where it couldn't be seen.

Quinn and his captors came to about five yards of Pardee and stopped there. A conversation ensued. It probably was about the money, because Pardee got down on a knee and opened the case. Then he backed off and one of the kidnappers came forward to examine the loot. This was the moment of truth. I knew that Pardee's heart had to be pounding as hard as mine.

The man checking the money took his time, examining bundle after bundle. I saw no sign of rage or displeasure when he closed the case. There was a bit more conversation, then the other kidnapper removed the constraints from Quinn's hands and gave him a shove in Pardee's direction.

Quinn and Pardee embraced as the kidnappers retreated with the money, jogging back across the sand. I was so happy I started to cry. It had gone off without a hitch! Incredible.

But my joy was premature. When I took a wider view of the lake, I noticed quite a few speedboats, perhaps half a dozen, converging on the island from different directions. I focused the telescope on one. It contained three uniformed officers. The other boats were the same. It was a trap, after all. The cops, who could have been in complicity with the kidnappers, had allowed the exchange to take place and were now closing in. Escape wouldn't be easy on an open lake.

I immediately got out my cell and dialed Pardee's number. Again we got a bad connection and he kept breaking up. "It's a trap!" I shouted into the phone. "Police boats! Police boats!"

I could see Pardee climb up on the foredeck of the boat

to survey the scene. "Roger," I heard him say before the communication ended. Now the question was whether he could make it to the south shore for our rendezvous before the cops closed in. I needed to get in the air, pronto.

Leaving the telescope, I turned to find two cops standing next to the chopper, rifles in their hands and grins on their faces. *Surprise,* they seemed to say, *the jig's up.*

It was a trap indeed, and I'd fallen in the pit right along with Pardee. The authorities probably had been lying in wait at various points around the lake, perhaps spotting me put down, then dispatched a couple of men to climb the hill and arrest me. My euphoria collapsed like an undercooked soufflé.

One of the cops, the older of the two, yelled something in Spanish. He was gruff-looking, with a heavy beard and drooping mustache. I didn't understand what he wanted, though I thought I heard the word "*pistola.*" He probably wanted me to drop my gun.

My mind raced as I tried to figure out what to do. The combination of panic and confusion left me feeling helpless. The man shouted again, more emphatically. I feigned ignorance, shaking my head as though I didn't understand what he wanted.

The other cop, who was younger and super skinny, kind of goofy-looking, put his rifle under his arm and made an exaggerated pulling motion at his belt to illustrate what they wanted. That gave me an idea.

Nodding like I understood, I slung the binoculars around on my back and began unbuttoning my blouse. The two men seemed shocked and the older one started yelling at me to stop, that that wasn't what he meant. The young guy wasn't so inclined to spare me the consequences of my confusion and told his buddy to be quiet, watching with great interest as I finished opening my blouse and yanking the shirttails out of my jeans. I indicated my bra.

"*¿Este?*"

The younger one nodded emphatically. "*Sí, sí,*" he said as the other man rolled his eyes.

Reaching behind me, under my blouse, I unfastened my bra, then lifted the cups off my breasts, exposing them. It was either this or God knows how many years in a Mexican jail.

The two men enjoyed my tease, especially the young guy, who started toward me as I twisted back and forth, displaying the goods. How dangerous could a woman resorting to sexual teasing be, after all?

The older guy said something to Goofy that sounded like a warning, but my would-be paramour kept walking toward me, shifting his rifle to his other arm, presumably to free his groping hand. He was between me and his buddy, maybe six feet away, when I let go of my bra and grabbed the automatic from my waistband in one quick motion. I had the muzzle pressed to his forehead before he could lift his rifle.

"Drop it, asshole!" I yelled.

Goofy's mouth dropped open and the rifle tumbled to the ground. I grabbed him by the shoulder and spun him around, pressing my gun against the side of his head.

"You, too, *compadre!*" I shouted at his pal.

The older guy wanted no part of this. Throwing down his rifle, he spun and charged back into the bush, leaving me to figure out what to do with Goofy. I couldn't shoot him. It wasn't in me to kill somebody in cold blood.

"Go!" I yelled, giving him a shove, hoping he'd take off after his friend.

Goofy took a step away, then spun around, trying to grab my gun. The sonovabitch was either embarrassed I'd gotten the drop on him, or he was just plain stupid. He had my wrist and was trying to wrench the gun away when I kneed him, dropping him to the ground. This time I slammed him in the head with the butt of my pistol, knocking him out cold.

I knew I'd lost valuable time, so I jumped in the chopper, my shirttails flying, my bra flopping. God knows what had happened to Pardee and Quinn while I was doing my striptease, but the quickest way to find out was to do an aerial reconnaissance. I took to the air as quickly as I could.

Down on the lake a boat race had developed. Pardee had opted to make a run for the near shore and was coming toward me with four police boats in hot pursuit and one each closing from the flanks. To make matters worse, enemy air power had joined the fray. A police helicopter was tracking Pardee's boat from above. Once they started shooting, Pardee and Quinn would be dead in the water.

The police helicopter was the most immediate threat, but I didn't have a gunner and I couldn't fly and shoot at the same time. Hell, I couldn't even fly and fasten my bra at the same time, though I did manage to get a couple of buttons on my blouse fastened.

Distracting the enemy chopper seemed the most constructive thing to do. Neutralize his air power. It was U.S. military doctrine and if it was good enough for the Pentagon, it was good enough for me.

I entered the combat zone from above, swooping down low over the water, headed straight toward Pardee and his pursuers. The chopper had to see me coming toward him. The tactic I chose was a good old-fashioned game of chicken. With both of us in position for a head-on collision, who'd blink first?

Under normal circumstances I didn't have the temperament for this kind of game, preferring guile over swagger and ballsy displays of daring, but the circumstances were anything but normal. And there was also the state of mind of the enemy to consider. The guy flying the police chopper was on a monthly salary and probably had two little kids and a pregnant wife. Long-term, he was looking at a comfortable pension. I, on the other hand, had a dog, a fiancé, a former husband and a stepson. Long-term I was looking at twenty or thirty years in prison. I hoped the guy was rational and saw that I wasn't worth dying for.

Fortunately, common sense prevailed over machismo. The guy broke away, peeling off a comfortable five seconds before collision. I looped back and saw that Pardee's lead was shrinking. The police boats were closing in fast and he still had a mile to go before he reached shore.

Turning my attention back on the police chopper, I could see that threat had to be neutralized first. I had no cannon or machine guns aboard, but I had something working in my favor—boldness and daring, born of necessity. So, figuring I had little to lose, I attacked, hoping suicidal tactics would drive him from the field. For the next minute or so I harassed him, darting at him like an angry hornet, the two of us twisting and turning, circling and diving over the lake. Time after time he swerved to avoid my determined efforts to collide with him. Finally I was able to get above him and force a soft landing in the water, putting him out of action.

Having achieved air superiority, I returned to the chase. Pardee was streaking along the shore now with two police boats only hundreds of feet behind him. I could see small-arms fire coming from them and Pardee firing back. Without air cover, the cops were vulnerable, so I swooped down on them, drawing their fire. I could hear the rounds piercing the skin of the bird, but without firepower of my own I was at best a distraction.

It was pretty clear that if Pardee put ashore, the cops would be on him and Quinn before I could evacuate them. Then it hit me. I'd extract my guys directly from the boat. I tried to raise Pardee on the cell phone, but to no avail. All I could do was get in as close as possible and hope that they would understand what I wanted them to do.

I'd dropped down right in behind Pardee's boat, at water level, so close that the splash from the wake was frosting my windshield with a fine patina of spray. Even so, I got my first good look at Quinn. He had several weeks' growth of beard, his shaggy hair shaggier than usual, his clothing grimy, but he looked wonderful to me.

The two of them looked at me, wondering, I could tell, what the hell I was up to. I made a grabbing gesture, hoping they'd understand I wanted them to grab the chopper's skids. With bullets flying, there wasn't a lot of time for charades, so I eased the bird forward so that I was directly above the boat. I hovered there several seconds to give them time to latch on.

I heard a clank on the underside of the craft. It was either a signal they were aboard or I'd bumped the boat. Assuming the former, I eased back a bit so I could get a look at the speedboat. It was empty. My boys were either dangling from my underside or they were in the drink.

There was no point in heading directly for shore because I knew the cops would be close behind. I decided to put some serious distance between us and our pursuers, even at the risk of the wind speed tearing my precious cargo away.

Figuring a couple of minutes at sixty knots would do the trick, I started searching for a landing zone. Half a mile ahead was a spit jutting out from the shore. It allowed ample clearance from the dense growth of trees and vegetation rimming the lake.

I reached the spot and hovered a few feet above the ground to allow Pardee and Quinn to jump clear, assuming they weren't being pulled from the water by the cops a few miles back.

Damn if the faces of my guys didn't suddenly appear at the side window. They pulled open the door and clambered aboard. Quinn, filthy but smiling, scrambled in first, then Pardee. My heart almost stopped when I saw his left arm hanging limp and dripping with blood.

"Get us the hell out of here, sweetheart," he shouted over the roar of the engine.

We were airborne even before the door was closed. I made a big arcing turn to the south that enabled us to look back up the shoreline. Half a mile astern, the Mexican armada had abandoned their pursuit, the craft congregating to lick their wounds.

We'd known Veracruz and other points along the coast were unlikely to be welcoming, so the plan was to head for the relative safety of the mountains and points south. I took the bird up over the hills, leaving the Presa Miguel Alemán behind.

The guys had scrambled into the cargo bay in back.

"Everybody okay back there?" I called over my shoulder.

"Perfect!" Quinn shouted. I could hear the glee in his voice.

"So, have a nice field trip at school, honey?"

He gave a hoot. Pardee came forward and, leaning between the seat, grasped my shoulder.

"Josie, that was perfect. We couldn't have practiced it for a month and done any better."

"How bad's the arm?"

"Just a flesh wound. Lot of bleeding, but not much damage. I wasn't sure how much longer I was going to be able to hang on to this thing, though. You put down just in time." Craning his neck, he gave me a kiss on the cheek. "You're worth your weight in gold."

"Yeah, every penny you pay me."

"I'll find a way to thank you, trust me," he said, caressing my cheek.

That sent a shudder through me, and I found myself wanting to kiss him back. Our farewell kiss that morning had left me wanting more, though I hadn't thought of it that way at the time. But now that we'd been reunited, my desire was far too intense to be denied.

"Hey, what happened?" Pardee said.

I glanced at him and saw him looking down at my blouse.

"The tropical heat get too much for you?"

I flushed and hastily fastened a couple more buttons. "I had a little adventure of my own," I said. "Now get in back and tell Quinn to put some pressure on that wound. If you don't get that bleeding stopped, you'll fly home as cargo."

"Aye, Captain."

Pardee retreated and I sat there grinning with glee. Quinn was hollering joyfully at being free, and Pardee was yelling right along with him. I gave them both a thumbs-up. Go team!

I felt pretty damned good, all right. We'd pulled off a miraculous rescue and I loved the excitement, loved my comrades, loved life. Combat will do that to a warrior. There was no substitute.

Twenty-four

Anybody who's lived more than a few decades can tell you the good times can't be taken for granted. The high we'd enjoyed of snatching victory from the jaws of defeat was soon followed by a big low. Pardee's arm wasn't the only thing spouting vital fluids. The bird had taken a round in one of its own critical arteries and I was losing oil pressure fast. I informed Pardee.

He replied in true Pardee fashion. "Nobody said this was going to be easy."

True. Bounty hunting was not suitable work for somebody looking for a sinecure. Still, I wished we could have enjoyed a little downhill sledding before having to plunge right back into the battle for survival.

We were above the first range of mountains and the Santa Domingo Valley lay ahead. Beyond the valley was a still higher range of mountains that rose to nine and ten thousand feet. By the looks of things we'd be lucky to make it out of this first range, especially considering the way we were losing power.

"I'm going to have to look for a place to put down," I told them.

Glancing back, I saw that Quinn had opened the first-aid kit and was bandaging his father's arm. Pardee looked pale and weak and undoubtedly needed fluids. All the more reason to find a spot not too remote from civilization.

The Santa Domingo Valley ran mostly east-west, which meant the collateral valleys ran mostly north-south. As we descended the southern slope of the range, we dropped right into one of those little valleys like a knife into a sheath. The bird died above a bean field and we dropped onto the edge of it with a bump. I took the opportunity to fasten my bra.

"Well, boys," I said to my guys, "it looks like we walk from here."

As we'd come down, I'd noted that the area was sparsely populated. The only building within sight was a small adobe farmhouse sitting under some cottonwood trees across the field. The first order of business, it seemed to me, was to make friends with the occupants. It was unlikely they had a phone to call the authorities—at least, that was what I hoped. Chance would play a big part in what happened next.

First thing I did was climb in back and give Quinn a proper hug. "Didn't I teach you to choose your friends carefully, young man?"

"It's not my friends who were the problem, Ma, it's my relations." Quinn had called me "Ma" when he lived with us to tease me. It was our little joke.

"You've got a point. But at least we did our damnedest to compensate."

"I'm eternally in your debt," he said. "Both of you."

"I just hope you don't live to regret those words."

Pardee was lying back, a big grin on his face, but I could tell he was hurting. And not just from pain. He needed to be hydrated.

"We got to get your old man something to drink," I told Quinn.

"Preferably a margarita, señorita," Pardee said gamely.

"Let's gather our stuff and get to that farmhouse," I said.

Our supplies and equipment were meager. We had two sidearms, the cell phones, a pair of binoculars, the first-aid kit and my duffel, which contained the lunch Vera had provided, and my things. Quinn had the clothing on his back. Pardee had his wallet, which was fortuitous, because that meant he had money. He also had his and Quinn's phony passports.

Abandoning the bird, we trudged across the bean field, me carrying the gear and supplies and Quinn helping Pardee, who could walk, but only with his arm slung around his son's shoulder.

As we neared the adobe house we saw chickens pecking in the dust, a big gray cat slinking along the side of the house, but no sign of human life. Then, when we were practically at the door, we heard singing inside. It was a man's voice, badly off-key and sounding distinctively drunk. The door was open, though the strips of plastic hanging in the opening to keep out flies also prevented us from seeing in.

"I'll handle this," Quinn said, helping his father to sit on the wooden bench by the door. "*¡Hola!*" he called.

Quinn had spent enough time in Mexico that his Spanish was fluent. He called out a few more phrases, then went inside. Moments later he came back out.

"There's an old guy in there, dead drunk on his feet. He wouldn't know me from the president of the United States."

"We can assume his hospitality, then?"

"Judging by his condition, we could pass ourselves off as aliens from outer space and he wouldn't know the difference."

"That's probably good," I said. "The question is, what does he have to drink besides tequila?"

"We'll have to look around. Be warned, Josie, it's not a pretty sight in there."

Quinn and I went inside. The old guy—grizzled jaw, potbelly, tangled gray hair—sat in a beat-up old armchair, wearing not a stitch. Hardly acknowledging us, he vaguely gestured in our direction with the bottle in his hand. The place was messy and rank. If I had to guess, I'd say our host was a recent widower, or maybe just a chronic alcoholic on a binge.

There was no electricity and therefore no refrigerator. There was only one room. Against the back wall was a bed and a chest. In the middle of the room sat a small table and two chairs, plus the armchair presently occupied by our host. The kitchen consisted of a stove, a sink and a pump for running water, plus a wooden stand that served as counter space. The shelves below were for dishes. Behind a cubby in the corner, which was covered by a curtain, was the larder. There was no bathroom. Undoubtedly the outhouse was in back.

I went to the pantry and found it surprisingly well supplied, mostly with canned goods, rice, dried beans, several bottles of beer and a case of soft drinks. I grabbed a couple of soft drinks and took them out to Pardee.

"I don't know why I'm feeling so shitty all of a sudden," he said. "But I do."

"Loss of blood. Drink up. You'll feel better."

Returning to the kitchen, I worked the pump until I finally drew some water, filling a large plastic glass. I took that to Pardee, as well. We were both startled by the sound of an engine starting out back somewhere. I went to the corner of the house and checked. Quinn came walking toward me.

"There's an ancient pickup truck back there in working condition. Maybe the old duffer would be willing to lease it to us."

"It's a cinch we can't hang around here for long."

The *patrón* entertained us with intermittent bouts of song and snoring, never fully coming to his senses except for garbled speeches that never lasted long. Because of the stench, we elected to stay outside. I checked the dressing of Pardee's wound. Quinn had done a pretty good job, but I cleaned it up and put on a fresh bandage after saturating the wound with liberal amounts of antiseptic.

Between the rest and copious amounts of liquids, Pardee had recovered somewhat, but was in far from tiptop shape. While I'd tended to him, Quinn shaved, except for a mustache, and borrowed a clean shirt from our nameless host. He needed a clean pair of pants as well, but the only extra pair in the *patrón*'s wardrobe were much too short in the legs. He opted to wash his own pants out, wearing them wet. He did borrow a straw hat from the farmer. Had his hair and eyes been darker, Quinn might have passed for a local.

This was important because we'd decided he would drive the truck and Pardee and I would hide in back. My red hair and fair complexion was a giveaway and Pardee's wound could be, as well. To avoid easy detection, we prepared a hiding place in case we encountered a roadblock. First we made a little pallet in the bed of the truck out of pieces of canvas and old blankets, then covered a hollowed-out place around it with chicken crates, covered by a tarp.

We dined on Vera's lunch plus a can of beans, sitting at a table and chairs in the dusty yard under the cottonwood trees. As we ate, Quinn told us how he'd ended up in this mess. He said that from the beginning something about the kidnapping didn't smell right—the swagger and indifference to danger the kidnappers exhibited, in particular.

That squared with Pardee's theory that they had acted in complicity with the authorities. Our best guess was that the guys who grabbed Quinn were allowed to keep the ransom in exchange for keeping the cops informed about communications with Pardee. While being held, Quinn had picked up bits and pieces of conversation supporting the theory.

The question was what to do now. Pardee had hoped all along that Quinn might be able to return home without facing charges for aiding and abetting us. He was, after all, a kidnap victim and couldn't be held responsible for Pardee's and my deeds, either now or a decade ago. Suarez might not like that, but Mexico had a free judiciary and there were limits to how far a governor could go. It was true they'd have every reason to question Quinn, maybe harass him some, but eventually they'd likely be forced to release him. With luck he might even avoid arrest altogether and slip out of the country unnoticed. But the question was, from where?

The nearest city of consequence that offered air service was Oaxaca. As the state capital, it was also Fernando

Suarez's stronghold, and because of that the least likely place for us to head. That led Pardee to believe it was the best place to go. My former husband did not lack for chutzpah. Plus he'd always had a certain in-your-face attitude when it came to his adversaries, figuring it was just as important to humiliate a morally corrupt opponent as beat him.

I, on the other hand, was more interested in getting home to Sky and Baron in one piece. When I told Pardee I wasn't so sure Oaxaca was a good idea, that Suarez was of no importance to me and I couldn't care less how he felt about our escapade, Pardee said, "Well, do you have a better plan?"

I didn't.

We decided to head for Oaxaca.

By the time we were ready to roll it was late afternoon, the sun already having dropped behind the mountains. We left our host five hundred dollars in cash for his hospitality and were reasonably confident the truck would be returned to him by the authorities. Quinn brought the battered vehicle around front and Pardee and I were in the process of crawling into our secret hiding place when we heard a bellow from the house.

Turning, we saw the *patrón* standing in the doorway. He was still stark naked, but somewhat more formidable with a shotgun in his hands. The sound of his truck's engine seemed to have brought him to life.

He bellowed at us and Pardee asked Quinn what he was saying.

"He wants to know what we're doing with his truck."

"Tell him we bought it and that the money's on his table."

Quinn tried to communicate with the old farmer, but the limit of his capacities seemed to be pointing the shotgun at us.

"I say we drive off," Pardee said. "Chances are the gun's not loaded. And even if it is, he'd probably miss at ten feet."

That was classic Pardee—playing a low straight like it was four aces.

"You might like that bet," I said, "but I don't."

"What are you suggesting? Surrender?"

"Maybe if I talk to him," I said.

"No offense, sweetheart, but I don't think the old boy will be susceptible to your feminine charms."

"We'll see." I walked slowly toward the old man, my hands out, palms open. "Hey, *abuelo*," I said. Grandfather.

The old farmer, with his potbelly, shriveled privates and skinny white legs, was not the most fearsome creature on earth, but he had a shotgun in his hands and it was pointed at my vital organs. If this dragged out very long, I'd be in need of an antacid, if not a heart transplant. Drunks were dangerous under any circumstances.

The *patrón* blinked at me like I was some kind of apparition.

"*Camión. Dinero,*" I said.

He shook his head like he was trying to clear it. He didn't have his finger inside the trigger guard and it looked to me like the rusty old piece didn't even have a trigger, but knowing—as we used to say in the army—that assumption was the mother of all fuckups, I played it like he'd be able to blow a whole in me the size of a *fútbol*.

"*Abuelo,*" I said, "*por favor. Dinero. Viene.*" Moving past him with calm assurance, I led the way back inside the house and he staggered behind me. I went to the table and pointed to the stack of bills we'd left.

The old man's eyes lit up. He handed me the gun and picked up the bills, trying to read the denominations. While he was preoccupied, I checked the chamber of the shotgun. Pardee was right. Unloaded. I don't know how he did it. Put the guy in ten situations like this and he'd guess right nine times. But it was that tenth time that always did in even the best of gamblers.

I went back outside, ambling over to the truck. "You were right. It was unloaded."

"How'd you find out, if you don't mind me asking?"

"A lot safer way than the one you proposed."

"The important thing, Josie, is that we got it right."

"Yeah," I said, climbing into the cocoon I'd be sharing with Pardee until God knew when, "but the question is how long will our luck hold out?"

We took off and soon discovered the vehicle wasn't much of a bargain. We could have used a courtesy up-grade, but with cops around the country probably on the alert, we were lucky to have any transportation. As my daddy used to say, "Never lament what you don't have be-cause it keeps you from appreciating what you do have." But after only half an hour on bumpy, unpaved roads in a vehicle without functional shocks and springs, I wasn't feeling very thankful.

Despite the obvious pain he was in, Pardee seemed con-tent. Our nest was about the size of a single bed and there was no Maginot Line separating us. There was no way our bodies weren't going to be touching, so I gave in to the in-evitable and lay my head on Pardee's good arm and told myself it wasn't personal.

He got brazen and gently pushed a lock of my hair off my forehead. "Kind of romantic, ain't it?"

"What makes you say that? The feather-soft ride or the chickenshit fragrance in the air?"

"Holding you in my arms again, sweetheart. There's no place on earth that wouldn't be romantic."

Unfortunately, he meant it. Even more unfortunately, I was kinda touched.

Twenty-five

When I'd signed on for this mission I hardly expected to find myself huddled in the back of a rusty old pickup truck on an old moth-eaten blanket while snuggled up against Pardee. Here I was, though, only days removed from Sky and my beautiful diamond engagement ring—a felon on the run in the arms of my former husband.

The irony was that it felt good—and not just because of the thrill of our adventure. There was no point in fighting it, though. Our survival was at stake. Pardee and I were simply hoping to live another day. I'd have to worry about what it all meant later.

It was dark when Quinn stopped somewhere for gas. Pardee and I lay very still under the chicken crates and the tarp. We could hear Quinn talking to the station attendant and the sound of a radio. Somewhere nearby children were at play, their laughter carrying in the stillness of the night.

Then we heard a dog. He was at the rear of the truck,

sniffing and whining before he started to bark. Apparently he'd picked up our scent and felt it was his patriotic duty to do what he could to bring the gringo desperadoes to justice. I thought of Baron. He was tenacious as all get-out when he was trying to warn me of impending danger. I hoped to hell that this dog wasn't as dedicated.

As Quinn tried to shoo the dog away, the attendant came to investigate. Conversation followed while we held our breath. Whatever Quinn said was convincing, apparently, because the man ran the mutt off. Disaster averted.

A few minutes later we were under way again and Pardee and I breathed easy. The truck's back window had been knocked out, so Quinn was able to talk to us whenever the clunking and banging caused by the rough road didn't make communication impossible. Wherever it was that we'd stopped must have been a fairly significant wide spot in the road because the pavement was much better thereafter and the ride quieter.

"That was close," Quinn hollered after we'd been driving for a minute. "Must have been your perfume, Ma. Not a lot of chickens wear that scent in these parts, I guess."

We all laughed.

"So, anybody hungry back there?" Quinn asked. "I bought some snacks."

"Get anything to drink?" Pardee hollered back to him.

"Coke and beer was all they had, so I got both."

"Anything wet would be great."

"Got some tortilla chips and candy bars, too," Quinn informed us.

Reaching back, he handed the provisions down through the gap between the cab and the first row of crates. Pardee and I were both excited. The chips were stale, the candy bars not much better and the drinks were only barely cool, but it was like a feast.

"Amazing how little it takes to put a smile on your face, isn't it?" I said to Pardee.

"Is that a comment on me or the meal?"

"I meant the food," I said, hoping he could sense my admonishing look despite the fact our surroundings were pitch-black.

"Sweetheart, any meal with you, no matter how modest, beats anything I had in a five-star restaurant with anybody else."

"Pardee, you're so full of shit."

"It happens to be a fact."

"You're just feeling charitable because I saved your bacon back there at the lake."

"Not true, Josie. Some of my fondest memories of you are the quiet meals we shared at the ranch. And it never mattered much what we were having. My mistake was taking you for granted."

The utter sincerity of his tone touched me. But it also made me uncomfortable. I took a long drink from the can of Coke. "Please don't say things like that," I said.

"Just being honest."

"I know you mean to be kind, but I wish you wouldn't."

I could sense the wheels turning in his head as he debated whether to press the matter or let it drop. He chose discretion. "Okay, sweetheart," he said, "whatever makes you happy."

We didn't talk much for a long time after that, my thoughts bouncing back and forth between Pardee and Sky and our predicament. It occurred to me that if we were caught and arrested, neither of them would be in my life, at least not for years to come. That was one way to solve my dilemma, I guess.

Because the space was so cramped, Pardee and I were lying right up against each other to begin with, but my melancholia started getting to me and I inched closer to him, finally putting my head on his shoulder. "Are we going to make it out of here in one piece?" I asked.

Sensing I needed reassurance, he drew me close. "I sure as hell hope so."

"I'm getting a bad feeling."

"Can't let yourself get down," he said. "You know that. Attitude is half the ball game when your survival is at stake."

I was perfectly well aware of that, of course, but I guess I felt the need to get a reading on Pardee's feelings. He sounded as upbeat and optimistic as ever, but we both knew we were in an extremely difficult and dangerous situation. When your plan gets off track and you start improvising, things become tricky. I wondered if maybe our run of luck was finally over.

Before long Pardee fell asleep and I started drifting off myself. We'd been doing a lot of climbing and the air was getting cooler. I was only half aware of throwing my arm across my ex's chest and snuggling right up against him. I guess I wanted to feel his warmth and affection without it meaning anything. Though he was half asleep, Pardee kissed the top of my head. I didn't mind at all.

I hadn't been asleep for long when the truck lurched and we suddenly slowed.

"Damn," I heard Quinn say.

Pardee stiffened and lifted his head. "What . . . what?"

"I think there's a roadblock ahead," Quinn said through the window. "At least the traffic's stopped."

"What are we going to do?" I whispered to Pardee.

"Is there a place to pull over?" he asked Quinn. "A side road or something?"

"Not really. The shoulder's narrow and there's a steep bank on our right."

"How far to the roadblock?"

"I can't tell. I can see fifteen or twenty vehicles ahead of us."

"Can you turn around?"

"It would be pretty tough. And there's a semi coming up behind us."

We could hear the sound of the big truck as it came lumbering up, its headlights showing through the holes in the tarp. Finally we heard the sharp hiss of the air brakes as it stopped. After that the only sound was the knock of its big diesel engine.

Pardee was up on his elbows, now in full alert mode. We inched forward for several yards and stopped again. "Quinn," he said, "look for a place to turn around. We've got to get off the road so Josie and I can get out and circle around the roadblock on foot."

"Okay." After a moment he said, "Hold on, there's a cop coming. Be quiet."

My heart rose in my throat. I felt like I was living in a John Le Carré Cold War novel and we were trying to escape from behind the Iron Curtain. Mexican cops weren't exactly jackbooted storm troopers, but they could be efficient, even brutal at times. Plus we were six hundred miles from the American border, which meant there were a lot of them between us and home.

Moments later we heard the cop's voice as he said something to Quinn. There was a brief reply and it seemed the cop moved on. We advanced a bit more, then Quinn said, "It might be tricky turning around. There are cops with submachine guns spread all along the road."

"We may have to take our chances and hope they don't do a thorough search," Pardee replied.

The next several minutes were excruciating as we crept forward a bit, then stopped, only to repeat the process again and again. I got my gun ready, but knew there was no percentage in trying to shoot our way out. Pardee confirmed this when he whispered in my ear that a shootout would probably be suicidal—even if we somehow managed to escape—especially if we killed some cops in the process. "Pray they won't look in here and find us."

I couldn't imagine them not at least lifting the tarp and shining in a flashlight. If they did, it would be all over. I took Pardee's hand and pressed it to my cheek. Yeah, I was scared, but I was feeling more than that. I had a very strong sense of doom, like we were at the end of our road.

With all the standstill traffic, the fumes were pretty strong, but I noticed a new acrid smell. It was a little like burning rubber.

"What's that?" I whispered to Pardee.

Before he could respond, Quinn spoke. "We've got a problem, Houston."

"What's the matter, son?"

"This old bucket of bolts is overheating. Steam's coming from under the hood and we're almost at the roadblock."

"Shit," I muttered. "When it rains, it pours."

The traffic moved ahead again, then stopped. Pardee leaned close and pressed his mouth to my ear. "I'm really sorry about this, sweetheart. I thought for sure we'd pull it off without a hitch. I just hate thinking I might have ruined your life."

"It's not your fault," I told him. "I came into this with my eyes open and if they let Quinn go home, I'll have no regrets."

"Not even because of Sky?"

"Well, yeah, that, of course."

"I'm sure he'll want to kill me."

"Let's hope he has a chance."

There was enough fractured light leaking through the tarp that we could see each other's faces. Pardee smiled sadly, his eyes glistening. He brushed my cheek with the back of his fingers.

"It's going to be costly," he murmured, "but these past several days have been my happiest since . . . well, since we split."

I think if I hadn't been so scared I might have cried right then and there. Before I could, the truck lurched forward and the engine immediately died. We heard voices from outside. It sounded like the cops were yelling at Quinn to get moving.

My Spanish is practically nonexistent, but Quinn seemed to be lamenting the fact his truck had broken down. The cops were pissed. One voice, the tone commanding, stood out above the others. It was probably the officer in charge and he was giving orders.

"They're going to push us off the road because we're blocking traffic," Pardee whispered.

We heard the cops moving behind the truck, muttered just inches from where we lay hiding. As they pushed, grunting and groaning, the truck bumped off the pavement and the cops went off, their voices fading.

"They told me to fill the radiator up once the engine cools down and get the hell out of here," Quinn said through the window.

"Then we're through the roadblock?" Pardee asked.

"They pushed us on through the barricade and off the road. I think they were so annoyed they forgot to do a search. I'm going to get out and open the hood."

I gave Pardee a fierce hug, I was so thrilled. Then I collapsed on the blanket with a sigh. "God, did we dodge another bullet or am I imagining it?"

"Let's not celebrate quite yet."

I lay there in our broken-down truck with the man from my ruptured marriage, my heart beating nicely. I knew we weren't out of the woods, but I was relieved, big time. My future seemed to be back in play again. The truck breaking down at just the right moment probably saved us. Maybe I would see Sky again before I was a middle-aged woman. And Baron, too! My poor puppy probably wouldn't have lived to see me free, if we'd been arrested.

I knew I couldn't get too worked up because we were far from safe. A lot of danger still lay between us and freedom. But it looked like we'd gotten over the first big hurdle and that was always a morale-booster.

But my joy was short-lived. Another problem developed of an entirely different nature. "Pardee," I said after we'd been waiting for maybe twenty minutes, "I've got to go to the bathroom."

"Now, Josie?"

"Yes, now."

"Well, you'll have to wait . . . or just go here in the truck."

"I can't do that."

"It's not like I haven't seen your bare butt before."

That was true enough, but I still didn't like the idea. "I'll try to wait. How long before we can start in again?"

"How's the engine doing?" Pardee asked Quinn.

Quinn got out of the truck, returning after a few seconds. "I think it's cooled down enough to add some water. The trick will be finding some."

"Let's get out of here as soon as we can. Your stepmother needs to use the john."

"I'll see if the cops have any water or a container to go find some."

Given the condition of my bladder, it seemed like Quinn was gone for an hour, but it was probably only fifteen minutes before he returned. He filled the radiator and then tried starting the engine. It turned over, but wouldn't start. I began considering pulling down my pants and letting fly. The trouble was we were facing downhill and it would be hard to avoid soiling our nest. I muttered under my breath, telling myself that a little hydraulic pressure was nothing compared to spending my best years in jail.

Quinn decided to ask the cops to give him a push so he could get rolling down the hill and start the engine on compression. My condition, meanwhile, had gotten worse. I lay there with my legs crossed, grimacing, as three or four policemen pushed us back onto the roadway. We started to roll, slowly gaining speed. When Quinn popped the clutch, the truck lurched and I very nearly wet my pants. The engine started on the second attempt and we were again rolling down the highway.

"Thank God!" I practically cried.

"Pull over when you safely can," Pardee yelled at Quinn. "I've got a dying woman on my hands."

A couple of minutes later the truck bumped off the pavement and came to a stop. As Quinn got out of the cab to come loosen the tarp, all I could think of was the time in kindergarten when I went running to the bathroom and didn't make it by about ten feet. I had visions of repeating the performance.

Once the tailgate was down, I flew out like a shot and plunged into the undergrowth, unzipping my pants as I went. There I was in the moonlight, my butt hanging over a big rock as I relieved myself, joyful that I'd made it.

My euphoria was shattered when I was suddenly illuminated by a flashlight beam coming from below, followed seconds later by laughter. As I scrambled to pull up my pants, I realized we'd pulled over above a hairpin turn in the road and several trucks had stopped at a turnout below us. I was in full view of half a dozen truckers. I ran back to Grandpa's truck, red-faced. Pardee and Quinn had heard the hooting and laughter and asked me what happened.

"I'm ready to turn myself in and throw myself on the mercy of the court," I said. "I don't want to do this anymore."

Pardee could tell I was embarrassed and, judging by the catcalls coming from below, pretty well figured out what had happened. "You may have the most famous ass in Mexico, my dear," he said, "but look at it this way—nobody's ever seen your face."

As I climbed back in the bed of the truck I thanked God that I'd been married to the man. In a million years I couldn't imagine having been through this charade with

Sky. He was a sweet guy, but my dignity would have been in shreds. No, if I'd had to go through a night like this with any man on earth, Pardee would be the one. Hands down.

It was a revelation.

Twenty-six

We rolled into the outskirts of Oaxaca shortly before dawn. Quinn had decided we deserved a few hours of rest in a motel and the chance to clean up, so he pulled into the Mexican version of Mom and Pop's Sleepy Hollow Motel. There were half a dozen cabins, each with electricity and running water—not necessarily hot. Ours had two beds. Pardee and Quinn got the double. I took the single, though I had several dozen bedbugs for company.

Morning brought a cold shower with a chip of soap, coffee in styrofoam cups and pastries from a café up the road, purchased and delivered by Quinn, who was proving to be quite useful. As family vacations go, it wasn't the best, but it was showing promise.

Quinn did have some bad news. On the TV at the café he saw a news bulletin about two American desperadoes, Napoleon Pardee and Josephine Mayne, a pair of Bonnie and Clyde figures on the loose in southern Mexico traveling under the names Denise Raymond and Robin Hood.

"Robin Hood?" I said to Pardee. I realized I'd never seen his fake passport. "Really?"

He shrugged. "Liked the symbolism."

I couldn't believe it.

"They had drawings of you which they showed on the screen," Quinn said. "Not very flattering ones, either."

"Great. Adding insult to injury."

Quinn said that according to the report the fugitive couple were said to have committed a series of crimes including air piracy, larceny, assault on police officers and attempted murder. They were believed to be traveling with Pardee's adult son, but no details were given about Quinn, except that he was being sought for questioning.

Quinn added that the governor, Fernando Suarez, made a personal appeal to the citizenry to be on the alert for the American couple and offered a reward of ten thousand dollars for information leading to their capture. "It's not a good time to be you," Quinn concluded.

"And probably not a good time to hang out waiting to see what happens," Pardee offered. "It's only a matter of time before we're recognized."

"Meaning whatever we're going to do, we'd better do it fast," I said.

"Exactly."

Quinn sat on the bed next to me. "I say the three of us stay together. We can drive all the way to the States, if need be. It seemed to work pretty well last night with me as the front man."

"It'd be a miracle if that truck has a few hundred miles left in it, never mind hundreds more of mountains and desert," Pardee said. "Anyway, we were lucky. The whole country's going to be on the alert, if it isn't already. That roadblock last night is just a sample of what we're facing. I still think going out by air is our best bet."

"Then let's get our butts to the airport," Quinn said.

"No, Josie's and my aliases are known, but the name on the passport I got you isn't. There's no reason you can't hop on a plane."

"What about you?"

"They'd pick us off before we could board the plane. We'll have to find another way."

"You don't have many options."

"I know, but we'll come up with something, son. Meanwhile, Josie and I are dangerous to be around, and the longer you stay with us, the more likely you'll be regarded as an accomplice rather than a victim. I want you to leave right away."

Quinn looked at me. I said, "For once, I agree with your father. Go into town, buy yourself some decent clothing and a little suitcase and get on a plane. If they do spot you, the worst that happens is they question you. The nice thing is you can tell them the truth right down the line, though you might want to say that Pardee did the driving and we forced you to hide in back with me."

"You'd have the boy lie?" Pardee quipped, giving Quinn a wink.

"It's the moral truth, Pardee," I protested, "and you know it. Anyway, if the passport you got him works for him as well as ours did for us, he may walk right through unnoticed."

"What are you two going to do?"

"I don't know," Pardee said. "What do you think, sweetheart? Do we hijack a plane, or do we make a run for it in the jalopy?"

I was genuinely torn. The nice thing about flying out was that it would be quick either way, whether it worked or not. Crawling home on the ground, mile by agonizing mile, through roadblocks and breakdowns with half the country on the lookout for us, would be like a slow death.

"Maybe we can play it by ear," I said. "After Quinn's gone we can go to the airport and get a reading on the situation. If it's an armed camp, we get the hell out."

Pardee stroked his grizzled jaw. "That works for me, but we've got to find a better place to hide out than this— someplace where we'd be safe for a day or two."

"I have an idea," Quinn said. "I have a friend from school who's from Mexico City, but her family's originally from Oaxaca. She told me about playing at the ruins of Monte Albán when she was a little girl. As I recall, her grandmother still has a rancho here, though she spends half the year in San Antonio. Maybe we could stay at her place."

"How trustworthy is your friend?" Pardee asked.

"I'd trust her."

"Could the grandmother be trusted?"

Quinn hesitated.

I saw something flicker over his handsome face that reminded me of his father. "Is this young lady a friend or a girlfriend?" I asked.

My dear, sweet stepson blushed.

I turned to Pardee. "My guess is they can both be trusted."

"How would you know?"

"Quinn, what's the girl's name?"

"Rosalinda."

"How long have you been dating?"

He grinned shyly. "Couple of months before I left Texas for the Yucatán."

"I'd say that's good enough," I said to Pardee. "If the grandmother doesn't want to cooperate, she'll say so."

"Is there some kind of female code of honor at work here?" he asked.

"Simple pragmatism. Just be thankful your son is more principled when it comes to women than you. I say you should call her, Quinn."

He looked at his dad. Pardee shrugged.

"Who am I to second-guess the brains of the outfit?"

We settled on a plan, deciding that Quinn, being the least conspicuous and most proficient in Spanish, would try to reach Rosalinda, then do some shopping. He'd pick up clothing for us as well as for himself, plus hair dye for me. It would take some doing to convert Pardee from Indiana Jones into an insurance salesman and me from Lara Croft into a kindergarten teacher, but we had to try. Pardee gave him one of the two cell phones we had, so he could communicate with us if necessary. We all hugged and Pardee and I wished Quinn luck. It was emotional because we knew we might not see each other again.

After Quinn left for town, I changed the bandage on Pardee's arm. It didn't look good and had to hurt like hell, but he hadn't complained once. Pardee was one tough hombre. I worked on him in the bathroom, with him sitting on the toilet. I guess my proximity was just too tempting and he gave me a little pat on my rear end.

"Get your hand off my butt," I ordered.

"Sorry, it looked inviting."

"It's not yours to play with anymore, Pardee."

"I thought we'd crossed a threshold."

"What are you talking about?"

"In the truck."

"You're confusing camaraderie with something else," I said, smoothing the last piece of tape on the dressing.

I left the bath and lay on one of the beds. Pardee came in and stared at me. I could tell he was contemplating lying down beside me but thought better of it. He plopped down on the other bed.

"Camaraderie?" he said, rolling onto his side, facing me. "That's what it was?"

"What else?"

I put up a brave front, but my cheeks colored. Pardee must have noticed because he zeroed right in, not chastened in the least. "Come on, admit it, Josie, these past few days have felt like old times. It's been fun, right? You've been feeling it, I know you have."

I sure as hell wasn't going to admit it, but what Pardee said was true. It *had* been like old times and I did miss it, maybe even including the way I was starting to feel about him. Not that I'd succumbed, but neither could I continue to pretend he wasn't having his effect. The question was how long it would last. I was betting not for long, so I held firm, as much out of fear of the trend as anything. "I'm committed to Sky and I love him."

"If you'd told me that last night, when we were in the truck, I'd never have believed you," he said. "I guess the world looks different to you by the light of day."

He was embarrassing me and I didn't appreciate it. "Those were unusual circumstances."

"Josie, we're not exactly lying on the beach in Carmel. This is a temporary respite at best. The police could come bursting in here at any moment."

"What are you suggesting, Pardee? That I should be clinging to you in fear?"

I don't know why I was being so combative. He hadn't been so far out of line as to deserve it. I guess I was just feeling insecure and didn't want to have to face the issue of my feelings. Momentous decisions shouldn't be made on the basis of things said and done at a time of crisis.

"Listen, I can understand your interest in Sky," Pardee said. "Besides being rich, he's a hell of a nice guy. And generous as all get-out. I can see why he'd be your friend. But marry him, Josie? Marriage is no small thing."

"Yes, I know," I said with a hoot of derision. "I found that out the hard way."

He looked like he didn't believe me. I turned on my side and faced him, the gap between the beds symbolic of a much greater chasm time had put between us. But no sooner had I reminded myself of that than I gazed—if not longingly, certainly anxiously—across the great divide.

"You're not living in the real world," I told him. "These last few days won't mean anything in the long run."

"Okay, I'm delusional, but I still love you."

I closed my eyes and rolled onto my back. "I asked you not to do that. It just makes it harder to be around you. It's not that long ago that I finally managed to put you behind me."

"Fine," he said. "I don't love you, then. I'm glad we're divorced. I've never been happier in my life since we've split. How's that?"

"That's not helpful, either."

"Christ, Josie, what can I say? I'm damned if I do, damned if I don't."

"The wages of sin."

"So that's it? You can't forgive me for my mistakes of the past? Is that the problem?"

I wanted to scream that *he* was the problem, but what was the point? Why was I arguing about this with a man I'd divorced five years ago, anyway? Why did I even care?

Then it occurred to me that maybe I didn't know what I wanted. The truth was I was more confused than ever. I was tempted to succumb, plain and simple. Why not admit it? Maybe I should just have sex with him, get it over with and put all the anxiety behind me. The constant tension, having to fight myself, wasn't any fun. Of course, I'd feel guilty and hate myself afterward.

But if, for some reason, it was wonderful, then I might as well know it. As in most things, the uncertainty was the real problem. What difference did it make if we had sex or not? Hell, it was easily enough rationalized. I'd definitely find out something about myself. And it would focus up my feelings about Sky and what I wanted in the future.

Still, I hesitated. I couldn't quite say, *The hell with it, let's screw.* Why? It wasn't because of Sky. That had been my excuse, but the truth was I was uncertain of Pardee's motives. I'd been burned once by him and that was enough. I couldn't be sure these professions of love weren't just a gambit. Pardee had an ego that wouldn't quit and this might be about nothing more than his need to prove he could have me if he wanted.

"If I ask you something important," I said, "will you tell me the God's truth?"

I waited and, when he didn't answer, I rolled my head in his direction. His eyes were closed, his mouth slightly open.

"Pardee?"

He didn't so much as twitch, though I could see his chest slowly rise and fall. My former husband gave a little snort then, and began to snore softly. I couldn't help laughing. The bastard was asleep.

Twenty-seven

I lay awake, marveling at the odd twists of fate in my life, until I finally dozed off, getting some much-needed rest. I didn't awaken until I heard the cell phone ring. Pardee groaned, but didn't appear eager to pull himself out of his deep sleep, so I reached over to where the phone lay on the table between our beds and answered it.

"Josie, it's me," Quinn said. "You've got to get out of there. The police will be there any minute. They've been moving down the highway, searching every motel, restaurant, bar and *pensión*. You don't have much time. Go now!"

"Should we meet you somewhere?"

"According to my map, there's a bridge a few miles from the motel. It's just off a secondary road which runs behind the motel. The police got the truck, so I'll have to find other transportation, but I'll meet you there as soon as I can. Don't waste a minute, though. Get out of there fast."

Pardee was trying to drag himself out of what looked like a drugged sleep, blinking at me as I ended the call.

"Come on, lover boy, we've got to get out of here," I told him. "That was Quinn. He said the cops will be here any minute."

That got his full attention and he rousted himself, though at first he was wobbly. While I threw our things in my duffel, he peered out the front window through the curtains.

"That call came just in time," he said. "A Jeepload of gendarmes just pulled up out front. We're not going out the door unless we want to shoot our way out." He stuffed his sidearm in the back of his pants.

The bathroom window was the only one that looked out the rear of the cabin. It was not large and it was high, but if we could get it open, we could crawl out. I unlocked it, but could only open it a crack. Pardee gave it a try with his good arm, but without much luck. Then he tried both arms and moved it a few more inches. I wedged myself in next to him and together we opened it about a foot and a half.

"That'll have to do," he said, as we heard shouts coming from the courtyard of the motel.

Pardee offered me his knee to boost me high enough to slither out the window. I shoved my duffel through the opening first, got my legs out, then my butt, dropping about eight feet to the ground. Pardee had to come out headfirst and I had to catch him. He ripped the dressing on his arm as he squeezed through the window, but that was the least of our troubles. About the time he got to his feet we could hear the cops banging on the front door.

I headed right for the adobe wall twenty yards from the row of cabins, but Pardee took the time to close the window so that our route of egress wasn't obvious. He wanted the cops to think we'd abandoned the place earlier. Finding several rusty barrels lined up against the wall, we climbed up on them and went over the top, landing in a patch of weeds bordering the nearby gravel road on the other side.

"Quinn said to follow this road to a bridge."

"Which way?" Pardee asked.

"He didn't say."

"You're the one with intuition, sweetheart. You pick."

I decided on the direction away from town, under the theory Quinn would have chosen a more remote location. It was more logic than intuition, but we had a fifty-fifty chance I was right. There was no time to discuss it, though, so Pardee took the duffel from me and we took off at a slow jog, picking up the pace when we heard shouts coming from the other side of the wall.

"What are they saying?" I asked.

"I don't think they spotted us. By the sound of it, they're searching the grounds."

After we'd gone a couple hundred yards, we were out of sight of the motel and slowed to a walk. Because of his weakened condition, Pardee was breathing pretty hard.

"How's the arm?" I asked, taking the duffel from him.

He held up his arm and I saw fresh blood on the torn dressing. "Not bad until that phone call," he said. "I'm going to have to talk to my kid about giving more ample notice."

"Let me try to fix it," I said.

I could tell his preference was to keep going, but we both knew I had to stop the bleeding. We went over to a big rock by the road and he sat while I did what I could to rebandage him.

"You really need to see a doctor," I said.

"I'll be fine, sweetheart. Honest. I could use a drink of something, though. I'm kind of parched."

It was late afternoon and the sun was dropping toward the mountains. Though it was warm, it wasn't sizzling hot. Pardee looked clammy and pale. I peered up the road. "I hope we're going in the right direction and that it's not far to the bridge."

"And I hope there's a taco stand nearby. You know how long it's been since we've had a regular meal?"

"That basket lunch yesterday at the naked old drunk's place, if you can call it regular."

"And it wasn't meant for three."

We heard a clip-clop, clip-clop and looked back the way we'd come to see a donkey cart approaching. It was driven by a girl of fourteen or fifteen. A boy, a few years younger, sat on the seat beside her. Understandably, their looks grew more inquisitive the closer they got.

Pardee, having been a natural with the ladies his whole life, hailed the pair good-naturedly. "¡Hola, amigos!"

The girl, pretty with long black hair, reined in the donkey. I saw that a goat was tethered in the back of the cart. Pardee began to converse with the girl and boy. It sounded to me like they were discussing the bridge. After a few cheerful exchanges, Pardee told me that we were indeed headed in the right direction and that the bridge was about three kilometers ahead on a larger road that crossed the river. "We've been offered a ride, if you didn't mind the company of a goat."

"I rode in the back of a truck with an old goat last night," I said, "and managed to survive. I don't suppose this will kill me."

"Get in the cart, lady," he grumbled, repressing a smile.

I climbed up into the cart and Pardee took the opportunity to slap me in the butt.

"Hey!" I protested.

"I got to live up to the epithet you've hung on me, don't I?"

"There are children present, Pardee."

Once we were seated, the girl flicked the reins and the cart started up the road.

"My guess," Pardee said, "is they live in a one-room shack with their parents and three brothers and sisters, which means they've seen it all. Kids like this get their sex education the natural way."

"Did you explain to them we're divorced and traveling together only because of extraordinary circumstances?"

"No, I just told them you're the love of my life."

When I gave him a look, he shrugged.

"Why pretend otherwise?" he said. "It's written all over my face."

We propped ourselves on opposite sides of the cart, facing each other, our knees touching. I wondered what he'd say if he knew I'd been on the verge of propositioning him when he'd fallen asleep. The thing was, I didn't know if I'd actually have gone through with it, but I'd seriously considered it and that in itself was significant.

The goat didn't seem thrilled with our company, giving us a walleyed look, indicating he was more wary of us than we were of him. He was a beautiful animal, white in color, with the longest, silkiest hair I'd ever seen on an animal.

The cart bumped along the road at a leisurely pace. Neither Pardee nor I said anything for a while, though he watched me intently. The circumstances were hardly conducive, yet a sexy feeling went through me.

"You know, Josephine," he finally said, "I forgot just how beautiful you are. Can you imagine that?"

"Ex-wives are easily forgotten."

"Oh, I remembered you were a fox well enough, but when I look at you now, I see that you're more gorgeous than I recall. How I could have let you get away is a mystery."

"Do you mean that, or is it just more of your bullshit?"

"I'm dead serious. As you recall, I wasn't exactly thrilled when you announced you were leaving me."

"You were losing your cook, housekeeper, gun bearer and reliable sex partner."

"Give me a break, Josie, you know I loved you."

"And it wounded your pride."

"I won't deny it, but that doesn't mean I didn't love you then and that I don't now."

"Let's say you manage to seduce me and we have sex. What would it prove? Certainly nothing about your feelings."

Pardee laughed, slapping me on the knee. "Ah, I see. You think this is about conquest."

"Getting me to bed would have to salve some of the pain of rejection."

He continued squinting at me in the late afternoon sun, a faint smile on his face. "Sweetheart, I'm not into short-term gratification."

"Since when?"

He chuckled. "Let me rephrase that. Not when it comes to you."

"I don't know whether to be flattered or offended."

"Josie, I think when we get out of this mess we need to reevaluate our relationship, take a fresh look at things."

"That is *so* unlikely."

"Why?"

"We could have sex until the cows come home and it

could be as good as it ever was, but that wouldn't change a damned thing."

"Who said anything about sex?"

I turned scarlet.

"Not that I'm opposed to the idea," he added.

"I don't even know why we're talking about this. It's ridiculous. Can we change the subject?"

Pardee began to laugh and I gave him a kick. His response was an endearing smile. That made me madder at first, but eventually I smiled back.

Pardee put his hand on my leg and gave it a squeeze. "I hope to hell we get through this," he said. "I really want the chance to prove to you I mean every word I say."

That touched me and I had to look away so that I wouldn't cry. "What is it about you, Pardee? I used to be able to count on you to be glib and irreverent. I think I liked it better when you made me laugh."

"So the new, more serious, sincere me doesn't do it for you, huh?"

"Not when I'm facing ten or twenty years in jail. I think I'd rather laugh."

I wasn't being facetious. In the years we'd worked together, Pardee had been the one to keep our spirits up when things got dicey. I think the funniest he'd ever been was that time we slogged through that tropical jungle in Venezuela after our guide deserted us.

I'd always liked it that Pardee was easygoing, though. It never felt like I was being judged—admired, yes, but never under critical scrutiny. I was always okay with Pardee, just as I was. Unless, of course, I was giving him a hard time. Most of the time, though, being with him seemed natural and just plain comfortable.

That was the good part. God knew we had problems. And I don't mean that chorus girl. She was more a symptom than a cause. What had destroyed our relationship and our marriage was that Pardee never fully revealed himself to me. The man could take, emotionally speaking, but he was reluctant to give. Once I'd said to him, "Having sex isn't sharing. Why can't you understand that?" His response was a dumbfounded look.

And yet, in retrospect, I may have taken for granted the fact that we had a lot going for us that was good. Like most divorcees, I'd concentrated on the negative. Lord knows, I never would have thought that riding in a donkey cart with a goat and Pardee for company would have opened my eyes to the fact, but dammit, that's what seemed to be happening. More was going on between us than I wanted to admit. The question—the damnable question—was what was I going to do about it?

About then we heard a siren in the distance and saw flashing blue lights on a vehicle coming around the long curve in the road behind us. It was followed by a plume of dust. Pardee and I looked at each other.

"Trouble," he said.

With the back of the donkey cart open, there was no hiding there. This time we were without chicken crates and a tarp, and our friend the goat was of little use. Without a word, we jumped out of the cart.

"*Gracias, amigos,*" Pardee called to the children. "*¡Adios!*"

We made a dash for the nearest structure, a small, open-sided hay barn about twenty yards from the road. We'd just ducked behind the neatly stacked bales of hay seconds before the police Jeep raced by, swinging wide to pass the donkey cart, its emergency lights swallowed by the dust cloud as it disappeared from sight. Pardee and I sighed at the same time.

There was a hollowed-out area in the middle of the stack of baled hay and he crawled into it and plopped down on the bed of scattered hay. I dropped down beside him and he took my hand.

"Josie, nobody can say we don't lead an exciting life."

"Maybe too exciting."

He rolled his head toward me. "You really think so?"

"One of these days our luck is going to run out."

"The hell. You and me are going on like this forever and ever." He propped himself up on his elbow and looked into my eyes. "We lead a charmed life, sweetheart. A very special one."

I reached up and touched his face, I guess in reaction to the tenderness of his tone. Then Pardee kissed me, and I kissed him back. It was a sensuous kiss, the kiss I'd been waiting for. In seconds we got worked up, going at each other with teeth and lips and tongues. I had a fistful of his hair; he had my blouse undone and started unfastening my pants when I came to my senses and stopped him, separating my mouth from his. We looked into each other's eyes, breathing hard.

"You haven't lost your touch," I said. "You can still turn me on. But I don't want to do it. Not here. Not now."

"The sex is not important," he said. "What I care about is how you feel about me."

"Isn't it obvious? Apparently I can't resist you."

"You know that's not what I mean."

I scooted away from him, sat up and leaned against the

wall of hay behind me. Pardee continued to lay where he was, staring up at the corrugated steel roof over our heads.

"You pissed?" he said.

"No."

"But you aren't happy."

"If you must know, I'm confused, not sure what to think."

"Maybe you're thinking too much."

"I'm engaged to marry another man."

"You'll have to put that on hold, sweetheart."

"Until I get out of jail?"

"Until I can convince you to trust me."

At least he understood the issue. I had to hand him that. But there were other things I had to consider, as well. I loved Sky and a few days of titillation and a kiss or two couldn't change that. So I still found Pardee attractive. What did that prove?

"You aren't saying anything," he intoned.

"I'm thinking you might be right. We should try to get through this before we worry about tomorrow."

"Damned by my own words. Okay," he said with a weary sigh. "Whatever."

"So, how are we going to get to the bridge?"

"Well, there seems to be a small army of cops swarming the countryside. Let's call Quinn. Maybe he can pick us up here instead of at the bridge."

"Good idea."

"You have the cell phone?" he asked.

"Oh, shit."

His brows went up. "You don't have the phone?"

"It must still be on the nightstand. In my haste to get out of there, I didn't think about it."

"Hmm . . ."

"Damn," I said, feeling just awful. "That was so stupid. I'm sorry. God, if that costs us, I'll just die."

"I didn't think about it, either, Josie."

"Yes, but I had it in my hand."

Pardee sat up. "What concerns me is that the police will get hold of it and maybe find a way to track down Quinn."

"Oh, Lord."

"They probably don't have the sophisticated equipment needed readily available, but I don't want to take a chance. The longer we delay hooking up with Quinn, the more likely he'll try calling us. I'd prefer to wait till dark, but maybe we should head for the bridge now."

"How far do you think it is?"

"I'd say not much more than a klick. If I climbed up on the roof, I might be able to see it from here."

"Lord, what if he isn't there?"

"We'll just have to do the best we can. You know as well as I we always end up running an operation by the seat of our pants. Why should things be any different this time?"

Twenty-eight

The bridge was only slightly farther from the hay barn than Pardee had thought. We encountered little traffic along the way—a few odd vehicles, four or five pedestrians and a wagon, but no more cops.

The gravel road we'd taken from the motel intersected a paved road fifty yards from the bridge, a modest structure that spanned a riverbed that was more imposing than the channel itself. There were a number of trees scattered along the riverbank. Nestled among them to the north of the bridge were a few shanties and trailers. The last rays of the setting sun reflected off the shiny metal of the trailers.

With the temperature dropping, we'd gotten our jackets out of the duffel bag. Both our sidearms had been in the bag as well and we decided to leave them there, but on top.

At the junction of the two roads there was a tortilla stand, consisting of little more than a piece of corrugated steel supported by four posts. Two women sat in plastic lawn chairs behind their propane stove, which rested on a folding table that also served as the counter of their fast-food establishment.

"Hungry?" Pardee said as we approached the intersection.

"Of course."

"Maybe they're selling soft drinks, too. Let's dine."

The women had been watching us and one, the younger and skinnier of the two, stood as we came up. Pardee greeted them, dropped the duffel at his feet and launched into a discussion, presumably about menu choices. After considerable conversation, he turned to me.

"How about a buttered corn tortilla and a warm juice squeeze?"

"Sounds wonderful."

He put in our order and the women went to work. Pardee and I peered down the paved road toward the bridge.

"Don't see any sign of him," Pardee said. "Quinn's either not here yet, or he's in the trees on the other side of the river."

"There are a few people on the bridge, but none of them look like Quinn. What are they doing? Fishing?"

"Yeah, they're probably from that encampment. I suspect these ladies are as well."

"So, do we wait here, or go over to the bridge?"

"After we eat, maybe I'll mosey on over and take a look around, just to make sure Quinn hasn't already arrived. The bad thing about hanging out here is that we're conspicuous should a police patrol come by."

"We could make like trolls and hide under the bridge," I said.

"The trouble is we'll need to be out so we can watch for Quinn."

"Basically we're in a quandary."

"Right."

That was the way I felt about my life. I missed Baron like crazy and Sky was so sweet I always enjoyed being with him. But the notion of sitting on my porch, watching the big rigs go down the highway, or even watching the sunset from Sky's deck overlooking the Pacific, seemed like somebody else's life, not mine. When in the grip of an adrenaline rush, normalcy was hard to imagine.

I did think longingly of that meal Sky and I had the night of our engagement, though. The chef had made a special effort and everything had been exquisite.

"Your corn tortilla is about to be served," Pardee said, bringing me back to southern Mexico and current circumstances.

The thinner woman handed Pardee a large buttered tortilla rolled in a sheet of waxed paper. It was a little like a giant ice-cream cone without the ice cream. He shooed away a buzzing fly and passed the tortilla to me. Then he took the second one she handed over. Two warm juice squeezes had been opened and were sitting on the table. Pardee gave me one and we clicked our bottles together.

"*Bon appétit*," he said, chugging down half the juice in his bottle.

I took a bite of the tortilla. It was plain, but not bad.

"Look at that sunset," he said. "Hell of a romantic setting for a romantic meal, huh?"

"Reminds me of some of the places you used to take me to dinner so I wouldn't have to cook," I said.

"Is that a jab?"

"No, just reminiscing," I said, repressing a smile.

He took a big bite of his tortilla, wiping his mouth with

the back of his hand as he chewed. "I guess it's progress that you're thinking back on our marriage fondly."

"That's one way to look at it, I suppose."

We ate for a while without saying much because we were so hungry. Pardee ordered another juice squeeze, paying for the meal with a ten-dollar bill. There wasn't a lot of traffic, but whenever we heard a vehicle approaching, we'd check it out pretty thoroughly.

"So, tell me, Josie, have you and Sky ever had an adventure like this?"

"No, our culinary adventures tend to involve gourmet meals."

"I bet not one of them was half this much fun."

"You have a tendency to glamorize roughing it, Pardee. My life with Sky is very comfortable."

"Comfort. Is that what you want?"

I shooed away a couple of flies. "Heaven forbid."

"Reverse things. Let's say you could be standing in the dust eating a tortilla with Sky, or you could be having a candlelight dinner with me in a fancy restaurant in Carmel. Which would you pick?"

"Which restaurant?"

He gave me a playful tap on the jaw with his fist. "Women are too damned materialistic."

"That must be why I lived with you all those years in a double-wide in the high desert, miles from civilization."

"I should have taken you to Hawaii that time you said you'd give anything for a week on the beach."

"I don't know if that would have made a difference, Pardee."

We watched a truck go by.

"You cook for him?"

"Sky? Breakfast often. Other than that, not much."

"Does he prefer it that way?"

"He has a cook and housekeeper. Doesn't expect me to do domestic chores unless I want to."

"Must be nice."

"That life has its advantages."

Pardee scrutinized me, really looking me up and down. After a while I started feeling self-conscious.

"What?" I said, pushing a wisp of hair back off my face. "Why are you looking at me that way?"

"No offense, sweetheart, but I really have trouble picturing you as Mrs. Astor. This is much more you."

"You mean eating a meal served on waxed paper while standing at a dusty crossroads with flies buzzing around my head?"

He chuckled. "No, when I say 'this,' what I really mean is being with me. Honest to God, why can't you see it? To me, it's as obvious as can be."

"Let's just get home in one piece, okay?"

"On that note, I think I'll go check out the bridge."

"Can't I come?"

"Why don't you stay and keep the ladies company? That way we won't have to lug the duffel. I'll only be gone a few minutes."

Pardee trudged off toward the bridge. I looked at the women and shrugged. The thin one offered me her chair, but I declined, thanking her. "*Gracias,*" I said using a big chunk of my Spanish vocabulary.

It didn't take Pardee long to get to the bridge, which he crossed to check out the far side. For a while he was out of sight, then I saw him coming back. It appeared he was attracting the attention of the men on the bridge. At about midspan he stopped and seemed to be talking to them. Seven or eight guys congregated around him. Pardee was either regaling them with stories about his pool hall prowess or he was in trouble. With twilight falling, it would have been easy enough for them to drag him off the bridge and empty his pockets and relieve him of his watch. And, with a bum arm, he wasn't in a position to put up much resistance.

It still wasn't clear what was going on, but I decided not to take any chances. I opened the duffel bag, got out my semiautomatic and stuffed it in the waistband of my jeans. Then I slung the bag over my shoulder, said *adios* to the women and headed for the bridge.

By the time I got there, it was clear Pardee was being harassed. The conversation was so intense that nobody noticed me until I was at the outer edge of the crowd. I could see then what was happening. A big heavy guy with a stubby ponytail and a leather vest had backed Pardee against the railing and was waving a pig-sticker with a six-inch blade in his face. They were talking in Spanish, so I had no idea what was being said. I dropped the duffel, deciding not to wait for a translation.

Pulling my gun from my belt, I hollered over the babble of voices. "Drop the knife, asshole."

My words brought the mob to a stunned silence. Heads turned and mouths dropped open at the sight of me and my gun, which I held with both hands, pointed at Dumbo. The crowd backed away, and the big guy, who I could now see had a deep scar across his cheek (a veteran of this sort of thing, evidently) grinned like he didn't believe whatever unintelligible words I'd uttered.

"Tell him to lose the knife, Pardee, unless he wants his belly to spout fluids."

Pardee did a brief translation, plucked the knife from his adversary's hand and tossed it over the railing and into the water, then he pushed past the guy and sauntered over to where I stood.

"Your timing is impeccable, sweetheart."

"What happened?"

"Señor Gordo wanted to sell me his sister, who apparently runs a comfort station in one of those trailers. When I declined his generous offer, he decided to collect a fee anyway."

"Well, it makes a good story."

"You don't believe me?"

"Pardee, if I'd routinely bet on you telling the truth, I'd have been in bankruptcy court long ago."

"Josie, that's the old me. I've reformed."

"You know, I'm getting tired of holding this thing. Tell the boys to run on home."

Pardee barked out an order in Spanish and the crowd moved off, some with fishing poles in hand, most heading for the near end of the bridge. The fat guy sneered, muttering under his breath as he went by.

"He was complimenting you on your figure," Pardee quipped.

"I bet."

With darkness rapidly falling now, we easily picked up the flashing lights of an emergency vehicle coming down the road on the far side of the river. Some of our friends noticed, as well, and they scampered away, perhaps thinking we were about to sic Juan Law on them. Little did they know.

Pardee picked up the duffel. "Why is it the cops always show up when you least need them?"

"Karma, probably."

We began hurrying back in the direction of the tortilla stand, only to see another set of headlights coming toward us. No flashing lights or siren, though. We expected the vehicle to cross the bridge, but it stopped before entering the span. Then, to our surprise, it began to turn around.

The vehicle, a silver blue Mercedes, was in the middle of a three-point turn when the passenger window went down and we saw Quinn's smiling face. With the cops approaching, he'd arrived just in time. "Want a lift?" he said.

We ran to the car and piled in the backseat. The Mercedes hurtled back up the road toward the highway. Quinn grinned at us over the seat.

"I decided to splurge," he said. "Got us a place with pool, a housekeeper and a cook. By the way, this is Carlos, our chauffeur."

"Good evening, sir, madam," the silver-haired man said.

I leaned back in the soft leather seats. Pardee put his hand on my leg.

"See, Josephine," he said, "I, too, can provide the good life. True love is only the beginning."

Twenty-nine

So what happened?" I asked Quinn as we sped along the highway, headed into Oaxaca. I knew he'd been busy because he'd gotten a haircut, a shave and new clothes. Unlike his father and me, he looked like anything but a fugitive from justice.

"I did my shopping as planned," he replied, "but when I went back to where I'd parked the truck, I found the cops there."

"The old man must have sobered up and reported his truck missing," Pardee said.

"That's what I figure."

"How did you know the police were coming to the motel?" I asked.

"I decided to take a bus back, thinking I'd be less conspicuous. And while I was walking from the bus stop, I saw an army of cops working their way up the highway, stopping everywhere, questioning people. I knew the jig was up. That's when I called you."

"I assume the wheels belong to your girlfriend's grand-mother," Pardee said.

"Yes, it's Señora Cachero Ostos's Mercedes. I called Rosalinda this morning and she promised to ask her grand-mother if we could have sanctuary. When I checked back she said everything had been arranged and gave me the phone number at the rancho so I could call for instructions. The housekeeper, Margarita, told me Carlos would come and pick me up in town at the tourist office near the cathe-dral. We met up, then drove out here to find you guys."

"We're damned lucky you've got generous friends, son," Pardee said, "because the truth of the matter is we're out of options."

"Rosalinda's family, especially her grandmother, is tak-ing a big risk helping us," Quinn said, "so I told her we wouldn't impose for long."

"And we shouldn't," Pardee said. "We have to put you on the first plane out of here. And Josie and I will leave as soon as we can figure out how we're going to do it."

"Plus your father's reinjured his arm," I told Quinn. "I think he should see a doctor."

"No, that'd be way too risky," Pardee insisted. "All I need to do is take it easy for a day or two and I'll be fine."

Quinn glanced back and gave me a wink. He knew his old man as well as I did.

"Señor," Carlos said, looking in the rearview mirror, "forgive me, but it is no problem if you stay with us for so long as you like, especially if you are injured. The señora wishes you to enjoy our hospitality. You will be safe at the rancho."

"That's very kind of you," I said. "And we're grateful. But harboring fugitives is a very risky thing."

"The señora is not a great supporter of the governor. It is our honor to help."

Pardee reached up and patted the man's shoulder. "*Muchos gracias, amigo.* My main concern is for my son. If you can get him to the airport for the first available flight, I'll be eternally grateful."

"This has been already arranged, señor."

"Margarita has me booked on a flight late tonight," Quinn explained.

I was elated. "Terrific."

I looked over at Pardee. His smile was almost as broad as mine. Our goal was within sight. He took my hand and gave it a squeeze. A warm feeling went through me, followed by a yearning. It was like at the hay barn. I wanted the man, no two ways about it. He caressed my hand with his thumb and it felt like the old days, as though nothing had changed. I realized right then I was not the same woman I'd been only a day ago.

Señora Cachero Ostos's estate was in the country, west of Oaxaca on the road to Monte Albán, the ruins where Quinn's friend Rosalinda had played as a child. Since Quinn's specialty was pre-Columbian culture, he took the opportunity to tell us about the place, which he described as one of the most spectacular archaeological sites in Mexico. Monte Albán, he said, had been founded sometime around A.D. 500 and was the Zapotec capital.

At one point, while Quinn and Carlos continued to discuss the Zapotecs, Pardee leaned over and whispered, "You can take the professor out of the classroom, but you can't take the classroom out of the professor."

"Your son is going to make important contributions to

our knowledge of the ancient world," I told Pardee, "and by saving him, we'll have made an important contribution, too."

"I can't argue with that, I suppose." He looked down at my hand. "Actually, Quinn could end up being *my* most important contribution. When you think about it, I haven't done much else for posterity."

They were the words of a proud father and a humble thing to say, but in my mind they had significance beyond that. That was not something that the Pardee of old would have admitted. No, the Pardee of old had used visits to see his son as cover for a night of fun with a chorus girl.

The Cachero Ostos estate was built on an oasis of lush vegetation in the high mountain valley, half a mile off the Monte Albán Road. Because it was practically dark when we arrived, we couldn't see the full grandeur of the setting. But after we entered a tropical forest of palms, the illuminated facade of the large villa, half covered with purple and pink blooming bougainvillea, could be seen. Built in the Colonial style, it was more gracious than spectacular, but definitely impressive.

"Oh, my," I said, as we came to a stop in the middle of the circular drive. I stared at the huge carved wooden doors. "We're coming up in the world, Pardee," I said. "No question about it."

We got out of the Mercedes and I was surprised to see how wobbly Pardee was.

"You okay?" I said, taking his good arm.

"Yeah, but I could use some liquid and a bite to eat."

Margarita greeted us at the door. She was a warm, accommodating woman with a very proper demeanor. Women of late middle age with an erect bearing, wearing silk dresses, tended to evoke an image of authority in my mind. But Margarita was every bit as gracious as Carlos. I couldn't believe our luck.

Margarita summoned a maid to come get my duffel and Quinn's packages. A tiny plump woman with a long black braid down the middle of her back came out the door. Seeing us, her eyes rounded. My first thought was that she may have recognized us from the news broadcasts—the gringo Bonnie and Clyde.

Margarita and the maid escorted us to the guest "cottage" located at the rear of the garden, just beyond the pool. "It's more private," the housekeeper said in impeccable English, "and I thought it would be better for you."

The maid deposited my duffel on a chair and left.

I didn't know what, if anything, Quinn had said about Pardee's and my relationship, but it felt like we were a married couple again, so I didn't give the matter a second thought. "Is the staff aware of who we are?" I asked Margarita once the maid had gone.

"They are very disciplined and very loyal. The elder servants have been here a long time and the younger ones were born here."

"For a guesthouse, this is very sumptuous," I said, looking around at the traditional Mexican decor.

To call it a cottage was understating the case. It was a house, larger than my place by more than half, though much of the floor space was taken up by a single great room, which included a dining area and comfortable sitting area opposite the fireplace. There was a single master bedroom with bath.

When I saw a smile flicker at the corner of Pardee's mouth, I knew he was thinking about what had very nearly happened at the hay barn. I had been thinking about it, too. It was pretty obvious that in the coming hours I would have important decisions to make.

"Your son tells me you were wounded," Margarita said to Pardee. "My father was a country doctor and, though I never was formally trained, I know a great deal about treating wounds. Would you like me to have a look?"

Pardee was willing and I was pleased because I'd been concerned about him, especially after he'd reinjured his arm. "Without you our goose would have been cooked," he told the woman. "We're very grateful."

"I'll have refreshments brought," Margarita said. "Dinner will be in an hour or so. Afterward Carlos must take young Mr. Pardee to the airport. But now let me have a look at your arm."

Margarita turned out to be a proficient nurse and had Pardee's wound cleaned and dressed in no time. After finishing, she left so we could get ready for dinner. Pardee stretched out on the big king-sized bed.

"I'll rest for a while, if you'd like the bathroom first."

He was keeping up a brave front, but he'd had a rough couple of days. The truth was, we were both lucky to be alive.

I got my cosmetic case and last change of underwear from my duffel and went into the bath. Twenty minutes later, when I emerged in one of the terry robes I'd found in the closet, Pardee was sound asleep.

I'd just returned to the front room when there was a knock at the door. It was Quinn, looking freshly scrubbed and handsome. He was accompanied by the maid, who had a tray of snacks and drinks, which she deposited on the table and left, but not before giving me a sideward glance.

Quinn had a large package in one hand and some hangers with a couple of dresses in the other. "Since your wardrobes are probably pretty much depleted, I thought I'd bring you the stuff I picked up in town. And Margarita sent these dresses. She says they probably won't fit, but that you're welcome to try."

"How sweet. Come on in and let's see what you've got."

The packages contained a suit, shirt and tie, socks and underwear for Pardee, a pair of shoes and a low-cut red dress with big white flowers on it for me. Quinn's taste in women's clothing left a lot to be desired, but it could also have been the selection available. I gave him an appreciative smile.

"Fashion is not my strong suit," he said, probably sensing I was less than enthusiastic.

"It's not your father's, either, so blame it on genetics." I took a look at the dresses Margarita had sent. Though beautifully made and obviously expensive, I could tell by looking at them that they were much too small. It was either dirty jeans or the red and white flowered dress. I chose to be unfashionable.

"I also got the hair dye you wanted," Quinn said, handing over the box.

It was a darker shade than I would have liked, but hey, beggars can't be choosers. I was fortunate to still have my freedom, a decent meal and a clean bed to look forward to. And, most importantly, I still had a chance to make it home in one piece.

Quinn told me we should leave our laundry in the basket

outside the door and the maid would come for it. "Dinner's in half an hour," he said, heading for the door, "and if the smells coming from the kitchen are any indication, we're in for a treat."

I took the clothing Quinn had bought for Pardee to the bedroom and woke him up, figuring he'd want to bathe. "And thanks to Quinn you'll have clean clothes to wear. Want me to run your bath?"

"Any chance I could get you to join me?"

"It's a very generous offer, Pardee, but I think I'll put on my new dress and take a walk around the garden instead."

"It'll be tough bathing with this bum arm."

"I'm sure you'll manage. And if you can't, we can always take you to the hospital."

"You're a hard woman, Josie Mayne."

"Like old times."

Pardee had a questioning look, which slowly evolved into a knowing smile. I hadn't meant to suggest anything specific, but my ex was quick to take it that way. I saw no point in disabusing him of his illusions. For all I knew, his instincts could turn out to be right.

"If you don't mind," I said, "I'll quickly put on my dress, then the bath is all yours."

I discovered the dress was too big in the bust, but I could live with that. The main problem was that it made me look like a hooker who was trying to put on airs. Before leaving, I ran Pardee's bath.

When I returned to the bedroom, Pardee had laid out his shorts, shirt, trousers, socks and shoes. "My, but don't you look beautiful," he said, checking me out.

"That's actually an insult, but I'll overlook it because I know you mean well."

"Huh?"

"Never mind, I'm going for a walk. Go jump in the tub. And watch that arm."

He grinned from one ear to the other. "I love it when you talk like a wife."

Flipping him the bird, I left.

The evening air was cool but pleasant. I could have used a light sweater or a wrap, but I was damned lucky to be walking around free in my garish dress. I wasn't about to complain.

I wandered along a lit pathway through the flower garden, stopping to smell some of the exotic blossoms. The air was rich with the fragrant scent. I felt relaxed, even happy, which was strange given our dire circumstances. Maybe I sensed Pardee and I were destined for a taste of joy before our final reckoning.

As I continued to move along a dark section of the path, I saw someone leave the main house. I instinctively stepped into the shadows. Moments later the plump little maid hurried past. She wasn't headed for the guesthouse. On an impulse, I decided to follow her. Call it intuition, but something about the girl bothered me. I felt the need to find out why.

The maid went through the woods to a cluster of outbuildings at the edge of the open fields. I assumed these were the servants' quarters. But there was also a stable and paddocks. I could hear the horses in their stalls.

The girl entered the door of a long low building that looked like a motel. It was undoubtedly her living quarters. Seeing nothing of particular interest in that, I knew I should probably turn around and head back. But something drew me to investigate further. I continued along the path until I reached the building the maid had entered.

It appeared there were perhaps half a dozen residential units. The first was dark, but light shone in the windows of the second, where the maid had gone. I decided to walk casually by and, as I passed the window, I glanced in and saw the girl speaking to an older man who sat at a table. I would have thought nothing of it except that they were both looking at the newspaper spread out before him. The girl was speaking with excitement and pointing to a picture on the front page.

I could hear their voices through the open window, but because they were speaking in Spanish I hadn't a clue what they were saying, until I picked out the word "*gringo.*" That, together with the maid's excitement and the picture, told me that my family was probably the topic of conversation.

Turning from the window, I hurried back along the path, half running, half walking until I reached the guesthouse. Entering, I found Pardee in his trousers, his hair wet and slicked back. He was struggling to put on his shirt over his bandaged arm.

"Ah, just in time," he said. "You wouldn't mind giving me a hand, would you, sweetheart?"

I helped him with the shirt and told him about the maid as I did.

"Aren't you making assumptions?" he said. "I don't doubt they were talking about us, but why shouldn't they? We're a curiosity and we're right here under their noses."

"We're a curiosity, all right. A curiosity worth ten thousand dollars to whoever turns us in."

"Josie, I do believe you're getting paranoid in your old age."

"And you're getting senile if you can't see there's a problem here."

"Okay, tell you what, we'll mention this to Margarita and see what she has to say."

That somewhat mollified me, but I still thought Pardee was being too casual. Now he was fingering his tie, giving me an I-could-use-a-hand-with-this-too look. "I never was good with ties, as you know."

I put the tie around his neck and under the collar of his shirt. Then, standing in front of him, I went to work on the knot. I could feel his eyes on me and knew he was enjoying the intimacy.

"Do you remember the last time you helped with a tie?" he asked.

I did. It was the only other time I'd ever seen Pardee wear one. It was on our wedding day. "Yes, I recall," I told him. "I was a lot younger then, and a lot more naive."

"If you were naive, what was I?"

"A lot more irresistible, for one thing."

"You're saying I've lost it?"

I cinched the knot up into the vee of his collar.

"Only relatively speaking. A woman with experience is more invulnerable than a girl with her illusions."

Pardee put his hands on my waist. I could feel their warmth right through my hooker dress and, after a few moments of his scrutiny, my heart began to bang against my ribs. The more intense his gaze became, the more I flushed.

"Invulnerable, maybe," he said, "but not invincible."

I couldn't help smiling at that. "Fortunately for me, we're due at the dinner table."

Pardee looked at my mouth. "Why fortunately?"

"Because knowing how hungry you are, I don't have to be invincible."

"I ate the snacks they brought, so I could last a few more hours without food."

"Quinn said the cook is just fabulous and is making us a meal to die for."

"You're enjoying this, aren't you?"

"What?"

"Making me choose between you and food."

"The meal is a sure thing," I said. "Maybe you should go with the bird in hand."

He took my jaw in his hand and said, "You aren't getting off that easily, lady. I've got plans for you." And then he kissed me.

I kissed him back, taking his face in my hands. Pulling back, I said, "You're quite a guy, Pardee. How many ordinary men can make their ex-wives weak in the knees?"

He gave me a happy grin. "I'm making progress, then?"

"If you weren't so damned sexy, I'd tell you to go to hell."

"Believe me, Josie, I'm flattered, but I'd rather you want me for the right reasons."

"Which are what?"

He reached out, gathered me close and said, "Since we split up I learned to express what's in my heart. I sure do wish you'd recognize the fact."

I'd rarely heard such candor, such openness, about feelings from Pardee. I guess because I knew him so well, I was skeptical. And yet, I was touched—maybe because I wanted to be touched. I bit my lip, fighting myself as I searched his eyes.

He kissed me again and I knew I was lost. But dinner gave me a reprieve. I wiggled free and said, "Come on, lover boy, we really do have to go."

Thirty

We had a lovely meal in Señora Cachero Ostos's dark wood-paneled dining room with the heavy oil paintings of saints in ornate gold frames. I watched Pardee as we ate, disbelieving of what was happening between us. Back home in California there was a man who I thought I loved waiting for me, yet here I was, ready to hop into bed with Pardee. Was it the circumstances, or was it him? We both knew that we could be coming down to our final hours of freedom. Maybe, in desperation, I wanted to make the most of whatever time I had left and grasp what happiness I could.

Sure I'd divorced Pardee. I'd known we weren't right for each other, but that didn't mean I'd stopped loving him. And now with the final grains of sand draining away, all I had left was love. That had to be the explanation.

From time to time Pardee would catch my eye and that sardonic smile of his—the one I'd seen at Pollo Gordo in San Antonio the first time I'd laid eyes on him—would play on his lips. He knew he had me then—even though at the time I hadn't had a clue—and he knew he had me now. What had changed in the interim was tens of thousands of hours together and hundreds of sexual encounters. There was no mystery in what was behind the smile, both the good and the bad, yet I remained a prisoner to it, as I remained a prisoner to Pardee. The man had my number. It was as simple as that.

The heartache I'd nursed since our divorce had been fading since we'd been together, and the urge to forgive him was now complete. The life I'd built back in California seemed as remote as our prospects of a safe return. All I had were these remaining hours with Pardee and I felt compelled to enjoy them to the max. I would make love with him again, perhaps for a final time, because I had no choice but to surrender.

But that would come later. First, we had to get through our farewell with Quinn. It would be tough. This could very well be the last time we'd see him for many years. So I tried to focus on him and the wonderful meal we shared as a family.

The cuisine was more European than traditional Mexican fare, which I suppose was a reflection of the pretensions of either the señora or her chef. It was scrumptious, though, and all three of us ate like pigs. We were probably not making the best impression on our hosts, and Lord knew, I didn't want Quinn to be embarrassed by his family. But let's face it, there's nothing like deprivation to instill an appreciation for good food and comfortable surroundings.

After our meal Margarita told us we had half an hour before Carlos would pull the Mercedes around front to take Quinn to the airport. He'd packed and his little suitcase was waiting by the door, so the three of us sat by the fire in the salon with its high, open-beam ceiling, drinking brandy and talking. The conversation reminded me of the day Quinn had left for college, with the anxiety and sadness and wistful feelings all around. Of course, the stakes were a lot higher this time, but our family of three was still breaking up.

"As soon as you two get home, we'll have a big dinner and celebrate," Quinn said.

"It's a deal," Pardee said. He left it there, but I knew what he was thinking—something like, *That's assuming Josie and I can figure out how to get out of here in one piece.*

"Right now the important thing is to get you safely on your way," I said.

"That's right," Pardee agreed. "Take the cell phone and call us as soon as you're on the plane. The reason Josie and I came down here was to free you and we want the satisfaction of knowing our effort wasn't for nothing."

"Hey, you're talking like this parting is forever," Quinn said. "It's only going to be for a couple of days."

"Nothing is for sure," Pardee replied.

I saw the concern on Quinn's face and didn't want him to worry. There'd be time enough for that when he got home. "Your father and I are professionals," I told him, "and we take our work very seriously. We'll have this game face on until we step off the plane back home."

Quinn nodded, somewhat reassured.

"But I've got a bone to pick with you," I said, trying to lighten the mood. "How can you have had a serious girlfriend for months without me having heard about it?"

"It's not that serious . . . yet," he replied. "Rosalinda and

I worked together in the Yucatán last year. We didn't start dating until last semester."

"Is she pretty?"

"What kind of question is that?" Pardee interjected. "Of course she's pretty. This is my son."

"She's pretty and really smart," Quinn said. "You'd like her, Josie."

"I would, too," Pardee said, sounding a bit defensive.

"I'm sure you would, Dad."

"Seems like she comes from a real nice family," I added.

"Same as Quinn." Pardee downed the rest of his brandy.

My stepson gave me a wink.

Margarita entered the room. "It's time," she said.

The moment I'd been both dreading and praying for had come. It was time to send Quinn home.

A few minutes later Quinn, Pardee and I stood out in front of the villa in the moonlight, waiting for Carlos to arrive with the Mercedes. I held Quinn's hand and Pardee had an arm around his shoulders. I tried to be upbeat, but it was hard. I wanted to think I'd see Quinn again, but I knew the odds were long. Despite my best efforts, my eyes filled with tears. I'd been determined to be positive, but now that the moment was upon me, I had to say what was in my heart.

"Listen," I said to him as the Mercedes came around the drive, "if you make it home and your father and I don't, come visit us, if they'll let you. And if they don't, then please write. I want to hear all about your eventual wedding, any babies you might have and all about your professional achievements."

"Listen, Ma," Quinn chided, wiping away my tear with the same tenderness as his father, "the old man doesn't die hard. And besides, I can't have my hypothetical wedding without the two of you there."

Wimp that I was, I began to sob, and my "kid" held me in his arms, patting my back.

"Come on, Josie," Pardee said, "get a grip. You're embarrassing me."

I gave him a withering look. "What happened to the new, more gentler you?"

"I'm just being practical, sweetheart. I need you tough and mean, not crying your eyes out." He gave Quinn a sly grin.

Sucking it up, I patted Quinn's cheek and said, "Take care of yourself, honey."

He hugged us both, then took his little suitcase and climbed into the Mercedes. Pardee and I stood at the huge wooden door of Señora Cachero Ostos's magnificent villa, watching him go. Pardee'd had his arm around my shoulders the day Quinn left for college and he had his arm around me now.

Once the taillights of the Mercedes had disappeared from sight, the two of us turned to go inside. As we did, I got a glimpse of a figure in the shadows at the corner of the house. It was the pudgy maid with the long black braid.

Margarita waited for us inside. I took the opportunity to ask her about the maid. "I have a very uneasy feeling about her," I said.

"Juanita is a very simple girl," Margarita replied. "I think she is in awe of you."

"You don't think her head might be turned by that reward Suarez offered? That kind of money could change her life, couldn't it?"

"If you would feel better, señora, I can speak with her."

"No, that would only upset her. If in your judgment there's nothing to worry about, then let's leave it at that."

"As you wish."

Pardee and I headed back to the guesthouse. As we walked through the garden, I took his arm. When we came to the pool, he stopped. Facing me, he held my hand. The moonlight reflected on the water, the shadows adding drama to his handsome face.

"Josie," he said, "I'm never going to be able to thank you enough for the sacrifices you've made coming down here with me. Regardless what happens, I'll deeply appreciate what you've done for as long as I live."

"I'm touched that you'd say that, but I hope this doesn't mean you've gone soft on me."

He laughed. "No, I'm as ornery as ever, but I have changed in certain respects. My heart is more open than it used to be. I've learned the importance of sharing myself. It was hard to do, but I've learned. Losing you taught me a lot, Josie. It was a very costly lesson."

"This is so unlike you . . . I'm not sure what to say, except that I'm glad and that I hope you're happier for what you've learned."

"I don't know that I'm happier, but I am wiser. And I'm convinced there's something important missing from my life." He brought both my hands to his lips and kissed them. "It's you, sweetheart."

It was such a sweet thing to say that my heart did a little dance. "You're amazing, but you should know I'm not going to be very good company until Quinn's safe," I said, hoping he'd get my point.

"I understand. I just don't know how many opportunities I'll have to tell you what's in my heart."

I could see that he shared my fears, though he wouldn't let himself dwell on it. The stronger he was, the more competent I became. That was the way it had always been. Looking at the face I'd known so well and once loved so much, I could tell he, too, realized that this couldn't be the defining moment. We had other, more immediate concerns.

"The next few hours will be agonizing," I said. "You should try to get some rest."

He rubbed my knuckles with his thumbs.

"You coming inside?" he asked.

"Actually, I think I'll sit here and enjoy the moonlight for a while."

"You want to be alone, in other words."

"If you don't mind."

He gave me a brief kiss and went inside. Once he'd closed the door, I stepped over to the edge of the pool, slipped off my shoes and sat, dangling my feet in the water. It was warm and I was half tempted to take off my clothes and go for a swim. Instead, I looked up at the moon, knowing that at that very moment hundreds of miles to the north Sky Tyler could be sitting in a deck chair outside his home, gazing at the moonlight on the sea. He would be thinking of me, I was fairly certain of that.

The incredible truth was that Sky was no longer foremost in either my heart or my mind. Pardee had reclaimed his place as the number one man in my life. What that meant exactly, I wasn't sure, but I could no longer deny that I still loved him, nor would all the resolve I could muster change that fact.

It could very well be that Pardee still wasn't right for me. He could end up as a man I'd love until my dying day, yet someone I couldn't live with, someone who drove me batty no matter how much I loved him. This experience had proven that the woman who'd come to Mexico with Pardee was the real me and that my true calling was sharing his wild and crazy life. Whether it'd be up close or from afar, whether constantly or occasionally, remained to be seen. All I knew for sure was that I loved the guy. I could only hope he wouldn't break my heart.

After searching my soul for twenty minutes more, I knew the next step would be to give in to what had probably been inevitable from the start. I should have known when Pardee showed up at the club it would end like this and that Sky's big diamond wouldn't change what I couldn't change myself. The tragic-sad fact was it might all be for naught. This would be Pardee's and my night together, maybe our last ever.

I went in the guesthouse and found him sitting at the table, cleaning our guns. I'd realized it before, but seeing him working on our weapons was yet another reminder that he would have made a hell of a soldier. He had the psychology of warfare down pat. He understood the importance of preparation and he had the best game face of any warrior I'd ever known.

This was the Pardee I'd been in awe of from the day we met, and if it wasn't the Pardee I'd fallen in love with, it was definitely the Pardee who seemed so comfortable and right for the woman I knew myself to be. The two of us were cut from the same cloth. I'd closed my eyes to the fact, but it was true.

"Hmm," he said, "I thought you might have decided to go skinny-dipping. I've been listening carefully for the sound of a splash, hoping I might sneak a peek."

"I thought about it, actually."

"I hope I wasn't what stopped you."

"As you said, you've seen it before."

"True, but I never tire of seeing you, Josie, whether naked or clothed."

How could I resist the man? I went over to the table and, standing behind him, put my arms around his neck, leaned down and gave him a kiss. "I think I missed you, too," I said, "without even knowing it."

"Better late than never."

"But I'm afraid maybe too late."

He looked at me over his shoulder. "This is the most down I've ever seen you, Josie," he said, patting my cheek. "You okay?"

I began to massage his shoulders. "I'm sorry, but I have this ominous feeling. I know you're trying to be your usual positive self, but I sense it in you, too. Or am I wrong?"

"It's because of Quinn, sweetheart. Once he's on that plane, the monkey will be off our backs."

"I hope you're right."

"You know, it'd help if we start figuring out how we're going to get out of this mess. What do you say we do a little brainstorming while we wait for Quinn's call?"

"Okay, but I want to ask you something first. And please tell me the truth. Do you really love me, or are you just lonely?"

He put down the gun he'd been holding and pulled me around and onto his lap. "I loved you before. I love you now. I'll love you always."

Tears bubbled from my eyes. "You are the most damnable man I've ever known."

"You didn't like my answer?"

"No, I liked it too much."

"You know what, Josie Mayne? I didn't understand you before and I don't think I understand you now. But maybe that's a good thing. It's probably why I love you."

This time I kissed him on the mouth. "Can we delay our council of war long enough for me to take a nice hot bath?"

"How would you feel about a bottle of champagne?"

"You planning on a run to the liquor store?"

"Margarita said the wine cellar is well stocked. Maybe she'd give me a bottle if I promise to send the señora a case."

"It's a good way to test her optimism, if nothing else."

The next couple of hours were right up there among the most difficult of my life. Worrying about Quinn, worrying about my heart, I think I wore a groove in the tile floor, pacing back and forth. I was in my robe. Pardee had built a fire and sat in an armchair, staring at the flames. One or the other of us occasionally said something, but mostly we were silent. The bottle of champagne Margarita had given him sat in the ice bucket waiting for Quinn's call. To work out a plan we had to be in a creative frame of mind and we were both too anxious to be productive. We put that off, too.

Every once in a while I'd come up behind the chair where he sat and I'd put my hand on his shoulder or massage his neck and shoulders. I'd given him regular massages when we were married. It was starting to feel like old times. And though it had been years since we'd made love, in a way we'd become lovers again. Quinn had reunited us for this mission and he'd reunited our hearts.

Finally, I got so anxious I went in to lie on the bed, hoping I could relax. I thought of my parents. I thought of Baron. I thought about everyone I'd ever held dear. At about the time Quinn's flight was scheduled to depart, the telephone rang. The guesthouse had a separate line and Quinn had the number so he could call us directly. Pardee appeared at the bedroom door. I reached over and snatched up the receiver. "Hello?"

It was Quinn. "Josie, they just closed the door and are pushing the plane back from the gate. There were cops in the terminal building, but not an army. Nobody said boo to me. I can't talk anymore, so see you back home. Tell the old man thanks."

I gave Pardee a happy thumbs-up. "We love you, honey!" I cried. It was half laugh and half sob.

I put the phone down and the next thing I knew, Pardee was on the bed and we were holding each other. I cried and he kissed my tears and told me again that he loved me. Then I did something I never thought I'd ever do again. I told Pardee I loved him, too. "And I want you to make love with me," I said. "The way we used to."

"Josephine, this just may be the happiest day of my life."

Thirty-one

I don't know what it was about Pardee pouring champagne bare-chested that got to me so, but it did. The combination had been my downfall in Las Vegas when we'd gone there on R&R together after our first trip to Mexico, and it was having the same effect on me now. As he carried two glasses brimming with bubbly to the bed, I thought of the lecture on the dangers of booze that my father used to give to me when I was a teenager. Dad would recite this little saying, which he got from a book of quotes. "First the man takes a drink,/ Then the drink takes a drink,/ Then the drink takes the man," he would say. "The same applies to a girl, only double."

Until Pardee had come into my life, I considered my father's saying sexist, but then I realized that Dad (or the author) truly understood the inherent danger of a man like Pardee. I can tell you this: It didn't take much inhibition to get aroused with my former husband at the controls. The thing that made him so effective as a lover was that he wasn't predictable. Pardee could be forceful or gentle, blatant or subtle. His manly, macho image completely belied his skill in the bedroom. I don't know who wrote that song about a man with a slow hand, but if it wasn't a woman, it was somebody who understood women about as well as Pardee.

I was lying on my side, propped on an elbow as he reached across the bed and handed me a glass. Then he carefully crawled onto the bed and lay next to me.

"Well, we've done it, Josie," he said. He looked about as happy as I'd ever seen him.

"Thank God."

"Now we can think about ourselves," he said.

"Amen to that."

"I propose we begin with a little thankfulness." He extended his glass toward mine. "To things getting back where they should be," he said, clicking my glass.

"In bed?"

Pardee shrugged. "Wherever we are will do, as long as we're together."

I was touched. "What a nice sentiment."

"It's more than a sentiment, sweetheart. It's the truth."

We each sipped our champagne. My eyes slid down his chest. A shiver moved down my spine. The chest was the same, but damn if that man didn't seem different. It used to be that I looked *at* Pardee. Now it felt like I could look *into* him. His veneer wasn't as hard as it used to be. There was an openness about him.

When he'd shown up at the club the night of my engagement to Sky, he seemed like the Pardee of old—arrogant, wisecracking, profane. "I'm curious about something," I said. "If you've been transformed by love, why is it just now beginning to show?"

"I knew I wouldn't be able to sweet-talk you into reconsidering a relationship with me because I had too much baggage. And I could see you wouldn't be giving up that big diamond easily, so I decided to be the guy I'd always been. After all, I supposedly came to see you about doing a job with me."

"Supposedly?"

"The problem was real enough, but I had some selfish motives, too."

"You mean rescuing Quinn wasn't the real reason?"

"Sure it was. But I was damned glad to have a good excuse to team up with you again."

I took a big sip of wine. "That really is despicable, you know."

"Give me another reason you'd have left Sky to come away with me."

"There isn't one."

"I rest my case."

I gave him the evil eye, but only halfheartedly. "I'm not mad, but I feel like I've been duped."

"It was for a very good cause. Two very good causes, as a matter of fact."

"Did you really want me that badly?"

"For years, sweetheart. The problem was I had a hell of a mountain to climb."

"And now here you are at the summit."

"Almost," he said with a smile.

Reaching out, he touched my lip with his finger. "You're still a damned fine-looking woman," he said.

"For somebody so old?"

"No, for somebody so divorced from me."

I laughed and kissed his hand. Then, scooting a little closer, I put my palm against the flat of his chest, savoring the sensation.

"This was what I missed most about you," I said, running my fingertip lightly over his nipple.

"That's all?"

I chugged a big gulp of champagne, then put down the glass. "The bounty hunting, too, of course."

"My fondest recollections of you are much more laudable," he said, tracing the vee at the opening of my robe with his finger.

When he passed over the swell of my breast, I shivered. "Which recollections?"

"Walking hand in hand to the top of the hill behind the double-wide to watch the sunset. Eating breakfast in bed after making love on a Sunday morning. The time we cleaned the stable together after the roan mare dropped her foal."

"Cleaning the stable?"

"I think about that all the time. We worked real hard and were sweating like the dickens. Both of us. I remember there were beads of perspiration all across your forehead, the late afternoon sun giving your face a golden glow. Your shirt was soaked and your hair wet at the temples. It looked darker than usual, which made your eyes—eyes as clear and blue as the morning sky—stand out all the more. At one point you stopped sweeping for a moment and leaned on your push broom to catch your breath. As you did, you wiped your brow with your forearm. You didn't notice, but I must have stared at your neck for a minute. It was so long and sleek and smooth. I had an urge to bite it."

I laughed.

"It's true, Josie. There were times when I wanted to swallow you whole because there never seemed to be a way I could get enough of you."

His voice and faint smile seemed so sad just then. I felt such love, such deep, abiding love, I thought for a moment I would cry. But I took a few deep breaths and managed to stay in control. "Why didn't you tell me any of this before?"

"I don't know. At the time it seemed too private to share. But I held on to it, I'll tell you that. Probably cried myself to sleep a hundred times thinking of that day, the image of you burned into my brain. Including your crazy legs, of course." His eyes glistened despite his smile. "I've missed you, sweetheart. Missed you one hell of a lot."

I finished the last of my champagne and sat my glass on the nightstand behind me. Pardee finished his off, too, and I took the glass from him. Then I scooted right up next to him so that we were practically nose to nose.

"You know what I'm thinking now, cowboy? I'm wondering why in the hell I ever left you." I kissed him lightly on the lips.

"You left me because I deserved it. But I think I deserve to get you back now."

"Oh, you do? Why's that?"

"Because I'm giving you everything I've got, everything in my heart. I know you didn't believe me when I told you I've changed, but I truly have."

He didn't have to convince me because I could see it—

or, more accurately, feel it. In fact, I felt things I'd never felt before with any man, including him.

Pardee kissed me then, a little more firmly than I'd kissed him. My heart started beating so hard it seemed he must have been able to hear it. Or feel it when he ran his index finger down the side of my throat.

I swallowed hard when his hand slid under the opening in my robe and cupped my breast. His thumb barely touched my nipple before it turned hard as a pebble.

He'd been gentle until now, the man with the slow hand, but I could see a mask of desire move across his face. There was a yearning for conquest in his eyes. With a sweep of his hand he loosened the tie of my robe and pushed back the flaps.

He looked me over with the same steamy intensity I'd seen so often before. For him this moment was five years in the making and paid for with hundreds of lonely nights of regret. He'd come to claim his woman.

When I fell back on the pillow, Pardee lowered his face to my breast, taking my nub in his mouth and caressing it with his lips. He circled the nipple a few times with his tongue, moved to my other breast, teasing it the same way before he dragged his tongue across my belly, leaving a trail of coolness in his wake.

My whole body throbbed, my fingers tingled, my muscles twitched. I was ready for him, but Pardee wasn't through. He pressed his face into my muff and inhaled my scent, bringing me to the edge.

I took his head in my hands and held him hard against me as my insides quivered. When his tongue found me, I gave a little cry, wanting him now more than ever.

I came once even before he entered me, then twice more. Before we were through we'd torn the bed up and I'd clawed his back and butt, trying to get all of him I could. I was a wild woman, and by the time it was over I knew I'd been thoroughly fucked.

"Lord," I said, struggling to catch my breath. The sweat was pouring off me. I opened my eyes to see the man who'd been my husband staring at me. "Will you remember this day, too?" I asked.

"Damned straight I will," he said, tapping my nose. "You?"

"Forever."

"No regrets, then?"

I looked square into his eyes. "We've had some fabulous times in the sack," I said. "None were better than this. But you want to hear something funny? This wasn't about sex."

"It *wasn't*?"

"Well, not entirely." I studied him for a long minute, then teared up. "You really made me feel loved." As I said it, my voice cracked.

He put his arms around me and gathered me close. "You *are* loved, sweetheart. More than you'll ever know."

I shed a few happy tears, but inevitably my fears began to creep in. I wondered if this would prove to be the last consensual sex I'd have for years. I wondered if this was all God would give us. Would it be a teaser or the crowning moment of a lifetime?

I had to ask Pardee what he thought because he had the best instincts of any man I knew. "Honey, is this the beginning for us or is it the end?"

He gave a little laugh. "You think this was all I wanted?

Josie, darling, this is only the beginning. I want much more than this, I want you to be my wife again."

It shouldn't have shocked me, but it did. *"Wife?"*

"Yes, I want you to marry me. We belong together."

I closed my eyes, stunned. I'd been worrying that what we'd just experienced was the tragic end of something beautiful, poignant and sad. Was I being unrealistic in not trying to think ahead, or was Pardee?

"Don't tell me you're thinking about Sky," he said.

I shook my head. "No."

"Then what's wrong?"

"Marriage isn't something we can decide about after one glorious night. We need to get home. We need to be together for a while."

He pondered that a moment and, apparently deciding it seemed innocent enough, he acted relieved. I saw every step of the thought process on his face.

"Then you'll come back to the ranch with me?" he said.

I don't know why, but the matter of where we'd go seemed academic. The much larger question was if we'd make it home at all.

"Just hold me," I murmured. "We can talk about it tomorrow."

Pardee kissed my forehead and I pressed my face into his neck, inhaling his scent. I'd said we could talk tomorrow, but if my fears won out, it might be that there'd be no decision about the future for a very, very long time. To put it mildly, the future was in doubt.

Thirty-two

The next morning I awoke alone in the bed, but feeling like a married woman again. I didn't know what had happened to Pardee. I'd slept so soundly I hadn't been aware of him leaving. That was nothing new, though. He was a morning person. On the ranch he often regarded breakfast as an early lunch break.

Not being in any rush to pop out of bed, I luxuriated in my sumptuous surroundings, fondly savoring my recollections of last night's lovemaking. Five years was a long hiatus, but as a lover, Pardee had no equal. I'd been well aware of what I was missing, but going without for so long had served to make our reunion all the more special.

What I liked best about it was the new dimension. My former husband was indeed more open and loving. The man might still have the heart of a thief, but he'd been transformed by losing me and I was the beneficiary.

I beamed, thinking about it. But I also knew my life had

been turned on its head. My engagement to Sky was over—if not officially, it was certainly dead in spirit. And what's more, Pardee wanted me to marry him again. Between that and being the object of a nationwide manhunt, I had a lot to think about. It was a classical good news, bad news situation.

Obviously, the next step was to figure out how we were going to save our collective ass. I also had to decide what I was going to say if Pardee raised the issue of us becoming a couple again.

One rose did not a summer make and I was well aware that the best intentions could crumble under the pressures of everyday life. Pardee and I needed time to find out how enduring our love could be. But first, we had to get home.

I heard the front door and, assuming it was Pardee, I sat up in bed, fluffing my hair and discreetly pulling the sheet up to cover my naked body. It was a good thing, because he wasn't alone.

Pardee stuck his head in the door and, seeing me waiting, said, "Oh, good, you're awake. How about some breakfast?"

He stepped back so that the plump little maid, who in my paranoia I'd decided was our nemesis, entered the bedroom with a tray. She did not make eye contact with me or say a word. Pardee directed her to put the tray on the foot of the bed, which she did and promptly left. Margarita's and Pardee's assurances notwithstanding, I still had a bad feeling about the girl.

Hearing the front door close, I put her from my mind. Pardee came and sat on the bed beside me. He leaned over and kissed me.

"You're beautiful," he said, "and last night you made me very, very happy."

"Likewise."

"Really, Josie?"

I caressed his cheek. "Really."

He searched my eyes for hints of my true feelings. That amused me, for I had spent many mornings during our marriage wondering about his.

"We have lots to talk about," he said. "Would you rather have breakfast first, talk first or do both?"

"How about both?"

"Okay," he said, retrieving the tray, which he put on the bed beside me.

There was a pot of coffee, orange juice, a basket of pastries and a fruit compote. It looked delicious. Pardee handed me the juice.

"Have you eaten, honey?"

"I had breakfast at the big house with Margarita. We discussed developments."

I took a drink of orange juice. "What developments?"

Pardee reached for a folded newspaper on the tray and handed it to me. "We've become really famous."

On the front page was a picture of our drunken farmer friend, standing in front of the chopper I'd borrowed from IGI. Next to it were the drawings of us. The likenesses weren't good enough that I'd fear walking down the main drag of Oaxaca because of it, but we were unique enough that we'd draw attention.

"What does the story say?" I asked.

"It's a pretty full account of what we've been up to. They've followed our trail from the downed helicopter and Grandpa's old truck to Oaxaca and the motel. We're believed still to be in the area and a massive search is under way."

I looked inside the paper to where the story continued. There was a picture of our old friend Fernando Suarez. "He looks all grown up now," I noted.

"But he hasn't forgotten his time in jail in Texas, thanks to us. According to the paper, he's made our capture a top priority. I guess because of his father, the story has gotten national attention. The country's top police official is flying down from Mexico City today to show support. He and Suarez will hold a joint press conference. They want us pretty bad, sweetheart."

The news didn't do wonders for my appetite, but I took a pastry and the coffee Pardee poured me anyway. "So what do we do?"

"I've been working on it," he said. "In fact, I've developed a plan and put the wheels in motion. Carlos told me Oaxaca is ringed with roadblocks. The only way out of here is by air."

"Surely they'll be watching the airport."

"Absolutely."

"Then?"

"We won't be flying commercial, sweetheart."

"What are we going to do, charter a plane?"

"Sort of. Last night while you were taking your bath, I made a call to the States. Don't get pissed, Josie, but I had a little chat with Tyler."

"You talked to Sky?"

"Yeah, I explained that we were sort of stuck using public transportation and that the guardians of the public peace weren't likely to be cooperative. I asked if there was any chance one of his corporate jets might be in the area this morning because we'd like to hitch a ride."

"You asked him to send a plane for us."

"I suggested that if he wanted to see you again, it might be a useful contribution to the cause. I'm hopeful that he'll have no problem with me tagging along."

"You did this before we made love?"

"I didn't want to burden you."

I flushed, seeing what he meant. "It isn't very considerate to ask a man for help, then turn around and screw his fiancée, is it?"

"No, and I didn't want to put you on the spot. That's why I didn't say anything before now."

My eyes flashed. "Is that why, Pardee? You didn't want to put me on the spot or you didn't want to mess up the seduction you had planned?"

"We were going to make love, Josie. I didn't see any reason to add to your anxiety."

"You seemed to deal with *your* anxiety over stabbing Sky in the back just fine. Don't you feel just a little guilty?"

"Hell, you were engaged to the man and he'd already loaned me money—"

"So what's the big deal in asking him to send a plane, then seducing his fiancée on top of it?"

"I don't mean to sound unkind," he said, "but which of us owed him more?"

It was a shot across my bow, but Pardee was right. My betrayal was much more egregious than what he had done. And he had probably done me a kindness by not making an issue of it before we made love.

"I apologize for being sharp," I said. "I guess I feel more guilty than I realize. I'm wrong to blame you for what's my sin."

"It wasn't a sin, Josie," he said, taking my hand. "We love each other. Had the circumstances been different, you would have talked to Sky."

"Yes, but asking for him to help me escape Mexico so I can be with you is the height of hypocrisy. What kind of woman does that?"

"That's why I called him rather than ask you to do it."

Pardee may have done me a kindness, after all. Still, I did not look forward to stepping off a plane only to tell Skylar I was breaking our engagement. It was almost as bad as the prospect of rotting in a Mexican jail. Almost.

"I guess I'll have to deal with that later," I said with a sigh. "So what's the plan?"

"Sky will have a plane at general aviation at eleven this morning. I don't know exactly where that is, so we'll have to find it. The field can't be too large, so it shouldn't be hard. The kicker, of course, will be the cops, lots of cops. Carlos should be able to get us to the airport without much difficulty. Nobody will expect us to be chauffeured in a Mercedes, though you never know. I figure the hard part will be getting from point A to point B once we're inside."

I checked my watch. "When do we have to leave here?"

"Carlos said around ten-thirty."

There was plenty of time, but I had to dye my hair and get dressed. Stuffing a pastry in my mouth, I threw back the covers and got out of bed. I intended to make a dash for the bath, but Pardee grabbed me, taking me into his arms.

"I haven't had a chance to give you a proper good-morning," he said, "or to tell you I love you."

I smiled and pressed my face to his chest. "I hope we haven't turned the karma gods against us," I lamented.

"The karma gods have had many chances to do us in," he said. "They always pass."

"But as my first husband used to say, 'You can't rely on luck to save your *cajones* forever.'"

"And second."

"Huh?"

"First and second husband. He's right about not being able to count on luck, by the way. But you know what? I personally will settle for just one more favorable roll of the dice."

I dyed my hair, all but crying when I looked in the mirror. My beautiful red hair was gone, swallowed up by inky black dye. I could tell Pardee hated it, too, but he didn't complain, noting instead that the dark hair looked better with the dress.

He put on his suit, sticking his gun under his belt. We looked at ourselves in the mirror and didn't know whether we looked more like desperadoes or circus clowns. Pronouncing ourselves as ready as we'd ever be, we bade the guesthouse adieu, knowing we'd have fond memories of the place that would be with us the rest of our lives.

We were halfway to the main house when Margarita came running toward us on the path, a stricken look on her face. "Señores," she said, "we are lost! The police have discovered you're here. They are coming to the rancho as we speak."

"How do you know?" Pardee said.

"I have a relative who is a state police official. He telephoned to warn me so that I can take precautions. You were right, señora," she said to me. "We were betrayed by someone on the staff. Perhaps Juanita. I am so sorry. I am responsible."

"Never mind that," Pardee said. "Does Carlos have the car ready? Maybe we can get out of here before the police arrive."

"It is not possible," Margarita said. "The veterinarian arrived a short while ago and said that there are roadblocks already established on the Monte Albán Road and that a large force of police are assembling a few kilometers from here. Even if you hid in the trunk, surely the car would be stopped and searched."

Pardee gave me a look, his expression dark. "This is shaping up to be a rerun of the Battle of the Alamo," he said. "We're outgunned and outnumbered."

"Margarita," I said, "is there another way out? Another road?"

She shook her head. "No, I'm sorry, the only access to the rancho is the Monte Albán Road."

"What if we go overland on foot? There must be a road somewhere to the north."

"Yes, but it is perhaps ten miles or more."

"It would take us half a day or more to get there," Pardee said. "And then what would we do? Call a taxi?"

"Wait," I said, "I have an idea. You have horses on the rancho, don't you, Margarita?"

"Yes, the señora's grandson keeps four riding horses in the stable. He frequently comes from Mexico City on weekends to ride with his friends."

"Would he mind if we borrowed a couple?"

"For an emergency such as this, I'm sure not."

"You don't plan to ride to the airport on horseback do you?" Pardee said.

"No, but if we can get to that road we have a chance. What if Carlos meets us there? We may not be able to get through a roadblock, but why couldn't he?"

"Josephine," Pardee said, putting an arm around me and kissing the top of my head, "you're a genius."

"Señores, there is a small village at the place where this road I told you about crosses a creek. To the west of the village a quarter of a mile is an abandoned gas station. The roof has caved in and it is in ruins. I will tell Carlos to meet you there. Later I will send men to retrieve the horses."

"Margarita, you're a lifesaver," I enthused, giving her a hug.

"You must go quickly," she said. "I will tell you how to get to the stable."

"I already know. It would be nice if Juanita and the other servants don't see us leave."

"They have all been summoned to the house and wait for me there. Goodbye, my friends. And I am so sorry for this trouble."

"Listen, Margarita," Pardee said, "if the police give you any grief about sheltering us, tell them your life was threatened." He pulled his gun out from under his coat and pointed it at her. "Now, where is the stable?"

Smiling, she pointed up the path.

Pardee and I took off at a run. We arrived at the stable breathless, and Pardee quickly checked the horses, selecting two for us to ride. I found the tack room and lugged out a couple of saddles and bridles. It was fortunate Pardee was an expert horseman because he had our mounts saddled up in minutes.

And none too soon. Even from the rear of the rancho compound we could hear the roar of the armada of police vehicles approaching from the road. Neither of us were dressed for horseback riding, but the situation couldn't have been more desperate.

We climbed into the saddles and took off to the north at a full gallop across the open plain. After we'd gone half a mile, Pardee reined in his horse and we stopped and looked back.

"Doesn't look like they have air cover, but when they discover we've flown the coop, they might call in some police choppers. I wish the terrain wasn't so damned open. We can be seen for miles."

"There's a tree line down there," I said, pointing to the east. "Looks like a creek bed."

"It runs north-south. Maybe it's the one that goes through the village Margarita talked about. Maybe we should follow it and if there are aircraft we'll have a better chance of finding cover."

"Lead the way."

Pardee again took off at a gallop, heading for the creek. Fortunately it was essentially dry, with only a tiny rivulet of water coursing the bed. We followed the creek north at a more measured pace. We had no idea how long it would take Carlos to circle around to the other road—assuming he was able to get past the police—but we had no other option but to press ahead and hope for the best.

We had gone perhaps three miles from the ranch compound when Pardee spotted a chopper coming from the direction of town. We reined in our mounts in a stand of cottonwood trees and watched the bird pass over a quarter of a mile or so to the east. Once the chopper was out of sight, we took off again, this time at a comfortable gallop.

"Keep your eyes peeled," Pardee hollered. "We want to see them before they see us."

I looked back frequently and it was a good thing because I spotted the helicopter only moments before we heard the *thomp-thomp* of its rotors, giving us the vital seconds we needed to find cover. This time the chopper flew directly overhead.

"He's checking out the creek bed," Pardee said.

"But he didn't spot us or he'd be circling."

"Right. It's hard to know whether they're conducting a general search or whether they know where we're headed. I guess we can't worry about it, though."

We came to a stretch where there were no trees of consequence for better than a quarter of a mile. It would mean a dash across open terrain. Stopping, we listened, hoping that we'd hear the chopper if it was still in the area.

"Race you to those trees," Pardee said with a grin.

We took off at full speed. Midway there was a fallen log that spanned the creek bed. Not every horse likes to jump, so all we could do was pray our mounts were courageous. I was in the lead and my horse jumped the log. Glancing back, I saw Pardee make it, as well. I reached the first stand of trees and stopped. Pardee reined in his horse beside me. Seconds later the chopper passed over us again, retracing its earlier route. We sighed with relief when it continued on.

"You were quite a sight with the skirts of that red dress flying," Pardee hooted. "Let's hope we don't see any bulls."

"Better a bull than another helicopter."

We made good time without any further sightings of aircraft, stopping once to rest the horses. After the animals had a good blow, we took off again. In half an hour the village Margarita spoke of came into view.

"I say we avoid the village and head cross-country for the abandoned gas station," Pardee said. "The fewer people who see us, the better."

It made sense to me. At this point peasants seeking the reward were probably a bigger danger than aircraft.

We didn't know exactly where the gas station was, but we got lucky and rode right up to it. There was no sign of Carlos.

The road was a minor one, not very well paved. The good news was there wasn't much traffic. Pardee took the horses around back and we sat on an old bench under the sagging overhang.

"Wouldn't you know it," he said, "not a Coke machine in sight."

We'd both worked up a pretty good sweat. I knew I looked like hell—even for a hooker.

"What's your guess?" I said. "Is Carlos going to show?"

"Fifty-fifty."

"How long do we wait before we start hitchhiking?"

Pardee checked his watch. "How much does Sky love you?"

"He'd tell the plane to wait until I showed up, or until they got word I was arrested."

"Then I say we err on the side of caution."

Half an hour passed with no sign of Carlos. I could tell Pardee was losing patience, especially when he got up and started pacing.

"I'm afraid the karma gods have finally bit us in the ass," he said. "Let's stop the next vehicle and try to bribe the driver to take us to the airport."

It was five minutes before the next vehicle approached. It wasn't a police Jeep as I had feared, given our luck. Instead it was a blue Mercedes.

Thirty-three

It was ten minutes to eleven and Carlos said we were only fifteen minutes from the airport. Amazingly we'd almost make it on time. Pardee said that arriving late was probably better. The longer we hung around the airport, the more likely we'd be spotted. The jet Sky had sent would wait.

As we guzzled down the bottled water Carlos had brought, he explained that he'd escaped from the rancho before the police arrived, but that he'd been detained at the roadblock for an hour. With no reason to keep him, they'd finally allowed him to go.

"But I'm afraid there is bad news, señores," he said. "On the radio they are reporting the airport has been closed and no one is allowed to enter."

"Sounds like Suarez is thinking right along with us," Pardee said.

"I will drive you as close as possible, but perhaps you must enter on foot."

The outlook was more bleak, the challenge more insurmountable, with each turn. I tried not to think about it, instead doing what I could to make myself presentable. Using Pardee's handkerchief and the bottled water, I gave myself a sponge bath. Pardee watched, seemingly enjoying himself.

"I don't know what it is about you and bathing, sweetheart, but I find it a turn-on."

I could see he was in his cheerful, upbeat mode, doing what he could to keep my spirits up. We soon were on the boulevard that led to the airport. My stomach was in a knot. Pardee took my hand.

As we cruised along, a siren sounded behind us and my heart stopped. I knew this was it. Carlos pulled over, but two motorcycle cops continued on past, followed by a big black limousine, followed by two more motorcycle cops.

"Holy Mother," Carlos said, "it's the governor."

I couldn't believe it. "What irony."

"He's probably on his way to the airport to meet that national police official," Pardee said. Then he snapped his fingers. "Hey, this might be the break we need. Carlos, catch up with them."

I looked at Pardee. "Are you crazy?"

"No, just brilliant, sweetheart."

"Get right up behind them," Pardee told the chauffeur.

"Why?" I said.

"We're going to become part of the entourage. A nice shiny Mercedes would likely be carrying the governor's aides, wouldn't it? We'll sail through the roadblocks with them."

I laughed with glee. It was ingenious. And sure enough, it worked. We made it through without a hitch.

Xoxocotlan International Airport was not large, nor particularly busy. The terminal building was modern, if small, with a curved facade and tall glass windows that rose nearly to the high, flat roof. There appeared to be two or three entrances with a few more cops posted at each. Suarez's limo pulled up in front and Pardee told Carlos to stop short of the terminal building, so our arrival wouldn't be so obvious.

Once the passengers in the limo entered the building, we thanked Carlos for all his help and bade him goodbye.

"Have a safe trip, señores," he called as we stepped out.

Pardee closed the rear passenger door. "I'd settle for a crash landing at any airport on American soil," he muttered under his breath.

I took his arm, wondering if the karma gods might not have reconsidered their decision. "Why don't we look around before we go inside?" I suggested. "We might be able to spot a private jet parked somewhere. How many are there likely to be?"

"Good idea."

There was a fair amount of vegetation around the building—flowering shrubs, palms and other trees. A cyclone fence enclosed the field. There was one commercial jetliner at the terminal building, which probably only had two or three gates at most. A smaller, propeller-driven commercial aircraft was parked on the tarmac, as well. From our vantage point we could see single- and twin-engine private aircraft in a more remote tie-down area, but nothing resembling a corporate jet.

"Our ride is either late or parked somewhere else on the field," Pardee said. "I guess we'll have to inquire inside, after all."

"I don't think both of us should go in," I said, "at least not together."

"You're probably right."

"How about if I give it a shot?" I said. "Might as well find out if this black hair is going to fool anybody. Besides, if they grab me you'll have a better shot making it on the lam than I would, so let's go with the odds."

"You never lacked for courage, Josie."

"I got my reckless abandon from you," I said.

"You mean I've left a legacy?"

"A small one," I chided.

Pardee liked that. He gave my cheek a pinch. "Break a leg, kid."

I headed for the nearest entrance, remembering one of Pardee's dicta—when outnumbered or in doubt, be brazen. So I swung it a little extra, hoping the cops would look at my ass, not me. I got to the door and had the full attention of the officers, porters and taxi drivers who were standing around. One of the cops opened the door for me.

I wasn't sure who to apply to, but the information counter looked like a good place to start. The girl behind the counter sat on a stool, reading a magazine. Being a shrewd observer of the human condition, she addressed me in English.

"May I help you, señora?"

"Where is the general aviation section of the airport?" I asked.

"You mean for the private planes?"

"Yes."

"There are two. On each side of the terminal, a few hundred meters away. The ones this way," she said, pointing the direction Pardee had gone to have a look, "are mostly local. The visitors go usually to the other one. Do you wish to lease a plane?"

"No, I'm meeting my husband, who's flying in from the States. He's said he'd be here at eleven, but I don't know where to look."

"I can call the control and see if a plane has recently arrived. Do you know the call number of the aircraft?"

"I'm afraid I don't. It's a corporate jet, that's all I can tell you."

"What is the name?"

"My husband's name is Sky Tyler."

The girl got on the phone. I didn't know if Sky would be doing this in his name or if he'd simply retained a pilot to come pick us up, but there couldn't have been all that many private jets landing in the past half hour.

The girl spoke Spanish to whoever was on the other end of the line, of course, and I couldn't understand what she was saying. I only hoped she wasn't speaking to airport security or the police. She ended her call.

"They tell me, señora, that there is an executive jet on final approach, the only one they know of. Perhaps there was a delay."

"That's probably Sky. Where would I go to meet him?"

"Back out the front of the building and two hundred meters that way. There is a gate. Tell the guard you are meeting a private plane."

"Thank you very much."

"My pleasure, señora."

Having the information I wanted, I headed for the entrance. As I approached the doors, I heard a commotion behind me. Turning, I saw a crowd of people walking toward the exit. I figured it must be Suarez and his guest, along with their aides and reporters. I hurried out the door, only to be pushed into the waiting crowd by one of the officers stationed in front of the building. Other cops cleared a way for the dignitaries.

Rather than run, I tried to melt into the crowd. Seconds later a dapperly dressed young man in a dark suit and a shorter, silver-haired man came out of the terminal building with the entourage. The better part of a decade had passed, but I recognized the younger man's sultry, brooding eyes. It was Fernando Suarez, all right.

My red and white dress was not exactly camouflage, but it was probably more obvious in motion than stationary, so I stood as still as I could. My back to the building, I applauded along with the others as Fernando Suarez stood at the doorway for a moment, waving at the crowd.

I don't think I took a breath until Suarez and his companion began to walk toward the limo. Thankfully, they were in conversation and didn't appear to be paying much attention to their surroundings. Or so I thought until Suarez came to a sudden stop not ten feet from me.

He looked at me. I smiled. His expression was questioning, then I saw the lightbulb go on in his brain. He gave a little laugh.

"Señores," he said, to no one in particular, "we are indeed honored. Unless I'm mistaken, we are in the presence of the infamous Josie Mayne." His brows rose superciliously. "Madam, is that you beneath the bad dye job?"

It was a classical "oh, shit" moment. There was nothing to say my life was over, so I fell back on instinctive politeness. "*Buenos días,* Governor," I said. "You seem to have come a long way since we last met."

"Indeed I have, Ms. Mayne. What a pity the same cannot be said of you. Still up to your dirty tricks, from what I hear. And where is Robin Hood?"

"You never know, Governor. But he does seem to pop up at the most unexpected times, doesn't he?"

It was wishful thinking on my part, but for once fantasy and reality coalesced. Out of nowhere came a sudden and violent burst of gunfire. People around me dove for cover, women screaming as bullets shattered the big plate-glass windows and slammed into the facade of the building.

Pardee charged up the sidewalk, firing away like a madman. The nearest officer was one of the motorcycle cops who'd brought up the rear of the motorcade. Pardee knocked him to the ground, screaming, "Josie!" as he continued to fire.

Somehow I had the presence of mind to run to where Pardee was climbing on the motorcycle. He tossed me the gun and I jumped on the bike behind him. We went roaring up the drive in a hail of gunfire. I felt a bullet rip through my billowing skirt, but somehow I wasn't hit.

"The jet's coming in up there," I yelled, pointing straight ahead. "They called to confirm. There's a gate. Look for the gate."

Within seconds we were there. Pardee stopped. A small hangar and office building stood on the other side of the fence. A few aircraft were parked in the tie-down area but nothing resembling a corporate jet.

"Where?"

"Maybe it hasn't landed. It was on its final approach when they called."

The sleepy guard stepped out of the little guardhouse. Back in the direction of the terminal building we heard sirens. The other motorcycles were in pursuit.

Pardee revved the engine and we roared through the gate, nearly knocking the guard down. We stopped briefly to scan the field and spotted a sleek private jet approach the end of the runway off to our left.

"That's probably him," Pardee said, glancing back at the gate. I looked, too. The motorcycle cops and a couple of police Jeeps were almost there. "It's a cinch we can't wait for our ride here. We're going to have to meet them at the end of the runway."

He gunned the engine and we took off again, doing a wheelie as we sped toward the far end of the field. The jet, meanwhile, had touched down. We were on the taxiway that ran parallel to the main runway. The jet zipped past us, but as it slowed we gained on it and soon we were alongside it. I waved frantically, hoping to get the attention of the pilot or somebody else on board.

I looked over my shoulder. Santa Anna's legions were in hot pursuit, sirens blaring. By the time the jet had finally come to a stop we were next to it and Pardee started banging on the side of the plane. I had no idea whether they'd open the door for us. It had to be against every aviation regulation ever written.

"We'll never make it," I cried, seeing the cops were only seconds away.

"Desperate circumstances call for desperate measures," Pardee yelled over the scream of the jet engines. "Get off, Josie. Our only chance is for me to divert them long enough for you to get aboard. Give me the gun."

I realized Pardee was going to sacrifice himself and I couldn't allow him to do it. We'd always been a team, always stuck together. I hadn't let him sink at the lake and I couldn't let him fall to the enemy now.

"Now, Josie!" he roared.

"No! I'm not going to leave you."

Pardee was in no mood to argue. He yanked the gun from my hand and swung his arm around, knocking me off the bike. I landed on my butt on the runway. "I think I'll take ground transportation home," he said with a grin. "Will you wait for me?"

"Yes!" I screamed over the roar of the jet's engines.

After a thumbs-up he thundered off, directly toward the oncoming cops. I got to my feet, watching the motorcycles and Jeeps scatter in the face of Pardee's suicidal frontal assault. The bastard was using my tactics from the air battle at the lake.

The jet's door opened a few seconds later and the boarding steps folded out. Sky stood at the door, his hand extended.

"Come on, darling," he said. "Quickly."

I looked back across the airfield. It looked like a demolition derby with cycles and Jeeps going in every which direction. I heard an occasional gunshot. I couldn't pick out Pardee in the melee.

"Josie, come on!"

I mounted the steps and walked into Sky's open arms. The flight attendant lifted the stairs and Sky took me to one of the club seats. I dropped into it, exhausted. Mostly I was terrified at the thought of Pardee being out there, mixing it up with a small army of cops. There was no way he'd survive. The worst thing was there was nothing I could do about it. Nothing.

As the realization hit me, I began to sob. My husband and I had been reunited, then, after one blissful night, we'd been torn apart.

Sky dropped to his knee beside me, looking me over. "Josie, you're bleeding," he said. "There's blood all over your skirt."

I looked down. There *was* blood on my skirt, but it wasn't mine. That bullet must have hit Pardee's leg. He hadn't said a word.

The jet's engines revved up. The pilot maneuvered the aircraft, presumably to get into a position for takeoff. Seconds later we moved rapidly back up the runway. Sky slipped into the seat across from me and I looked out the window. Most of the vehicles were gone. I could see a motorcycle on its side and a cop sitting on the ground next to it. They couldn't have dragged Pardee off already. The skirmish must have moved to another location.

I gave Sky a woeful look. I'd escaped, but my heart hadn't. It was still with Pardee.

Sky reached over and took my hand. "Black hair's not bad, Josie, but I was kind of partial to the red curls."

I tried to smile, but I couldn't. A couple of minutes later we were airborne.

Sky looked like he couldn't have been happier. I could tell he was disappointed I wasn't as stoked as he was. He had no way of knowing I was sick at heart because I'd lost more than a comrade in arms; I'd lost the man I loved.

"Pardee sacrificed himself, maybe his life, to save me," I said, my eyes bubbling up. I wiped my nose.

"He's a brave man."

"I'm afraid of what they'll do to him."

"If he survives and there's a trial, we'll do what we can for him, darling. I promise you." I knew he meant it. That was the kind of person Sky Tyler was.

The pilot made a big sweeping turn to the north. I

looked out the window at Oaxaca. On the road from the airport I could see the flashing lights of emergency vehicles, headed into town. A whole string of them. It looked like they were moving at a pretty rapid clip. That couldn't be the police still in pursuit of Pardee, could it? I knew the guy was lucky as well as good, but it was hard to believe he'd survived that gun battle on wheels.

No, that couldn't be Pardee. But even as my head told me there wasn't a chance, I hoped with all my heart that it was him and that he and the karma gods were still on good terms.

Thirty-four

I was too distraught for intelligent conversation and Sky was understanding enough to give me space. Half an hour into the flight home, I pulled myself together enough to talk to him. I knew I could have put off the conversation we needed to have, but Sky deserved the truth and he deserved it now.

"There's something I have to tell you," I said, drawing him to the seat beside me.

"What's that, darling?"

My heart pounded like mad, knowing how much my words would hurt him. Sky was a wonderful man and I did care for him, but not the way I cared for Pardee.

"I've betrayed your trust, Sky," I said, my voice shaking. "I was unfaithful to you. I slept with Pardee. I still love him and I want to be with him." I drew a breath. "I didn't intend for it to happen. I didn't want it to happen. But being with him proved to me that we belong together."

Sky was very still. He searched my eyes. "And he feels the same?"

"Yes, he wants me to marry him again."

Sky swallowed hard. "Will you?"

"God, for all I know he's dead or they're dragging him off to prison as we speak. But that doesn't affect the way I feel. Whether I ever see him again or not, I know my heart and I have an obligation to tell you. I'm certain of that."

I made myself look in his eyes. He was surprisingly calm. After a moment he said, "I kind of expected it, to be honest. Seeing the two of you together, I sensed unfinished business."

"I guess it was inevitable. But I'm so very sorry for your sake. You deserve better because you're a wonderful man and a very special person."

His head dropped. I put my hand on his shoulder.

"I hope you don't hate me, but I can't blame you if you do."

"Sometimes love isn't reciprocated, I realize that. But I couldn't hate you, Josie, no matter what."

I cried then. I cried for Sky, for Pardee, for myself. Life was sometimes tragic. In this case it was tragic for us all.

Sky proved the size of his heart by helping me to learn Pardee's fate. We were still a thousand miles from home when he got on the phone to try to find out what had happened to the gringo fugitive who caused such a ruckus in southern Mexico. Getting such news was not easy. Word of criminal events in foreign countries tends to make its way to us very slowly, if at all.

The first reliable information we got came out of a press source in Mexico City and that wasn't until after we'd landed at home in Monterey. The word was that Pardee had indeed escaped immediate capture and was on the loose. I was thrilled, but I knew he was still in deep trouble. Our friends were no longer in a position to help him; he was essentially without resources and no closer to home than before.

Sky had the limo take me to my place from the airport, but before he said goodbye, he promised to follow up his inquiries and would let me know the minute there was word about Pardee. After that initial report out of Mexico City the information well went dry. The only news I heard was that the manhunt was in progress. There'd been no sightings, no gun battles or narrow escapes. Pardee, it seemed, had dropped off the face of the earth.

I worried that he'd died of his wounds in some godforsaken hideout in the mountains, though he might have simply been on the lam, eluding the authorities. I wondered if he could be making his way home mile by painful mile, or if I was simply deluding myself.

I called Quinn that first night to tell him what had happened, but he'd already gotten word from Rosalinda that his father was unaccounted for. I asked about Margarita and Carlos and he said Señora Cachero Ostos had already dispatched a prominent lawyer from Mexico City to look out for them. The sole casualty of the operation seemed to be Pardee. Quinn was as anxious about that as I. We both knew this was likely to end badly.

The hours, as they say, turned to days and there was still no word about Pardee. With each passing day, I grew more pessimistic, fearing that the wound he'd suffered may have been fatal. Quinn and I wondered if we'd ever learn of Pardee's fate.

Little by little Baron's and my life returned to the way it had been before, except that Sky no longer played a central role in our existence. We spoke on the phone every few days and he said he'd always be there for me. I could tell he would have taken me back, had I indicated that's what I wanted, but I knew it could never be. My heart was with Pardee, alive or dead.

It was a hot, sultry night about three weeks after my return from Mexico that the final act occurred. I was at my kitchen table, painting my toenails, eating chocolate and listening to my favorite Clint Black tape when Baron, who'd been a bit more clingy since my return, perked up his ears and went charging to the front door, barking like crazy. That usually meant somebody, if only a possum or a polecat, was out in the yard. I went to the door and stepped out onto the porch.

I could see a vehicle, a pickup, had stopped at the top of the drive. A man got out and came ambling across the yard in the moonlight, slow and easy. Baron raced to meet him, yapping with puppy glee. The guy had on a cowboy hat and he had a bit of a limp. The limp I hadn't seen before, but I thought I knew the gait. I started trembling and my heart immediately went into overdrive. When the light from the house fell on Pardee's shadowed face, I let out a cry and went running down the steps.

We collided on the lawn and we went spinning around and around, me squealing and crying and carrying on. Finally we stopped turning and I took his face in my hands. "I thought you were dead, you bastard."

"For a while, I thought I was, too, sweetheart."

"What happened?"

"I couldn't die until I found out whether you'd have me

again, Josie. I didn't know what you'd do once you got home and I knew there was only one way to find out, so here I am."

Baron was doing a dance, as excited as me. Pardee bent over and scratched his ears, then gave me a sly smile. "I see you got back your red hair."

"Sort of."

"So, how you been?"

"Dying with worry." I reached up and touched his face. "It's really you? You're not a ghost?"

"No, but I am fifteen pounds lighter than when you last saw me."

"You could have called me to say you were all right, you know."

"It's only been the last few days that it was even possible, Josie, and since so much time had passed, I thought I'd bring the news of my survival to you in person."

I took his hand. "Come on inside. Have you eaten? Are you hungry? Can I fix you something?"

"I'll be content just to sit and look at your pretty face."

We climbed the front steps, Pardee favoring his leg.

"It's so nice out, how about if we sit on the porch a spell?" he said.

We sat on the bench against the front of the house, Pardee stretching out his leg. He took my hand and kissed it. Baron, the shameless cur, rested his chin on Pardee's knee.

"You get shot pretty bad?" I asked.

"Let me put it this way: When I passed out finally, it was in the right woman's arms. That's all I'm going to say about that."

"Oh, so that's why it took you three weeks to get home."

Pardee grinned. He wouldn't explain, nor would I ever

hear the whole and absolute truth. It wasn't in him. I'd get three or four different stories and the more times I talked to him about it, the more versions I'd hear. Pardee had to keep you guessing. "I've learned to open my heart, Josie," he told me, "but a fella's got to maintain his mystique. I know you and you're not the type of gal who'd settle for an ordinary guy."

He was right about that, yet I was curious about what had happened during those three weeks after I'd left Mexico. I wasn't going to twist his arm, though. Keeping things a little off balance was Pardee's way. Though sometimes it infuriated me, I kind of liked it.

Quinn later told me the story he was inclined to believe was that Pardee had made it to the coast, then talked his way onto a tourist bus full of American schoolteachers headed for Acapulco. Given his medical condition, I sort of favored the version that had Pardee resting up in the home of a Mexican midwife and her little son. Maybe that was my romantic bias talking rather than a nose for the truth. But there were other possibilities—rumors around the skip-chase business involved wild tales, including a commandeered fishing boat and even the succor of a noted film star doing a drug rehab in Mexico. I guess the truth doesn't really matter beyond the fact that Pardee made it home to live another day, chase more bounty and me.

"I see you don't have on Sky's ring," he said, not disguising his satisfaction. "I guess that means that night we spent together wasn't a one-night stand after all."

"Did you think I'd forget you as soon as I got home?"

"Millionaires don't fall off trees, sweetheart. There was no guarantee things wouldn't look different to you once you were back in the California sunshine."

"If you can say that, you don't know me very well." I studied him. "Or are you trying to tell me you're the one having second thoughts?"

"Lord, no. If it weren't for me wanting to get back to you so bad, I'd probably be dead. I'm here for your answer, Josie. As you recall, I asked you to marry me."

He was dead serious—as serious as I'd ever seen him—and I was thrilled. But if he insisted on keeping a few of his old tricks in his bag, I would, too. I wasn't about to make it easy for him. "My answer's still the same," I replied. "We need to spend time together and see how it goes."

We fell silent then and for a while just stared off into the night. The air was rich with the smell of jasmine and the sound of frogs. From time to time we could hear a big eighteen-wheeler going down the highway. Pardee stroked Baron's head.

"So, will you come back to the ranch with me, Josie?" he asked.

"Even that's a big step," I said, sounding as ponderous as I could. "Is that really what you want or are you testing the waters?"

"As far as I'm concerned, we can leave tonight, tomorrow, whenever you give the word, sweetheart. All I want is for us to be together. All three of us."

"Hmm." I pondered that. Then, leaning over, I said to my dog, "What do you think, Baron?"

He woofed, adding a funny little bark at the end. It wasn't his usual straightforward reply.

"Yeah," I said, shaking my head. "I should have known you'd take his side."

Summer nights are hotter than ever thanks to these July releases from Avon Romance . . .

The Marriage Bed by Laura Lee Guhrke

An Avon Romantic Treasure

Everyone in society knows that the marriage of Lord and Lady Hammond is an unhappy one. But all that is about to change, when John, Lord Hammond, begins to see what a beautiful woman he is married to. Now he prays it's not too late to win back the love of his very own wife.

The Hunter by Gennita Low

An Avon Contemporary Romance

In order for Hawk McMillan, SEAL commander, to succeed in his latest lone mission, he needs a tracker, and the best woman for that job is CIA contact agent Amber Hutchens. But when their mission requires Hawk and Amber to risk everything, they've got too much at stake to stay far away from danger . . . or from their passion.

More Than a Scandal by Sari Robins

An Avon Romance

Lovely Catherine Miller has always been timid—until the treachery of unscrupulous cousins threatens her childhood home. To save it, she steals the identity of the notorious "Thief of Robinson Square" who, years ago, preyed on pompous society to help the poor.

The Daring Twin by Donna Fletcher

An Avon Romance

When Fiona of the MacElder clan is told that she must wed Tarr of Hellewyk so the two clans can unite, she is furious. Fortunately, Fiona's identical twin sister Aliss is on her side. The two boldly concoct an outlandish scheme—to make it impossible to tell who is who—and it works. The only trouble is, one of the twins accidentally falls in love with the would-be groom!

Avon Romantic Treasures

Unforgettable, enthralling love stories,
sparkling with passion and adventure
from Romance's bestselling authors